STOLEN
GIRLS

Also by Patricia Gibney

THE STOLEN GIRLS

A Detective Lottie Parker Thriller

PATRICIA GIBNEY

GRAND CENTRAL
PUBLISHING

New York   Boston

Copyright © 2017 by Patricia Gibney

Cover designed by Richard Augustus. Cover photographs © Arcangel Images. Cover copyright © 2020 by Hachette Book Group, Inc.

Grand Central Publishing
Hachette Book Group
1290 Avenue of the Americas, New York, NY 10104
grandcentralpublishing.com
twitter.com/grandcentralpub

Originally published in the United Kingdom by Bookouture, an imprint of StoryFire Ltd., in 2017
First North American edition: February 2020

Grand Central Publishing is a division of Hachette Book Group, Inc. The Grand Central Publishing name and logo is a trademark of Hachette Book Group, Inc.

The publisher is not responsible for websites (or their content) that are not owned by the publisher.

The Hachette Speakers Bureau provides a wide range of authors for speaking events. To find out more, go to www.hachettespeakersbureau.com or call (866) 376-6591.

Library of Congress Control Number: 2019946026

ISBN: 978-1-5387-0196-6 (mass market)

Printed in the United States of America

OPM

10 9 8 7 6 5 4 3 2 1

For Aidan
A true soldier, a peacekeeper
My husband, my friend
Rest in peace

PROLOGUE

Kosovo 1999

The boy liked the peacefulness of the creek, midway between his home and his grandmother's. Despite the roar of water flowing down the mountainside, it was quiet today. No gunfire or shelling. He looked around as he dipped the bucket into the spring water, making sure he was alone. He thought he heard a car in the distance and glanced behind him. Dust was rising from the twisting road. Someone was coming. He hauled up the bucket, spilling the water. The screech of brakes and the sound of loud voices propelled him to run.

As he neared home, he dropped the bucket and fell to the ground, lying flat on his belly, gravel tearing into his bare skin. He had left his shirt hanging on a rusty nail sticking out of a concrete block back where he was working with Papa. They'd been trying to mend the shell damage on his grandmother's house. The boy knew it was futile, but Papa insisted. At thirteen, he knew better than to argue. Anyway, he had been happy to spend a day with Papa, away from his chattering mother and sister.

On elbows and knees he crawled over the dusty roadway into the long scrub grass at the edge. Only a few yards from his house, but it might as well have been a mile.

He listened. Heard laughter, followed by screams. Mama? Rhea? No! He pleaded with the sun in the cloudless sky. Its only answer was a burning heat on his skin.

More rough laughter. Soldiers?

He inched forward. Men were shouting. What could he do? Was Papa too far away to help? Did he have his gun with him?

The boy crept on. At the fence, he parted the long brown grass and leaned in between two posts.

A green jeep with a red cross on an open door. Four men. Soldier's uniforms. Guns slung idly across their backs. Trousers *around ankles. Bare buttocks in the air, humping. He knew what they were doing. They'd raped his friend's sister who lived at the foot of the mountain. And then they'd killed her.*

Fighting back his useless tears, he watched. Mama and Rhea were screaming. The two soldiers got up, straightened their clothes as the other two took their places. More laughter.

Clamping his teeth onto his fist, he choked down sobs. Shep, his collie dog, barked loudly, circling the soldiers hysterically. The boy froze, then jumped, cracking his front tooth against bone, as a gunshot echoed up against the mountain and back down again. He let out an involuntary cry. Birds shot up from the sparse trees, merged as one, then flew in all directions. Shep lay unmoving in the yard beneath the makeshift swing, a tire Papa had put up on a branch when they were little children. They were still children, but they didn't play on the swing anymore. Not since the war.

An argument broke out among the soldiers. The boy tried to understand what they were saying but couldn't avert his eyes from the naked, dust-covered figures, still alive, their screams now muted whimpers. Where was Papa?

He stared, feeling hypnotized, as the men pulled on surgical gloves. The tallest one extracted a long steel blade from an old-fashioned scabbard attached to his hip. Then another one did the same. The boy was frozen with terror. Watching transfixed, he saw the soldier crouch behind his mama and drag her up against his chest. The other man grabbed eleven-year-old Rhea. Blood streamed down her legs and he quelled an urge to find clothing to hide her nakedness. Weeping silent tears, he felt powerless and useless.

One man raised his knife. It glinted in the sun before he drew it downward, slitting Rhea from her throat to her belly. The other man did the same to Mama. The bodies convulsed. Blood gushed and spurted into the faces of the abusers. Gloved hands thrust into the cavities and tore out organs, blood dripping along their arms. The other two soldiers rushed forward with steel cases. The bodies dropped to the ground.

Wide-eyed with horror, the boy watched the soldiers quickly place the organs of his precious mama and sister into the cases, laughing as they snapped them shut. One took a marker from his pocket and casually wrote on the side of the container and another turned and kicked out at Rhea. Her body shuddered. He looked directly over toward the boy's hiding place.

Holding his breath, eyes locked on the soldier, the boy felt no terror now. He was prepared to die and half stood up, but the man was moving back to his comrades. They packed the cases into the jeep, jumped in and with a cloud of stones and dust rising skyward, drove back down the mountain road.

He didn't know how long he stayed there before a hand clamped down on his shoulder and pulled him into an embrace. He looked into a pair of heartbroken eyes. He hadn't heard the frantic running or the frenzied shouting. The vision of the disemboweled bodies of Mama and Rhea had imprinted themselves as a photograph in his mind. And he knew it would never fade.

Papa dragged him toward the bodies. The boy stared into his mother's eyes. Pleading in death. Papa took out his pistol, turned his wife's face into the hot clay and shot her in the back of the head. Her body flexed. Stilled.

Papa cried, big, silent tears, as he crawled over to Rhea. He shot her too. The boy knew she was already dead. There was no need for the bullet. He tried to shout at Papa but his voice was lost in the midst of the turmoil.

"I had to do it!" Papa cried. "To save their souls." He pulled the two bodies, and then Shep, into the house. With determination in his steps he hurriedly emptied a jerry can of petrol inside the door and threw in a lighted torch of dry reeds. Picking up his gun, he raised it toward the boy.

No words of fear, no movement. Yet. The boy was immobile

until he saw Papa's work-stained finger tremble on the trigger. Instinct caused him to run.

Papa cried out, "Save yourself. Run, boy. Don't stop running."

Looking over his shoulder as he went, he saw Papa turn the gun to his own wrinkled forehead and pull the trigger before falling back into the flames. They ignited in a whoosh of crinkling, falling timber.

The boy watched from the fence as the life he had known burned as bright as the sun in the sky. No help came. The war had caused everyone to fend for themselves and he supposed those living in the other houses along the road were hiding, terrified, awaiting their own fate. He couldn't blame them. There was nothing they could do here anyway.

After some time the sun dipped low and night stars twinkled like nothing was wrong. Without even a shirt on his back he began the long, lonely trek down the mountain.

He did not know where he was going.

He had nowhere to go.

He did not care.

Slowly he walked, one foot in front of the other, stones breaking through the soft rubber soles of his sandals. He walked until his feet bled. He walked until his sandals disintegrated like his heart. He kept on walking until he reached a place where he would never feel pain again.

FRIDAY NIGHT,
MAY 8, 2015

Ragmullin

CHAPTER 1

It was the dark that frightened her the most. Not being able to see. And the sounds. Soft skittering, then silence.

Shifting onto her side, she tried to haul herself into a sitting position. Gave up. A rustle. Squeaking. She screamed, and her voice echoed back. Sobbing, she wrapped her arms tight around her body. Her thin cotton shirt and jeans were soaked with cold sweat.

The dark.

She had spent too many nights like this in her own bedroom, listening to her mother's laughter with others in the kitchen below. Now she remembered those nights as a luxury. Because that wasn't *real* dark. Street lights and the moon had cast shadows through paper-thin curtains, birthing the wallpaper to life. Her dated furniture had stood like statues in a dimly lit cemetery. Her clothes, heaped in piles on a chair in the corner, had sometimes appeared to be heaving, as the headlamps of cars passing on the road shone through the curtains. And she thought that had been dark? No. This, where she was now, was the true meaning of pitch black.

She wished she had her phone, with her life attached to it— her cyber friends on Facebook and Twitter. They might be able to help her. If she had her phone. If only.

The door opened, the glow from the hallway blinding her eyes shut. Church bells chimed in the distance. Where was she? Near home? The bells stopped. A sharp laugh. The light flicked on. A naked bulb swayed with the draft and she saw the figure of a man.

Backing into the damp wall, scuffing her bare heels along the floor, she felt a tug on her hair and pain pinpricked each follicle on her head. She didn't care. He could scalp her bald as long as she got home alive.

"P-please..."

Her voice didn't sound like her own. High-pitched and quivering, no longer laced with her usual teenage swagger.

A rough hand pulled her upward, her hair snarled round his fingers. She squinted at him, trying to form a mental picture. He was taller than her, wearing a gray knitted hat pierced with two slits revealing hostile eyes. She must remember the eyes. For later. For when she was free. A thrust of determination inched its way into her heart. Straightening her spine, she faced him.

"What?" he barked.

His sour breath churned her stomach upside down. His clothes smelled like the slaughterhouse behind Kennedy's butcher's shop on Patrick Street. In springtime, little lambs succumbed to bullets or knives or whatever they used to kill them. That smell. Death. The cloying odor clinging to her uniform all day long.

She shuddered as he moved his face nearer. Now she had something to be more frightened of than pitch-black nothingness. For the first time in her life, she actually wanted her mother.

"Let me go," she cried. "Home. I want to go home. Please."

"You make me laugh, little one."

He leaned toward her, so close that his wool-covered nose touched hers and his sickly breath oozed through the knitted stitches.

She tried to back away but there was nowhere to go. She held her breath, desperately trying not to puke as he gripped her shoulder and pushed her to the door.

"Stage two of your adventure begins," he said, laughing to himself.

Her blood crawled as she hobbled into the barren corridor. High ceilings. Peeling paint. Giant cast-iron radiators snatched up her faltering steps with their shadows. A high wooden door blocked her progress. His hand slid around her waist, pulling her body to his. She froze. Leaning over, he shoved open the door.

Forced into a room, she slipped on the wet floor and fell to her knees.

"No, no..." She swung around frantically. What was going on? What was this place? Windows sheathed in plexiglass kept daylight at bay. The floor was covered in damp heavy-duty plastic; the walls were streaked with what she thought looked like dried blood. Everything she saw screeched at her to run. Instead, she crawled. On hands and knees. All she could see in front of her were his boots, caked in mud or blood or both. He hauled her up and prodded her to move. Rotating her body, she faced him.

He pulled off the balaclava. Eyes she had only seen through slits were now joined by a thin, pink-lipped mouth. She stared. His face was a blank canvas awaiting a horror yet to be painted.

"Tell me your name again?" he asked.

"Wh-what do you mean?"

"I want to hear you say it," he snarled.

Catching sight of the knife in his hand, she slithered and slipped on the blood-soaked plastic before falling prostrate before him. This time she welcomed the darkness. As it glided over the tiny stars flickering behind her eyes, she whispered, "Maeve."

DAY ONE

Monday, May 11, 2015

CHAPTER 2

They were at it again. Loud and cheerful. Alto and tenor competing with each other, starling and wood pigeon. Bird shit floated down in front of the open window, just missing the glass.

"Shit," Lottie Parker said; her favorite swear word, the irony not lost on her. She tugged the window shut, making the room even more hot and airless, but she could still hear them. She flopped onto the damp duvet. Another night sweating. She would be forty-four next month, at least six years, she hoped, from the age when she could put it down to menopause. So it had to be the monster heat.

Her eyes were dry from lack of sleep, and then her phone alarm buzzed.

Go time. Work time.

And Lottie Parker wondered how she would cope today.

* * *

"Where are my keys?" she shouted up the stairs half an hour later.

No answer.

Eight bells rang out from the cathedral situated in the center of Ragmullin, half a mile from her home. Late. She tipped the contents of her handbag onto the kitchen table. Sunglasses—necessary; wallet—empty; receipts—too many; bank card—lost cause; phone—would ring any minute; Xanax...Help. No keys.

Opening a blister pack, she swallowed a pill, even though

she had promised herself not to slip into old habits. What the hell, she'd been awake most of the night and needed a shot of something. It was months since she'd touched an alcoholic drink, so a pill was the next best thing. Maybe even better. She poured a glass of water.

The stairs creaked. Seconds later, Chloe, her younger daughter, stormed into the kitchen.

"We need to talk, Mother."

She called Lottie *Mother* just to antagonize her.

"We do. But not now," Lottie said. "I've to go to work. *If I ever find my keys.*"

She rummaged through the detritus on the table. ID, hairbrush, sunscreen, two-euro coin. No keys.

"Is that all you've got to say?"

"Jesus, Chloe, give me a break. Please."

"No, Mother. I won't. Sean's going round like a zombie, Katie's... not herself, I'm a mess and you're a madwoman the minute you have to return to work."

Lottie stared helplessly at her daughter and kept her mouth shut in case she said the wrong thing. These days everything she uttered appeared to send the sixteen-year-old into either a sulk or a tantrum. And Chloe wasn't finished yet.

"You need to do something. This family's falling apart and what does all-important Mrs. Detective Inspector do? She goes back to work."

Chloe scraped back her unruly blonde hair, piled it on top of her head and wrapped it up with a bobbin. It stuck out in places and loose tendrils framed her face. Lottie went to smooth it but her daughter stepped away.

"I'm trying," Lottie said, slumping on a chair. She'd spent the last few months trying to build her family back up after tragedy had struck while she had been trying to resolve her last case. She'd thought things were a lot better now. How wrong could you be? "You've had me at home for the last few months. Granny is coming over later to have dinner ready when you and Sean get in from school. She'll keep an eye on Katie too. What more can I do? You know I have to work. We need the money."

"We need *you*."

What could she say to that? Adam would have known what to say, she thought, remembering her dead husband's gift for finding the right words. But he was never coming back. Four years dead come July, and she still struggled without him.

Chloe picked up her school rucksack. "And I hate this shit-hole of a town. What hope have I of ever getting away?" She banged the front door on her way out.

"Want a lift?" Lottie shouted to a shadow.

No keys. Shit! Now she'd have to walk to work. Swiping her hand across the table, she knocked the contents of her handbag to the floor.

The doorbell rang. She jumped up and ran into the hall.

"What did you forget?" she asked, opening the door.

It wasn't Chloe.

CHAPTER 3

The girl was dressed in a navy sweater despite the morning warmth.

Stepping into her footsteps, a good fifteen strides behind her, he assessed her long legs. Not muscular, but beautifully slender. Blonde hair lolling on top of her head in an untidy bun made her appear taller and leaner. She had large breasts for a teenager, beneath her loose school uniform. He knew this because he'd seen her wearing a tight long-sleeved T-shirt in Danny's Bar at the weekend. Unnoticed in the heave of hot bodies spilling pints in the beer garden, he had been close enough to touch the V of her back, just above her buttocks. He had removed his hand quickly though he'd wanted it to linger, to trace the vertebrae beneath the light cotton, to let it wander lower. Her hair was hanging loose that night, long and voluminous, with a few strands nestling in the curve of her breasts. Every detail registered, stored in his mind, for him to return to whenever he wanted.

Now she walked slowly and he had to keep several paces behind. She strolled up Gaol Street and onto Main Street. The school was another ten-minute walk from there.

He forced himself to concentrate on the end target. She needed saving. Because he knew why she wore long sleeves. Soon she would search the depths of his eyes, begging for a happy release from her pain.

He smiled contentedly, following her along the street, watching her swing her rucksack from one shoulder to the other. She must be very hot by now; too hot. Lost in his thoughts, he almost missed her stopping and turning around.

Dipping his head, he overtook her.

He kept walking. Normal pace. Had she noticed him? A glance over his shoulder to see why she had suddenly halted. Perhaps she had sensed him. Would she recognize him as a dangerous Lucifer or a guardian angel? He would know soon enough.

At the old harbor he crossed the road, avoiding the few girls chattering at the school gates. He walked along the canal bank and idly watched a swarm of flies hover above the stagnant waters. A sleek brown shadow lurked in the depths—a predator searching for prey? He was aware that menacing pike swam in these waters with their large gaping mouths, fangs gnashing and snaring unsuspecting trout and bream.

His excitement had been tempered. For now.

His little fish had escaped him. For now.

But he would continue to prowl the shadows, waiting to snatch his chance. Like the pike with its open mouth, he could be patient.

CHAPTER 4

Lottie stepped back from the front door.

The young woman standing on the step was a stranger. A white silk scarf wrapped around her head, a hijab framing a gaunt face. A small boy was clutching her hand tightly. He stared up at Lottie with scared brown eyes. A cracked-plastic cream-colored jacket over a cotton blouse and jeans did little to hide the woman's thinness. Lottie noticed that despite the oppressive heat she was wearing heavy brown boots.

"Can I help you?" Lottie asked wearily.

"*Zonje.*"

"Sonja?"

The young woman shook her head. "*Zonje*...madam..." A shrug of her shoulders.

"Oh. *Zonje* means madam. Got you now." Lottie stepped forward, closing the front door behind her. "Look, I can't stop. I'm in a hurry, I need to get to work."

The woman didn't move. Lottie sighed. This was all she needed. Next she'd have Superintendent Corrigan shouting down the phone to hike her arse into work. Was the woman begging? She thought of the coins she'd tipped out of her bag. Maybe they would do the trick.

"*Ju lutem*...please." The woman looked at her imploringly, her broken English soft and accented.

"I've no money," Lottie said. Almost true. "Maybe later." Not true.

With a shake of her head, the young woman lifted the little boy into her arms. "Please," she said, "help."

Sighing, Lottie said, "Wait here."

Back inside, she picked up a coin from the floor. When she turned round, the woman was standing behind her. In her kitchen.

"Jesus! What are you doing?" Lottie held out the two euros. "Here, take this." She waved her hand toward the front door.

Declining the money, the young woman tugged a crumpled envelope from her jeans pocket and offered it to Lottie. She shook her head without taking it.

"What is it?" she asked. Was it one of those notes begging for money? The morning was going from bad to worse.

The woman shrugged and the little boy whimpered.

Feeling the stirring of an instinct within, Lottie pulled out a chair and gestured for the woman to sit. The boy climbed on to her knee and nestled his head into the silk scarf.

"What do you want?" Lottie asked, picking up her stuff from the floor and dumping it all back in her bag. She hurriedly tapped out a text to Detective Sergeant Boyd telling him she was going to be late, asking him to cover for her. A streak of guilt itched beneath her skin. She hadn't had time for her daughter earlier and here she was entertaining a stranger. But something was telling her to listen to what she had to say.

The girl spoke rapidly in a language Lottie couldn't understand.

"Hey, slow down," she said. "What's your name?"

A head shake, shrug of shoulders. It reminded Lottie of Chloe. What age was this woman? Looking at her more closely, she thought she might be anywhere between sixteen and her early twenties. No more than a girl.

"I'm Lottie. You?"

Deep brown orbs appeared to question her for a moment before their flecks of hazel brightened, lighting up the face.

"Mimoza." The girl smiled, white teeth glinting in the morning sun beaming through the window.

Getting somewhere at last, Lottie thought.

"Milot." The girl pointed to the boy.

"So, Mimoza and Milot," Lottie said. "What do you want?"

Maybe she should offer tea. No. She needed to get rid of them as quickly as possible. Her phone beeped. Boyd. She glanced at the text. *You are dead late. Corrigan's on the warpath.* Nothing new there.

Sean, her fourteen-year-old son, sauntered into the kitchen. "Who owns this?" he asked, holding up a raggedy stuffed rabbit with long chewed ears.

Milot held out a hand and grasped the toy.

Sean mussed the boy's hair. "What's wrong, bud?" He crouched down. "Why you crying?"

Shrinking into Mimoza's chest, the child pursed his bottom lip over his top one while his little fingers slid up and down the rabbit's worn label.

"Can you play with him for a few minutes?" Lottie asked. "Before you leave for school? Chloe's already gone ahead."

Sean nodded and bounced a hurling ball from one hand to the other. "Wanna play ball?"

The child sought his mother's approval with his eyes and the girl nodded. Sliding from her knee, Milot followed Sean through the back door out into the garden. Lottie stared after them. It was the most she'd heard her son say in a month. She smiled across the table at the girl. Maybe allowing her into her home had had some use after all.

"Son?" Mimoza asked.

"Yes," Lottie said.

"Milot my son," Mimoza said.

She looked too young to have a child, Lottie thought.

"I have little English. Is hard to explain to you. Easy for me to write in my language." She passed over the envelope.

Lottie glanced down. It was sealed, with foreign words written on the outside.

"How am I supposed to know what this means?"

The girl said, "Find Kaltrina. Help me and Milot escape. Please, you help?"

"Kaltrina? Who's she? Escape what?"

"I cannot tell much. I write down a little. You read?"

"Of course. Is someone threatening you? Where do you live? What's happened to this Kaltrina?"

The girl pointed to the envelope. "All there. Sorry it not English. I afraid."

"How do you know who I am? Why did you not call in to the police . . . the police station?"

The girl shrugged. "It not safe. You help?"

Lottie sighed. "I'll see if I can get someone to translate it for me. That's all I can do at the moment." She glanced at the clock. She was going to be dead late for her first day back to work after almost four months off.

The girl caught her eye, stood up quickly and called the boy. Sean ushered him into the kitchen. The little fellow's cheeks were flushed. Mimoza smiled up at Sean, took her son by the hand and went to the front door. It closed behind her with a soft click.

"Did you find out anything from him?" Lottie asked.

Sean shrugged. "He's a great little hurler." He sauntered up the stairs toward the cavernous security of his room.

"Hurry up, Sean. You're going to be late for school. And don't wake Katie."

Picking up her bag with an exasperated shake of her head, Lottie stuffed Mimoza's envelope inside and then noticed her keys hanging on the hook at the door. She took them and stepped out into the morning sunshine.

Reversing her car out of the drive, she noticed Mimoza and

her son walking to the end of the road. Before they turned the corner, a smaller girl joined them, linking her arm into Mimoza's.

When she arrived at the junction with the main road, Lottie glanced around and noticed a black car pulling away from the curb at great speed. It drove along the outside of the line of traffic, squeezed in and disappeared. Had someone been waiting for her mysterious visitors?

As a break in the traffic appeared, she maneuvered her car into the line of early-morning commuters, still thinking about Mimoza and her son. How did the other girl fit into the picture? Maybe the letter would explain it all.

CHAPTER 5

It was too hot for a jumper, but Chloe had been in such a state she hadn't been able to find her long-sleeved uniform shirt. She resigned herself to sweating her way through the day in the heavy wool garment.

Pausing opposite Dunne's Stores car park, she wiped away the perspiration bubbling on her forehead and debated skipping school. A man brushed past her and she was aware of him looking at her sideways, but she took no notice of him. The knot of anxiety in her chest was threatening to explode. Taking a few deep breaths, she continued up the hill, greeting other girls on the way, a smile plastered firmly in place.

At the bridge over the old harbor, she glanced down, almost casually, into the dark green canal water and realized she couldn't face school. With exams a month away, she knew she needed to be in class, but she couldn't do it. Not today.

The knot in her chest slowly untied itself as she hurried along the towpath, away from the ceaseless carefree chatter of the gaggle hanging around the school gate. She walked with unseeing eyes until she reached the small bridge where the canal linked up with the supply. Her dad had once told her the river was called the supply because it supplied fresh water from Lough Cullion to replenish the canal. God, she missed her dad.

Turning left, she walked along the riverbank for a few minutes before sitting down on the long grass, losing herself in the depth and height of the reeds. Opening her rucksack, she extracted from her pencil case a razor blade wrapped in soft white tissue.

She knew life was cruel. They'd lost their father, and then a few months ago Sean had almost died too. Her younger brother would never be the same again, tarnished with the memories of what had happened in that cursed chapel to him and Jason, Katie's boyfriend. Katie was damaged too; even though she tried to act normal, Chloe knew her scars ran deep.

Did Katie blame their mother? Chloe hoped not, but she couldn't rid herself of the feeling that Lottie was somehow at fault; she hadn't acted fast enough at the time to save the boys, and Jason had died.

Chloe was a fixer and now she felt helpless. She couldn't fix her family. She couldn't fix herself. She couldn't fix anything. She turned the blade over and over in her hand.

Lifting her face to the rising sun, she allowed the rays to burn her face before rolling up her sleeve. Selecting an unblemished patch, she brought the sharp piece of steel down into her young skin. One slow slash. Not too deep. Not too shallow.

The sight of the bright red blood, bubbling at first then flowing over the paleness, soothed her. Digging in a little deeper, she felt the pain, fought tears and slumped back into the arid grass.

The reeds rustled. She sat upright, looking around, but there was silence. She felt like someone was watching her but she couldn't see anybody. Pulling down her sleeve, she gathered her belongings and shoved them into her bag. Was she imagining things? Was the noise just water rats foraging among the reeds? Ugh! She shivered in the heat and set out along the gravel path, wondering where she could hide out for the day.

Checking her phone, she posted to the Twitter hashtag #cutforlife. The feeling that someone had been watching her refused to disappear. She slung her rucksack over her shoulder and began to run.

CHAPTER 6

The narrow roadway made the job difficult, but at least it was a one-way street. The three-story apartments on the right-hand side cast a thin shadow, averting the rays of the morning sun.

He had been late for work so he had to make up time before the boss arrived. New water pipes had been laid on Friday, and as the work moved along the street they'd filled in parts of the road with temporary tarmac, while other parts took a light dusting of clay covered with iron sheeting. Quick and simple, the boss had said. No one would know the difference. Now they had returned to take up the temporary material, pour permanent filling over the pipes and lay tarmac on the road.

He drilled the jackhammer into the clay, working as quickly as he could, even though the machine generated so much heat. As dirt rose and settled, a flash of blue a little further down the trench caught his eye. He stopped to wipe away a solitary bead of sweat from inside his safety goggles, then switched off the machine altogether. Dropping it to one side, he lifted up his plastic eye protection and stared. Was it an animal of some sort? He hadn't time for this.

That was when he noticed a glimpse of pale skin and a wisp of black hair. Falling to one knee, his safety boots securing him to the sliding soil, he tore at the clay. The crown of a skull emerged from the dark earth. He had no thought for forensics or police or anyone who would want to preserve the ground. Feverishly he wiped away more earth.

Andri Petrovci was not a fearful man. He had seen many bodies: people starved, butchered and burned in his homeland.

He shouldn't have been shocked by this one, but something about the alabaster skin, spotted slightly green with decomposition, and the jet-black hair, sent shivers up and down his spine. And triggered a moment he had tried to forget.

With the final trace of soil cleared from the head, Petrovci sat back into the mound of dirt, oblivious to the honking horns, incessant shouts and increasing frustration of drivers held up with the stop/go sign thirty meters away.

The victim's eyes were closed, mouth shut tight in a tiny pout. Her slender neck rose from the stained blue cotton material that had first alerted him.

Angry yelling bored sharp shards into his consciousness.

"Dumb Polack!" a man shouted, leaning out of his car window. "Go back to where you came from."

Stupid ignorant Irish. He wasn't Polish. Tightening his solid fingers into balled-up fists, he thumped them against his forehead.

Car doors slammed and footsteps squelched in the bubbling tar. It was too hot for May. A heatwave, the forecasters were saying. He was used to heat. He was used to bodies. He was used to violence. But this girl, lying here in unconsecrated ground, abandoned below the busy street, reminded him of another girl, now long dead. This girl was not long dead. Despite the beginnings of decomposition, he imagined her as fresh as the cherry blossom petals floating from the trees to the pavement, into the melting tarmac. He thought he'd left all this behind. But he knew death didn't recognize boundaries. It followed you like your own shadow.

He looked down again at the still face of the girl and briefly wondered if her eyes were blue.

CHAPTER 7

It was hotter inside the police station than outside. Detective Inspector Lottie Parker stretched her tall, lean frame and smoothed down her white cotton blouse. Still no sign of the builders being anywhere near finishing her office. She'd have to slum it for a while longer in the general office.

Opening the door, she stepped into the familiar setting, dropped her bag on the ground beside her desk and glanced at the clock. Just gone nine. An hour late. Not the start she wanted. There was no sign of Superintendent Corrigan. That was a relief.

"I could've sworn I left a mess," she said, turning up her nose at the tidy desktop. A new ceramic mug with hand-painted red poppies held her pens.

She looked over at Detective Sergeant Mark Boyd and arched her mouth in an unasked question.

"You could at least thank me," Boyd said, turning round in his chair, brown eyes sparkling with welcome. His shirt hugged his lean body tightly. Not a bead of sweat anywhere; he always looked impeccable.

"How am I supposed to find my password?" She put her mobile phone on the desk and tipped over the keyboard where she usually kept the Post-it.

"You'll have to remember it."

"Ah, lovely," she said. "Thank you, Boyd, for all your help."

Boyd's dark hair, flecked with steel gray, was shorter now. His face was still thin and hungry-looking, his ears sticking out slightly. Lottie pulled open a drawer. Files lined up and color-coded. She had only been away a few months and already his neatness had run amok.

"Welcome back, Inspector." He gave a mock salute. "Missed you too."

Closing the drawer with an unnecessary bang, she powered up the computer, racking her brain for her password. She couldn't remember it after four minutes, let alone four months. Trying to make conversation while searching, she asked, "How are you doing since the—"

"The wound healed up quickly," Boyd cut in. "Mentally? I'm as screwed up as ever."

"Thought I was the mental one. Password?"

"Under the mug."

She tapped in the code. "Thanks."

"How are things at home?"

"Sean's back at school. Well, he goes in most days. It's a running battle. He's seeing a therapist," she added, running a hand through her newly cut hair.

"You should see one too," Boyd replied

Lottie shrugged. "You're as good as any therapist, Dr. Phil."

"My middle name." Boyd laughed before putting on his solemn mask. "Seriously, though. Sean's a good kid but he's been through a lot."

"Yes, he has. But I think teenagers are more resilient than us adults." She hoped he wouldn't ask about Chloe and Katie. She didn't want to talk about her children and their problems; she just wanted to bury herself in work. She'd taken enough leave as it was.

She hoped Sean and the girls would be okay without her around all day. But she couldn't stay at home any longer; the last few months had slowly eroded the edges of her resilience. There was only so much advising, washing and cooking she could do. At least she'd got the kids out of the habit of eating junk food and takeaways. Today she wanted to ease back into office life gently. Get her feet safely under the table. Take it in her stride.

"Body found on Bridge Street." Detective Sergeant Larry Kirby thrust his head around the door, his bulk following a second later. His plaid shirt was rolled to the elbows, and pearls of perspiration trickled down his wide forehead. He pushed back his mop of bushy hair and stopped when he saw Lottie.

"Jesus, boss. Welcome back," he panted.

"Sandals?" Lottie stared at his white-socked toes.

"Gout," Kirby said.

"But white socks with sandals?"

"Missed you too, boss."

"Where's Lynch?" Lottie asked. Detective Maria Lynch was the other core member of her team.

"At the scene. The guys working on the new water main unearthed the body of a female."

"First day back and you're welcomed with a body." Boyd smirked as he followed Kirby out of the door.

Lottie sighed. Taking a handful of the carefully filed folders from the drawer, she scattered them over the desk and spilled a few pens from the mug on top of them. Now she felt more at home.

She picked up her bag and popped her mobile inside, catching sight of the envelope from her earlier visitors. That would have to wait.

She marched out behind her detectives. She had work to do.

* * *

Tar oozed from the ground. The morning heat burned bare arms and brought freckles out on pale faces. Having come through the worst winter since records began, Lottie thought they were possibly on the brink of the hottest summer yet. She stepped out of the air-conditioned car and the humidity swamped her. Putting on her sunglasses, she was glad she'd applied sunblock to her fair skin.

"Got your sunscreen on?" she asked.

"Yeah." Boyd locked the car and fell into step beside her.

She glanced sideways at him. Was he being offhand with her? He'd put on his sunglasses, so she couldn't read his eyes. Their personal history had a habit of interfering with their mutual civility. Maybe it was because now that she was back at work, he was no longer acting detective inspector, and was once again only a detective sergeant.

As they approached the outer cordon, uniformed police redirected traffic back down the one-way street, succeeding in generating tailbacks throughout the town. Tempers rose as quickly as the sun in the sky, and Lottie's blouse was already saturated. She stole another look at Boyd in his cool cotton shirt and navy trousers. He hadn't even loosened his tie. How did he succeed in looking so chilled? She shook her head. It was beyond her.

The road narrowed. Vehicles caught up in the traffic jam before the diversions had been put in place attempted to reverse, creating further gridlock. The fact that a body had been found did nothing to calm tempers.

They ducked under the crime-scene tape on Bridge Street, a narrow tributary road snaking past the football stadium, over the river, around the shopping center, narrowing where it linked to the main thoroughfare. Traffic lights blinked at the end. To the left, Barrett's Pub, with boarded-up windows and weather-beaten paintwork, and a cul-de-sac. Apartments on the right, products of the boom years, some with timber planks covering windows. Had she sleep-walked through the good times? No wealth had come her way. Looking up at the dusty three-story block, she thought perhaps she was better off. But these apartments offered her an immediate problem: numerous people to interview. Door-to-door inquiries could take days.

She glanced around for CCTV. A broken camera hung by its wires from the wall above the back door of the pub.

Detective Maria Lynch, long fair hair swishing in a ponytail, was busy inside the inner cordon, where a partly excavated trench lined the cul-de-sac. Three men in hi-vis singlets, safety helmets askew, smoked cigarettes in a group at the corner. Uniformed police were taking notes. Lottie looked away from the group, realizing that Lynch had approached her and was speaking.

"...young woman."

"What?" Lottie tried to focus.

Lynch continued reading from her notebook. "We're waiting for the scene-of-crime officers to arrive before the body can be fully excavated. The state pathologist has been notified." She closed the notebook. "With this traffic, God knows how long it will take her to arrive."

Lottie made her way toward the temporary tent erected over the trench. Standing outside it, she could smell decay and decomposition.

"It's too hot to leave a dead body here for any length of time," she said, carefully picking her way across abandoned tools.

"Too warm for the live ones," said Boyd, peering over the edge of the trench from a vantage point on the road. "Fucking hell."

"What?" said Lottie and Lynch together.

"My shoes," he said, extracting a foot from the sticky tar. He stepped on to a large stone poking out of the ground.

Lottie was impatient for the SOCOs to arrive. She wanted to see what they were dealing with. She glanced again at the group of men at the corner. One of them excused himself, stepped to the side and lit another cigarette.

"Who is he?" she asked, indicating the man.

Lynch consulted her notes. "Andri Petrovci. He unearthed the body. Almost killed her a second time with his jackhammer. He just missed the head by a few inches. A flash of color in the clay stopped him."

Lottie averted her eyes as Petrovci caught her staring. She couldn't help but notice that his face was riddled with old scar tissue, running from his left ear lobe to his bottom lip.

Turning her attention back to the tent, she said, "I'm going in closer to have a look." She pulled protective gloves from her bag. Marching toward the tent, she glanced over her shoulder at Petrovci standing on the corner, and shuddered. She wondered how a pair of eyes could hold so much pain.

* * *

Light gleamed through the tent opening when Lottie pulled back the flap. Lynch had provided her with the requisite protective clothing, which she had pulled on along with the gloves, a mask over her nose and mouth, and covers on her shoes. Steel plates had been laid so as to preserve the already contaminated scene.

Careful not to disturb anything, she crouched into the confined space, noticing the victim's face first. Dark eyebrows. A wisp of black hair on a smooth forehead. No sign of trauma. Eyes closed, the feather-fine skin of the lids already blistering with the beginnings of putrefaction. A silver stud in one ear. Had she lost the other one? This, more than anything, touched Lottie. No matter how many victims of crime she came across or how many bodies she viewed, it was the little things that made them human.

"Strangled?" asked Boyd, hunching down beside her. He

too had donned protective gear. "Better wait for the pathologist," he said.

"Fuck that," Lottie said and swept a dark tendril of hair from the victim's forehead. "Dear God, she's no more than a child."

"Eighteen to mid twenties, I'd estimate," Boyd said soberly.

A sudden shout made them both jump.

"Get out of my crime scene!"

Jim McGlynn, head of the SOCO team, stood at the tent entrance, glaring at them.

"Nice to see you too," Lottie said, and realized she'd only ever seen McGlynn in his crime-scene outfit.

"Out now, the pair of you."

"We've not touched a thing!" Lottie said defensively.

"You should know better, Detective Inspector." He brushed past her and began setting up his equipment.

Boyd scurried away. Lottie inched back against the tent wall, allowing the technical guru to get on with his job. McGlynn ignored her as he worked. She kept her mouth firmly shut, just in case. When he finished photographing he began slowly sweeping away the gauze of clay from the victim's chest. The collar of a blue garment appeared.

The click of high heels out on the road alerted Lottie to the arrival of Jane Dore. The state pathologist dressed quickly in her protective garments and pulled off her four-inch heels. Sliding her feet into a pair of moccasin slippers, she covered them with overshoes. Lottie moved to one side, towering above the other woman. They exchanged greetings as the pathologist joined McGlynn.

"Young female. No fissures or ligature marks," Dore declared, running her fingers along the victim's throat, having first assessed the scene.

McGlynn was methodically brushing the rest of the clay

from the corpse. Gradually the entire body appeared. From her vantage point, Lottie noted that the clothing was made from cheesecloth. Undone buttons revealed braless breasts with blue veins like a road map.

A small mound protruded from below the ribcage.

She felt her mouth drop open. "She was pregnant."

The suffocating air instantly chilled around them. Lottie felt her clammy skin rise in goose bumps.

"It might just be decomposition," Jane cautioned.

"I don't think so," Lottie said, and she knew Jane didn't think so either. "How long has she been dead?"

"Hard to say. Decomposition is slower when the body's not exposed to the elements. But it's been unusually hot. Two days. Maybe. Rigor mortis has left the body, so I'd say more than forty-eight hours. I'll know more when I get her to the Dead House."

The Dead House, where the state pathologist performed her postmortems, was the mortuary attached to Tullamore Hospital, forty kilometers from Ragmullin.

"Was she killed here?"

"First I need to determine cause of death, Inspector," Jane said formally. "But looking at the soil and the location, I doubt this is where she was killed."

"Keep me informed."

"Of course."

Walking out of the tent into the blazing sunshine, Lottie hurriedly removed her outer clothing, dumped it in a brown evidence bag and called Maria Lynch over.

"Get uniforms to carry out door-to-door inquiries. Someone must have seen the body being buried." She glanced up at the shaded apartment windows. "Be thorough, and I want those contract workers in the station as soon as possible for statements."

"Yes, Inspector," Lynch said, and busied herself giving orders to the assembled guards.

"See if Barrett's Pub has working CCTV," Lottie said drily, eyeing the broken camera dangling by its wires. "And Kirby, get someone to search those trash cans." She pointed to the commercial-sized bins lining the alley, the stench of rotting rubbish mingling with the smell from the tent.

Kirby nodded.

"First forty-eight hours are crucial," Lottie said, "and I believe we've already lost those."

CHAPTER 8

Back at the station, Lottie joined Boyd in Interview Room 1. It was as claustrophobic as she remembered. No windows. No air con. So much for architects. And the renovations were still unfinished.

There would be plenty of people to interview in this case and it could take days. She wanted to start with the men working on the site.

Andri Petrovci was currently sitting at the table secured to the floor with bolts, his large fingers clenched in fists and his brown eyes drooping. Fatigue or fear?

"So, Mr. Petrovci, where are you from?" Lottie asked. She wanted to get started straight away.

"I from Kosovo." A deep, penetrating voice.

"How long have you been in Ireland?"

"I come to work," he said. "Maybe a year, maybe more."

"You've been in Ragmullin all that time?"

"Yes. No."

"You seem unsure," Lottie said.

"I arrive. I work in Dublin. Then I come to Ragmullin."

Lottie smiled as he struggled with the pronunciation of her town. She struggled with her town full stop, no matter what you called it.

"Why Ragmullin?"

"Job. Water main work."

"Where do you live now?" This was going to take forever.

"Hill Point. Small room."

Lottie knew the estate. Hill Point consisted of a series of

apartment blocks, constructed in a crescent, skirting the canal and railway. A few shops, a day care and a doctors' surgery. A low-market complex trying to be upmarket and failing miserably. She focused on Andri Petrovci.

"The body of the girl you discovered, do you know anything about her?"

"No."

"Tell me about the trench you were digging. When did this work start?"

"Three days ago, we lay pipes. Filled it in…how you say… temporary. Today we come back to fix."

"Fix?"

"Put back road. Understand?"

"I think so," Lottie said.

"So no one was working on that site since Friday?" Boyd asked.

"We do different street, then come back. Traffic… management?"

"Can you tell us anything else?"

"I know nothing," Petrovci said, lowering his head.

Further probing questions revealed little of interest to the investigation. Lottie felt a familiar growth of frustration swelling in her chest.

"Will you consent to having a sample of DNA taken? Just to rule you in or out of our investigation." It was probably a useless exercise, she thought. He had already contaminated the body.

He looked defensive. "Why? I do nothing wrong."

"It's just procedure. Nothing whatsoever to worry about."

"I not know. Later. Okay?"

"I'd prefer to get it out of the way, Mr. Petrovci."

"I not see reason for this. But okay."

Lottie instructed Boyd to arrange the buccal test, a simple swab to determine DNA for analysis. Boyd nodded and read Petrovci back his statement.

"You're free to go. For now," Lottie said. "We have your contact details and we may need to talk to you again."

Boyd switched off the recording equipment and began sealing up the DVDs. Lottie followed Petrovci with her eyes as he moved to the door. Wide shoulders, muscles taut beneath his hi-vis singlet.

He turned his head. "Little one... in the clay. Too young to die." He opened the door, exited and pulled it closed silently behind him.

Lottie stared at Boyd as he shrugged his shoulders.

"I'll get the next one in," he said, and followed Petrovci out of the door.

* * *

When they'd interviewed all the workers from the site, Superintendent Corrigan put his head around the door and said, "Incident room. Now."

Lottie followed him, watching the light glint off his bald pate, wondering how often he had to shave his head to maintain such an even sheen. In the incident room, an unwelcome surge of shivers shot up her spine as she recalled her last case. Same room, different murder. A free-standing noticeboard held a death-mask photograph of the victim. A rough drawing of the area where the body had been found and a large map of the town were pinned on a second board. Officers were busy on phones and typing up reports from the ongoing door-to-door inquiries.

Superintendent Corrigan rubbed a hand over his head, pushed his spectacles up his fat nose and said, "Inspector Parker, you are the senior investigation officer on this inquiry." He stared at her through one eye. The other was red and half-closed. An infection? Hopefully it wasn't contagious. She took a step back, just in case.

"Thank you, sir." Past experience had taught her to say as little as possible in Corrigan's presence. A habit of uttering the wrong thing in front of him had got her in trouble too many times.

"But all the press stuff goes through me first," he warned. "Don't want a feck-up like last time, do we?"

"I want to get straight to it, sir. Maria Lynch is working on the jobs book and Boyd is going to review the transcripts of the interviews we've just conducted."

"Kirby? What's he at?"

"I'll let you know shortly." As soon as I find him, she added silently.

"You know my views on cases like this. Ragmullin district handles it. No feckin' need for the city to be involved. But after the almighty balls-up you made of your last case, I'm not sure I can keep their noses out of this for long. So wrap it up quickly. Without feck-ups. Okay?"

"Sure, sir." She couldn't help wondering what was wrong with his eye. Had Mrs. Corrigan lost her temper and thumped him?

"And stop feckin' staring at me."

Lottie sighed. So much for her quiet first day.

* * *

Kirby was sitting at his desk shuffling through a bundle of interview transcripts from the apartment residents, one foot resting on top of a stack of files with his sandal beside it.

"I was looking for you," Lottie said, wrinkling her nose.

"You found me." He quickly slid his toes into the sandal. "I was about to bring this lot into the incident room."

"Does the pub on the corner of the street where the body was found have CCTV?"

"Take a guess, boss."

"Doesn't work?"

"Correct." Kirby scratched his wiry mop of hair. "Why go

to the bother of installing all that equipment and then not maintain it? It's beyond me."

"And none at the apartments either?"

"Nope."

"What about the town CCTV at that location?" she asked hopefully. "Anything there?"

"Cutbacks? Budgets? I don't know, but half the cameras don't work. They're only on the main streets anyway."

"Great." Lottie tried not to let her disappointment show, but it was a setback.

She spent the afternoon reading every report her detectives had highlighted for her. Boyd sat doing the same while intermittently organizing pens in a straight line on his desk. But there were no clues as to who the girl might be or who had murdered and buried her beneath the streets of Ragmullin.

At 4:15 p.m., Lottie's phone rang. Jane Dore, the pathologist. Lottie listened carefully before disconnecting the call. "Jane has the preliminary report ready."

"No flies on her," Boyd said.

"Your choice of words amazes me at times." Lottie shook her head, grabbed her bag. "I'm going to Tullamore."

"Do you need me to—"

"No, I don't need you to come with me. I know how to drive. Keep sifting through that lot. I want to know the name of the victim."

"I can't magic it out of thin air."

"Just find out who she was."

"Yes, boss. Why do you have to go all the way over there? Can she not email the report?"

"Can you not do your own work and I'll do mine?"

Lottie swung her bag over her shoulder and hurried out of the office before she lost her temper with him. Heading to the car, she hoped the damn air con worked. Chance would be a fine thing.

CHAPTER 9

"What did you say?" Lottie asked.

"Gunshot," the pathologist repeated.

"No way." Lottie shook her head in dismay.

"It's all preliminary at the moment," Jane Dore said, curt and professional as always.

"Preliminary will do for now," Lottie said.

A forty-kilometer drive to Tullamore and she had sweltered through every one of them. At least in the Dead House it was cold. And round here it was like a million miles away from the scenery she'd viewed along the road. Green trees, luscious in their growth, grass verges blossoming with buttercups and one of the many midland lakes glittering in the distance under the heady sun. That was before she hit the motorway of speeding vehicles and diesel fumes rising in the air. Now she would welcome that oily smell to help dispel the odor shrouding the Dead House.

They sat on chrome stools at a bench. The victim lay beneath a sheet on a steel table behind them.

"Entry through her back. No exit wound. X-rays show a bullet lodged in a rib. I'll send it to the lab and the ballistics people can examine it."

"She was shot. Shit," said Lottie. "I can't remember when we last had a shooting in Ragmullin."

"And I found what looks like a bite mark on the back of her neck. I've swabbed the area for saliva and taken impressions. I'll send the images to you."

"Will you be able to get DNA from the swab?"

"Not sure. It was very clean. Wait and see."

"Any sexual assault?"

"Evidence of vaginal tearing. So it's probable but not conclusive."

"Anything from her clothes?"

"Nothing. I believe she was undressed before she was shot. The wound presents as very clean. It may have been washed."

"The bullet hole? He washed it after he shot her?"

"It's clean. Someone washed it. I've also taken scrapings from beneath her nails. They might yield results. But don't depend on it."

"Why did he undress her, shoot her, wash the wound and then dress her again?" Lottie shook her head. What was she dealing with?

"Maybe he's a *CSI* freak."

"Who is she, Jane?"

"That's your job, Lottie. All I can tell you is that she was aged between sixteen and twenty and was pregnant at the time of her death. Allowing for the intense heat we've been experiencing and the rate of decomposition, I'd estimate she was murdered two days ago, three max."

Lottie thought of Petrovci's statement. They'd initially dug the trench three days ago. Had this girl been buried after that and been lying under the street since then?

"So she wasn't killed where we found her?"

"Lividity on the body suggests she was moved after death. The area where she was found would not allow the killer the freedom to undress her, shoot her, et cetera. She was definitely killed elsewhere. There's something else too." Jane jumped down from her stool, steered Lottie to the autopsy table and pulled the sheet from the body. "See this scar?" She pointed to an arc circling the victim's left hip, from her abdomen around her back.

"I see it," Lottie said, keeping her eyes away from the gaping vacuum where the pathologist had removed the fetus.

"The suturing is very neat," Jane said.

"What happened to her?"

"She'd had a kidney surgically removed."

"Why?"

"Perhaps she donated it to a family member? I don't know."

"Was the surgery recent?"

"I'll have a better idea when I do more tests. At the moment, I'd estimate surgery was no more than a year ago. That's all I can say until I go in again."

"And the pregnancy?" Lottie asked. "How far along was she when she died? Can we get DNA from the fetus?" She wondered if she was dealing with a reluctant father brandishing a gun, or a crime of misspent passion. Her gut told her it was something completely different. She trusted her gut. Most of the time.

Jane glided over to a second table. Lottie followed. Taking a deep breath, she braced herself. She wasn't squeamish and didn't mind looking at bodies. But an unborn baby? This was different.

"Here's her baby. It was about eighteen weeks' gestation at time of death. A girl."

Jane slowly drew back the sheet. Lottie gasped at the sight of the smallest baby she'd ever seen, curled on one side on the cold steel. She gulped back tears; composed herself. Glancing sideways, she noticed Jane hastily wiping her eyes. In the short time she had known Jane Dore, the pathologist had hardly ever registered any emotion.

"I've carried out a lot of autopsies in my time, but this... this is monstrous..." Jane's voice trailed off in the raw Dead House air.

"Sometimes I think there's nothing left to surprise me," Lottie said, "but there's always one more horror awaiting discovery." She turned away, picked up the reports and stuffed them in her bag.

"Find whoever did this," Jane said, her voice soft and flat.

Lottie didn't answer. But there was a new determination in her step as she left Jane in the Dead House and headed back to Ragmullin. As she drove, all she could see was the tiny baby with its miniature webbed thumb secured in its little mouth. She didn't think she would ever be able to dislodge that image from her memory.

* * *

Dropping the pathologist's preliminary report on Boyd's desk, Lottie thought he looked as haggard as she felt.

"We've canvassed the entire area, the pub, the apartments, everywhere. No one saw anything," he said.

"Typical Ragmullin."

She sat at her desk, recalling the case from late December that had crawled into January. A town where no one saw anything, very few said anything and those who did never told the whole truth.

"So what'd Jane have to say?" Boyd picked up the reports.

"The victim was definitely shot."

"What? Shot? This is bad, Lottie."

"I know." Gun crime was low to nonexistent in Ragmullin. Not like in the cities, she thought, where gangland crime was usually conducted at the end of a pistol. "She was definitely pregnant when she died."

"Bollocks!"

"And—wait for this—at some stage she'd had a kidney surgically removed."

"God. I hope it was by consent."

"Hard to know at the moment. Jane has to complete the postmortem yet."

"Pregnant, shot and a kidney gone. That girl has been through some horrors," Boyd said, scratching his head, looking lost. Lottie knew the feeling.

"The victim was undressed before she was shot, then the wound was washed and she was re-dressed."

"Why would someone do that? It's mad."

"Insane. Anyone fitting her description on the missing persons list?" Lottie inquired, masking a yawn. Her first day had been much more hectic than she could have imagined.

"Nothing to match our girl. But if she was over eighteen, I doubt she'd be on it yet anyway."

"She's been dead two days, maybe three. Eighteen weeks pregnant. Someone, somewhere, is missing her. The father of her child, for instance."

"Maybe she told no one. The pregnancy could be the result of a one-night stand."

"Or could be in a relationship with a married man and something went wrong and he shot her."

"We *could* release the postmortem photograph."

"You saw her face. We can't put decomposing flesh into the public domain." She grabbed the pathologist's report from Boyd and scanned through it. "Not yet, anyway."

"It was just an idea," he said.

"A stupid one."

She knew he wanted to retort, but the seriousness of what they were discussing didn't warrant it. She said, "Jane notes here that based on the girl's bone structure, she could be Eastern European, possibly of Balkan origin."

"How could she make that call?"

"She studied anthropology."

"So was the victim here illegally?" Boyd said. "It'd make our job all the harder to identify her."

"She could be a refugee or asylum seeker," Lottie said. "They're documented."

She recalled a local outcry a few years ago when the Department of Justice leased out the defunct army barracks.

It had been converted into a direct provision center for asylum seekers. A storm in a teacup, her mother had said. It had all died down.

"It's worth checking," Boyd said.

"Put it on tomorrow's to-do list."

"Sure."

"And we need to interview Petrovci again. First, though, I've to conduct a team meeting before everyone escapes for the night."

CHAPTER 10

It was after eight o'clock when she eventually arrived home from work. Silence greeted her. Her mother, Rose Fitzpatrick, who'd been looking after the kids, was long gone. Lottie thought how they were all doing a good job of avoiding each other recently.

"Anyone here?" she shouted up the stairs.

No reply.

Entering the kitchen, she groaned. The sink was piled high with glasses and plates. Back to what was normal before her sabbatical from the force. But at least her family had been fed. At one time Rose would have left the house sparkling clean. Lottie wondered what she'd done to cause the change.

"Does anyone know how to wash a mug in this house?"

No answer. Talking to herself. Again.

Everywhere was unusually quiet. In a fit of panic, she raced up the stairs and plowed into her son's room.

"What's up?" Sean asked, removing headphones. He quickly tapped his computer and the screen faded to a photograph of a sunny beach.

"I'm home," Lottie said, feeling relief flood her cheeks.

"So?"

"How was school?"

"Boring as usual." The boy replaced his headphones and waited for her to leave.

Pulling the door behind her, wondering if she should have checked what he was up to on the computer, she poked her head round Katie's door. Her elder daughter appeared to be asleep.

Leaving her, Lottie glanced into Chloe's room. Chloe was sitting at her small desk, buds in her ears and a stack of school books in front of her. Lottie waved a hand in front of her.

Without raising her head, Chloe said, "I'm studying."

Leaving her alone, Lottie returned downstairs to see if there was anything left in the cupboards worth cooking. Nothing.

Slumping into the comfort of the kitchen armchair, she noticed the paint peeling above the cooker. The house needed redecorating. She lowered her eyes to avoid the sight of grease gathered in small black dots along the wall just below the ceiling. The day had drained the energy from her body. Maybe a sleep would energize her enough to clean up the mess. She closed her eyes.

* * *

Chloe locked her bedroom door, wrapped up her ear buds, put away her books and took her noise-reduction headphones from the wardrobe. With the window open, she let the night breeze flutter over her body as she tapped the Spotify app on her phone.

After she'd run from the canal, she'd spent most of the day in the library, listening to music, staring out of the window. At 4:30 p.m., she had strolled home, knowing her granny would have left by then.

A knot of anxiety gripped her chest and she tried to catch her breath. She wanted to tell her mother how she felt. How this fear of helplessness threatened to overwhelm every thought she had. But any time she tried to say something, the words wouldn't form. And there was no talking to Lottie now that she was back at work. As for Katie, God only knew what was going on in her mind since Jason had been murdered. She'd refused to go back to college and spent her days moaning.

Looking over the fresh cut on her upper arm, Chloe

wondered what her mother would do if she found out about that. The panic rose in her throat and she tried to control her breathing. In. Out. In. Out. She needed the blade. Yes, the physical pain might ease the thoughts swamping her brain.

A message alert flashed up on her phone screen. She tapped it. A new post on #cutforlife. She opened it up and engaged on the forum, breathing a sigh of relief. She wouldn't need to use the blade tonight.

* * *

A deserted street at midnight was probably not the most sensible place for a jog, especially with a killer about, but after waking up in the armchair, Lottie needed air and exercise to clear her head and help her sleep that night.

Deliberate, methodical steps, counted in her head. Her iPhone was equipped with a step counter, but she couldn't be bothered setting it up. Anyway, she'd heard it chewed up battery life. With the phone nestling in her bra, she slowed her pace as she made her way uphill by the county council offices. Her breath came in sharp gasps. Unfit, she thought, even though she'd been jogging daily while off work.

Taking a right at the top of the street, she suddenly stopped. Froze. Drawing in a breath, she turned around. Her body trembled as her heart palpitated. No one. Slowly she started jogging again. Imagining things, she thought.

Monday nights were quiet in Ragmullin. No stragglers heading from the pubs to nightclubs; even the taxi rank outside Danny's Bar was desolately tranquil as a lone driver leaned against his cab, smoking a cigarette.

Unable to cast off the feeling of being followed, she decided against shortcutting through the town park and headed up by Friars Street instead, where the duo of ancient monks cast in bronze appeared watchful with their solid eyes.

The jog wasn't working in terms of clearing her head. Images of the girl's body decomposing beneath the street and the tiny baby on the stainless-steel table in the Dead House refused to wane.

Glancing to her left, toward Bridge Street, she noticed the crime-scene tapes hanging limply, blocking off the road. She walked across the deserted street to stand outside the tape.

At the corner, the SOCOs' tent flapped, forlorn in its solitude. A uniformed police officer stood beside a squad car parked at the gated entrance to the apartments. He saluted her. Lottie acknowledged him with a nod, hands on hips, getting her breath back.

"Quiet night?" she asked.

He shrugged: *What do you think?*

She knew it was necessary to guard the site until everything was checked. Anyone could interfere with it. The killer might even return, though she supposed he was more than likely far away from Ragmullin at this stage. At least she hoped he wasn't hanging around town, ready to strike again. But wherever and whoever he was, she would catch him. The image of the unborn baby girl flashed anger into her heart. No one was getting away with this murder.

There it was again. She swung around, sure that someone had been at her shoulder.

"Did you see anyone just there?" she asked the officer.

"No, Inspector, I did not."

"Okay. Thanks."

Deciding she'd had enough of the murky night air, she ran by the unlit community college and headed for home. The thought of a cool shower and bed stimulated her tired limbs.

It was getting bad when she started to imagine things.

CHAPTER 11

The room was too small for so many. Two bunk beds, a nightstand and a wardrobe with no doors. Floorboards worn and bare, cracked paint, and cobwebs claiming the dusty corners of the ceiling.

Two girls slept soundly in the beds opposite Mimoza Barbatovci, their soft snores breaking the silence. They had stepped out of their clothes, dropping them on the narrow floor space in the middle of the room, and crawled naked beneath thin sheets, falling asleep immediately.

The unlit lightbulb swayed above Mimoza's head. Nighttime didn't come as quickly here as in her homeland. The evenings dragged through a slow dusk. Even then the dark never fully succeeded in pulling down the night.

Curling her body into itself on the bottom bunk, she nursed her bleeding arm. The skin was broken in two crescents above her elbow. She didn't like it when he bit her. It was always painful, but this time he'd drawn blood. Hopefully she wouldn't catch a disease from his putrid saliva. He had made sure she suffered for leaving this morning. And now he had taken poor Sara, who'd only been trying to help her and little Milot. So much for giving the security guard at the gate a blow job. He had allowed her to go out, but the others had come after her anyway. They must have followed her. Or followed Sara. Did they actually know where she had been? She hoped not. And now she and Milot were back here. Incarcerated. She should have run when she had the chance. But where could she have gone? What was done was done. She'd kept her mouth shut. She hoped Sara would too.

Pain itched between her legs. No matter how much she scrubbed herself afterward, she was sure something remained, feeding off her insides. She tried to ignore the soreness and thought of other things worrying her.

She hadn't seen Kaltrina for days. No one would tell her where her friend had gone. Terrible things happened in this place, Mimoza knew that. Most people were too afraid to utter a word, but Kaltrina had opened her mouth. And now she was gone.

All she could hope for was that the detective lady would help. She had thought it too dangerous to go to the police station; how could she make them believe her? So she'd taken a chance and gone to the address, the one written on a piece of paper he'd given her with the badge. Before he had abandoned her in their homeland. It seemed like a lifetime ago and she didn't want to think about him now.

The door opened and Sara limped in. She stood in the middle of the room, a black statue in the moonlight. Mimoza smelled the same horrible odor from the young girl, that still clung to her own body. Sara had been punished for helping her.

"Don't cry," she said, rising up on her elbow, wincing in agony.

Sara wrapped her arms tightly around herself and stared through the window, tears shimmering on her face.

"Come. Lie beside me." Mimoza reached out and grasped the girl's hand. It was slick with sweat. Sara turned and lay down beside her.

Cradling her, Mimoza was careful not to wake her son, who was snaked against the wall in her bed. She soothed Sara like she'd done with her little boy earlier.

Sara heaved with sobs until they eventually petered out, but her body still shuddered every few seconds and Mimoza listened to the shattered breathing until the girl drifted at last into a fitful sleep.

Milot stirred, murmuring.

"Shh," she said.

The sheet rustled with her movement. Gently she traced a finger over his forehead, whispering a soft lullaby in his ear. She loved him so much, her spine tingled. He was all she had left in the world. And he'd been dragged with her on her long, harrowing journey. Was it her fault it had turned into a tortuous nightmare? He was her son, and if she'd made a mistake, she would rectify it.

"Where will it all end?" she mumbled in her mother tongue.

With no answer to her question, sleep evaded her, and she was still awake when she heard the door open. As Sara was dragged to the floor, Mimoza tried to catch her. Familiar rough hands pushed her away and Sara was pulled out into the hallway, screaming.

When the door slammed, Mimoza cradled her weeping son, silently praying for one small mercy.

"Please don't let them harm my Milot."

CHAPTER 12

He lifted the iron sheeting with his gloved hands, tugging it to the side of the trench. With a shovel he quickly dug out the loose clay. When it was deep enough for his intended purpose, he walked the short distance back to his white van.

The temporary *Men at Work* signs he had erected at both ends of the narrow street a few minutes earlier ensured uninterrupted work. It was 4 a.m. and Ragmullin was asleep. The intermittent vibrations of cars along Main Street caused him little concern. No one was coming down this road. Rear shop entrances to his left and a car dismantler's yard to his right. A small block of half-empty flats further down. All lifeless in the dead of night.

With a quick glance around to be doubly sure he was unseen, he unlocked the rear doors, dragged down a narrow ramp and wheeled out a wide wheelbarrow covered with a piece of dark green canvas.

Making his way in the dark to the hole, he removed the canvas and tipped the wheelbarrow. The body tumbled into the ground. He laid her out and began shoveling the clay on top of her. Her pale skin darkened with each soft thud of earth. When he had finished, he hauled the iron cover back in place as silently as possible, though he was sure there was no one around to hear a thing.

He checked his surroundings one more time before lifting the canvas and placing it on the wheelbarrow, then hurrying back up the street to his van. When he had everything inside, he pushed up the ramp and went to collect the signs. Back in the van, he smiled to himself as he headed away. He was getting closer and closer to his target.

Job done.

* * *

Kosovo 1999

He didn't know how many days he had walked or how long he had lain in the bushes. But his trousers were soiled and his feet bleeding. He looked at the darkening sky and listened to the many trucks passing by on the old dirt road. Why couldn't he remember? Why was his mind full of black holes?

"Hey, young fella, what you doing down there?"

He hadn't heard the truck stop. Curling into himself, he prepared for the gunshot. Maybe it would solve everything for him. Feeling a hand grab him by the shoulder, he yelped like a helpless dog.

"Don't be afraid. You're safe with us."

A slight wind kicked up, blowing a cool breeze over his bare chest. He understood a little English. He'd learned it at school. That seemed so long ago. The man was dressed in an army uniform. Another soldier glared down from the cab of their big green truck.

"Are you lost, son?"

He'd called him son. But he wasn't anyone's son. Everyone was dead.

Looking up at the soldier, the boy was surprised. He had a face like Papa. Before Papa had... Before the war.

The soldier glanced at his comrade. "Bring him with us?"

"Well, hurry up. We've been driving since Macedonia. I'm fucked."

"Come on then."

The soldier lifted the boy and the driver hauled him into the cab. Sitting between the two of them, the boy scrunched his elbows into his body, making himself as small as possible.

"You hungry?"

He nodded.

"Here you go. Have a bag of Tayto crisps. Got them sent over from home."

The boy wished the soldier would stop talking. He opened the bag and began munching. He was starving. How long since he'd eaten? Another black hole.

"You don't talk much," the soldier said. "Eat up. We'll be at the chicken farm soon."

The boy did as he was told.

DAY TWO

Tuesday, May 12, 2015

CHAPTER 13

The birds were singing a tune only they recognized. The dawn sunlight eased through a slit between the windowsill and the blind. A shard of light cut across the bed like a steel knife.

Lottie plumped up her pillow and listened. The two wood pigeons began their harmony at the end of her garden. A mug of coffee in bed would be nice, she thought. Some chance of that happening. Adam used to leave a mug beside her, feather his lips over her forehead and silently close the door as he headed to work. But it was now almost four years since he had died and she was left with his shadow, living in a silent movie stuck in rewind mode.

As the seconds churned, boring into her consciousness, she felt the familiar and uneasy loneliness that accompanied her memories. Wasn't it about time she got over Adam? Everyone seemed to think she should be back to her normal self, whatever that might be. But now her life was like a black-and-white photograph, fading to sepia with time, and she struggled to find color to inject into it.

She slammed her fist into the duvet and gritted her teeth to keep the tears away. It was no good. She was still angry at Adam, at his cancer, for dying and leaving her alone with three children. For not giving her the time to ask him what he wanted her to do with the rest of her life without him by her side. For not being stronger in the face of her grief. "God damn you, Adam Parker!" she cried aloud.

Throwing back the duvet, she jumped out of bed, fleeing her jumbled thoughts, and ran to the shower. As the water flowed in a swirl of suds down the drain she knew her attitude wasn't good enough. Pull yourself together, woman, she scolded, and consciously she did just that. She was stronger than her memories.

"Strong Lottie, that's me," she said to the steamed-up mirror.

She dried and dressed herself, and was ready to face whatever the day had to throw at her. And then she realized she was late. Again.

* * *

"You're late," Boyd said, slamming a cabinet drawer. Files, stacked on top of it, slid to the floor.

"Really? I could've sworn I was *dead* late." Lottie sat at her desk and powered up her computer. "Who are you now? My mother?"

"How is your mother?"

"Boyd, you know right well not to go there." She shoved her handbag under her desk and lifted the poppy-painted mug. She read her password, keyed it in and said, "Any updates?"

"No identification of the victim yet," he said, picking up the files, sorting them alphabetically.

"Do you ever stop?" Lottie asked.

"What?"

"Trying to keep everything in order." She waited for her computer to wake up.

"Just because you're 'sloppy Lottie' doesn't mean we all have to be." He slotted files into the drawer.

"Boyd, will you sit down, for heaven's sake!"

"Okay, okay."

"I meant to tell you. Yesterday morning I had a visit from a young woman and a little boy."

"What are you talking about?" Boyd stood with a file in each hand.

So much had happened yesterday, Lottie had completely forgotten about the girl and the letter until this morning. She took the envelope from her bag and slipped out a folded page.

"It's written in a foreign language," she said, passing it over to Boyd.

He took it. "How am I supposed to know what this says?"

"We need to get it translated."

"Why do we need to do that?"

She ignored him and peeked into the envelope, surprised to see something wedged at the bottom. She was about to take it out when Superintendent Corrigan appeared like an apparition at the door.

Corrigan opened his mouth to speak, but before he could utter a word, Lottie said, "Yes, sir, I'm coming." She stuffed the envelope back into her bag.

* * *

Seated, slightly squashed behind his desk, Superintendent Corrigan said, "Jamie McNally is back in town."

"What? Does Boyd know?" Lottie sat down uninvited. Shit, she thought. A few years ago, Boyd's wife Jackie had left him for McNally, who was known to the police as a small-time criminal. Last she'd heard, the couple were residing in Spain.

"I don't know," Corrigan said, removing his spectacles to rub furiously at his sore eye.

Lottie grimaced as she watched him. "He'll go mental."

"Inspector, you and I know Sergeant Boyd never goes mental. He's the calmest one in the station."

"Will I tell him?" Lottie asked. If McNally had come back to Ragmullin, she wondered if Jackie had returned also. How would Boyd handle it? She didn't like to dwell on that.

"I don't care who tells him, but we need to find out why McNally's back and what he's up to."

"I'll put Kirby on it straight away, sir."

"Do that."

"When did he arrive?"

"Our intel says Wednesday of last week. This is all I need." Corrigan replaced his spectacles on the bridge of his nose but his finger searched beneath the glass to continue rubbing.

Lottie flinched.

"What?" he asked.

"I think you need to see a doctor about your eye, Superintendent."

"You're starting to get on my nerves now. I've to listen to that shite from the wife. I don't want to feckin' listen to it from you too, do you hear?"

"Yes, sir."

"And put someone on McNally's tail."

"On it already."

* * *

After instructing Kirby to find out anything he could about McNally's whereabouts, Lottie slumped back at her desk and began reading the accumulated case reports. Time enough to tell Boyd about McNally. Maybe Jackie hadn't returned. But should she consider McNally as a possible murder suspect? He had history. Maybe not murder, as far as they knew, but history all the same. What the hell was he doing in Ragmullin?

"Still no hits on the missing persons list. No one resembling our girl." Boyd tapped angrily on the keyboard.

"Someone, somewhere is missing her," Lottie said. Her T-shirt clung to her skin, a rivulet of sweat pooled between her breasts and the wire of her bra burned into her ribs. The unease she'd felt earlier in the morning returned with a sharp stab of anxiety in her chest. She took a few deep breaths. It didn't work. She blinked as the room slipped in and out of focus. Oh God, she thought. I have to be strong. I can handle this shit. Fuck it.

Opening her bag, she unzipped the small internal pocket. Her emergency pill was there. Popping open the blister, she quickly swallowed the pill, grabbed Boyd's bottle of water and washed away the chalky taste. Last one, swear to God, she silently prayed, and handed back the water.

"Keep it," Boyd said, waving her away.

She knew he'd seen her surreptitiously taking the pill and ignored his derisory look. "Any word from ballistics?" she asked, knowing it could take weeks.

"No."

Sighing, she noticed Boyd had dumped the letter on her desk. The foreign words seemed to mock her. Where had the girl and her son come from? And how could she help them?

"I think we need to find this Mimoza. She mentioned her friend was missing, so it's possible she might know who the victim is."

"That's some leap in deduction."

She waved the letter at him. "Did you have any luck translating this?"

"Sorry, I didn't try."

"No worries," she said and started to type the words into Google Translate. It wasn't making sense. She got up and rummaged through the stack of paper on Boyd's desk.

"Hey, I sorted those," he said, trying to pull them out of her reach.

"I'm just looking for the phone number for that guy who found the body. Andri whatshisname." She continued to flick through the reports, opening files, leaving pages curled and untidy.

"Petrovci?"

"Yes, him."

"Why do you want to ring him? Isn't he a suspect? A person of interest? I thought we were going to interview him again today."

"He found the body. That's all. Ah, here it is."

Boyd shook his head. "I hope you're not going to do what I think you're going to do."

"You know me too well, Boyd."

"I'm serious. This is—"

"Career suicide? I know. But look at it this way. If he had anything to do with the murder, the letter might scare him into confessing. Or something." She hesitated for a moment before tapping the number into her phone. For some reason, she wanted to see Petrovci's reaction to the letter. Right or wrong, she was going to run with it.

Boyd noisily stacked his files back in order on his desk. "You're on a kamikaze mission. Day two back at work, Lottie. Day two. Don't do this."

She listened to the call ringing before being cut off.

"Suicide," he muttered.

"Shut up," she said, and waited a moment before trying the number again.

CHAPTER 14

Andri Petrovci, with his boss Jack Dermody, loaded the work van and headed for Columb Street. The road management crew had been late arriving on site to divert the traffic and vehicles now trailed slug-like through the town. It took them half an hour to reach the new dig.

This piecemeal pipe-laying to appease the retailers exasperated motorists who didn't know where an excavation would spring up next. The contractors were like summer weeds sprouting in a smooth lawn, Petrovci supposed, unwanted and generally making a nuisance of themselves.

As he checked the temporary traffic lights at the Main Street junction, his phone vibrated. He didn't recognize the number, so he disconnected the call and shoved the phone back into his trouser pocket. When he looked up, a small fat man was rushing toward him.

"Hey, you! What do you think you're doing?" said the red-faced man, his ginger hair a beacon to the sun.

Twisting round, Petrovci looked down at him and shrugged. He kept walking, brushing by the man, who only reached his shoulder. The man grabbed his elbow.

"Problem?" Petrovci asked.

"How are the trucks going to deliver to my yard?" The man pointed to the car dismantler's depot. "Bob Weir. That's me and that's my business."

Petrovci swiped the man's chubby fingers from his arm and strode onto the site. He knew Bob Weir from Cafferty's Bar. Got a few earfuls one weekend as he'd tried to sip his Guinness in peace. But Weir's voice had soured his pint so he'd left it on the counter and made his way home. Racism was rife in Ragmullin, he concluded. But they were only words. In his homeland, he had encountered racism at the barrel of an AK-47.

As he picked up his tools, his phone vibrated again. This time he answered rather than having to listen to Weir's ranting at the roadblock.

* * *

The letter lay on the green-Formica-topped table in front of Andri Petrovci, along with a plate of chips. Mugs of black coffee for Lottie and Boyd.

Lottie kept her eyes on the workman's downturned shaved head. "Do you know the language it's written in?"

He had agreed to meet her once she'd said they didn't have to go too far from the site. The Malloca Café on the corner was quiet, even though it was lunchtime. Louis, the owner, stood behind the counter glaring at them. He probably blamed the contractors for decimating his trade.

Boyd, sitting with his arms folded, was frowning. She should have come alone—she knew he didn't approve of this course of action—but he was in his persistent-mole mood, so she had relented.

"I busy," Petrovci said. "Boss, he not happy."

"Mr. Petrovci. Just tell us what the note says. DS Boyd will write everything down. Then you can go back to work," Lottie said.

He picked up the note. "Not signed."

"No," she said curtly. She wasn't about to tell him where it had come from.

He studied the page. She studied him. Thick fingers with dirty broken nails. Behind long dark lashes his brown-black eyes appeared couched with pain. The caverns of his sunken cheeks might be from hunger, or maybe it was his nature. And the scar. An uneasy shiver slid down Lottie's spine and her smile drowned on her lips in a sea of confusion. Was it a mistake involving him? Boyd thought so. She hoped not. Her last case had landed her in enough trouble without her making the same mistakes this time.

"The note is in Albanian," he said.

"Can you read it?" Lottie asked.

He shrugged.

"Please," she urged.

"The person who write say not free to leave. Want your help. Find missing friend Kaltrina. Help escape."

Lottie leaned forward, keeping her eyes on his. "Escape? From what?"

"I only know what it say. This friend Kaltrina, not seen for few days."

Lottie turned and looked at Boyd. Could Kaltrina be their dead girl?

"Anything else?" she asked.

Petrovci shook his head. "Need your help. That all." He pushed the page toward Lottie. "I go now?"

"Wait. It must say something else. Was this Kaltrina pregnant?"

His eyes darkened. "I tell you what is written."

Learning nothing from his stony expression, Lottie said, "Can you tell us where you were this weekend and what you were doing?"

"You arrest me?"

"Just asking a few questions." Lottie felt Boyd's eyes boring into her. She refused to acknowledge him.

Petrovci said, "I at home. Alone. Okay? I go now."

"We will need to take another formal statement from you. Don't leave town."

Standing up, Petrovci gestured for Boyd to get out of his way. As he eased out of the seat, Lottie noted that he was a good head taller than Boyd, who was over six foot. He walked out, hi-vis vest billowing in the breeze orchestrated by the swinging door.

She saw Boyd watching her looking after Petrovci. He shook his head slowly.

"What?" she snapped.

"Big mistake. Big mistake." He folded his notebook into his trouser pocket. "You shouldn't be interviewing a suspect in a fucking chipper's. And you had no right to show him that letter. You learned nothing from him, and what if this Mimoza really is in trouble? Did you think of that? Maybe your construction worker there is the source of that trouble. You need to stop and think before you act."

He walked out, leaving Lottie to pay the bill.

Mistake? Shit.

*   *   *

"I wonder if our murdered girl is this missing Kaltrina," Lottie said, walking behind Boyd, trying to make conversation.

She caught up with him as he swung his jacket from one shoulder to the other. The street was steaming with clogged traffic going nowhere. Dust from the roadworks swirled around; noise from heavy machinery polluted the atmosphere, raising temperatures higher than a mercury barometer.

"The note doesn't mention she was pregnant, so your guess is as good as mine." Boyd shifted his jacket once again.

"I don't do guesses."

"But you go to potential suspects for help."

"Give it a rest, Boyd."

"Okay, but when Corrigan gets wind of this, I don't want to get caught in the down-draft." He walked on ahead of her.

"How can we find out if the body is that of this Kaltrina?" She caught up with him again.

"So far no one has been reported missing. No one reported abducted."

"I need to find Mimoza for more information."

"Lottie?"

"What?"

"Don't involve this Petrovci character. We know nothing about him."

"He read the note for us, didn't he?"

"You have no idea what is in that note. He could have said anything."

"I'll get it translated," she said. "Properly this time."

"Don't make the same mistake as last—"

"Oh my God, you're the proverbial broken record."

They turned the corner. The twin-spired cathedral soared upward like a majestic bookend at the top of the street. The murder at the end of December within its marbled walls might have been a fading memory to most of Ragmullin's citizens but Lottie could not forget. It had set off a train of events, solving her personal family secret about her long-lost brother, Eddie, and in the course of many mistakes she had almost lost her son. She shivered.

"Are you all right?" Boyd asked.

Gripping her arms tight to her body, Lottie shrugged off his concern and hurried into the station. She couldn't help thinking she had made an error of judgment involving Andri Petrovci.

CHAPTER 15

Back in the office, sitting at her desk reading her way through various reports on the murder, Lottie looked up to see Kirby struggling to get in the door, a large watermelon gripped to his chest, dribbles of perspiration slipping down his face from his bushy, in-need-of-a-cut hair.

"Is it raining?" asked Boyd.

"We're so funny today," Kirby mocked, slapping the watermelon onto his desk. It started to roll. He caught it before it smashed on the floor.

"What's that for?" Lottie asked.

"Thought we might have a game of football. Any of you geniuses know how to cut up this thing?"

"Google it," Lottie and Boyd said together.

"Fuckers," said Kirby.

Turning her attention away from Kirby as he went off in search of a knife, Lottie said, "When we find Mimoza, we'll show her a photograph of the dead girl."

Boyd slammed a bunch of interview transcripts down on his desk without answering her.

"Just thinking, boss, the victim might be one of those asylum seekers," Kirby said, returning from the canteen brandishing a bread knife. "They're housed up in the army barracks and she might not have been reported missing yet." He leaned down to Lottie and whispered, "No sign of McNally."

She nodded her thanks. "We were wondering the same thing yesterday evening. Why do you think she could've been resident there?"

"She hasn't been reported missing by anyone, has she?" Kirby set about dissecting the watermelon on his desk.

"No," Lottie said. "So she's probably not a local, and we've checked the national missing persons list too."

"There was a fierce commotion a few months ago in the media about the accommodation at the army barracks," Kirby said. "Overcrowding or something." Juice splattered up from the melon. "When the barracks closed down, everyone was afraid it would be overrun with vagrants," he continued, pips caught in a day's growth of stubble. "Then there was more of an outcry when the Department of Justice set up the camp."

"Camp? Kirby, you are the most politically incorrect person I know."

"You know what I mean." Kirby sucked on the watery fruit.

"We've no evidence the victim is from this... what do they call it?" Lottie said.

"Direct provision center. We've no idea where the hell she's from." Kirby offered a slice of melon to Boyd, who declined with a shake of his head.

Lottie typed a few words into her computer. "Says on the DOJ website that the guy in charge of the direct provision center is Dan Russell, ex-army officer. Interesting to note too, the Ragmullin center is one of the government's latest outsourcing projects." She continued to read.

"Experimental so," Boyd said. "God knows what it's like."

"Like a concentration camp. That's what I heard." Kirby squelched the fruit, rivulets leaking from the side of his flabby lips. "All women and children. The men are located at another center somewhere. Longford or Athlone. Families split up."

Lottie ignored their banter. "Let's pay a visit to Mr. Russell," she said to Boyd, anxious to flee Kirby and his obnoxious eating habits.

"Wonder if Russell knew your Adam," Boyd said.

CHAPTER 16

Ragmullin army barracks, built in 1817, had changed little in almost two hundred years. Lottie and Boyd entered through a door beside the main gate and showed their ID to a security guard. Up ahead, the old guard hut was empty and the jail, which during the civil war had held IRA leader General MacEoin captive, also looked bereft of human habitation. The security guard pointed out directions. Lottie and Boyd followed the cobbled path and entered a building marked "Block A," situated beside a small chapel.

Climbing the wooden stairs to Russell's office, Boyd asked, "Are you all right being here, Lottie?"

"It's a bit weird, but I'm okay."

She knocked on the door, feeling claustrophobic in the narrow corridor.

"Enter," came the command from within.

With formalities over and seated at his desk, Lottie studied Dan Russell. He was the quintessential ex-army man. Uniform-like suit, slate gray, black tie and immaculate white shirt. She placed a photograph of the dead girl on the desk. She had no qualms about showing him a postmortem picture.

He glanced down. "I don't know her." His voice was as sharp as his appearance. He looked up from the photograph, directly at Lottie. He had navy-blue eyes and was older than she'd first thought—perhaps late fifties—with a mustache perched above a thin upper lip. "I'm exceptionally busy, Inspector," he said. "You do realize I've had to reschedule my day to fit you in."

"Yes, and thank you. Appreciated," Lottie said abruptly. Tell me if you know the girl in the photo and I'll get out of your sleek black hair, she thought.

"You're on a wild goose chase." A smile tickled the edge of his upper lip.

"I beg your pardon?"

"What makes you think this person might be from here?"

Lottie counted the pictures hanging on the wall behind him. In stressful situations, she counted things. Gave her time to breathe. It stemmed from a trauma in her childhood when she'd used it as a coping mechanism.

"Do you recognize the dead girl? That's all I'm asking," she said at last.

"She's dead?" The lip drooped. Shock? Surely he knew it was a postmortem photograph.

"Yes, she's dead," Lottie said. "Murdered."

"And I'm your first port of call?" Russell's eyes narrowed.

"I don't think she's local and it's possible she's a refugee or an asylum seeker as she's not yet been reported missing. We thought you might recognize her as someone who's been here and—"

"I have to stop you there, Inspector." He held up his hand as if she was a lowly private under his command. "Let me explain. This center houses desperate people escaping war in their own countries. Syria, Africa, Afghanistan. You name it. They come from many troubled lands. They stay here while their documents are being processed. During this transition period they have access to food and shelter until we find ways of dealing with their circumstances." He took a breath and exhaled. "I don't want to appear disruptive to your investigation, but frankly I'm astonished that you have the audacity to suggest one of our inmates might be this murdered girl."

Lottie let him rant, casting an eye toward Boyd. He raised a quizzical brow. Inmates?

"Is this a prison?" she asked.

"No. It's a direct provision center. I thought I'd explained that. It's a government initiative, run by my company."

"A private company?" Lottie asked.

"Woodlake Facilities Management. Look it up."

Lottie bristled. "I only want to establish if you know who this victim is."

"I don't know her. I'm sorry." He slid the photo back across the desk.

"Can I ask around?" Lottie chanced. "Someone might recognize her."

"That won't be necessary," Russell said. He retrieved the photograph. "I'll keep this and do the asking. If I discover anything, you will be contacted."

"Thank you. Another thing. Do you know anyone called Kaltrina?"

His eyes flickered slightly. "No. Should I?"

"Just wondering."

Doubting she would hear further from him, Lottie handed over her card anyway. Though it was sweltering despite an old fan, the room suddenly felt icy.

Russell stood. Lottie rose too.

Boyd remained seated, chewing the inside of his lip. "How about the name Mimoza? Ever hear that?"

Lottie kicked him, but it was too late. She caught the look darting like the tail of a fleeing rat across Russell's face before he flashed his pearly-white teeth.

"There are a lot of people residing here," he said. "My job is to oversee the facility. It's a very busy place and I don't have much direct contact with the inmates."

That word again. And it was clear to Lottie that he had recognized the name Mimoza.

Before she could question him further, Russell continued,

"They come from many countries but unfortunately most of them look alike to me, so I can't say I know who you're talking about. Sorry."

"Then we need to talk to someone who does know," Lottie said firmly.

"No, Inspector." He looked at her sharply. "I will check on your behalf."

Silently she admitted defeat. For the moment. She would try getting a list of names herself. They had to be logged on some database. Gesturing for Boyd to leave, she hurried down the wooden stairs behind him and out into the blistering sunlight.

* * *

Outside the gates, Lottie wondered why they hadn't seen any evidence of people milling around the barracks.

"It's eerily quiet," she said. "Do you think everyone's locked up in their rooms?"

"I doubt it," Boyd said, "but Russell's a tough nut."

"If any evidence turns up to suggest the dead girl was a resident, we'll get a search warrant."

They trekked across The Green, once a bustling market area for cattle and sheep, now a makeshift shortcut into the town center. Girding the grassy expanse were terraces of jaded 1950's houses. Minuscule gardens fenced with rusted ironwork appeared neat but generally devoid of humanity. Too hot for the aged residents to venture outside. Lottie didn't blame them.

"I hope Russell's in this mess right up to his shiny arse," she said.

They crossed the road at the edge of the green and headed across the canal footbridge.

"Why?"

"He calls the residents inmates. Does he think he's a prison governor?"

"He knew the name Mimoza—that much was obvious."

"Yes, Boyd, and I hope you haven't caused difficulty for her if she is in there."

"If he knows her, why didn't he admit it?"

"There's something he's not telling us. I can feel it."

Boyd leaned over the bridge and lit a cigarette. "You want one?"

"I do, but I've quit."

"Again?"

"Oh, shut up and light one for me."

Lottie inhaled and stood on the bridge contemplating the cloudy green waters below. A man walked along the cherry-blossom tree-lined towpath, with a husky pup on a long lead. He waved and she waved back.

"Who's that?" asked Boyd.

"I've no idea."

They smoked their cigarettes in silence.

"Why didn't you ask Russell if he knew Adam?" Boyd said eventually.

"I wouldn't give him the satisfaction, the bastard." She took a long, hard drag on the cigarette. "I'm going to get Lynch to check Russell out."

* * *

When he was sure the detectives were well away from the front gates, Dan Russell made a phone call.

Three minutes later, a man with crooked teeth was standing in his office.

Russell said, "Fatjon, I've had the local guards in. They've discovered a girl's body. Has that got anything to do with you?"

"I know nothing about a body."

"Good. Find out what that bitch Mimoza has been up to and make sure she keeps her big mouth shut."

Fatjon said, "She left the compound yesterday morning. Bribed one of the guards with her cute little ass." He laughed. Russell glared.

"Did you find her? Where did she go? Did she say anything to anyone?"

"We found her and that girl she hangs round with strolling on the other side of town. I had a word with her. Threatened to take her boy away."

"I asked for a low-profile operation and what do I get?" Russell stood up suddenly and paced the wooden floor of his office. "Fucking incompetent Arabs."

"They're not Arabs."

"They're fucking eejits, that's what." Russell, his head an inch below the fan, continued his march.

"Sir?"

"Grill her again. One of the detectives mentioned her name. She's done or said something. If she refuses to talk to you, send her to Anya. A few days with her legs around a pimple-backed, rutting Ragmullin pig might change her silent tune."

"Thought we were told to keep her for—"

"Don't question me!" Russell ceased pacing and stood toe to toe with the crooked-toothed man. "I trust no one." He flared his nostrils. "Not even you."

Fatjon kept his silence.

"I want results," Russell said.

"Yes, sir." Fatjon turned to leave.

"Today."

"Sir? The boy? What will I do—"

Russell whirled round on his patent pointy-toed shoes. "I don't give a flying fuck how you do it, but you better keep him quiet. And safe. That's an order. Deal with it without any more dramatics."

"Yes, sir."

When Fatjon had gone, Russell smoothed down his mustache, picked up the dead girl's picture, tore it in half and fed it into the shredder beneath his desk.

Once his breathing had returned to normal, he looked at the card. Detective Inspector Parker. He knew he had to stop the nosy nuisance. He had too much to lose to have her fuck it all up now. He fingered the card and wondered about the name. Parker. She couldn't be related to Sergeant Adam Parker. Could she?

CHAPTER 17

"So whose toes did you step on this time, Inspector Parker?"

Lottie stood in front of Superintendent Corrigan. "Sir?"

"I've had a call from the Department of Justice, the RIA."

"The IRA?"

"Don't play smart with me, Inspector. The Reception and Integration Agency. Apparently you've upset their coordinator here in Ragmullin, a Dan Russell."

"Really? I thought I was very polite. Sir."

"What are you up to?"

"It appears that when I step on toes, the guilty invariably jump around holding theirs, squealing."

"What are you on about?"

Lottie took a deep breath before speaking. "I didn't give Mr. Russell any reason to contact the department, this RIA. In any case, he's managing the center as a private enterprise. A new initiative, so I'm told."

"What did you do, Inspector?"

"I showed him a photo of our murder victim. I wanted to know if she came from his facility, as he calls it."

"Why in God's name would you think she came from there?"

"No one has reported our dead girl missing. No reported abductions. No sightings. Nothing. If she's not local, I thought, on a hunch, that maybe she was here illegally, or possibly an asylum seeker. If it's the latter, the direct provision center's the logical place to ask questions."

Lottie debated telling Corrigan about the visit from

Mimoza, but decided he was irate enough already without adding to it.

"A hunch? One of your gut feelings? Those feckin' things that got you and me into trouble last time. Tread softly, Inspector, very softly. I saved your job before, not so sure I can do it again. Please keep your feet firmly on your own side of the table."

Corrigan was a good man but Lottie knew there was only so much shite one person could shovel at him. And he'd already had a trailer load from her.

"Any word on McNally's whereabouts?" he asked.

Lottie had heard nothing further from Kirby. "Not yet. I'll get to it."

"You do. Now go and find our killer."

Off the hook for the moment, Lottie wanted to find out everything she could about Russell. Now that he had complained about her, she had him firmly in her sights.

* * *

When she got back to her desk, she began writing up the Dan Russell interview. She hated paperwork but it was a core responsibility of her job.

"That fellow got under my skin," she muttered, unable to concentrate.

Popping her head over her computer, Maria Lynch asked, "Who? Superintendent Corrigan?"

"Him too. But I'm talking about Dan Russell. He runs the direct provision center in the old army barracks." Lottie could hardly hear herself speak above the drone of the photocopier. The place was never quiet.

"Heard rumors about that DPC place," Lynch said, undoing her ponytail and running her fingers through her long hair.

"What kind of rumors?" Lottie was interested. She didn't know much about the asylum-seeker or refugee population in Ragmullin.

"My husband, Ben, you know he lectures in languages at Athlone Institute?"

"Of course I do," Lottie said.

"Some of the grad students teach English to the refugees and asylum seekers from time to time. They've told Ben that place is run like a prison camp." She wrapped her hair up in a bobbin.

"Dan Russell appears to be getting above his station. Do a background check on him, please." Lottie stood up and went round to Lynch's desk.

"Sure."

"And could you do me a favor?" Lottie held up a copy of Mimoza's note. "I need this translated."

"What is it?"

"It was given to me yesterday by a frightened young woman who called to my home. She had very little English and I can't be sure of the accuracy of Andri Petrovci's translation."

"You showed it to Petrovci?" Lynch looked up incredulously.

"I did."

"Do you think that was wise?"

Not you too, Lottie thought. "Wise or not, that's what I've done."

"Hope Superintendent Corrigan doesn't find out you involved a suspect in something unrelated to the murder."

"He won't if people keep their mouths shut." Lottie stared directly into Lynch's confident little face. And if you tell him, I'll know, she thought, because she was sure Boyd wouldn't rat her out. She handed over the letter, then went in search of Kirby.

CHAPTER 18

The cathedral bells chimed four times in the near distance.

Pulling Milot behind her, Mimoza walked across the yard to the cookhouse. The guard at the gate waved a hand in salute and smirked. A feeling of disgust assaulted her. Yesterday she had done what she needed to do. Sometimes you had to sell your soul to the devil and hope he would rent it back to you. Shaking off the memory, she pushed open the door and escaped inside.

The cookhouse was buzzing with flies. Through glass-paneled walls, sunshine radiated unhindered over the women seated at wooden tables. Crockery clunked against trays and the chatter was a muted drone. Mimoza spied Sara sitting alone and made her way toward her.

"What are you eating?" she asked, dragging Milot up on her lap. Four p.m. was too early for dinner, but if you didn't eat now, you got nothing until breakfast time. And she was hungry.

Sara's bony shoulders twitched as she twirled her fork around the puddle of watery spaghetti. Her eyes were too big for her petite dark face, her hair in raggedy plaits, swirling around her thin neck. She sucked the stringy pasta into her mouth. Suddenly Mimoza didn't feel hungry anymore.

The canteen chatter dropped and rippled to silence as the glass door at the end of the room opened and two security guards made their way toward Mimoza's table. Her body began to shake and she clasped her arms around Milot, pulling him to her chest protectively.

The men halted. One of them gripped her shoulder, hauling her to her feet. Still she held on to the boy. Panic threatened to suffocate her. The man's hand tightened on her shoulder, bone on bone. Cold shivers of steel cut through the cauldron of fire raging in her heart. With one swift movement he unlocked her hands from the boy and dragged her away.

Milot cried out and the other guard pushed him toward Sara.

Looking over her shoulder, Mimoza wailed, "Sara! Look after him."

She saw her son kicking wildly, attempting to follow her. The guard caught him by the arm, jerked him backward, sitting him firmly on Sara's lap.

She could hear his screams long after she had been taken across the courtyard and thrown into the concrete room with no windows.

Lying in the dark, Mimoza quelled her tears and tried to figure out what was going on. Feeling naked without her son by her side, she listened because she couldn't see a thing. Footsteps approached, the thin shaft of light slipping beneath the bottom of the door darkening as someone walked by. The footsteps faded. She strained to hear. No traffic, no birds. Deathly silence. Nothing permeated the solid walls.

She lay on the floor with only her heartbeat for company.

* * *

The man with the crooked teeth slammed his fist on the table.

"I ask for one thing," he said to the two men in front of him. "And you mess it up."

"You said bring that Mimoza witch to be questioned."

"I did, but not in front of a full canteen and a screaming boy. Now they have all seen. How can I make her disappear? There are too many witnesses. Imbeciles."

The two guards remained tight-lipped.

"Bring her to the interrogation room without causing a scene."

"Yes, sir."

Pacing the room, Fatjon came to a halt in front of the men.

"And do something about the boy. I can hear him screaming from here."

The pair left quickly.

Where had that bitch Mimoza gone yesterday? Who had she spoken to? He needed to know, and soon. The big plan could not be jeopardized at this stage—not by a sniveling whore and her snot-nosed brat. There could be no more mistakes. But knowing his boss, someone would pay for mistakes already made.

Fatjon bared his overlapping teeth at his reflection in the window. He had to make sure it wasn't him.

* * *

Mimoza heard the return of footsteps. The door opened, bringing with it the amber glare of fluorescent lights. Rough hands grabbed her and shoved her out.

Up concrete steps and along a corridor of bare brick walls, single bulbs lighting the way. Five doors, then they stopped outside the sixth. The guards pushed her into a room similar to the previous one. A red-topped table with two chairs reminded her of her mother's sparse kitchen a lifetime ago. She banished the memories before they could reduce her resolve to be strong. She had Milot to think of now. Standing erect, she hoped her posture would instill bravery.

The man with the crooked teeth stood in the center of the room.

"Where did you go yesterday morning?" He walked around her, so close, the musk of his body clinging to her skin as he moved.

"I bring Milot to town. Ice cream. He want ice cream." Her eyes darted around as she tried to lock down her fear.

"At seven a.m., huh? Truth," the man shouted, one of his teeth catching the light. "Tell the truth."

"I am."

He pushed her onto a chair. A lamp on the table flashed in her face.

"Look at me." He thumped the table. The lamp shook. Mimoza did too.

"I c-can't see you." The brightness blinded her. Perspiration trickled down her nose. Be strong, she silently pleaded with herself.

There was another man sitting at the other side of the table. She hadn't heard him enter. She couldn't see him properly because of the light from the lamp. His hands rested on the Formica. Did she recognize those hands? Something familiar? She couldn't think with the light glaring in her eyes. When he moved his head, his unshaven chin jutted toward her.

"Who are you?" she asked as he continued his silent vigil.

"Who I am is not your concern." He spoke in her native tongue.

"I told you where I went," she said.

His voice. She thought she knew it. But where from? She recoiled into the hard chair as he stood up and moved behind her. He banged a chair down beside her and sat. His canvas trousers six inches from her knees. Reaching out, he ran a finger along her cheek. She flinched. The touch of his skin scuttled her blood through her veins. She was sure he could see her heart trying to leap out through her ribs. His hand trailed around the back of her neck and he screwed her hair in a knot. Pain leapt up her skull as he tightened his hold, pulling her face close to his. She smelled the sourness of his breath. Bile rose in her stomach and she struggled to keep it from releasing. Still she could not see his face.

"I do not like to be crossed." His spittle rested on her lips, her cheeks. She forced her eyelids up and the vomit down. "I do not like liars." With a jerk he released her and she fell back on the chair. "I do not like you."

And then she did puke, a straight projectile flow of vomit onto his shirt.

She welcomed the slap to her jaw and the thump to her forehead as she slumped to the ground, spitting acrid liquid out of her mouth.

"You are a bitch," he said. "I will make you suffer. I will make your boy suffer."

"No, please no." Heat blazed through her body. "Not Milot. Don't touch him."

Three sets of black boots on the concrete floor merged before they were raised and aimed at her stomach.

She welcomed the pain if it could save her son. She welcomed the stars swimming behind her eyes, if only to blot out the face she thought she knew.

And at last she welcomed the relief of darkness.

CHAPTER 19

Lottie eyed Boyd over the top of her computer and smiled. He cocked his head to one side and she noticed the slight upturn of his lips, the beginning of a question.

"I'm only after noticing. Are you growing a beard?" she said. The soft stubble, flecked with gray, matched his cropped hair.

"No law against it last time I checked," he replied and returned to his work, averting his hazel eyes from her inquisitive green ones.

She wasn't letting him get away that lightly. "Did someone say it would suit you?" She noticed a flush creep over his cheeks. Was there a woman in Boyd's life? She hadn't considered this.

"You're jealous, Inspector Parker."

He stood up and walked over to her desk. She leaned back in her chair and studied him. The sun sneaked a streak of light over his face.

"Doesn't matter to me one way or the other," she lied, turning away. She tapped loudly on her keyboard.

"You'll break it."

"Feck off, Boyd."

"You *are* jealous," he said, and rotated her chair so that she was facing him.

"If I knew what there was to be jealous of then maybe I might be, but as I don't know anything, how can I be jealous?"

"The riddle queen of Ragmullin," he laughed, giving her chair an extra spin.

She stamped her feet to the floor, halting the chair's

movement, and stood up. "Well, am I right? Is there a woman telling you to grow scruff on your face?"

For an instant she was sure she read a sadness written in capital letters in his eyes before he shrugged his shoulders, went back to his desk and began tidying his files, which were already neatly lined up end to end.

"You break my heart, Lottie Parker. You know that. You show no interest in me unless…"

"Unless what?" Suddenly the office was too hot. "Unless I'm full to the gills with alcohol?" she prompted, indignation coloring her cheeks.

"Sorry, I didn't mean that. I never know where I stand with you."

"Like I already said…"

"What?"

"Feck off, Boyd."

"Right so." He slammed the files into the drawer and stomped out.

Lottie looked around at the empty chairs and equally empty office. *Was* she jealous? Of what? Or whom? Boyd hadn't admitted anything. And why should he? He owed her nothing. I'm going mad, she thought. Stark raving mad.

Boyd stuck his head back around the door.

"We've got a call," he said, beckoning her with a nod.

"What?" Lottie stayed where she was.

"Might be a crime scene."

She gave the keyboard one last thump before hurrying after him. Beard or no beard, she realized she needed Boyd. Whatever else happened, she needed him as her friend.

* * *

After negotiating the water main works on the narrow street outside the car dismantler's depot, Lottie and Boyd were directed in through the gates. Met by the owner, Bob Weir, they walked along a gravel path lined with battered cars stacked five high, scarred metal shimmering in the sun.

Lottie sniffed the late-afternoon air, inhaling a noxious whiff of oil and rubber. She pulled her T-shirt from the waist of her jeans and flapped air against her clammy skin.

"Down this way," Weir said, ducking under a platform of disassembled vehicles.

She wondered if they should be wearing hard hats. None had been offered. She and Boyd had to bend in two to get under the platform.

"Over there," Weir said, pointing to the furthest corner of the yard.

The entire depot seemed to shudder as a train in the station beyond the wall picked up speed and exited on the Sligo line. Following the direction of Weir's plump index finger, Lottie scoured the ground until her eyes rested on a dark congealed pool. She held out her hand, keeping Weir back.

"Council wouldn't let me demolish it," he said.

Lottie eyed him quizzically.

"The wall. I wanted to erect a proper one. It's ancient, falling down and disintegrating in places. Dangerous, so I thought. But a dipshit planner said it was something to do with heritage or some other shite. Cost me a fortune to stabilize it. And there's still enough holes and gaps to make it a fucking shortcut to the station and Hill Point Flats over there."

She saw what he was talking about. Easy access for cider parties. Or murderers. Hoping he wasn't wasting their time, she walked past him, over to the puddle. Tar oozed underfoot and clung to shards of gravel already embedded in the soles of her shoes. She hunkered down to the pool, slipped on gloves. Dipping her finger, she scrutinized the rusty color and beckoned Boyd over.

"Blood," he said, stating the obvious. As usual.

"Could be animal," she ventured. Holding her fingertip to her nose, she sniffed, getting a metallic odor.

"I had pest control in only a few weeks ago," Weir protested, his face as red as his hair.

Straightening up, Lottie stepped carefully over the pool, her eyes traveling the length of the wall behind it. It would be easy for someone to scale the corroded stones.

"Told you, didn't I?" Weir said, smirking.

"You did." Lottie turned to him. "Thanks for calling this in."

"Well, I felt it was my duty, seeing how you found a murdered girl yesterday."

"It might lead to nothing, but I have to treat this as a crime scene for the moment." She turned to Boyd. "We have to evacuate the depot. Immediately."

Boyd got on his phone and called in reinforcements and the SOCO team.

"You can't be serious," Weir said, looking like he was sorry for reporting it.

Lottie said, "I'm very serious. Is this place locked at night?" It didn't make much difference, she thought. Access was manageable—up and over the wall.

"It's locked and a security van passes every fifty minutes or so. You mightn't think it, Inspector, but this lot is very valuable." Weir smeared his face with an oily hand.

"I don't doubt it." She skirted round the puddle. Running her fingers along the old stone wall, she marveled at the original workmanship.

"Nineteenth century, so I'm told," Weir said.

"Boyd?" Lottie called him over. "I think this might be a bullet hole. McGlynn will need to see it. And get uniforms to clear the place."

"Ah for Jaysus's sake." Weir paced in small fat circles. "This is my business. You can't do that."

"I can and I am," Lottie said. "You too. Out."

As the depot owner marched away across the yard, chuntering to himself, Lottie pointed to the wall. "Is it a bullet hole?"

Boyd inspected the mark. "Possibly. Could be our primary crime scene."

"Our victim still has the bullet inside her."

"Maybe he missed with the first shot."

"We'll let SOCOs make an impression of the hole and poke around to see if there's a bullet in there."

"You know what else it could mean, Lottie?"

"Yes. There's another body somewhere."

They stayed on site until Jim McGlynn and his team appeared, suited up, equipment cases in hands.

"Out, the both of you," McGlynn ordered. "Contaminating my scene."

"We didn't know it was a crime scene, and it still might not be." Lottie turned away.

"You know better, Inspector. Protective suits or go."

Boyd tugged her elbow. "Come on. There's nothing else to do here."

Lottie had to agree.

* * *

"Blood and a bullet hole. So where's the body?"

Lottie rinsed her hands under the tap in the makeshift kitchen. Boyd flicked on the kettle and leaned against the wall, arms folded, watching her. She dried her hands.

"Well?"

He shrugged. "It must be related to the girl in the morgue, one way or other."

"I hope it is, otherwise we might have a second victim."

"There's no body there, as far as we know."

"When the whole area is searched, every car and scrap of a car, we might find more evidence." She got two mugs and spooned in coffee.

"No milk," said Boyd, shaking an empty carton.

"There's definitely something there."

"Definitely no milk."

"Not *milk*," Lottie said. "At Weir's depot. It's easily accessible, despite his so-called security."

"So what?"

"Ideal dumping ground or murder site."

"It's in the middle of town. How could someone discharge a gun there? It'd be heard a mile away."

"Pick the right moment. Say, when a train is entering or exiting the station—you heard the noise. And if the gun's equipped with a silencer, it's just a loud pop."

"Ballistics will confirm or otherwise."

"And we need the blood type." Lottie eyed the black coffee in her mug. "Still no identification for our victim?"

"Nope."

Sipping the scorching liquid, she felt comforted by Boyd's proximity even though he was wearing his serious face. She glanced at her watch and decided to call it a day.

"I'm heading home. I'll download a few files to a USB and study them there."

"Still content with breaking the rules?"

"Yep," she said.

"Need any help?" His face broke into a wicked grin.

"You never give up, do you?"

He smiled wryly. "I'm getting there, Lottie. Believe me."

And as she poured her coffee into the sink, she believed him.

CHAPTER 20

The house was tidy for a change. Katie and Sean had already eaten and were watching something loud and bloody on Netflix. Chloe had secreted herself in her room. Lottie was too tired to have an argument, so she let her be and fried a rasher and egg for herself.

After eating, she took out her laptop, inserted the USB and opened up Jane Dore's autopsy report. Could the unknown girl have been killed in Bob Weir's yard? She would love to have the ballistics and DNA reports but knew it could take days, even weeks. Unless Jane could pull a few strings, something she'd done before.

Scanning the report, Lottie skipped over the technical data and noted the victim's vitals. Pregnant. Undernourished. Sexually active. Organs and brain normal. Bite mark on neck. Impression molded. Swabs taken. Left kidney surgically removed. Precise sutures. Assume medical professional or at least surgically trained. Victim aged between eighteen and twenty-five. Possibly Eastern European or Balkan, determined by bone structure.

She closed the laptop and read through her handwritten notes. What had the girl's story been? What motive could someone have for killing her? When had she had the kidney removed, and why? Had the killer known she was carrying a baby? Was it the killer's child? Six-million-dollar questions. She needed to unravel the girl's life to determine the answers. Hard to do when she didn't have a name. Maybe, after all, they would have to release the death-mask photograph to the general public. Not a nice prospect. Especially if it meant she'd have to talk to Mister Congeniality himself, television news reporter Cathal Moroney. Perhaps she'd pass that one to Corrigan. Might be safer.

Exhausted and unable to think clearly, she put away her work and headed up the stairs to bed. She paused outside Chloe's room, knocked on the door and waited.

"Go away," Chloe said.

"You said we needed to talk. I'm here now." Lottie kept her hand on the handle but didn't venture in. "Are you okay?"

"I'm tired. Goodnight."

So am I, Lottie thought. "Goodnight so," she said. "Chat in the morning."

She went to her room and lay on the bed, wondering if she was a bad mother not to have gone in and talked with her daughter. No, she thought, it would only end in a row. She eventually fell asleep to the sound of Chloe crying softly in the room next to hers.

CHAPTER 21

The man shifted slightly in the long dry grass where he had been lying for the last hour and a half. He fixed his night-vision goggles and binoculars in line with the window, then returned to his rigid position. The railway tracks were a mere meter behind him, but he had no worries. The next train was not due until 6 a.m.

Stars twinkled high above and street lights cast a yellow hue into the night sky. He ignored his surroundings and concentrated on his target.

With the blinds up and curtains hanging out through the open window, he had a clear view inside. Her light was off but through his hi-tech equipment he could decipher her slender form lying atop her tossed duvet.

He conjured up her youthful beauty. Every strand of her blonde hair sparked electricity throughout his body. The smooth sheen of her face and the rise and fall of her breast—all images he registered and filed away for future perusal.

He didn't want to be aroused. That wasn't the object of his crusade. He was not the tempest; no, he was the calm after the storm. He would bring her peace. She would bring him peace.

As he shifted uneasily, the hardness in his groin making his position unbearable, the grass around him rustled in the stillness. He froze. No one ventured down here at 4:47 a.m. Not on the canal and definitely not this far along the railway tracks. Slowly he lowered the binoculars and turned his head, coming face to face with a bright-eyed fox. He laughed. The animal scampered away.

A sign. Time to quit for the night. He packed up his equipment, slung the bag over his shoulder and hurried the length of the track, his hand thrust deep in his trousers, feverishly stroking himself. He knew there was only one way to truly gain relief, to expel the demons from within. Perhaps he should move her up his timeline, he thought, expelling small groans of pleasure with each breath.

Such was his fever of anticipation for the girl, when he arrived home, and before he could even unlock the door, his desire ejaculated in an orgasmic explosion.

He would sleep tonight.

* * *

The hood over Mimoza's head smelled of vomit. She knew she was in the boot of a car, but they hadn't traveled far when it stopped. Still in town, she felt. Please let Milot be cared for. No matter what they do to me, let my son be okay, she pleaded silently in the darkness. She thought she could smell his apple shampoo. Her chest constricted in panic. She had to be strong. For Milot.

Dragged from the car, she was pushed up a flight of steps and through an open door. When the hood was wrenched from her head, she ascertained that the vomit was her own. It had dripped and hardened along her chin and on her chest. Her breath came low and fast as she tried to calm herself.

A tall woman stood over her, arms folded, stiletto-clad feet wide apart. Mimoza struggled to her knees. A gray stripe streaked an intimidating line along the center of the woman's black-haired crown. A red dress floated out from the folds of flesh and a nipple protruded.

"Up," the woman said in Mimoza's language.

"Wash?" Mimoza asked, rising to her feet.

"Don't speak unless instructed." The slap cracked the skin below her eye. As she reeled backward, rough hands grabbed her. The man with the crooked teeth. He spoke rapidly, turned and left.

At once Mimoza knew what type of place she was in and what was expected of her. She had been forced to work in such a place once before. Following the woman, she trailed through a patterned-wallpapered hall and up uncarpeted stairs. At the top, four doors, faux-pearl bracelets hanging on the handles of three. The woman opened the one without a bracelet, ushering Mimoza into a tiny bathroom. Soft music drifted from the ceiling.

"You pee. Two minutes."

"Wash?"

The smack of a hand caught her on the side of her head.

"Dare to answer back and you will be punished. Two minutes." The woman left, pulling the door closed behind her.

As a key turned in the lock, Mimoza stripped off her soiled clothing and sat on the toilet. Blood mixed with urine spilled from her body, and with it, excruciating pain, a reminder of Crooked Teeth Man's violent sex attack before he'd brought her here.

Despite her distress, all she could think of was that she was trapped in one prison while her son was in another.

"Oh Milot," she said aloud, "I'm so sorry."

* * *

Kosovo 1999

The mosquitoes wouldn't leave him alone. All his life they'd blighted him. He pulled the net tighter around his head and swatted his hand through the air. No good. Couldn't sleep. He was lying on a bunk in one of the soldiers' billets. They had been nice to him, allowed him to stay with them. On condition he stay quiet until they had time to tell their commanding officer.

He thought it might be around 3 a.m. but he wasn't sure. He heard the multitude of mice scratching surfaces all around him. He hated them. Hoped they wouldn't breach his curtain. He was more afraid of the vermin than being killed. If he was going to survive on his own he would have to learn new skills. Reading and writing and hauling buckets of water wouldn't help him. What did the future hold for him now? Not much, he supposed.

The door opened and the soldier who had given him the packet of crisps came in.

"Can you not sleep?"

The boy shook his head.

"The doctor will have a look at you in the morning. Where were you heading to anyway?"

The boy shrugged his shoulders. He couldn't answer because he didn't know. He'd never been further than his own village. Maybe he could say he was going to Pristina. Maybe he'd get work there. He was tall so he could pass for older than thirteen. He looked up at the soldier. He had kind blue eyes and a sweep of blonde hair on his forehead.

The boy said, "Pristina."

The soldier said, "What's your name?"

The boy remained mute.

"Here's a bottle of water. Drink, then sleep. I'll have to inform the captain about you in the morning. He'll decide what to do."

The boy sipped the water and closed his eyes. A quiet blackness descended, and to the sound of hungry mice and buzzing mosquitoes he fell asleep.

DAY THREE

Wednesday, May 13, 2015

CHAPTER 22

It felt good to apply a streak of Katie's lipstick over her lips—
her own was now a broken smudge in the bottom of a tube—
and to run a comb through her hair. She was enjoying being
back at work. Feeling alive again, she slapped away a pang of
guilt. Escaping from her family and the troubles they threw
at her wasn't the trait of a good mother, was it? But she had to
get on with it. She still had to talk with Chloe. She slipped the
lipstick into her bag and turned to see Sean enter the kitchen.

"Anything to eat?" he asked, gazing into the refrigerator.

"You're up bright and early," Lottie said. "There's cereal in
the cupboard."

Sean squeezed a milk carton and shook it. "Might be
enough," he said, and went to get a bowl and the box of cereal.

"You're looking very smart today."

Conversation with Sean was strained at the best of times.
She hoped he might open up a bit more now that he was seeing
a therapist. Coping with what he'd gone through in January
had not been easy. Lottie knew he needed time to be himself
again, but she wasn't so sure that Katie needed the same. The
girl had retreated into herself and looked awful. Lottie knew
all about grief, but she hadn't the words to comfort her own
daughter.

"Same rotten uniform," he said, munching. "I had a shower."

"Must be a girl."

"Mam, that's gross."

Lottie smiled as she watched her son spoon cornflakes into
his mouth, slurping milk like a toddler. His blonde hair fell

across his blue eyes, once bright and sparkling, full of life, now stony and strained. Stopping herself from rushing over to brush his hair back with her fingers, she touched his arm instead.

"I'll see you this evening. Have a nice day at school."

"Mam! How can anyone have a nice day at school?"

On the drive to work, Lottie thought about her job. She didn't know what it would throw at her from day to day, and now that a girl had been murdered along with her unborn baby, it was her task to bring the killer to justice. Once she had solved this murder, her children would get all her attention.

As Lottie entered the office, Lynch jumped up, brandishing a page in the air.

"I got one of our technical guys who's an ace with languages to have a look at the letter."

Lottie sat down, her good mood evaporating. "Anything different from what Petrovci told us?" she asked.

"Basically it's the same. Someone called Kaltrina appears to be missing and the writer of the letter needs your help to escape."

"From what, though?"

"You know what I think?" Lynch brushed her hair out of her face.

"That the Kaltrina mentioned in the note could be our dead girl. But no one fitting her description has been reported missing in the last week."

"I spoke about it briefly with Ben last night," Lynch said, adding quickly, "without giving away anything confidential, of course. He thinks we should check if the girl who came to your house is in the direct provision system. Kaltrina too. Numbers have been increasing in recent months, with the refugees swarming through Europe. It's possible that's where they're from."

"They are not insects, Lynch," Lottie said harshly.

Kirby raised his head from his corner, unlit cigar in his mouth. "The government can't house our own people, let alone migrants."

Lottie gave him an icy glare. "You should know better than to talk like that. And if you want to smoke that cigar, get the hell out of here."

"Sorry, boss."

Kirby dragged his bulk through the door, leaving Lottie clenching her fists and shaking her head.

"He's only saying what others think," Lynch said.

"I can do without that kind of attitude. And I'm sure you know that human rights groups condemn the type of inappropriate language you used a moment ago. So be careful."

Lottie held Maria Lynch's stare. Her detective broke away first.

"Anyway, Ben told me that his department funds translators to work with the refugees and asylum seekers."

"Any of them up in the army barracks?"

"I don't know."

"Can you find out?"

"I'll try."

"Okay. Did you dig into Dan Russell's past yet?"

"I'm working on it." Lynch clicked on something on her computer. "Wait a minute. Have a look at this."

Rushing across the cluttered office, snagging the leg of her jeans against the corner of a box file, Lottie leaned down and peered at the screen.

"Missing person report." Lynch tapped her pen. "Filed late last night."

Lottie read quickly. "Maeve Phillips, aged seventeen. Possibly missing since last weekend, according to her mother, though only now being reported." She felt the blood drain slowly from her cheeks. "I wonder if—"

"If she's our Jane Doe?"

"If she's related to Frank Phillips."

"Who?" asked Lynch.

"The criminal. He fled to Spain a number of years ago."

Lynch wrinkled her nose in disgust. "I hope she's not related to that scumbag."

"Give me the address and I'll go talk to the mother. Where's Boyd?"

"At your service." He walked into the office. Slung his jacket over the back of his chair, rolled up his shirtsleeves and sat.

"What's up?" Lottie asked, raising an eyebrow. Boyd was never late. Ever.

"Nothing. Couldn't sleep in the heat. Then I couldn't wake up after I eventually nodded off sometime around five."

"You need a woman," Lynch said.

"You could be right," Boyd said.

"Shut up, the pair of you," Lottie said. Stuffing the missing person report in her bag, she grabbed him by the elbow. "I think you need fresh air."

CHAPTER 23

Mimoza's eyelids fluttered open. She had no idea where she was. Her body ached and pain thumped through her head. She lay naked on a sheeted mattress, staring at the ceiling.

Drawing her legs to her chest, she wrapped her arms around them and rested her chin on her knees, like Milot did when he was sulking. Then the memories swamped her consciousness and despair threatened to overwhelm her. Diverting herself from her inner distress, she scanned the room. A nightstand, a red-shaded lamp and a teddy bear with a blue bow tie sitting forlornly on the glossed wooden surface. Washbasin with a dark towel on a rail attached to a wall. Heavy flowery curtains drawn closed, blanketing a window. The embossed velvet roses on the wallpaper appeared to be struggling to escape their thorny prison.

She eased her aching limbs from the bed and investigated what might be behind the door of the wardrobe to her right. The only items it held were red and black sheer nylon negligees.

Slumping back on the bed, she wondered what they had done with Milot. How could she survive without her son? If only she was sure he was safe, perhaps she could endure the life to which she had been condemned. Reality attacked her as brutally as the boots that had kicked her. She hoped Sara could care for Milot until she escaped from this hole.

The room was hot but her skin prickled with goose bumps. This was not the first time she had been in a brothel, and hadn't she been subjected to violent sex attacks in the center? She'd endured such torture in Pristina, too, before she had been rescued, and then, when she'd thought she was safe and secure, she'd been abandoned, pregnant. Sighing, she tried to shut out the memory.

She had thought about trying to report the abuse she'd suffered in the center, but Kaltrina had warned her that things like that always got covered up and no one would believe her. Her only hope was the cryptic letter she'd given to the policewoman.

She lay on the lumpy pillow and listened to the sounds of everyday life beyond her confined space. A train trundling along tracks in the distance, the joyful screeches of children in a playground far beneath her, and the slow drone of traffic. Was she still in Ragmullin? She didn't know and didn't care. She only cared about Milot. She thought again of the tall policewoman and prayed she hadn't thrown her letter in the bin. But she knew she probably had.

With trembling hands covering her eyes, willing strength into her body, Mimoza braced herself for what lay beyond the door, for who would walk through it, for what they were about to subject her to. Yes, she was ready for all that. But first she had to know her son was safe.

A key rattled in the lock and the door shifted open.

"Get up," said the woman from last night.

"Where is my son?"

"To you he is dead. To us he is an asset. Maybe someone like him as a bum boy? Now you shower."

Mimoza allowed herself to be led to a bathroom down a narrow hallway. As the water drummed against her bruised ribs, she vowed she would escape the clutches of the elephantine woman who stood sentry outside. Was she spying through a crack in the door?

"Look all you want," Mimoza shouted, though she supposed her voice was drowned out by the water gushing from the shower.

When a flabby arm grabbed her by the hair and dragged her to the ground, she still continued her internal mantra. *I will be strong.*

* * *

Andri Petrovci woke up late. It was twenty minutes past nine. He'd forgotten to set the alarm. His boss, Jack Dermody, would have plenty to say. Slowly he rolled out of bed, his brain drumming a beat against his skull. He rubbed his shaved head with a trembling hand. Another night of turbulent nightmares.

Turning on the tap, he heard the glug, glug of water slowly releasing before it flowed freely, splashing up against his naked torso.

He washed his face free of the night and brushed his teeth. He dressed in his work clothes and left with a backward glance at his neat living space, quietly closing the door on his private world.

CHAPTER 24

Lottie was familiar with Mellow Grove. Her last case had brought her to the estate a couple of times. Looking around, she concluded that someone in the council must have had an odd sense of humor when they named it.

The Phillips house stood at the end of a terraced row, near a football pitch, the only abode in need of a coat of paint. The pebble-dash, probably once cream in color, was now a weather-beaten brown. The curtains were closed.

She pushed the rusted gate inward. The rectangle of lawn looked like a meadow awaiting harvest.

"Could do with a bit of a clean-up," Boyd said. Lottie rang the doorbell. "It's open," he added.

She was about to reply when she noticed the door was indeed slightly ajar. Tentatively she pushed it inward. Speckled green and gray linoleum covered the floor, faded white down the middle; the stairs were squeezed to the right, a multitude of coats overloading the banisters. The light was on. Probably from the night before.

She ushered Boyd in and called, "Anyone home? Hello?"

Hearing a cough from behind a door at the end of the short hallway, Lottie knocked and entered.

"Mrs. Phillips? I'm Detective Inspector Parker and this is Detective Sergeant Boyd. Can we have a word, please?" She flashed her ID.

The woman sitting at the table nodded and with a cigarette between tar-stained fingers beckoned for them to sit down.

On the short drive over, Lottie had tried to imagine what

type of mother could wait almost five days to report her teenage daughter missing. Now the answer sat in front of her.

Clearing crumbs from a chair, Lottie sat, glancing quickly at her surroundings. Boyd remained standing. The kitchen was dim despite the fluorescent tube flickering overhead. Flies sizzled in the plastic shade. Oppressive heat accentuated the smell of rotting vegetables emanating from a cupboard below the sink—itself piled high with dishes caked in dried food. A swarm of fruit flies rose toward the light. Lottie couldn't see any fruit.

"So have you found the little wagon yet?" Mrs. Phillips poured a liberal amount of vodka into a pint glass. Without adding any mixer, she took a large gulp, burped, and sipped. She put down the glass, the shake in her hand clearly visible.

"You only reported your daughter's disappearance last night." Lottie counted to three, keeping her anger in check. "Why the delay? Can you fill me in on the details, Mrs. Phillips?"

"Call me Tracy. Details? Wha' details?" Her words slurred into each other.

"When did you last see Maeve?" Lottie fought off an urge to find a cloth and wipe down the table. She kept her arms firmly folded, away from the dirt.

"My husband, the bastard…"

"What about him? Is Maeve with him?" Lottie hoped so, then the case could be stamped closed without the need to enter this hovel again. She was sure she heard something rustling around the bread bin on the counter.

"I doubt it," Tracy said, "but everything is his fault. Left me when Maeve was seven years old, he did. Ten years I've been on my own with her. Did my best. Honest to God. Slaved to bring that girl up well and how does she repay me?" Her eyes glazed over as she gulped more alcohol. "She's gone. Run away. Ungrateful little bitch…" Hiccups obliterated the remainder of her words.

"Where can I find your husband?" Lottie asked.

"Some whorehouse in Malaga, I'd say."

So the girl's father *was* the criminal who had fled the country. This wasn't going to be easy.

Struggling to remain focused on Tracy Phillips, Lottie's eyes were constantly drawn to the chaos surrounding them. A pot, congealed beans on the rim, stuck out obliquely from the overcrowded sink. And the bottles…She counted eleven empties on the gray granite-type counter. Five half-full pasta sauce jars, one brimming with cigarette butts, within the menagerie of clutter on the table. Bolognese and cigarettes definitely didn't mix, she decided. Wrinkling her nose at the acidic odor, she dragged her gaze back to the thin-jawed woman.

As she watched Tracy through the smoky haze, a jolt shook Lottie. It was like looking through a skewed mirror at an image of what she herself had almost become in the months following Adam's death. Drunk by midday, operating in a vacuum, normality disintegrating around her like the ash falling from Tracy's cigarette.

She had been pulled back from the brink, but she knew Tracy was precariously perched on the lowest rung of existence. Who was going to save her? Not Maeve, if she had indeed run away from this crumbling lifestyle.

"She's never been away this long before," Tracy said, lighting another cigarette from the one in her hand. She doused the first in the pasta jar. "Sometimes she stays with friends. Anywhere is better than here. That's what she says." She swept her hand around the kitchen, trailing ash everywhere. "She was supposed to be back by now."

"When exactly did you last see her?" Lottie felt her patience disappearing as quickly as her sympathy.

"Friday morning. She went to school. She's in transition

year. Said she was staying the night with ... Emily or someone. Sometimes she stays away longer, so I wasn't really worried."

Too drunk to care, thought Lottie. This was like extracting teeth, but the molars visible in Tracy's mouth convinced her the woman hadn't seen a dentist in decades.

"Today is Wednesday, for God's sake! Why wait until last night to report it?"

"I needed groceries." Tracy lowered her eyes, looking down at her shaking hands.

"What?" Boyd exclaimed.

Tracy rose with a wobble and opened a cupboard. Empty. Lottie noticed the woman wore cheap cotton pajamas and two-euro plastic flip-flops. She looked sixty but was probably closer to forty. Her dark hair was a tangled mass of grease, ragged unintentional dreadlocks, like Amy Winehouse without the eyeliner.

"Your daughter normally shopped for you?" Boyd asked.

"Yeah. I was out of ... things."

Vodka probably, Lottie thought. Someone must have bought her the half-liter that stood on the table; she doubted Tracy Phillips had the energy to dress herself to go to the shops. Then again, she most likely ventured out in her nightclothes.

"Vodka?" Boyd sneered.

Lottie glared at him.

Turning her head away, Tracy sat down.

"Did you ring Maeve?" Boyd snapped. "I'm presuming she has a mobile phone."

Tracy doused her cigarette in the clogged jar, lit yet another and gulped her vodka, eyeing Boyd over the rim.

"You think I'm a good-for-nothing drunk, don't you? You're right. But I do my best for that girl and now I'm reduced to this ... this mess." She drank some more and looked up. "Anyway, the school rang me yesterday evening. That's how I knew something was up. No matter what happens at home, my

Maeve goes to school." Another deep inhalation and a cloud of smoke encircled them. "I'm ringing her every five minutes. Nothing. Her phone's dead. I don't know where she is."

Lottie had expected lots of tears. There were none. Tracy Phillips had probably used up her quota long ago.

"Do you have a photo of Maeve?"

Tracy handed over her phone. Lottie took in the pale face framed with long black hair on the cracked home screen. A tiny diamond stud adorned her nose. It could possibly be the dead girl. She showed it to Boyd. He nodded.

Lottie said, "Can I send this to my phone?"

"Fire ahead."

"Did Maeve ever have a kidney removed?" Boyd asked.

"Jaysus! Why would you ask me that? No, of course not."

"We're building a profile," Lottie said quickly, checking she had received the photo. "Another thing," she said. "I have to ask this. Could Maeve be pregnant?"

Tracy's eyes shifted upward through the haze of cigarette smoke. "You bitch! Just 'cause I'm way below your class, you think my girl opens her legs for anyone. You can fuck off with your dirty questions."

Lottie said, "I'm not passing judgment. I just need to know everything about her."

Tracy slurped her drink and gave a resigned nod. "To answer your question, I don't know."

"Her room, can I see it?" Lottie hoped the girl was neater than Tracy. "Has she a computer?"

"A laptop," Tracy said, pointing to the stairs. "Her door says 'Keep Out.' Not too original, my Maeve."

"Does she have a boyfriend?"

"If she does, she didn't tell me."

"So you're not sure?"

"I can't be sure, can I? What mother can be?"

Indeed, thought Lottie, following Boyd out of the depressing kitchen and up the stairs.

* * *

Unlike the kitchen, Maeve's room was clean but untidy. Like any normal teenager's bedroom, Lottie thought. Tracksuit bottoms turned inside out, along with a collection of underwear, crowded the floor. A single bed, plain cream duvet thrown back as if the girl had just rolled out. Dressing table overflowing with perfume bottles and tubs. Makeup, every shade of eyeshadow and eyeliner.

"Twenty-seven," Lottie said.

"Twenty-seven what?" Boyd asked.

"Bottles of nail polish. This girl likes her nails." She continued counting. Five perfumes and six body sprays. A flowery scent hung in the air. Lottie inspected a tin. Impulse, Forest Flowers. She sprayed it.

Boyd said. "Spray a little around the kitchen, will you?"

Jackets hung from the back of the door, jeans jumbled up on the floor. Lottie flicked through the hangers in the wardrobe. School shirts, skirts and a few blouses. Right at the end, a dress, hanging in a clear zipped cover, appeared out of place. Extracting it, she held it up.

"Bit fancy for a seventeen-year-old." Boyd raised an eyebrow at the garment swinging in Lottie's hand.

"Seventeen-year-olds have unusual tastes," she said, thinking of her own girls' multicolored clothes. She unzipped the plastic.

"Wow," Boyd said, stepping closer.

The fabric flowed out of the wrapping, blue silk, bling-studded bodice, halter neck.

"One hundred and fifty euros," Lottie said, inspecting the label swinging from the waist.

"How could she afford that?" Boyd flicked through the remainder of the clothes.

"Perhaps someone bought it for her."

"Or she stole it."

"Boyd, you don't even know the girl. How can you make such an assertion?"

"I've seen the mother."

Lottie shook her head. "Maeve might have a part-time job. I'll ask when we go downstairs." She hung the dress back in the wardrobe, but first she plucked off the label, put it in a small plastic evidence bag and popped it in her pocket.

She found the laptop under a pillow on the bed. It was a cheap model, charging.

"Dangerous," she said, unplugging it from the socket. She put the small computer into her bag.

"You can't take that," Boyd said.

"I'll ask the mother."

A chair piled high with clothing revealed a stack of paperbacks beneath. Wedged halfway down, Lottie noticed a card sticking out. A birthday card. *To Maeve, love Dad.*

"Her father's still in contact with her," she said.

"I reckon she's with him," Boyd said, shutting a drawer noisily. "I'd fly the coop to escape this hellhole too."

"This hellhole, as you call it, is her home and is probably preferable to a life of crime with her dad." Why was she defending Tracy?

"Come on," she said, placing the card in a plastic evidence bag. Just in case. "I want to ask Tracy about that dress."

* * *

Lottie nudged Tracy Phillips.

"Wha'? What d'ya want?" Tracy squinted. "Oh. It's you. Still here?"

"Can I take Maeve's laptop to have a look at it?"

"Why'd you want it?"

"Just to run a check on it. Might tell us where Maeve is."

"Suppose it's okay so."

"There's a new dress in her wardrobe. Any idea where it came from?"

Tracy sat up straight, looking from Lottie to Boyd. "Dress? She must've bought it."

"It's expensive. Where would she get the money? Her father? Has she a part-time job?"

Tracy seemed to struggle with what Lottie was saying. Too many questions at once?

"She hasn't got a job, but maybe I don't know my girl very well."

"I'll need to talk to her friends."

"What friends?"

"Maeve's friends. Do you have any names?"

"Emily...something. Works in the Parkway Hotel after school."

"Do you want me to assign a family liaison officer to stay with you?" Lottie asked.

"I'm fine on my own." Tracy rested her head on her folded arms on top of the greasy table and promptly fell asleep.

Shutting the door behind them, Lottie wondered how long it would take for Tracy Phillips to self-destruct.

CHAPTER 25

Lottie dropped off Maeve's laptop at the station for analysis and instructed a trace to be put on the girl's phone. She wasn't sure if Maeve was actually missing, but at least they could put a report out on social media. Someone might know where she was. She printed the photo from her phone and enlarged it on the photocopier. Holding it up to the death-mask photo of the murder victim, she squinted to see if there were any similarities.

"She didn't have her kidney removed," Boyd said, standing at Lottie's shoulder.

"So her mother says. But anyway I don't think Maeve is our dead girl."

Lynch appeared with a one-page printout. "This is all the history I can find on Dan Russell. It's not a lot. Just gives his army service and the date he left, and the year he set up his company, Woodlake Facilities Management. All above board."

"We'll see," Lottie said. "Will you have a look at this too?" She handed Lynch the tag from the dress. "Check the barcode to see if there's any way of tracing where it came from."

"Sure."

Drawing Lynch to one side, out of Boyd's earshot, Lottie said, "Get on to the lads in the new Drugs and Organized Crime Bureau and try to establish where Frank Phillips is hiding out. I need to speak to him about his daughter."

Making her way back to her desk, she wondered if Jamie McNally had anything to do with Frank Phillips. If he had, Kirby would find out. It seemed too much of a coincidence,

McNally being back in town. A girl gets murdered and another goes missing. She didn't like coincidences.

Her thoughts were interrupted as she read through the sparse data on Dan Russell. Something had caught her eye. Grabbing her bag, she made for the door. "I'm going to see Russell again."

"Want me to come?" Boyd asked.

"No. You process the information on Maeve Phillips. Circulate her photo to the media and see what comes back from her computer. Follow up on the murder interview transcripts. See if you can spot anything I might have missed. Grab some lunch. I'll be back in less than an hour."

Kirby blocked her escape at the doorway. "I called the security company Bob Weir employs to carry out nightly checks when his yard is closed."

"And?" Lottie hauled her bag onto her shoulder.

"They only do a drive-by on alternate nights. According to their logs, there's nothing to report."

"Great. So whoever knows about the nights the van patrols has a free run to do whatever they like."

"The search of the yard is complete. Nothing else turned up."

"Follow up with ballistics on that bullet hole in the wall and see if they have anything yet on the bullet from the dead girl."

"Will do." Kirby stood back to allow her to leave.

This time Lottie got out before anyone else could halt her progress.

* * *

Flashing her ID, she asked to see Dan Russell. The security guard let her through the door at the main gate and phoned Russell to announce her arrival.

This time, she took in her surroundings. A barren square,

once the ground for army transport, was flanked on three sides by four-story accommodation blocks and offices. A glass-walled cookhouse skirted to her left. It looked empty. To her right stood the chapel and gym. Adam had once told her that two men were executed behind the chapel in 1921, the bullet holes in the wall a reminder of a volcanic time in Irish history. She hoped that it was indeed history. She didn't fancy finding any recent bullet holes there. The thought jolted her back to the present and the scene at Weir's yard. As she looked around, an uneasy feeling of disquiet lodged in her breast. What was she missing?

She entered Block A, climbed the flight of wooden stairs and knocked on Russell's door.

"Inspector Parker. What can I do for you?" Russell brought her inside and smiled.

Too nice, Lottie thought. She'd have to be careful.

"Mr. Russell—"

"Call me Dan," he interrupted. "And please sit."

She stared back at him. What was he up to? She sat opposite him.

"I'm afraid I drew a blank on that dead girl's photograph. She's not from here. I'm sorry I'm no help to you."

His statement didn't surprise her, but his change in character did. He was actually being apologetic!

"And the other girl we mentioned. Mimoza. Does anyone know her?" she asked.

"Nothing to report there either, I'm sorry."

Lottie tried again. "What about this girl. Do you recognize her?" She placed the photo of Maeve Phillips on his desk. A long shot, but worth a try.

He glanced at it. "No. Should I? Is she dead also?"

"I hope not." She hadn't detected any flicker of recognition from him.

Thinking of the background check they'd conducted, she decided to come straight out with it.

"You left the army in 2010. I would've thought that having risen to the rank of commandant, you would have pursued the higher echelons of the force. Why did you leave?"

He stood up, walked around to the front of the desk and sat on the edge of it. His knees were inches from hers. She didn't budge.

Leaning toward her, he said, "What difference is it to you? It's my business." He was so close she could smell his minty mouthwash.

"Just thought it odd."

"Checking out my CV?"

"I'm just curious." She held his gaze, not a bit unnerved by his tense, staring eyes. "So why *did* you leave?"

"I'd enough of the army life. I wanted new adventures. So I set up my company, Woodlake Facilities Management, and landed this job."

"You didn't do any more overseas tours after Kosovo. Why not?"

"Why is that of interest to you?"

"Just wondering."

"Speaking of Kosovo, your name, Parker, it rings a bell."

"My late husband served there in the late nineties. You may have met him." Suddenly Lottie was anxious to hear about Adam, despite her misgivings over Russell.

"I met a lot of army personnel in my travels."

He stood up and walked to the wall of photos, moving from one to another. She knew he wasn't really looking at them. He was making up his mind just how much he wanted to tell her. The bastard.

He turned and stood with his feet planted wide. "I'm a while out of the army. But now I come to think of it, I do remember him. Tall, well built. A good soldier."

"He was a brilliant soldier," Lottie said.

"Oh yes, I could tell you a thing or two about him. Perhaps we could have a chat over a coffee? Dinner maybe?"

"You're joking!" Lottie said in surprise

"On the contrary, I'm quite serious. I think you should have dinner with me."

She thought his statement sounded like a threat.

"I don't eat very much." Where had that come from?

"Am I making you uncomfortable?" Russell asked. He moved back to his desk and sat down.

"Not at all." But you're playing silly-bugger games with me, she thought. "Why won't you answer my questions and tell me about Adam?"

"I've no problem answering your questions." He smiled. "I've told you, I don't know the dead girl and I don't know any Mimoza. Now, while I'm disappointed that you've declined my invitation to dinner, I must get on with my work. Was there something else you wanted?"

"Actually there was. Do you have an interpreter working here?"

"Yes, we do. George O'Hara. Very talented young man."

"Is he attached to Athlone Institute?"

"No, he's freelance."

"Really?" Shit. She had wanted an opportunity to speak to someone not in Russell's employment.

"It works out much cheaper."

"I'd like to meet him."

"Why would you want to do that?"

"I might have some work for him. I've time now if he's around."

Russell steepled his fingers and looked at her. "Ah. Unfortunately he won't be in until Friday."

"I'll call back then." It might be worth meeting this George

O'Hara. Maybe she'd get more sense out of him than she'd got from Russell.

Russell was chewing on the inside of his lip and looking furtive. Shifty. That was how she'd describe him if asked. Or maybe she was imagining it. Must be the heat.

Opening the door, she said, "If there's something illegal going on here, I intend to find out."

Russell laughed, and Lottie noted how this reaction might strike fear into an unsuspecting person. Not her, though; it merely strengthened her determination to get to the bottom of whatever scam he was involved in. Because she was bloody sure he was up to something.

Once outside again, she knew what it was that had nagged her when she first arrived. The place was empty. No children running around or women watching over them. Silence.

Walking resolutely out through the gate, she headed back toward the station. At the canal bridge she glanced down and quelled a ridiculous urge to walk barefoot through the cherry-blossom petals sheeting the pathway in a pink carpet. She felt like she wanted to strip off the uneasy feeling she'd experienced in the barracks. Had Russell been implying there was something she should know about Adam?

* * *

The man drew into the shadows as Lottie left the block housing Dan Russell's office. He hunkered down and patted the dog's head to keep the mutt quiet.

The detective was going to be a problem. But not for him if he could help it.

He just needed to speed up his work.

He would be okay. But she would have to be watched.

CHAPTER 26

Three years ago, her stilettos clipping out the front door, long black hair swishing behind her with purpose, Jackie Boyd had exited DS Mark Boyd's life.

Now he watched openmouthed as she dashed into Books and Things. She had never read a book in her life; hadn't done much of anything except complain about everything that crossed her line of vision. She was beautiful, not in an understated sort of way, but extravagantly gorgeous. And he'd been such an eejit, he hadn't been able to hold on to her.

She had liked excitement and danger, so he supposed that was why she'd hightailed it off to Spain with her lover. Jamie McNally, suspected smuggler of drugs and God knew what else. "You're so boring," she'd said in one of their arguments before she left. And she was probably right. But he had loved her and done what he could with what little he had, stretching his savings to their limit for a wedding at Ashford fucking Castle. The wedding had been so expensive they couldn't afford to buy a house afterward. His one-bed apartment wasn't good enough for Jackie. She had spent most weekends in Dublin partying with her friends, leaving Boyd alone in Ragmullin, and eventually she'd been swept off her high heels by Rat-Face McNally.

Boyd had kept her departure under wraps for a while, but Ragmullin, though it was a big town, was still small enough that you couldn't go unnoticed from being married to being single. Humiliated and ridiculed, with the threat of a major investigation into the scandal, he'd relied on his close work colleagues for support. There had been an inquiry regarding his nonexistent association with McNally, but nothing had come of it. *He* hadn't been the one cavorting with a criminal. Outwardly he accepted the slaps on his shoulders; inwardly he tried to consign Jackie to his past. Venting his anger on his bike, pedaling like a madman, didn't make him feel any better, but it did dull the void in his heart. A void into which he had tried unsuccessfully to entice Lottie Parker. But she'd stepped over it like a rain-filled puddle and danced around the edge, sometimes getting her feet a little wet but never jumping right in.

Seeing Jackie heading into the store, her hair shorn so short her neck appeared swanlike, stopped Boyd in his tracks. Why was she back in town, and where was lover boy McNally?

He watched from his vantage point as he exited the shop, unwrapping a pack of cigarettes, letting the cellophane catch in a slow breeze. She looked around nervously, lit a cigarette and inhaled deeply. Clipping down the street, she turned right, to the Brook Hotel. And Boyd, unable to help himself, followed her.

* * *

As he walked into the hotel lounge, he saw her sitting in a booth. Leaning against a pillar, he watched her. She must have spent the last few years in the sun, he thought. She had changed. A lot. Her skin was like an old brown leather handbag, and her eyes appeared dull and lifeless. But she'd maintained her perfect figure.

She looked up and they stared at each other. No smile. He thought about turning and leaving, but did neither. He walked up the wooden steps, careful not to slip in his haste, and sat on a stool opposite her.

"Hello, Marcus."

Boyd cringed. Jackie had never called him Mark, his birth

name. Too common, she'd said, the irony lost on her. So she'd rechristened him Marcus. He hated it.

"It's Boyd to all and sundry now," he said. "How're you, Jackie?"

"I'm fine," she said, laying the menu on the table. He noticed her fingers twitching. Itching for a cigarette? Nervous?

"What brings you back to Ragmullin? If you'd warned me, I would've rolled out the red carpet."

"Sarcasm never did suit you."

Boyd put a piece of gum into his mouth and chewed. "So, are you going to tell me?"

"Nothing to do with you, if you really want to know."

The waitress arrived with a notepad.

"Just a coffee," Jackie said. "Something has taken away my appetite."

"Nothing for me," Boyd said.

He leaned back and remembered just in time that he was sitting on a stool. His knees ached. Could he chance moving over to the seat beside her? No way. Maybe he should just get the fuck out of here, away from his not-yet-ex-wife.

He said, "Was it too hot for you in Spain?"

"What do you think, Detective Sergeant Boyd? Heard from one of my friends that you didn't make inspector. Sorry about that. Was your reputation sullied by my indiscretions?" She crossed her long legs, her light dress sliding up her thigh. "No need to answer that." A smile glided across her face. She knew how to hurt him, knew how to tip his anger off the scale.

Boyd shook his head. "So did you leave McNally on a sunbed somewhere?" he asked.

"Do you speak in questions all the time? I don't have to answer any of them. Unless you want to arrest me?"

"You should have stayed under whatever rock he dragged you to. I don't need to see you around here."

"It's a free country, last time I checked."

"I'd better go, if you don't mind." He stood up.

"Why would I mind? I didn't invite you."

"Just stay out of my way." He walked away before the rage, swelling like lava, overflowed into something he would later regret.

"Marcus?"

He paused on the bottom step of the booth.

"You stay out of my way too."

"Keep McNally out of my face," he said, "and you won't see me."

He left the hotel and headed for Cafferty's Bar. He needed a pint before he faced Lottie.

* * *

Jackie Boyd knew it had been a risk returning to Ragmullin. But she had wanted to come, and following lots of cajoling and partaking in a few things she didn't particularly like in bed, Jamie had relented. She'd known there was a strong possibility she would run into Marcus, and somewhere in her subconscious she had thought he might be able to help her. Before she could dwell on it too much, Jamie was sitting in front of her.

"Was that Detective Sergeant Boyd I saw leaving like Batman?" he mocked.

"He appeared out of nowhere," she said, taking the coffee cup from the waitress who had materialized at her side.

"I hope you haven't been screwing around behind my back."

"I can't help it if people I used to know happen to bump into me." She knew she had said too much the second the words left her lips.

"Were you talking to him just now?"

"He said hello. I told him to get lost. He left." She hoped Jamie accepted this. She didn't want a row. Not here. Not in public. "How did you get on?" she said quickly, changing the subject.

"I'm calling to the house later. See if I can find out anything. If you're finished, let's go. I don't want to be seen."

She wondered why he was out in a public place if he didn't want to be seen. Wishing she had time to still her nerves with the coffee, she left the correct money on the table and stood up. McNally caught her by the elbow and steered her down the steps.

He pulled her close. "Stay away from your ex or you'll have me to deal with. You hear?" He bit down on the lobe of her ear.

"Of c-course, Jamie," she stuttered. "Of course."

CHAPTER 27

Lottie glanced up as Boyd slunk into the office shortly after three o'clock.

"Liquid lunch?" she asked.

"Leave it. Just for once." He sat at his desk.

"What's the matter with you?" She noticed he was looking unusually disheveled, his cotton shirt soaked with perspiration.

"I said leave it."

"Have it your own way." There was no getting through to Boyd when he was like this.

Scanning her notes on Maeve Phillips, she considered handing the file over to another team to heighten its profile. She had plenty on her desk already to contend with. She was no closer to discovering who the murdered girl was; there were no results from Weir's yard; no sign of Mimoza and her son. But she couldn't ignore the fact that a girl was now missing.

"You never drink at lunchtime." She couldn't help herself. Boyd was acting so out of character, he was almost someone else.

He sighed. "Jackie's back."

So that was it. If anyone could drive Boyd to drink, it was Jackie. Why hadn't he divorced her? He must still have a spark for her. If she was Boyd, it'd be a knife, not a spark. But she wasn't, and Boyd had a soft heart. Shit, she thought, I should have warned him about McNally. Now she felt really bad.

"You saw her?"

"Met her, actually."

"What does that mean? Was lover boy with her?" she asked,

without thinking. Kirby still hadn't found any sign of Jamie
McNally. Maybe Boyd could get some information on the
criminal's whereabouts through Jackie.

"Wait a minute. Did you know McNally was back?" he said.

"I'm sorry. I didn't want to tell you until we were sure.
Superintendent Corrigan had information that he returned to
Ireland last Wednesday. Kirby was trying to locate him. To
date he's come up empty." Shit, she was making a balls of this.
"So... you don't know if McNally's with her or not?"

"To be honest, Lottie, I don't give a shit."

"Rubbish"

"Ah, just give me a break. I don't want to go over this."

"Why? Don't be an eejit. Three years ago Jackie broke your
heart and nearly lost you your job."

"I couldn't give her what she wanted. It was all my fault."

"Yes, for marrying her in the first instance."

"That was my choice."

"And you *still* have a choice. Stay away from her."

"Lottie?"

"Yes?"

"Mind your own business."

"Okay." Lottie relented. For now. Perhaps she should have
warned Boyd that McNally was back. Bad judgment on her
part? No, she'd been trying to protect him.

"Will you find out where we can get a list of the residents at
Dan Russell's facility?" she asked. Boyd looked like he needed
an OCD-type job to get him back concentrating on work.

"I'll check with the Department of Justice. Though if the
facility is outsourced, I'm not sure they'll be able to help."

"Try it anyway."

With a sigh, Boyd nodded.

"They have a freelance language tutor in the DPC. George
O'Hara..." she began.

"Don't even think about it."

"Okay so," Lottie relented. "About the dress we found in Maeve Phillips's room," she said. "From the code on the tag, Lynch discovered it's only available online. She's checking with the company now. Hopefully we can trace the transaction."

Boyd sat up straight. "We'll never trace it."

"Be optimistic. There's enough pessimists around without you turning into one." She slammed the desk.

"Got something!" Maria Lynch interrupted them, dragging a page from the printer. "The dress was bought from Dinkydress on April first. Paid for by credit card. They won't say who owns the card, but it was delivered by courier to Maeve Phillips, 251 Mellow Grove, on the fifth."

"She had that dress over a month and never wore it. Wonder what it was bought for? Any credit cards in her own name?" Lottie asked, reading the page.

"She hasn't even got a bank account," Lynch said.

"Someone bought it for her. Might be a boyfriend. See if you can get the company to release the name."

"How?"

"Make something up. I think whoever bought that dress may be Maeve's mystery boyfriend. If we find this boyfriend, we might find Maeve. We need to be concentrating on the murder of the woman found under the street."

"Will I hand this missing person case over to someone else, so?" Lynch asked.

"No. We need to make it high priority. Find out if Maeve Phillips has a passport, and I want to talk to this friend of hers, Emily. I need to be sure Maeve's disappearance isn't linked to the murder."

"Hardly likely, is it?" Boyd said.

"Ticking the box," Lottie said.

"As long as it's not a wooden one with a brass cross on

top," Kirby said, raising his head from behind a mountain of paperwork.

"That was anything but funny." Lottie ran her fingers through her hair and wondered if Kirby had a point.

* * *

Emily Coyne was chatty and full of life. Lottie caught up with her at the Parkway Hotel, where she worked afternoons, after school.

Flouncing onto a chair in front of the two detectives, Emily's eyes shone with excitement through pink-rimmed spectacles. Auburn highlights in her curly hair flashed every time she turned her head, which was often.

"Thanks for talking to us," Lottie said.

The girl stared. "Oh, Mrs. Parker. I hardly recognized you. How's Chloe?"

Lottie wondered if Chloe was in Emily's year at school, and if so, did she know Maeve?

"She's fine, thanks."

"Cool," Emily said.

"We're concerned about your friend Maeve Phillips."

"Maeve? Why? What she do?" The curls remained stationary long enough for the curve of her mouth to dip downward. "Nothing serious, I hope."

"We're trying to locate her," Lottie said, feeling slightly dizzy at the girl's constant gesticulations. "Any idea where she might be?"

Emily puffed out her cheeks and widened her eyes. "At home?"

"She's not there. Do you think she might be with her father?"

"That yoke. She hates him."

Lottie digested that for a moment, then asked, "When did you last see Maeve?"

More facial contortions and flicking of long nails before Emily said, "Let me see. Last Friday at school."

"Didn't she stay over at your house for the weekend?"

"No. She was all excited, like. I think she has a boyfriend. Said she'd see me Monday with all the gossip. But she hasn't been to school this week. Oh shit. I hope she's all right."

Lottie said, "Is it unusual for her to miss school?"

Emily made a face. "Yes, it is actually. I should have been more worried about her, but I've been so busy studying and working here and all." She dropped her head. "Maeve rarely misses school, which is odd seeing as how her mum is..." She paused. "I don't mean to disrespect her mother, but she drinks a lot."

"I know that."

"I tried ringing Maeve. Text and Snapchat too, but I got no reply on anything. I wasn't concerned about her, though. Should I have been? Do you think she's all right?"

Ignoring the girl's inquiries, Lottie asked, "Do you know anything about Maeve's boyfriend?"

"She only hinted she was seeing someone. Never mentioned a name or anything. I asked but she wouldn't tell me."

"And you're sure she hasn't been in contact with you since Friday?" Lottie had been hoping Maeve had stayed with Emily, or at least told her where she was going.

"I only saw her briefly then. We're in TY together but the class splits up on Fridays for our project."

"TY?" Boyd asked.

"Transition year," Lottie explained. "After they complete their Junior Certificate, students have a choice of taking an extra year for projects." She turned back to Emily. "What kind of project are you doing?"

"Helping people understand languages a bit better. All boring stuff really."

"And Maeve's doing this too?"

"Yes, and she was all excited on Friday. Like I said, I don't know why."

"So you definitely didn't see her after that?"

"No. You have me worried now. Where do you think she is?" Concern seemed to put a damper on Emily's antics.

"I thought you might know, but obviously…" Lottie rose to leave.

"Wait." Emily tugged her bag. Lottie resumed her seat. "Maeve was online a lot. Tinder and Facebook. Snapchat and Twitter too. More than any of us. I think her fella might be someone she met that way."

"Okay," Lottie said. "If you think of anything else, contact me." She handed over her card.

"Yup. I'll ask around too. I can be like a private detective."

"Emily, we will do the investigating. But if you hear anything, ring or text me."

"Whatever." The curls bounced around even more. "Mrs. Parker?"

Lottie paused. "Yes?"

"You should ask Chloe about Maeve. They're friends as well."

* * *

"I'll drive," Lottie said, at the car.

"Fine by me," Boyd said.

"I'd say you're over the limit."

"Oh, I was way over my limit three years ago."

"I'm not talking about Jackie."

"Neither am I."

Lottie unlocked the car and got in. "Boyd, I'm very concerned."

"I feel sick." Boyd buckled his seat belt. "Hope I'm not getting the flu," he complained.

"Grow up. It's your lunchtime pints mixed with the heat.

I'm convinced now that Maeve is missing. I'm just not sure if she ran off freely or not. I'll need to set up a task force to oversee it. Even with the murder investigation ongoing, we have to keep this high-profile."

"She'll be with her online boyfriend. No need to panic."

"She'd have told her best friend." Lottie started the car. "Teenagers stick together, tell each other everything. If Emily doesn't know where Maeve is, then no one does."

"What about Chloe?"

"I'll talk to her this evening, but she's a year behind Maeve in school, so she mightn't know much about her."

Boyd shook his head. "You think Maeve's been abducted, don't you? Come on, Lottie. Don't jump to conclusions. The evidence points to the fact that the girl ran away."

"Ran away with what? You saw her home. They have nothing."

"She has a criminal father who is more than likely loaded and you're panicking because you didn't do the right thing when Jason Rickard went missing."

Lottie slammed on the brakes. Luckily there was no one behind her. She quickly maneuvered the car onto the hard shoulder opposite the old tobacco factory. Twisting round, she shot Boyd a scathing look.

"That was below the belt. Way below."

He appeared to shrink beneath her glare. "Shit, I'm sorry. But in all honesty, don't you think it's true?"

"Fuck you, Boyd."

Gritting her teeth, she floored the accelerator, swerving into the lane without a glance in the rearview mirror, and roared the car back to the station.

She was mad at Boyd because she knew he was right.

* * *

Lottie rang Jane Dore, but the pathologist had had no word from ballistics regarding the bullet found in the victim.

"Any favors owed to you?" Lottie asked.

"Cashed them in last time when I bumped that DNA sample to the top of the queue for you," Jane said. "No identification yet?"

"No. We also have a missing local girl, but I'm nearly positive it's not her. I'll email you her photo, just so you can rule her out."

"Okay, send it on."

"Do you think our victim could have been shot at the car dismantler's depot?" Lottie asked.

"I'm having the bloods checked," Jane said. "And I found a particle of moss lodged under a fingernail."

"Moss? But she was buried in clay and dirt."

"I'm having it analyzed at the moment."

"Let me know as soon as you have results."

"I will."

"Moss," Lottie repeated as she ended the call. Her head ached. Looking around, she noticed she was the only one left in the office.

CHAPTER 28

Lottie had let Boyd out of the car at the front of the station while she parked round the back. He had grabbed Kirby, who was on the steps having a smoke, and steered him down the street to Cafferty's. The pub was quiet at 5:30 in the evening.

"Don't mind the boss. She's chewing everyone's arse," Kirby said.

"It's not that," Boyd replied. "Jackie's back."

Kirby averted his eyes. "That's all you need."

"Tell me about it."

Kirby sipped his Guinness. "Look, Boyd, I knew your ex-wife was trouble the first time she wiggled her boobs at me."

"She's still my wife, if only in name," Boyd corrected him. "To hell with this sparkling water. Hey, Darren. Put on a pint for me."

The barman set about the slow art of pulling the perfect pint of Guinness.

Kirby said, "You're blind to all things dangerous and criminal when the gorgeous Jackie's in your vicinity."

"Playing the philosopher doesn't wash with me."

"You know McNally is back in town?"

"I do now, but I didn't see any sign of him nor did I hang around to hear her story. Not that she had any intention of telling me anything."

"Was it weird seeing Jackie after so long?" Kirby finished his pint with three gulps and signaled for another.

"Weird?" Boyd thought for a moment. "That's one way of putting it after three years. Scary, I'd say."

"You're not afraid of Rat-Face McNally, are you?"

"Afraid of what he's doing back in Ragmullin more like. Trouble tracks him like a second shadow."

"We need to get on to Europol and see if they can tell us what he's been up to."

"We're not the CIA, Kirby."

"Hmph," Kirby grunted.

"I'm not even sure Jackie's still with him."

"Wishful thinking?"

Darren, the barman, arrived with the pint. While Boyd was counting out the money, Kirby picked up the glass and started drinking.

"I'll have the other one ready in two shakes," said Darren with a wink.

"You're a greedy bastard, Kirby. Anyway," Boyd said, "I don't want to talk about Jackie."

"Fine by me. But you'd like to get your leg over her again, wouldn't you?"

The barman arrived with the second pint.

"Shut up and let's get shit-faced," Boyd said.

"I'll drink to that," Kirby replied, raising his glass in a mock toast.

CHAPTER 29

Chloe was lying on her bed, bright red headphones clamped to her ears, still wearing her uniform. She was thumbing through her phone.

"Can I have a word?" Lottie walked into the room and sat on the edge of the bed. Chloe jumped up, pulled the Beats down to her neck and slipped the phone under her pillow. Lottie took this as assent.

"How are things? You seem to be in bad form all the time. Why?"

"Just stuff. You wouldn't understand."

"I'm worried about you; try me."

"No. Way. What do you want?"

Sighing, Lottie asked, "Do you know Maeve Phillips?"

"What if I do?"

"Chloe, please do me a favor and answer the question."

"Okay, Detective Inspector. Yeah. I know her."

"Any idea where she might skive off to?"

"No. Is she gone AWOL?"

"I got the impression she wasn't the type of girl to go AWOL, as you put it."

"Maeve is a drama queen, always looking for attention."

Lottie knew a couple of other drama queens, both living in her house.

"So it's not unusual for her to go missing, is it?"

"Not really. She has friends in Dublin. Sometimes she heads up there on the train. Gets sick of looking after her alcoholic mother, so she says."

"She hasn't been seen since last Friday," Lottie said.

"Don't think she ever went off for that long before. Usually a day or two."

"Emily Coyne thinks she has an online boyfriend. Know anything about that?"

Chloe hesitated. Just a fraction. Lottie caught it.

"Emily is a gobshite. I'm not BFFs or anything with her or Maeve. They're a year ahead of me."

"I know. So how are you acquainted?"

"We hang out online sometimes."

"Facebook?"

Another hesitation, then, "Yeah."

Lottie had the feeling Chloe was being purposely evasive. "If she wanted to leave home, do you think she might go to these friends in Dublin?"

"I *said* I don't know."

Lottie stood up, went to the door and looked back at her daughter. When had she lost her? Chloe used to be the child she could depend on, the sensible one. Had life in the Parker house become too much for the teenager? Her mood had definitely altered recently. Since Lottie had been off work? At home all day going stir-crazy and making her kids just as crazy? But she sensed it was related to the events that happened in January. Or maybe it went back even further, to Adam's death. She knew how devastating it had been for the whole family. But she thought Chloe had coped better than the others. Maybe she'd been wrong about that too.

Chloe chewed her lip for a moment, then, as if having a change of heart, she said, "I thought Maeve was supposed to be staying with Emily for the weekend."

"Emily says she didn't stay with her. Tell me, what's Maeve like?"

"She's okay," Chloe said. "A bit of a loner. Before you ask, she doesn't do drugs or any of that shit."

"This boyfriend of hers…"

Chloe shrugged her shoulders. "She's always online. Has her phone glued to her hand, even in school."

"Same as you, then." Lottie smiled. "We'll interrogate her Facebook account."

"Is nothing sacred anymore?" Chloe groaned.

"And we'll check any other social media sites she might be using."

"Whatever." Chloe pulled the Beats over her ears.

"I'll be getting my guys to probe all her online accounts, but maybe you could have a look and see if you notice anything unusual or odd that might escape us old people."

Lottie walked out onto the landing, followed by the thump of music from the headphones.

"Your room could do with a hoover," she said with a backward glance.

Chloe closed her eyes and waved her away.

Conversation over.

* * *

When she was sure her mother had gone downstairs, Chloe logged on to her phone and searched Maeve's Facebook page. No updates. She tapped on Twitter, clicked her lists. Nothing. She keyed in the hashtag #cutforlife and scrolled. No posts from Maeve since last Friday. Odd. Normally she posted every day, every minute some days. Luckily they hadn't told big-mouth Emily anything, because she would surely blab. There was enough strife in her life without her mother finding out about this.

She expelled a loud breath. Life was such a bitch. She hated having to keep secrets. Why had Maeve told her anything?

She should have gone off to do whatever it was she wanted to do without bringing Chloe into it.

The panic was back. Cutting through her chest. Hauling off her headphones, she threw them on the pillow and sat upright. She rolled up her sleeve and trailed her fingers along the inside of her elbow, feeling the scabs healing over old cuts. Her fingernail caught the edge of a fresh crust, pulling it away from her flesh. She watched a dark blob of blood bubble then settle. She knew what she needed to do.

Jumping off the bed, she searched in her rucksack for her pencil case and sat back on the bed. Extracting the tissue with its sharp implement inside, she listened again to ensure no one was outside her door. She didn't need Sean snooping around. He would surely call their mother.

Very little space remained on her arm. She pulled down her trousers and felt along the soft skin of her inner thigh. It was virgin white and smooth to the touch. Squeezing the flesh, she brought the blade down hard and sharp. A small groan eased from between clamped lips as the pain cut into her.

She knew it was wrong, but somehow it felt right. Later she would tweet about it and hopefully *he* would see it. After all, the hashtag was his idea.

She smelled the cooking from the kitchen downstairs and suddenly she felt hungry. She knew she had to clean up before eating but still she lay supine on the bed. As the blood trickled from the wound, she thought about Maeve. Where on earth was she?

* * *

"What's this?" Sean asked.

"Chicken stir-fry," Lottie said.

"Where's the chicken?"

"Just eat it."

Katie looked ill as she picked through a tangle of noodles

concocted from the remnants of Lottie's last grocery shopping expedition.

"Katie, will you shop for food tomorrow? I'll leave some cash and a list."

"Okay," Katie said.

"How was school?" Lottie asked Sean.

"Okay."

Sometimes conversation in her house reminded her of interviewing a suspect who had taken the "no comment" route. Tough going, she thought.

After the dishes were cleared away, she decided to go for a run and perhaps drop in on her mother en route. She went to her room, and once she had changed into her running gear, she stood at the top of the stairs and listened.

Loud shouts emanated from Sean's room as he fought with his online friends over his football game. Silence from Chloe's. Lottie put her hand on the handle of her door, but decided to let the girl be. She'd said enough for one evening.

She left the house and ran out into the heat of the evening.

By the time she reached her mother's house, sweat was dripping down her back and drenching her Nike top. Panting, she leaned on the neatly trimmed hedge, considering whether she should call in or not. Probably not. Her relationship with her mother was fractured, to say the least. And in some ways it had deteriorated since the body of her murdered elder brother had been discovered almost forty years after he had disappeared. Hadn't she had enough hassle for one day? She'd see her mother tomorrow.

Before she could turn away, the front door opened.

"Are you going to stand out there all evening or are you coming in?"

Rose Fitzpatrick, with her short, sharp silver hair, seemed to intimidate the doorway. Lottie stepped away from the hedge.

"I'm out for a jog. Better keep going or my muscles will seize up." She didn't need a confrontation.

"For God's sake, come in." A command.

Sighing, Lottie pushed open the gate and walked up the pathway to the bungalow that had been her family home. It hadn't changed in the twenty-plus years since she'd left it to marry Adam. She often wondered if she had married so she could escape her mother. She walked through the hall and into the steaming kitchen. Even though it was near eight o'clock, the smell of cooking filled the air.

Her mother unplugged the kettle and brought it to the tap.

"No tea for me. I'll have a glass of water. What's in the pot?" Lottie asked, pulling out a chair and sitting at the table.

"I'm helping Mrs. Murtagh with her soup kitchen."

"Really?" Lottie sat back, eyebrows raised. She hadn't known her mother was in contact with the old woman, who had been a witness in her last case. "Does she still live in Mellow Grove?"

"Of course she does. Why?"

"I'm dealing with a missing girl from there. I wonder would Mrs. Murtagh know something about it?"

"She knows everything about everyone but her mind is so addled I'm not sure you'd get anything worthwhile out of her."

"Will you ask her? A little inside information is always a good thing. Maeve Phillips is the girl's name. Her mother is Tracy and her father is Frank."

"The criminal?"

"One and the same."

"He's not been seen in Ragmullin for years."

"I know."

"I'll chat to Mrs. Murtagh about the family. I'll let you know if I find out anything." Rose smiled, then her mouth flatlined. "You blame me," she said.

"Blame you for what?"

"It wasn't my fault, Lottie, no matter how you care to dress it up. Your brother Eddie was always a handful. After your father...did what he did..." The sound of water flowing from the tap into the kettle drowned out her last words. "You've no idea what it was like. Living with that stigma."

"That stigma was my dad," Lottie whispered. Biting back tears, she stood up, walked over and flicked off the kettle switch. "I have to know what made him do it. Was it work? A case he'd been working on, maybe? What made him put a gun to his head and pull the trigger?"

She could almost see her mother's brain clicking over her words. Moving away, Lottie sat down, cupping her face in her hands. The room filled with an uneasy silence until the kettle began to hiss once again.

"There's a lot you don't know and I think it's better for all of us if it stays that way," Rose said.

"What are you talking about now?" Lottie said through her hands.

"Nothing. I'll keep an eye on my grandchildren during the day and make sure they get at least one decent meal. And you leave the past alone." Rose poured boiling water into a teapot and looked around for the lid.

Twiddling her fingers around the white cotton tablecloth, Lottie glanced up at her mother. Rose Fitzpatrick looked every one of her seventy-five years. Having a forensic scientist identify a bundle of bones wrapped in linen aprons and decades-old flour bags as the body of her long-lost son had been earth-shattering.

"I appreciate all you're doing for my family, honestly I do," Lottie said. "But I have this hole here in my heart and I think I can only fill it if I find out the truth. Until then, I can't leave it be. One day I'll know why my dad killed himself."

"There was a lot going on back then," said Rose. "I can't tell you why he did what he did, because I don't know why." She turned her back on Lottie and stirred the pot of soup on the hob.

"I'm sorry," Lottie said.

"So am I."

"And I do love you, in—"

"In your own way. I know, Lottie. I love you too."

"I'm going home now."

"Do that, girl."

Lottie shook her head wearily and left her mother there, shoulders trembling, stooped over the stove. She ran out into the warm night and didn't stop running until she reached the end of her own road across from the greyhound stadium. As she stood on the curb, a dark saloon car purred up beside her.

"You'll kill yourself running in this heat," Dan Russell said, lowering the window.

Lottie gaped at him, sitting in his Audi. Typical car for a smart-bastard. "What are you doing? Following me?"

"Just passing. On my way to the center."

"So you work day and night?"

"When I'm needed."

"You must be very busy with the recent influx of refugees." She stood with hands on hips as he leaned out of the window with the engine running.

"There isn't enough room for the agreed quota, let alone this new batch. We're doing our best."

New batch? Lottie cringed. He was talking like people were nothing more than sliced bread. "How many are you housing?"

"At the moment we have fifty-four more than we can comfortably hold."

"How do you manage?" She noticed how he never fully answered her questions.

"Extra camp beds. It's crowded."

"Overcrowded?"

"Unofficially, I'd say yes. Officially, it's not quite a health-and-safety issue yet."

"You only have females and children there, is that right?"

"Yes, the men are in various other towns dotted around the country."

"It seemed very quiet when I was there this afternoon. Where is everyone?"

"Oh, they have lots of activities. Did you decide about dinner?"

She laughed. "You're persistent, to say the least."

"Of course."

"I don't think dinner is appropriate, Mr. Russell."

"Dan, please. How about tomorrow evening?"

She remained where she was. Thinking about it, she decided she could possibly garner some information from him over dinner, to assist the murder investigation. A bottle of wine might loosen his tongue. As long as she stayed on sparkling water, it would be fine.

"Be a daredevil," he pressed.

"Maybe," she said.

"Excellent!"

"I'm not agreeing to anything. Give me your number and I might ring you tomorrow." Two could play at being evasive.

He extracted a business card from the glove compartment, scribbled on it and handed it over. "That's my personal mobile number. I look forward to your call. But let's say provisionally that I'll pick you up here tomorrow evening at seven." His fingers brushed hers as she took the card.

Walking to her front door, she wiped her hands down her top, feeling decidedly grimy from his touch. What would Boyd say about that little encounter? Russell was playing a game of poker. She knew that. But could she read his hand over his shoulder without him knowing? That was her task. She knew she was up to it.

CHAPTER 30

Boyd and Kirby stood outside the bar, too many hours to count since they'd entered the establishment, leaning into each other under the clear starlit sky. Boyd tried to light a cigarette and failed. Kirby lit it for him.

"I know a great place to get a ride," Kirby said, his bushy hair damp with perspiration against his scalp.

"So do I. There's a taxi rank at the top of the street," Boyd said, inhaling his cigarette at last.

"You're as drunk as a skunk," Kirby said. "Come on, I'll bring you to the best little whorehouse in Ragmullin. I think you're due a night in the saddle. Two fingers to Jackie and... well, you know who."

Boyd realized Kirby was talking about Lottie. He stared up at the street lamp, seeing two where there should only be one. The door of the Chinese takeaway across the road swirled into three. Jesus, he was well and truly pissed.

"Think I'll go home," he slurred.

"Don't be a spoilsport." Kirby walked on ahead up Gaol Street.

Boyd followed in the middle of the narrow road, walking on the white line. Was he tagging along because he wanted to get laid?

"Please God, don't let me remember all this in the morning," he pleaded as Kirby hailed a taxi and poured him into it.

* * *

Boyd awoke to find himself sitting on the floor at the top of a flight of stairs. A short corridor lay before him, with doors floating in and out of focus around him. How did he get up the stairs? Did Kirby drag him here? He glanced at his watch. Jesus, it was 12:35 a.m.

He shook his head, trying to remember, and groaned with pain. Cafferty's. Drink. Lots of it. Pints and shots. Dear God, he'd been drinking shots. He scanned his surroundings blearily. A girl stood half in, half out of a door at the end of the corridor. Staring at him.

He could see she was beautiful even though she was slipping in and out of focus. Eyes like saucers, dark hair falling across them and down along a bare shoulder. But she looked too young, and immediately he felt it was all wrong. Wrong that he was here, wrong that she was here. She should be in college or somewhere. Anywhere but here.

"I have to go," he said.

Her eyes questioned but her mouth remained sealed, lips quivering. Too much red lipstick.

His stomach heaved. God, he was going to puke.

Easing his spine up along the wall, shuffling his feet until he was standing. He clutched the banister of the stairs. Steadied himself.

She put out her hand. To help him? For money? Had he to pay her? For what? He'd done nothing. Had he? No. He was sure he hadn't. He searched for his wallet, thinking how Lottie would have plenty to say about this if she found out. Kirby better keep his mouth shut or he'd kick the shit out of him.

"Can't pay you," he said, not liking the sound of his own voice in the penetrating silence. Christ, he had to get out of here.

Still she said nothing. Stayed where she was. Unmoving.

"'S not your fault," he slurred. "Mine." He pushed his wallet toward his trouser back pocket, then carefully, one step at a time, walked down the stairs and along the hallway. He pulled back the linked chain and opened the front door. Warm night air greeted him as he moved outside.

Shutting the door behind him, he walked down the steps hoping it was a dream. Maybe a bad dream, but just a dream.

* * *

Mimoza waited until she heard the front door close, downstairs, then crept from her room over to where the man had been. His wallet was on the floor. Picking it up, she ran back inside, shutting the door with a soft thud. She had needed the toilet but had forgotten to go when she'd seen him lying there. Drunk and unconscious. When he'd woken, fear had held her to the spot, frozen in time. And then he was gone.

Glad he hadn't been allocated to her, she wondered idly which one of the other girls had missed out on being puked on.

She went to the wardrobe. After placing the wallet on a shelf, she pulled on clean underwear and shuffled back to the bed. She yearned for the comfort of oblivion. The bliss of a long uninterrupted slumber to drown out her fears and terror. Her eyes closed and the door opened. Another client began unzipping his trousers before she could raise herself on to her elbows. Slowly she removed her underwear and spread her legs for the impatient man. He groaned in rhythm to her moans. He in pleasure; she in pain.

* * *

Lottie couldn't sleep. She twisted and turned. Glanced at the digital clock: 1:15. Got up, pulled on her jogging pants again and a light hoodie. Prowling at night was becoming a habit. Bad habit. She wondered if Boyd was in bed. Maybe she'd call over.

Running quickly through town, she was sweating by the time she reached his apartment. As she rang the bell, a car drew up on the pavement and stopped. The door opened and Jackie Boyd stepped out, dangling keys in her hand.

"Well if it isn't the woman who stole Marcus's job."

Lottie ignored the gibe. Jackie looked tired and haggard. Good, but who am I to judge? she thought.

"Hello, Jackie. What brings you back to Ragmullin?" And what was she doing at Boyd's at this hour?

"I've some things to discuss with my husband. Not that it's any of your business."

Lottie smiled wryly. "I'll let you get on with it so."

She moved away from the door. Jackie walked by her and turned. The cloying scent of an expensive perfume suffused the night.

"I don't think he's at home," Lottie said. "By the way, I hear McNally's back in town. Where is he?"

"Definitely none of your business," Jackie said, jabbing the doorbell with a bitten nail.

"It had better stay that way," Lottie said and hurried down the path, away from the constant ringing of the doorbell.

Suddenly she felt very tired.

CHAPTER 31

Chloe checked Twitter once more. No posts from Maeve.

Tomorrow, she thought, if I hear nothing by tomorrow, I'll tell Mam everything.

She plugged in the charger, placed her phone on the night-stand and fixed her headphones. As she stared at the ceiling, her room was lit up momentarily by the last train passing high up on the tracks behind the house. She wished she could shed her clammy PJs and sleep naked. But there was no privacy in her house. If she locked the door at night, her mother would be banging it down asking her what would she do if the house went on fire?

As if.

The heat of the day settled into her room, suffocating her. Opening the buttons on her pajama top, she allowed the air from the open window to ease over her body. Only for a few minutes, she thought, and hummed to the music blasting in her ears.

She must have drifted off to sleep, because suddenly she was thrust awake by a horrible feeling that someone was watching her. She pulled her top closed. Yanking off her headphones, she glanced around in the darkness at the shadows dancing on the walls. She jumped up and dragged the curtains across the window, blotting out the moonlight. Falling back onto her bed, her skin crawling with a cold sweat, she saw a figure standing in the doorway.

She screamed. "Mum, help!"

"Shut up, you silly cow."

"Jesus Christ, Sean. You frightened the shite out of me." Chloe bolted toward him, pulling on a hoodie.

"I thought I heard someone at the front door," he said.

"Open it and see," Chloe snapped, relenting immediately when she saw the hurt skim over his face. "Sorry, bro. I'll go have a look."

Sean had been through too much. She needed to cut him some slack. She went back and unplugged her phone, glancing at the time. After 1:30. Late for callers.

"Is she home?" she asked.

"Who?"

"Mother...Mum."

"She's out."

"Go back to your PlayStation or whatever you do in that den of yours." She smiled.

Sean's face relaxed. "I'll go with you," he offered.

"Okay."

Together they hurried down the stairs and Chloe opened the front door.

"There's no one here," she said. Barefoot, she walked out to the front wall. Looked up and down the road. "No one."

"I definitely heard the bell."

"How could you hear anything with those monster headphones?" Chloe pointed to where they were hanging around Sean's neck. "World War Three could erupt and you'd hear nothing. You imagined it."

Marching back up the stairs ahead of Sean, she glanced into her mother's room. Empty.

"Wonder where she is."

"Probably out on a case," Sean said.

"What's all the noise?" Katie said, coming out of her room.

"Nothing. Go back to sleep. The two of you."

Chloe closed her bedroom door. Lying on her bed, she

wondered if someone had in fact been at the door. And she remembered the feeling of being watched just before Sean burst into her room. Clutching the sheet to her throat, she turned out the lamp. But she couldn't sleep. She posted on Twitter all night long, hoping *he* would reply. Where was he? And for the hundredth time that night she wondered: where was Maeve?

* * *

The man moved out of the shadow of the neighbor's garden and smiled to himself. She'd looked so beautiful with her frightened face and flowing hair. Maybe he should have stayed there at the door. Waited for her to open it. Grabbed her round the waist and pulled her body into his. The thought spread a feeling of longing from his chest to his groin, and he hurried to where he could sate his salacious appetite.

CHAPTER 32

Tonight was different. Maeve Phillips felt it, even though nothing had yet been said. She hoped whatever was in store for her didn't involve the room with all the blood. She'd tried not to think of it since she'd collapsed there and been dragged back to her cell. Her prison cell.

How long had she been here? A few days? A week? She had no idea. But now something was going on. Rushing footsteps up and down the corridor outside her door. Muffled voices, low whispers, then shouts. The voices sounded male but she couldn't be sure. She wished they'd at least left the light on. The narrow gleam from beneath the door offered only shadows.

She closed her eyes and wished for the thousandth time that she had her phone. Would Emily or Chloe be missing her? She'd told Emily she'd fill her in with all the gossip on Monday. What day was it today? No idea. She had lost all concept of time. If her own mother failed to raise the alarm, Chloe surely would do so. She was a detective's daughter; she would know what to do. She'd miss her at school. She'd miss her on Twitter. Or would she? Maeve wept at the hopelessness of her situation. She had been so trusting. So stupid. As she wiped away her tears, she was grateful for one small thing. So far he hadn't hurt her. But how long until he did?

The door opened loudly. She darted up.

"Let me out. Please. My mother needs me." She stretched out her hand toward the figure in front of her.

He grabbed and twisted her arm up her back until she screamed.

"Calm down, little darling. Tonight is your lucky night."

* * *

Kosovo 1999

He slept for the twenty-kilometer drive into the city of Pristina. The jeep jerked to a stop, causing him to wake with a jolt. The door slammed and the captain jumped out.

The boy stared up at the sign over the door of the building: Klinikë. Most of the surrounding tall buildings had satellite dishes pulsating from their walls like varicose veins. There were so many, he stopped counting.

His eyes drawn to the two-story clinic, he asked, "Is captain ill?"

"He has to see if the doctor will check you over." The soldier reclined the seat and closed his eyes.

The boy closed his too. He didn't want to be looking at the two girls curving their legs around a lamppost doing their best to attract the soldier's attention.

The captain returned. "Come with me," he said, gesturing the boy out of the car.

Looking at his soldier friend, the boy pleaded with his eyes.

"You better go, lad," the soldier said, straightening up. "I'll be waiting here for you."

The boy clambered over the seat and climbed out of the door. He didn't know why, but he had an unnatural feeling of terror, even worse than when the men had raped and murdered his mama and sister.

Gulping down his fear, his eyes filling with tears, he read the letters on the green canvas badge taped across the soldier's chest. He didn't understand what they said but the letters imprinted themselves on his brain. He knew he would remember his friend for the rest of his life. However long that might be.

DAY FOUR

Thursday, May 14, 2015

CHAPTER 33

Lottie had walked to work rather than driving, in a bid to clear her head after a restless night. It hadn't worked.

Following the morning conference with her incident team, she briefed Superintendent Corrigan with information for his press conference. She was glad he was still handling the media, because she had no immediate wish to renew her acquaintance with Cathal Moroney.

"You don't have much of anything, do you, Inspector?" Corrigan turned up his nose at the page of scant notes. "Any evidence suggesting the body could be this missing Maeve Phillips?"

"No evidence, sir. I don't think it's her."

"You should hand the missing person file over to a new team so you can concentrate on finding the murder victim's identity. After all, you are the senior investigation officer."

Tell me something I don't know, she thought. "I'll hold on to the missing person for a few days, sir."

"A few days, then hand it over. I'm going to release this photo to the press."

"Maeve Phillips's photo?"

"No, the unidentified murder victim. Didn't I just say we need to find out who she is? The way I see it, you have nothing so far. A whole lot of nothing gives me feckin' nothing to tell the media."

Lottie couldn't disagree. "Right, sir."

Walking down the corridor to her office, all she could think of was the photo of the black-haired girl with the diamond stud in her nose. Maeve Phillips.

Back at her desk, she noticed the report detailing the examination of Maeve's laptop. Nothing unusual had been discovered. English essays on Word and maths on Excel. The laptop wasn't set up for internet. Maeve must do her online stuff on her phone, she thought. Where was her phone?

"Kirby, did we find anything on the whereabouts of Maeve Phillips's phone?"

Kirby lifted his head from his computer. "It's taking a while because it's switched off. I'll try spinning a few lies and see where it gets me."

"Any word on those friends of hers in Dublin?"

"I got a colleague in HQ to check them out. All sound people but none of them has had any contact with her for ages."

"Dead end there so. Any luck with the school?"

"No one has seen her all week. Principal rang the mother. Stupid bitch didn't appear to know her own daughter was missing."

"No need for name-calling. Tracy Phillips is an alcoholic, and alcoholism is a disease, in case you didn't know."

"Sorry, boss." Kirby ducked his head back to his work.

Lottie wasn't letting him away that easy.

"Did you find out where Jamie McNally is?" That made her think of Boyd. Where was he this morning? Maybe Jackie had hooked up with him after all.

"He's gone to ground. We've a record of him entering the country last Wednesday. Nothing since. Jackie Boyd's been spotted around town. No sign of McNally."

"He wouldn't leave Jackie in Ragmullin unattended. He has to be nearby. Keep digging."

"Will do." Kirby stood up with a mug in his hand and wobbled.

"Hard night?"

"You could say that."

"Do you know where Boyd is?"

Kirby shook his head and escaped out the door without a word.

"What's going on around here?" Lottie asked, raising her arms to the ceiling.

Lynch lifted her head. "Must be the heat."

Opening up her emails, Lottie clicked on the murdered girl's postmortem report and read it again. Who are you? Why has no one reported you missing? Why did the killer wash your bullet wound?

"Any DNA results back?" she asked Lynch.

"Not yet. SOCOs found no bullet in Weir's wall. So whoever fired the shot took the bullet with them."

"Or it's the one in the victim. If not, there has to be a reason for it."

"Someone shooting rats? Probably Bob Weir himself."

"Do you honestly think he'd have called it in if it was him? He doesn't like the disruption," Lottie said.

"You're right," said Lynch. "Did you do anything else about that letter you got from the girl, Mimoza?"

"She hasn't been in contact since. Maybe she was taking a risk or something." Now that Lottie thought about it, she got an uneasy feeling that she'd neglected it. "Wonder where she is now."

"And who is she with?"

"Probably with the girl who was waiting for her at the end of my road. Very mysterious." Lottie twiddled a pen between her fingers, thinking back to Monday morning. So much had happened since then.

"What I'd like to know is why she came to you," Lynch said.

"I have no idea. But it's a bit odd that the note's written in Albanian and the guy who found the body is from Kosovo. Isn't Albanian one of the official languages in that country?"

Saying this aloud made Lottie think about it for a moment, and she felt the beginnings of a churning in her stomach. She said, "Maybe I should have another word with Andri Petrovci."

"Maybe you made a mistake involving him with the note," Lynch said.

"Maybe you haven't enough work to be doing."

"I've plenty, thanks."

"Do it then, and let me get on with mine."

"I was just saying—"

"Don't, Lynch."

Lottie shoved back her chair, picked up her bag and got out of the office before she said something that would result in a harassment tribunal.

CHAPTER 34

Mimoza eased herself out of bed and walked slowly to the washbasin, tugging back the curtain to allow in light. A brick wall, maybe a foot from the window, blocked any view. She looked down. Too high up to jump. The gap too narrow anyway.

Dampening a cloth, she rubbed away the dried semen from between her legs. Why did this place allow unprotected sex? The main attraction, she supposed, for frustrated old men and the young uninitiated, who didn't want or couldn't wait to slide the rubber on before ejaculating.

Searching the wardrobe for clean underwear, she glimpsed the man's wallet that she'd picked up last night. She took it out, opened it up and quickly counted the money with trembling fingers. Less than a hundred euros. Bank cards and an ID badge. Her eyes widened in surprise as she slowly read the words. Detective Sergeant Mark Boyd. Her translation wasn't good, but she was sure that meant he was a policeman.

If only she'd known who he was. If only. Would he come back for his wallet? She hoped so, because Mimoza knew this detective might be her only escape route from captivity. Especially since it appeared the woman police officer had done nothing with her note.

She would have to come up with a plan before he returned. She was sure he would come back for it. Once he remembered where he had lost it. He might wait until after dark, so nobody could see him, unless of course he had an official reason to return.

Could she put a message inside the wallet? But what to write with and on? She spied the few items of makeup on the small nightstand. The eyeliner pencil would have to do. She unscrewed the cap and checked it was working by marking the palm of her hand with a black line. Sitting on the bed, she looked at the bulky curtains. Too heavy. But her sheets were white cotton.

She stood up. This might be her only hope. But he had been so drunk, would he even remember her? She had no other option but to try it.

Dragging the sheet loose from the mattress and biting down on the material while yanking at it with trembling hands, she felt it give, heard a tear. Dust mites floated into the air as she inspected her handiwork. The rip was close enough to the hem and she tore a strip from one edge to the other. Then she carefully folded the end of the sheet back around the bottom of the mattress, hoping no one would notice her destruction.

Flattening out the strip on the bed, she took the eyeliner pencil and began to write, in her own language because she couldn't write well in English. When she'd finished, she folded it into the smallest wad she could manage, slipped it into the cash flap and placed the wallet on the floor under the bed.

Looking round her tomb-like abode, she silently prayed that this Detective Boyd would remember where he had been last night. And she hoped he would be brave enough to return. It might well be her only hope of ever seeing her son again.

CHAPTER 35

The morning heat was giving way to a welcome breeze, raising dust into the air at an alarming rate. Lottie clamped a hand over her mouth and walked around the barrier toward the man in the yellow singlet.

He stood up tall from his work and wiped a gloved hand over his forehead. Removing his protective goggles, he tipped back his safety helmet.

"You not allowed here. Danger," he said, and stepped out of the trench to the road.

Lottie hoped her smile might melt some of his antagonism, but he remained tight-lipped and grim. Shit.

"I was wondering if perhaps you'd thought any more about the note? The one written in Albanian."

"No."

"You sure you don't know anything about the girl mentioned in it, Kaltrina?" She studied his face, waiting for a reaction. It was marble-like. Unmoving. Even his eyes didn't blink. Staring. Silence. Except for the constant buzz of flies in the heat.

"Help me out here, Andri," she said, hoping her informality might work on him.

"Why you want help? You police. You look."

"I don't speak the language. You do."

"What you want?"

"Ask around? Ask your people."

"My people? Who you mean?"

Lottie tried a smile. "We think the girl you uncovered in

the ground is a foreigner. No one has reported her missing. We don't know who she is. We are stuck. Please, can you help?"

"No."

"No? Why not?"

"I not do work for you." He tugged his helmet forward onto his forehead, pulled on his goggles and stepped back into the trench.

Walking away, swatting the flies, Lottie was just about to text Boyd to come and meet her when a message came through from Dan Russell.

Detective Inspector. Seven tonight. I'll pick you up at the greyhound stadium. Don't forget.

She sighed. Perhaps if she met him, she could figure him out. What was he really up to? She sent him a brief text agreeing to his plans and hurried back to the office, all thoughts of a late breakfast disappearing.

At her computer she read up as much as she could discover on Russell, which wasn't a whole lot more than Lynch had found out. Thirty years in the army, rising to the rank of commandant, retiring in 2010. He had established his business, Woodlake Facilities Management, in 2012. It seemed to be making a handsome profit. She closed down her search, thinking how he had traveled just about far enough under her skin to start an itch. And she didn't like how that felt.

She wondered again if Russell had ever served with Adam. He'd answered her question evasively when she'd asked, but there was no way of finding out anything online, though Russell's overseas dates seemed to confirm that the two men had been in Kosovo at the same time, serving under the NATO flag on peacekeeping duties. She clicked into an article about the Kosovo conflict. Mimoza had written her letter in Albanian, so it might have a tenuous link to the investigation. Flicking from article to article, she scanned them without fully absorbing the stories of human tragedy and murder.

When eventually she raised her head, it was lunchtime. A morning wasted. She phoned Boyd. He said he'd meet her in Cafferty's. She grabbed her bag.

"I'm going to grab some lunch," she told Lynch, who had buried her head behind a mound of door-to-door reports. All yielding absolutely nothing.

* * *

Boyd was standing at the counter in Cafferty's with house-special sandwiches and a pot of tea for two when he discovered he didn't have his wallet.

"When did you have it last?" Lottie asked when he returned to their small round table in a corner of the bar.

Every morning, once he had dressed, he put his wallet into his trouser pocket. He couldn't remember doing it this morning. He couldn't remember even seeing his wallet.

"It's Kirby's fault," he muttered, eyeing the overflowing sandwich, his appetite suddenly taking a dive and the contents of his stomach rising up his throat.

"Are you all right?" she asked. "You look a bit green. I know Kirby is used to benders but I don't think you are. And you've missed a morning's work."

"If I want a lecture I'll visit my mother, thank you very much."

"Touché."

Boyd bit into the sandwich and swirled around a mouthful of tea to wash it down.

Lottie laughed. "You know what you need?"

"No, but I've a feeling you're about to tell me."

"The hair of the dog."

"You'd know all about that, wouldn't you?" he said. Wrong thing to say. Too late now.

Lottie slammed her cup down on the saucer, stood up and marched to the counter. Her voice rang across the bar to where Boyd was sitting.

"Darren, can you wrap up this sandwich? I think I'll have it back in my office." She pushed her bank card across the counter. "You can take for everything, as my esteemed colleague appears to have mislaid his wallet."

Boyd caught Darren's wink as he scanned Lottie's card on the machine.

"Was there a session here last night?" she asked.

"Oh, the usual crowd." The barman was noncommittal.

Boyd shook his head, cringing with the pain shooting up behind his eyes.

Lottie took the receipt, her card and the tinfoil-wrapped sandwich. Boyd searched his pockets once again before gingerly getting up from his stool.

"Maybe you should file a report," Lottie said and let the door close behind her as she stepped out into the midday heat.

Boyd knew she was wondering what he and Kirby had got up to last night. If he had anything to do with it, it would be one night she would never know about. Not that he could remember much about it himself.

He'd better talk to Kirby. And soon.

First, though, he just needed to rest his head for a few minutes.

"Will I wrap yours up too?" the barman asked, pointing to the sandwich with one bite gone out of it.

"Don't think I can stomach food today," Boyd said.

"Some session the two of you had, if you don't mind me saying."

"I'd agree with you if I could remember it. I didn't by any chance leave my wallet behind, did I?"

"I cleaned up last night and I was first in this morning. No wallet. Did you go to *Bed* after here?" Darren asked, referring to the nightclub.

"I wish," Boyd said. "My own bed."

"The two of you were last to leave, so I reckon you lost it wherever you went after here. Maybe you left it in a taxi?"

Boyd rested his head against the leather of the seat and shielded his eyes from the sun squinting through the dusty stained-glass window.

"Kirby, you bastard," he whispered, the full realization hitting him. He remembered exactly where they'd gone after leaving the pub.

The doe-eyed girl had robbed him.

CHAPTER 36

Entering her code on the inner door at the station reception, Lottie met Kirby coming down the stairs, Maria Lynch bobbing behind him.

"Come on, boss." He grabbed her by the elbow and steered her back out the door.

"What the—"

"The contractors. They've found another body. Columb Street."

"What the hell? I was there this morning." She dumped her sandwich into the bin outside and jumped into the car with Kirby and Lynch.

Speeding away, Kirby switched on the siren and flashing lights. They screeched up Main Street on the wrong side of the road. The lunchtime traffic came to a standstill. Swerving round by the chipper, he pulled up outside Weir's yard.

Andri Petrovci was pacing around in circles, running his hands up and down his arms, his safety helmet pushed right back on his shaved head.

Jumping out of the car, Lottie ran toward him. She felt his fingers dig into her arms as he grabbed her.

"Another one. What is going on?" he said.

Sidestepping the barrier, Lottie instructed Lynch to calm Petrovci down while Kirby called for backup and got uniforms on to the site to seal off the area, corral the contract workers and erect a tent over the body. She spied Boyd coming up the street from the other direction. When he reached her, they both pulled on protective gloves and moved to the opening in the road.

Flies buzzed and circled. The stench hit her first. Gasping, she swallowed a breath, composed herself and looked down.

"Dear Jesus," she said.

"Another woman," Boyd said.

Lottie thought he looked decidedly greener than he had earlier.

"So it is," she said softly.

Hunkering down, she peered at the blistered, decomposing flesh swarming with maggots.

"Dead a few days."

"Our missing girl?" Boyd asked. "Maeve Phillips."

"I hope not," Lottie whispered. But there was no way she could be sure.

Sweeping back a handful of clay, she noticed that the face appeared to be in worse condition than that of the first victim. Black hair, eyes closed, with bulging, crawling lids. Teeth bared through stretched-back lips. Died screaming? Was this Maeve Phillips? No glittering stud pierced the nose. She didn't know what she'd hoped for.

Further down, the soil was heavier. Boyd helped brush it away from the clothing, though Lottie knew they should wait for the SOCOs.

"Looks like a bullet exit wound there, dead center," she said.

"SOCOs are on their way." Kirby loomed at her shoulder. "Is it the Phillips girl?"

Lottie inspected the girl's hands without touching her. "I don't think so. Look at the nails."

"Very short," Boyd said. "Bitten to the bone."

"A girl who has twenty-seven bottles of nail varnish doesn't bite her nails," she said.

"If she'd been in a stressful situation for a few days, then maybe her nails were the least of her troubles."

"I grant you that," Lottie said.

Uniformed officers were working quickly around them, erecting the tent.

"How did she get in the ground?" Boyd pointed to the body, now partially uncovered.

"She hardly put herself there."

"I know, but—"

"Boyd. Enough."

Lottie stood up and turned. Andri Petrovci was staring at her, his hand shading his eyes from the sunlight. A second body unearthed by him. Sheer bad luck, or something else? She intended to find out.

"Bring him to the station for a statement," she told Lynch.

"Someone has to have seen something this time," Boyd said.

Looking around, Lottie noted that one side of the street was lined with the rear entrances to Main Street shops. To the right was Weir's yard. Further down, a gate to a small block of apartments.

"Door-to-door again," she ordered. "And check if there's any—"

"CCTV," Kirby interrupted. "Yes, boss."

Boyd rubbed a hand around his chin. "This is bad. Very bad."

"You epitomize the understatement, Boyd. Every time."

"Just saying."

"This is worse than bad. It's horrendous."

"I know, and—"

"Why don't you make yourself useful? It might get rid of your hangover. Close down the whole area. Cordon it off. No entry or exit. And interview every last person you can find."

"But—"

"No ifs, buts or ands," Lottie said, wheeling round on her heel to face him. "We found a bullet hole and blood in Weir's yard over there, a body buried under the street here, and we're nowhere near finding out the identity of the first victim, let alone a suspect. So I don't want to listen to any shite."

She marched off without waiting to hear his protestations.

* * *

"Detective Inspector Parker! A statement?"

Lottie glared at the crime correspondent for national television, Cathal Moroney, who was standing on the station steps. He lunged forward, his cameraman pointing a lens into her face.

"How did you find out?" She moved right up to him and quickly recoiled at the reek of sweat. "I've only just heard about it myself," she added.

A look of confusion scrolled down Moroney's face and she immediately realized her error. Shit and double shit.

"Heard what, Inspector?" He flashed his famous megawatt smile.

"What were *you* talking about?" Trying to divert the inevitable.

"You tell me, then I'll tell you."

Lottie shoved by him and stomped up the steps. Moroney tugged at her elbow, pulling her backward

"Shit-head," she said. "Switch off the camera."

Moroney hesitated for a moment, then gave a nod. With the camera off, he stood, arms folded, waiting.

"What do you want me to give a statement about?" Lottie forced calmness into each syllable.

"The photos released this morning. One of a dead girl and one of a missing girl."

Now that she knew where he was coming from, she wondered how she could steer him onto a different route, make him forget her outburst.

"I'm sure Superintendent Corrigan has issued a full press release."

"Isn't Maeve Phillips the daughter of the criminal-in-exile Frank Phillips? Is her disappearance linked to organized crime?"

"This is not the inner city."

"But Phillips's family lives round here. Has his daughter's disappearance anything to do with the murder victim found on Monday?"

Lottie tried to edge by him. He wasn't budging.

"Ragmullin will get a bad reputation now, won't it?" he persisted.

"If you broadcast any shite about this town, Moroney, I'll personally break every one of your show-biz white teeth." She nudged his shoulder and hurried up the steps.

Moroney followed her. "Lottie, what were you talking about a few minutes ago? You were asking something about how I found out so fast."

Turning, she jabbed a finger into his chest. "Don't you ever call me Lottie. I'm Detective Inspector Parker to you. And you can follow that inquisitive nose of yours around until you find out for yourself."

She stormed into the station and tried to bang the door. It glided shut. She hadn't even that satisfaction.

* * *

Sitting at her desk, Lottie ran her hands through her hair. Things were getting out of control. Where to start? Maybe a good place would be with Andri Petrovci.

Her phone vibrated and she saw Chloe's name flashing. She answered the call.

"Maeve's photo is all over Facebook. Everyone at school is talking about her."

"Anyone know where she might be?"

"The girls are saying nasty things. But don't believe what you hear. Maeve isn't like that. She's having a hard time at home."

"What kind of things are they saying?"

"That she's a slut and stuff."

"So no one said anything helpful?"

"No. I checked through her Facebook friends list and I can't see anyone who might be this boyfriend."

"We're working on that. How's Katie doing this morning?"

"Like a briar as usual."

Lottie smiled. "I'll see you later. Do plenty of study when you get home. Not long until your exams. June is only round the corner."

"Jesus, do you have to do that?"

"What?"

"Constantly remind me. I don't need added pressure from you."

Lottie looked at the phone as Chloe cut her off. Now look what she'd done. But for the moment, she had enough on her plate without worrying about Chloe's sulks. Another murder on top of the first one, and not a single suspect. Plus a girl who had apparently disappeared into the ether.

Glancing at Maeve Phillips's photo, she didn't think the girl was the most recent body buried in the road. So where the hell was she? Who was this second dead girl? Who was the first one? And why had they both been the targets of a murderer?

Her desk phone chirped. The desk sergeant.

"Andri Petrovci is in Interview Room One."

CHAPTER 37

With Boyd, Lynch and Kirby still at the scene, Lottie commandeered Officer Gillian O'Donoghue, one of the brighter uniformed officers, to sit in with her. Once the recording disk was in place and the formalities were over, Andri Petrovci was first to speak.

"So much of this in my home country. I not want to see it here. Understand?"

"Yes, but it's odd that it's you who has found two bodies. Do you find that strange?"

"Not my fault. I work here. This what I do. I dig. I fill. I work." He shrugged his wide shoulders halfheartedly, and Lottie couldn't help thinking that for all his size, he seemed childlike. "Who are these women, Inspector?"

"Do you have any idea, Mr. Petrovci?"

"Sorry. I not know. You police. You know?"

Lottie's phone vibrated. Chloe again. She ignored it. Then she remembered she had the photo of Maeve on her phone. She opened it up and slid the phone across the table to Petrovci. All the time keeping her eyes locked on his face.

He gulped. Stood up, visibly shaking. "Please. I go. Now."

"Sit down." At last she'd got a reaction out of him. "Do you know her?"

"No. You no understand. I go."

"Come *on*." Lottie felt she was on to something here. "How do you know her? Where did you meet her?"

"No. Is she one of them? In the ground?"

"You recognized her. Tell me."

His shoulders sagged. Locking his fingers together, he bowed his head. Silence. She heard the slight movement of his hi-vis vest with the rise and fall of his breaths.

"Who is she?" His voice so low she could barely hear him. "In photo. You know?"

"I know who she is," Lottie said. "What do *you* know about her?"

He shook his head as if the movement could dispel some demon from his brain. He did not speak.

"Andri, you can tell me. Where is she?"

He looked up. Lottie tried to see into the depths of his eyes, to read what was written there. All she saw, penetrating the surface, was pain. What had happened to Andri Petrovci? And what had he done to Maeve? A slow anger began to boil in the pit of her stomach, knocking her sympathy out cold.

"I know nothing." He unclenched his hands and folded his arms.

Lottie took a breath and set her mouth in a fake smile. "You mentioned you saw a lot of death in your own country. Tell me about it." Changing the subject away from Maeve in an attempt to wrong-foot him. No such luck.

"Inspector, I work on water main. I dig road. I find bodies I not put there. I not kill them. Please, I go now?"

"First tell me what you know," Lottie insisted.

"I know nothing."

"Yes you do. Is Maeve in danger? What did you do to her?" Shit, she'd let the girl's name slip. No harm really, she thought. It was already in the media.

He folded his arms. "You not let me go. Get me lawyer," he said, and closed his mouth into a thin line.

Lottie sighed heavily. All she had were suspicions. No proof that he'd done anything. They were still awaiting results from his DNA sample. She could hold him in custody. Assign a solicitor. Then what? Hours of nothing.

Persisting with questions for another five minutes got her nowhere. He refused to speak. She had nothing to hold him on.

Making her decision, she said, "You can go."

Officer O'Donoghue switched off the recording equipment and sealed the disks. Petrovci unfolded his arms, stood up and walked out of the room without a word. As he left, Lottie wondered if he actually did know Maeve Phillips. He'd appeared to recognize her photo. Perhaps he had seen the social media alerts, or was he the invisible boyfriend? He had to be near thirty years old and Maeve only seventeen. How to get him to admit to it?

Leaving O'Donoghue to sign off on the technical and written reports, she rushed up to her office, grabbed her bag and raced down the stairs and out of the station.

* * *

Chloe looked at her phone in disbelief. Her mum had refused to take her call. Just when she'd decided she was going to reveal all to her. She had thought it would be easier telling her on the phone rather than face to face.

Now she decided she wasn't going to tell her anything. Nothing at all.

She would deal with it herself. She only needed to get her fixer mojo back.

CHAPTER 38

Boyd was well and truly fed up with Lottie Parker. He'd spent all afternoon deflecting flak from the businesspeople in the Columb area of town, and she hadn't the balls to appear back on site. Even Jane Dore had been wondering where she had got to. At least the body was now on its way to Tullamore and SOCOs were busy with the site.

"How's the door-to-door going?" he asked Kirby when he caught up with him outside the gated apartments.

Kirby wiped sweat from his forehead. "Not too many people at home. I'll have to hang around with uniforms until later on. And this gout is killing me." He pointed to his feet. "What're you up to?"

"Just finished here. Need to see if I can find my wallet."

Without waiting to hear what other tales of woe Kirby had to tell, Boyd headed up the street. Crossing the footbridge spanning the railway, he ran across the road and over the new canal bridge leading to Ragmullin's landscape deformity. Hill Point Flats. Apartments if you wanted to be fancy about it, he thought.

The buildings looked blander in daylight. Not that Boyd could remember much from the night before. Red bricks streaked white with mildew; super-sized satellite dishes protruding from windows along the five floors; urine-stained stone steps leading up to the door. As if to reassure himself that he wasn't entirely mad, he tapped his pockets once more. Definitely no wallet.

Ringing the doorbell, he looked around anxiously, hoping

no one would see him. But parents were picking up children from a day care and bedraggled shoppers struggling with grocery bags across a paved area. Did they not know what was going on under their very noses? He ducked his chin to his chest and pressed the bell again.

A stream of foreign words preceded the opening of the door. Looking at the woman, Boyd wondered, had he met her last night? He wasn't even sure it was the right place. Apartment five, block two, Kirby had said.

"Excuse me." He flashed his sincerest smile. "I think I lost my wallet here last night. I was wondering if you or any of the girls found it."

"Hmph!"

Arms folded across saggy breasts beneath a black T-shirt. Jeans, too tight, in tan leather boots. She looked anywhere from fifty to a hundred. Framed with long black hair, her face sagged in mounds of white flesh. Boyd physically shook himself. What had he been thinking of letting Kirby bring him here? Not thinking at all, that was what. God damn you, Kirby, he silently swore.

The woman looked him up and down. "With the fat man? Yeah?" A low, gravelly voice. Hundred a day, probably.

"Yes," Boyd replied. "Sometime after midnight. I think. My wallet?"

She laughed then, breasts wobbling under the knitted ribs of her T-shirt, cheeks flopping up and down.

"No wallet. I sorry," she said when the guttural chuckles ceased.

"Can you look again? Please?"

"Not here."

Boyd glanced over his shoulder to make sure no one was watching before he grabbed her wrist and pulled her close. "I'm with the police and I'm asking you to look for my wallet."

"Police? Hah! No frighten me. I show your boss, yes?" She pointed to the small camera nestled in a cobwebbed nook above the door.

If it even works, Boyd thought, but he released her, shook his head and walked back down the steps. It was useless. Now he'd have to declare his ID card lost and apply for a new one. He only hoped it wouldn't end up in the wrong hands. That scenario didn't bear thinking about.

At the bottom step, he turned. "I will have to tell my superiors about this."

The woman paused before beckoning him with a curled finger. The door creaked inward. He hurried back up.

Inside, she slammed the door behind him. The vivid flowers on the wallpaper shouted out at him. Jesus, he thought, what the hell brought me to this place? The woman sidled past him in the narrow hallway. He flinched from the touch of her skin. She opened a door and ushered him into a small room. Worn couch and a small coffee table scattered with magazines normally stored on the newsagent's top shelf.

"Wait." She pulled the door closed behind her.

He had no other choice.

* * *

"Bitch, where is his wallet?"

Mimoza shrugged her shoulders and stared at the woman who called herself Anya. Shrinking into the pillow, she scrunched her knees to her chin and wrapped her arms about her legs. She had to act innocent with this woman or she might never get to see her son again. She couldn't let Anya know she had found the wallet or she might check inside it. Better if she just found it herself.

"Tall, skinny man. Here last night. Policeman. Lost his wallet. I ask other girls. They not see him. You see him?"

Mimoza shook her head.

Anya grabbed her by the arm. "My girls, they see nothing. You. You with big eyes. I know you see something."

She released Mimoza's arm, flicked down the sheet and pulled the pillow out from behind her before slapping her across the back of the head. Mimoza squeezed her eyes shut as Anya dragged her by her hair to the floor. The woman flipped the mattress. Finding nothing, she stooped down and peered beneath the bed.

"Ha!" she squealed.

Holding her breath, Mimoza watched Anya open the wallet. Silently she prayed that the hidden note would not be discovered. She watched as Anya removed a fifty-euro note and folded it between her breasts. Seemingly satisfied, she closed the wallet and left the room.

Mimoza began to pray. She prayed that the tall, skinny policeman would help her.

* * *

"Today lucky for you."

The woman waved the black wallet in front of Boyd's face. For a moment he thought she might snatch it away as he reached for it. But she relinquished her prize easily. He checked to make sure his ID was still in its flap before shoving the wallet into his pocket, vowing never again, no matter how drunk, to venture through the doors of a brothel.

Outside, he chanced a glance up at the windows. The curtains were drawn. It might as well be a deserted building for all the life it exuded. He remembered the wretched young girl with her pleading eyes and a sadness settled into his heart where moments earlier he had felt anger. As he walked in the cool evening breeze toward the footbridge, he wondered what her story was. He knew he had enough to be doing without worrying about her, but he considered it might be wise to contact some of the lads working in the vice squad. Yes, that was what he would do.

* * *

At first Lottie couldn't see Petrovci anywhere.

Fearing she had lost him, she decided to turn left toward the canal and caught sight of his yellow singlet immediately. She broke into a run. By the time she reached the brow of the hill, he was almost at the town's main bridge, having made his way through the cherry blossoms along the canal pathway. She knew he lived in Hill Point and that seemed to be where he was headed.

Glad of the rising breeze, she hurried on, gaining on the tall foreigner with each step. He never looked behind him, so she was sure he hadn't noticed her. Waiting for a moment under the old stone bridge to allow him to cross the footbridge up ahead, she was sure he was heading for his flat. She couldn't remember the exact block or apartment number so she speed-dialed Lynch. Then, with the phone clamped to her ear, she walked on as nonchalantly as she could, keeping Petrovci in sight.

Lynch read out the full address as Lottie walked. When she put the phone away, Petrovci was nowhere in sight. Her breath caught in her throat. Where had he got to?

That was when she saw Boyd.

He was walking around a corner, across a cobbled square, meters away. Without knowing why she was doing it, Lottie ducked behind a set of concrete steps. Boyd was hurrying away from the general area where Andri Petrovci lived.

She should have stepped out and confronted him. Asked what he was doing. Should have just said, "Hello, fancy meeting you here." But she didn't. She remained hidden as he passed by with his head bowed, seemingly deep in his own thoughts.

Straightening up, Lottie froze. Was there someone behind her? She felt a whisper of air on her neck. She held her breath, closed her eyes. Shivers engulfed her body and her hands trembled violently. A dribble of perspiration rolled down her nose. She sniffed it away. It felt like minutes but it was only a couple of seconds before she turned. No one.

She looked all around. No one near. No one running away. Her imagination? In those few seconds, all motivation for following Petrovci evaporated.

Coming out from her hiding place, she advanced up the steps to get a better view. She noticed how close Hill Point was to Weir's car dismantler's yard. Scanning the height of the stacked junk cars, she thought how it would be an ideal hiding place for a body. Now that the whole area was cordoned off and out of bounds to the public, she decided there would be no harm in getting each and every bit of scrap metal searched again. Thoroughly this time.

Assuming Petrovci was now ensconced in his flat, Lottie knew she had no authority to knock on his door, to search his home, but she would keep him firmly fixed on her radar.

She headed back to the station wondering about Boyd. Had he been one step ahead of her, marking Petrovci as a prime suspect? Or was his not-yet-ex-wife Jackie residing around here? Lottie thought it was probably the latter. She intended to ask him.

CHAPTER 39

"Got it," Boyd said, throwing his jacket over the back of his chair.

"Your wallet?" Kirby asked. "You went back up there? You're an eejit."

"Don't even talk to me." Boyd began tidying up the paperwork on his desk. "Did you get anything from the residents in the Columb Street area?"

No answer.

"Jesus, Kirby, out with it."

Kirby scratched himself. "You told me not to talk to you. Anyways, there's one flat with a wall-mounted camera, at the front gates of the block. I'm going back up there later to see if the resident is home. Might be something on it."

"If it even works. Who lives there?"

"Willie 'the Buzz' Flynn. Retired from the local newspaper. Must be eighty if he's a day."

"Buzz Flynn? What'd he be doing with CCTV?"

"He was always getting robbed. I advised him to get the little camera set up a few years back."

"Good. We could do with a break," Boyd said.

"Fancy a pint?" Kirby wheezed as he rotated his chair.

"Not that kind of break...Oh, forget it." Boyd flicked off his computer and swallowed a mouthful of water from a bottle.

"One pint."

"No. Never again. Not with you, anyway." Boyd drained the water, squashed the bottle, screwed on the lid and threw it into the recycle bin.

"Don't be an arsehole." Kirby shuffled his feet into his sandals and bent down to buckle them. "You got your wallet back; what're you complaining about?"

"That place, where we went after the pub. We should be raiding it, not servicing it. Fuck's sake. Makes me feel like a lowlife shit."

"Live and let live. That's my motto."

"It's not right."

"What're you going to do about it? Call the vice squad? The National Immigration Bureau?"

Boyd paused, thinking.

Kirby said, "They've bigger fish to fry than a little whorehouse in Ragmullin. There's one in every town in Ireland. The bureau is after the sharks, not minnows." He bent down to rub his sore foot.

Boyd stood up, banged his chair against the desk and headed for the door. Looking back over his shoulder, he concluded that Kirby was a sorry excuse for an officer. But wasn't he himself just as bad? He hadn't slept with the girl but he couldn't shut out the image of her melancholic eyes.

With one last shake of his head in Kirby's direction, he left for home. Hopefully he could get some peace and quiet there. And ditch his lingering hangover.

CHAPTER 40

There was no sign of Boyd, Kirby or Lynch in the office when Lottie arrived back at the station. She sat at her desk to write a report of her interview with Andri Petrovci. Her own thoughts and assumptions. Just in case all hell broke loose during the night and she couldn't remember it in the morning. Anything was likely to happen. Officer Gillian O'Donoghue had left a transcript on her desk. Lottie read over it again. She was convinced Petrovci knew something about Maeve Phillips.

Before going home she checked in with the staff in the incident room. A few detectives were talking on the phones. No sign of her own crew.

On the whiteboard, the photo of the latest dead girl had been pinned up. The face seemed too decomposed to be of any help in identifying her. Lottie hoped the body might give them a clue as to who she was and who was carrying out the killings, if it was the same perpetrator. Of course it was. How many psychos were out there burying bodies under the street? Only one, she hoped. Maybe Jane Dore had had time to prioritize the PM. Lottie rang her to check.

"Nothing of interest at the site," Jane said. "But the victim has a gunshot to her back, exited just below the chest. Unfortunately the heat accelerated decomposition but I can determine that she has a scar from her abdomen up over her hip and around her back. Just like the first victim."

"Oh my God. And was the bullet wound washed, like the first victim?"

"Looks like it. I'll start the PM in the morning. Eight a.m. if you'd like to attend?"

"I'll be there," Lottie said. "Why can't you do it now? I can be there in half an hour."

"No can do. Wonder of wonders, I've a dinner date at seven."

"Delighted for you," Lottie said. Shit, she'd forgotten all about Dan Russell, her own dinner date. A quick look at her watch: 7:15. Oh well. There was no time for it now. "See you in the morning, Jane. Enjoy your night out."

Calling over a couple of the detectives, Lottie instructed them to organize another search of Weir's yard in the morning.

She glanced up at the board.

A second body with a washed bullet wound and a scar. Another missing kidney?

"Dear God, I hope not," she whispered to herself but she knew it was more than probable.

As she left, she wondered if she should ring Russell to apologize but then thought that leaving him hanging might be better for him.

* * *

As she walked toward the greyhound stadium, Lottie saw Dan Russell sitting in his big black Audi. On double yellow lines, engine running. It was a race evening and traffic was building.

She crossed the road. He lowered the window. Hunkering down beside the door, she said, "Got delayed at work."

"Half an hour late. You could have given me a call."

"I should give you a parking ticket."

"How about dinner tomorrow?"

"Honestly, you know what, I'm actually too busy at the moment. We've found another body, so let me ring you when things die down." She stood up to go.

"Another body?" he repeated. "That's awful. I'll drop you to your door."

Oh what the hell, Lottie thought, and went around to the other side of the car. The coolness of the interior was welcome. Rich bastard.

He said, "Where's your house?"

She pointed to the estate across the road. He swung the car in a U-turn and she directed him where to stop.

"So this body you found, is it a murder?"

"I'm not at liberty to say."

He stared straight ahead. "Are you going to question me about this also?"

Not wanting to give him any information, she decided to change the subject.

"You mentioned you remembered Adam. Did you work with him?"

Russell idled the engine. "I did, actually. Overseas."

Silence filled the car. Since Adam's death Lottie had alienated herself from Adam's military friends, though somehow she doubted Dan Russell had been a friend.

"Tell me more," she said.

"How about you give me a shout tomorrow," he said.

"Why are you stalling?"

"There are things you should know about your late dear husband. Things you might not want anyone else knowing. But I'm not going to speak about it now."

She got out of the car. "You can forget about dinner. I'd rather starve." She slammed the door.

He rolled down the window electronically. "I honestly think it would be a mistake not to listen to what I have to say."

Leaning against her front wall, she watched as he put the car in gear and drove off. No screech of brakes or dust cloud rising in his wake. His slow departure made his words feel all the more threatening. Dan Russell was playing her, playing some sick game, and she didn't want to be part of it.

But she knew she would eventually listen to what he had to say, no matter how compromising it might turn out to be.

* * *

The takeaway pizza had been a hit with the kids. At last Lottie had witnessed smiles on all three faces. For a few minutes. It was after nine by the time she'd tidied the kitchen and folded away the washing her mother had hung on the clothesline during the day.

"I'm going to sit in the garden to check over my emails for a bit. Shout if you need me." She stood in the hallway and listened. Murmurs of assent greeted her.

With a cup of tea and a chocolate biscuit, she sat at the patio table, iPad on her knee and the moon visible in the still bright sky. She had tried to keep busy so she wouldn't think about Russell and his words. She thought instead of a second murdered girl who might be missing a kidney. She knew that until the pathologist confirmed it or otherwise, there was no point in speculating.

The sound of a loudspeaker from the stadium permeated the air along with the hum of a lawnmower droning in tune to the whistling birds, nesting for the night. Glancing around her garden, she wished she had green fingers. It could do with flowers, color, a total makeover. Adam used to tend it. She hadn't time. Sean? He was too engrossed in his PlayStation to be bothered. Sometimes he cut the grass but only if she bribed him.

Sipping her tea, she flicked through her iPad. Couldn't concentrate. Adam. She would love to know more about his time in Kosovo. He'd traveled there in 1999, just as the war had finished, with an advance international unit under

NATO command, and he'd returned there again a year later. Two trips and he'd spoken little of his time away. Or maybe he had and she hadn't been listening. Back then, she realized, she'd been too consumed with work and two small children to be interested in Adam's tales. Chloe had been less than a year old the first time he'd traveled. They'd debated it at the time, but they'd needed the money. And Adam was military to the core, so she wasn't going to be the person to put a halt to his overseas tours of duty.

"Mam!"

Chloe stood at the back door, her face white, mouth open.

"What is it?" Lottie jumped up, ran to her. "Are you okay?"

A little boy poked his head from behind Chloe's knees.

Lottie pulled up short, eyes wide, her breath catching in her throat.

Chloe said, "He was at the front door. All alone. Crying."

Kneeling down, Lottie held her hand out to the boy. "Milot?"

He retreated back behind her daughter's leg.

"Milot, honey. What are you doing here? Where's your mother?"

The boy stuck his thumb into his mouth. No tatty rabbit. How did he get here? Where had he come from? A multitude of questions swamped her brain. She looked up at Chloe.

"Did you see anyone else? How did he reach the doorbell?"

"He knocked."

"There had to be someone with him. Did you look?"

"I saw no one when I opened the door, just the little fellow."

"You sure?"

With a shrug of her shoulders, Chloe lifted Milot into her arms and strolled inside. Grabbing her phone, Lottie followed.

"Who do you call about this?" Chloe asked. "At this hour?"

Lottie poured milk into a mug and offered it to Milot. He

turned his face to Chloe's shoulder, refusing the drink. He was wearing only a scruffy white T-shirt and navy shorts, his feet stuffed into soft white shoes with no socks. It was a balmy night but not warm enough for a child to be wandering the streets half-clad.

Who should she call? The clock showed 9:15 p.m. The Child and Family Agency would need to be contacted. But there was distrust between the agency and the police from a previous incident. She couldn't thrust Milot into the hands of strangers. Anyway, his mother could be in danger. Lying hurt somewhere? Dead? Surely Mimoza hadn't abandoned her son?

Quickly Lottie checked the child. No obvious bruising or cuts. No sign of trauma, except for his tears. She held his little hand. Skin so soft, but no soft toy.

"Talk to me, Milot. Where is your mum?"

He stared at her, tears trekking down his cheeks, then stuck his thumb into his rosebud mouth again. He wasn't going to tell her anything. Did he even understand her? Could he speak English at all? She didn't know. Shit.

Pink petals were stuck to his hair and she gently picked them out. Cherry blossom. Had he walked? His little white shoes were dusty. She examined them. Tiny stones clogged the rubber soles. He'd walked, she deduced. Escaping from something or someone? She wished he would talk. Her heart broke for the child.

Katie appeared, pale-faced, at the kitchen door. "What's going on?"

Lottie explained, and the girl took Milot into her arms. "Is he staying the night?"

Katie's demeanor had brightened, and without further thought Lottie made her decision. "Yes, he's staying." There was no way she could turn the boy over to social services, not tonight. She'd be in trouble for this.

"He can sleep in my room," Katie said, cuddling the little boy. Chloe scowled.

"I'll get a duvet for him and we'll sort this out in the morning. Is that all right with you?" Lottie said.

Katie nodded. "Come on, little man. Wait till I show you my room. Oh Mam, he's shivering. The poor little thing."

Lottie touched his arm. So he was.

Bundling the boy into her arms, Katie caressed his back, his head nestling into her shoulder.

"I'll follow you up in a minute," Lottie said.

She had to think this through.

She needed to talk to Boyd.

* * *

Chloe shut her bedroom door and stretched full-length on her bed, mad at the way Katie had shoved her aside and taken the little boy.

She thought of Maeve and wondered what else she could do to find her. She had messaged everyone who knew her. No one had seen or heard from Maeve. No new posts on Twitter, and her Facebook page looked sad without updates.

There was one person who might know, but she was hesitant to make contact with him. Too risky? Yes, it was. Then again, Maeve could be in trouble. She really should talk to her mother first, but she didn't even answer her phone call earlier in the day.

Sitting up, she tapped her phone. Before she could change her mind, she took a photograph of her toes and sent him a Snapchat message.

He replied immediately: *Meet me. Town park. Ten minutes.*

CHAPTER 41

The call went straight to voicemail.

"Boyd, will you for feck's sake answer your phone." Lottie hung up.

She had folded a duvet around Milot on Katie's bed. The girl lay beside him, stroking his hair. Eventually he closed his eyes. Hoping she was doing the right thing by keeping him at her house, knowing she had the child's interests at heart, Lottie crept back down the stairs. Sean had returned to his computer game and she assumed Chloe was studying with headphones on. No sound from her room.

By half past ten, unable to stand it any longer, she grabbed her keys and headed for Boyd's apartment. Hopefully Jackie wouldn't be there. "So what?" she told herself. "I'm a big girl. I can handle it."

* * *

"I shouldn't have come." Chloe flopped onto the park bench in the furthest corner, behind the children's playground. She'd sneaked out of the house while her mother had been on the phone in the kitchen.

"It's all right," he said and took two cans of Diet Coke from his jacket pockets.

Sitting up straight, Chloe flicked open her can and smiled nervously. "So do you know where Maeve is?"

He inched closer beside her. She scrunched up along the bench.

"I won't bite," he said.

"I'm not so sure this is a good idea," she said.

"Why not?"

"My mother ..."

"Forget your mother."

Chloe shrugged. "I'm worried about Maeve. I thought she might have told you if she was going away or something."

"Or something? Like what?"

"I know she fancies the arse off you."

"Really? I don't think that."

"Maybe I should go," she said, flicking the tab on the can up and down, breaking her nail.

"I want to talk to you," he said, moving right up beside her.

Chloe felt her heart beat a little faster as their knees touched and he lifted her hand. He began stroking her fingers, one by one, endless, even touches.

"As long as you're not going to confess to being an ax murderer or anything." She pulled her hand free, now conscious of the seclusion around them. Not even a bird sang in the branches overhead.

"Be serious," he snapped.

She thought she caught the hint of a shadow drooping over his eyes, but when he raised his head, he smiled again.

She said, "I am serious. I'm all ears."

"Ears? My sweet girl, you are so much more than ears."

Chloe got up and walked around the tree beside the bench, sipping her Coke.

"Can't you stay still for a moment?" he said.

She stopped her pacing.

He stood up. "My one request is that you never, ever tell anyone about me," he said, his voice sharp.

"What do you mean?"

"About me knowing Maeve." He walked over and stood in front of her.

"Okay." Chloe gulped loudly. He was freaking her out now.

"Good," he said, and his shoulders relaxed.

"Where *is* Maeve?" she asked, feeling the bark of the tree cutting through her thin cotton T-shirt.

He shrugged. "She didn't tell me. And you must not tell anyone about us either."

"I don't know anything to tell. You asked me here. I thought you'd know where she is." Chloe didn't like where this was going. She should leave. She ducked under his arm.

Too late. She felt him grab her hair and pull her back against the tree. His fingers tipped up her chin and his lips locked firmly onto hers, stemming further words from her mouth. Tears gathered at the corners of her eyes before exploding down her cheeks as he thrust his tongue into her mouth and sucked until she couldn't breathe.

Bringing her knee up, she hit him between the legs with every ounce of energy she could muster. He drew back with a yell.

"Bitch!"

"Let me go!" she screamed, twisting away furiously from his grasp. "My mother knows I'm here."

"Fuck your mother!"

Tears flowing freely, Chloe began to run.

He shouted after her. "I will know if you tell anyone. You witch."

She kept running until she reached home. Her mother's car wasn't in the drive. Thanking God for small mercies, she flew up the stairs and into her room.

She got out her blade. Without searching for a perfect site, she hurriedly stuck the sharp edge into her arm and dragged it toward her elbow. Blood oozed. Sinking to her knees, she tore off her top and bra and turned the blade to her breast. She lifted up the mound of flesh and drew the sharpness over her ribs. Gritting her teeth, she kept her scream in her throat.

She climbed into bed shivering and pulled the duvet over her head. She didn't care that there was blood everywhere. She needed to feel the intensity of the pain. She deserved it. Every sharp dart. She had gone willingly to him but he'd told her nothing about Maeve. Had he done something to her?

That look in his eyes. That had made her more frightened than anything else.

Even more frightened than having to hide the bloodstained sheets from her mother.

* * *

Peering through the patterned pane of glass on the upper half of the door, Lottie waited for Boyd. She heard the hum of his turbo bike slowing down.

He opened the door. "Hey, Mrs. Parker. Nice surprise. Come in."

"I want to talk to you. Something's happened."

Boyd headed for the kitchenette. "Fire ahead."

"Sit down and listen," Lottie said, looking at him. He wore tight tracksuit bottoms and no T-shirt. She could see the muscles across his chest and the scar where he'd suffered a potentially life-threatening knife injury months earlier.

"It must be important," he said, producing small bottles of water.

Lottie longed for something stronger but took the water and unscrewed the cap.

"It is. Put something on," she said, and sat down.

Boyd laughed but went to the bedroom and returned wearing a loose white T-shirt.

"Now, what's bothering you?" He sat beside her.

"The boy, Milot, turned up on my doorstep earlier."

"Who?"

"The child who was with the girl Mimoza at my house on

Monday morning. He just appeared at my front door around nine o'clock tonight."

"Holy shit. Where is he now?" Boyd spluttered, eyes open wide. "No, please don't tell me he's still at yours."

She nodded.

"And you haven't contacted the Child and Family Agency either?"

She said nothing.

"You'd better give them a call," he insisted. "Now."

Lottie sipped her water. "Who'll be there this late? Come on, Boyd. Be practical. I'll call them in the morning."

He shrugged. "You're hoping his mother comes looking for him, aren't you?"

"She might have dumped him," Lottie said. "Oh, I don't know what to think." She put down the water. "I'd love a proper drink. Do you have any wine? Or vodka? Even a beer?" She could really do with a Xanax. She'd been weaning herself off them, denying she was taking the odd one.

Boyd ignored her request. "The boy. How old is he? Tell me more."

She sighed. "He's only three or four years old. He knocked at the door. Chloe brought him in. I reckon he walked. His shoes were grubby and there were cherry-blossom petals in his hair. Someone left him at my door, but I've no idea who or why."

"So where's his mother?"

"Wish I knew. He was crying and he hadn't his toy rabbit with him. Something's happened to Mimoza, I think, and Milot escaped—ran away."

"Don't be so melodramatic. How did he know the way to your house?"

"Like I said, someone probably brought him, or maybe he remembered the way and came alone."

"It's dark. I don't think he'd remember." He gulped his water noisily. "Has he been reported missing?"

"I rang the station. No reports. Something's not right with all this."

"I agree, and something's not right with you. Get the boy placed in care. Tonight."

"I can't. Not tonight." A yawning silence sprung up between them before she changed the subject. "I spoke briefly with Jane Dore this evening, about the second girl we found."

"And?"

"She's doing the PM in the morning, but she said the body has a similar scar to the first girl."

"Missing a kidney?"

"I'd imagine so but we won't know for sure until Jane completes her work. It's getting very scary."

"Jesus, someone is going round Ragmullin taking out organs and then shooting the victims. Unbelievable."

"I know." Lottie drained her water and stood up. "I'd better go."

Boyd wiped the damp ring on the table with his hand. She smiled.

"What's so funny?"

"You."

"Glad you feel that way because I wouldn't like to be in your shoes when Superintendent Corrigan finds out you kept a lost boy in your house overnight."

"Who's going to tell?" She went toward the door. "You know the history with that agency. I can make him see my point of view. By the way, I meant to ask you—"

The doorbell rang. Lottie glanced at the time, then at Boyd. He shrugged. She opened the door.

"Hello, Jackie," she said.

Jackie Boyd smiled coldly, took a long drag from the

cigarette in her hand before dropping it to the step and crushing it with the heel of her stiletto. Long legs, clad in leopard-
print jeggings, edged inside.

Stepping around her, Lottie headed for her car. She'd been
about to ask Boyd what he'd been doing at Hill Point that
afternoon. Maybe now she had the answer to her unasked
question.

CHAPTER 42

For the second night in a row, he'd raped her. But he hadn't broken her. No way. He'd only succeeded in strengthening her resolve to get the hell out. Somehow.

When he was done, he tied her hands behind her back and pushed her into the room. Maeve dropped to the floor, her body numbed from the rape, and banged her head against the concrete. The man had his balaclava on, but she had already seen his face. She knew what that meant. She'd read about these types of abductions online, never in a million years thinking she could be one of the statistics.

"Bastard," she cried. "Let me go."

"Feisty tonight, missy," he sneered as he dressed himself. "Not so brave when I put this down your neck." He cupped his penis beneath his jeans. "Not so brave when you saw my slaughter room."

"If you were going to kill me, why haven't you done it yet? You prick." She stared at his eyes gleaming through the knitted slits. "Untie my hands, I need to pee."

"Use the bucket."

"Fuck you and your bucket." She spat at him, kicking out.

He pulled a knife from the back of his jeans and flicked it beneath her chin.

"What do you want with me?" she whimpered, her bravado dissipating.

"Soon. You will find out soon. Your time is almost up."

He turned and left, slamming the door behind him.

Lying on the ground, resting her head on the rough concrete,

Maeve vowed she would get out alive. Surely by now her mother had raised the alarm. Unless she was drowning in one of her drunken stupors.

But Maeve knew in her heart that Tracy Phillips really only thought of herself.

* * *

A fist smashed into her face. Mimoza screamed.

The woman, Anya, was standing over her. Another smack. Bone crunching. Blood flowing. Wrenched out of her bed, she fell to the floor.

"Bitch. Get up. You leave. Now."

Dragging herself to her knees, Mimoza crawled to the open door. A kick to her buttocks sent her crashing into the small corridor. A polished black boot nudged at her nose. Pulled to her feet, she squinted through her unbruised eye into the face of the man with the crooked teeth.

She found herself being twisted around and a blanket thrown over her head. Hauled up onto his shoulder, she was carried down the stairs, out the front door and down steps. A car engine revved. Flung into the back seat, she fell to the floor when it screeched in a turn and sped off.

The policeman must have found the note and begun asking questions, she thought wildly. And that had scared her captors.

A cold reality dawned on her. Now that they were moving her, the policeman wouldn't find her.

And she would never see her son again.

* * *

Lottie knocked on Chloe's door. She thought she'd heard her crying when she returned from Boyd's.

"Go away. I'm trying to sleep."

Lottie put her head around the door. "You sure you're okay?"

"I'm fine."

"Okay, goodnight, pet."

"Goodnight."

Lottie closed the door and peeked into Katie's room. The little boy was curled up with her daughter's arm resting lightly over him. Tomorrow she would have to sort him out with the social services agency. She prayed Corrigan wouldn't find out that she'd kept him here overnight.

"Turn off that game," she said to Sean's closed door.

"Five more minutes."

"It's a school night."

No reply.

In her own room she undressed without switching on the light. Pulling on a long T-shirt, she lay on the bed and closed her eyes. Sometimes all she could do was pray to a God she didn't believe in to spare her family from the horrors she had to witness in her job. Two girls without names and an unborn baby were lying tonight in Jane Dore's Dead House. Maeve Phillips was still missing. A frightened young boy was sleeping across the landing. She had no idea where his mother was.

And Jackie was back in town, stalking Boyd.

* * *

Kosovo 1999

It wasn't very clean inside. Not for a clinic. But there had been a war. That must be the reason, the boy thought.

He followed the captain though a swing door into a narrow corridor. At the end, an open door.

"Ah, thank you." A man in a white coat rose from behind the desk and shook the captain's hand vigorously. "You never let me down."

"*Take a blood sample, Doctor. See if he's any good to you. The lads at the chicken farm have seen him. He can't disappear. Not yet, anyway.*"

The boy watched as the doctor took a syringe from a steel tray and pinched his arm. When a vein rose, he jabbed in the needle. The boy scrunched his eyes until the implement was extracted. When he looked, it was full with his blood. A plaster was applied and his elbow bent upward.

"What now?" the captain asked.

"A few days. Come back with him then."

The two men shook hands and the boy felt a nudge in his back as he was shoved out of the door.

In the corridor he came face to face with another boy not much older than himself, leaning with one foot up against the wall, arms folded. One eye slanted into a wink as he unfolded his arms and drew a hand across his neck in a slicing motion.

"Don't mind him," the captain said.

But he did mind him.

He didn't want to ever see that boy again.

DAY FIVE

Friday, May 15, 2015

CHAPTER 43

He had tied her to the bed. The rope cut through her thin wrists and blood oozed on to the sheets. Mimoza could move her legs, nothing else. He was by the window, naked, clutching a smoldering cigarette. Gray rain sleeted against the glass and he seemed to be looking beyond it into the black-clouded sky.

Gulping down her fear, she asked, "What you do to Milot?"

Crooked Teeth Man had asked her over and over again about her son. All night long. Where was he? Where would he go? What had she told him to do? Relentless. But Mimoza was immune to the physical pain he inflicted. It was the ache in her heart that threatened to break her. Milot was gone. And they didn't know where he was. She wished she could ask Sara, but wouldn't they have already broken her little friend? Maybe Sara had escaped with him. She hoped so. She clung to that hope. Tears flowed down her face. She couldn't wipe them away.

The man turned, went to stub out his cigarette in the ashtray, seemed to think better of it. Mimoza held her breath as he brought the glowing butt to her face. Squeezing her eyes shut so she wouldn't see, she screamed as he thrust the cigarette into the soft flesh of her cheek.

"Where is your boy?" he snarled through gritted teeth.

She passed out with the sound of thunder outside and the echo of pain shooting through her ears.

CHAPTER 44

Thunderous rain woke Lottie at 6:30 a.m. Triple flashes of lightning, followed by a monster thunder clash, transformed her bedroom into a kaleidoscope of brilliance. A child cried. Somewhere in her house. What?

"Dear God!" She jumped out of bed in a tangle of pillows and duvet as she remembered. Milot.

Her door opened and Katie rushed in, the little boy screaming in her arms.

"Mam, what will I do with him? He's terrified." Her daughter's face was chalky white.

"Make him breakfast," Lottie said. "I'll be down in a few minutes."

She dragged herself into the shower, washed quickly and dried herself while trying to find something to wear. Everything was everywhere.

By seven o'clock, Milot was calm enough to eat a bowl of cornflakes. The storm seemed to have passed over, though the rain was incessant. Lottie glanced at the clock. Tullamore for the postmortem at eight. Would she make it?

The front door opened and Rose Fitzpatrick marched in, rainwater dripping from a clear plastic coat. She deposited a carton of milk and a loaf of bread, its wrapper wilting, on the table. Katie escaped out the door and up the stairs.

"And who is this?" Rose nodded toward the boy.

Shit, thought Lottie, how was she going to explain Milot to her mother?

"It's a long story. Work-related."

"What have you done this time?" Rose said, arms folded.

"Nothing. I'm dealing with it."

"Like you always do." Rose's voice cut through the air.

Lottie ruffled the little boy's hair and picked him up as Rose put the milk in the fridge. Shifting him onto her hip, ready to bring him upstairs to Katie, she said, "I'm running late. I appreciate you coming over. I really couldn't manage without your help. But there was no need to be here so early." She eased toward the door. "By the way, did Mrs. Murtagh have anything to say about the Phillips family? Maeve's parents?"

"Just that Frank stocked up his ill-gotten gains in Spain and headed there when Maeve was a child," Rose said. "Left Tracy to struggle raising the girl. Here, give him to me. Poor little mite. I'll look after him until you sort out a placement for him."

"If you're sure?" Lottie handed Milot over and was astounded when the boy sat placidly on her mother's knee. "Thank you."

"I'll do a spot of hoovering later," Rose said, stroking Milot's hair. "When did you last clean this house?"

Lottie didn't answer. Truth was, it was so long ago, she didn't even know where she'd put the hoover.

* * *

In the car, Lottie rang the station and rescheduled their team meeting to 10 a.m. Driving through the spray rising from the motorway, she wondered how she could juggle her day to fit in everything she had to do.

The windscreen wipers struggled to keep up with the deluge. As she left the motorway, her phone rang. Chloe.

"I can't go to school today."

A clap of thunder seemed to crash against the car.

"Why not? Feeling sick?"

"I think I've a temperature."

"Stay in bed." Too stretched to argue, Lottie added, "Granny's there if you need anything."

"I know. She's flying round the house hoovering like a witch with a broom."

So she'd found it. Lottie laughed. "Thanks for that image."

"By the way," Chloe said, "don't forget Sean has to see his therapist today."

As she pulled into the Dead House car park, Lottie thought how life didn't seem to get any easier.

The wind picked up as she ran up the path to the door and warm rain pelted into her face. Of course she had no coat.

* * *

The myriad of antiseptic and antibacterial washes and sprays could not mask the mortuary smell. Though the tiled and stainless-steel room was sterile, the overriding odor was pungent ammonia.

"Still no idea who the first victim is?" Jane asked. "The pregnant girl?"

"No." Lottie tightened the loops of a surgical mask around her ears before pulling a gown on over her damp clothes. "It's so frustrating. If we could identify her, we'd have a starting place. As it is, without knowing anything about her, we've nothing to go on and no suspect to target."

"I think you might have the same problem with this one. I'll keep the technical and medical lingo for my reports. She'd been dead maybe four days; because the weather has been so hot, it's difficult to be exact. I'll examine the blowflies and larvae. I'd estimate she is aged between eighteen and twenty-five and at first glance I can't see any tattoos or identifying marks. Apart from the scar I told you about. She is very undernourished also."

Standing well back, Lottie allowed Jane and her team to

get to work. She concentrated on the pathologist detailing the victim's outer clothing into a recording device. Blue cotton blouse, pleated short black jersey skirt, no tights or shoes.

"All clothing intact," Jane said, examining the blouse for a bullet hole.

The victim had no bra but was wearing cheap white cotton knickers.

"Inside out," Jane added. One of her assistants bagged and labeled the clothes.

"Bastard undressed her, shot her, then re-dressed her," Lottie said, banging one gloved hand into the other. "You'll confirm if he washed the wound? And if there's evidence of sexual assault?"

Jane nodded.

"Anything yet on the analysis of the moss from the first victim?"

"As soon as I have anything I'll send it on. And before you ask, I will be checking this victim for it too."

She turned the body on its side.

"Bullet's gone right through her. Entry through the back and exit through the stomach. Certainly looks as if it has been cleaned. If you find the crime scene you might find the bullet," Jane said, continuing to examine the blistered skin.

If that burst, Lottie thought, they would be swamped in putrid odors. She noticed she'd been holding her breath.

"Is it possible she was shot at Weir's yard?" she asked from behind her mask. But they'd found no bullet there, she reminded herself, though the body was unearthed close by.

"The blood taken from the yard will be checked against this girl's DNA and you'll be informed of results."

"Thanks." Lottie knew the process could take weeks.

Jane pointed to a scar trailing from the girl's abdomen up over her left hip and around her back. "This is similar to the first victim. I'm sure that when I go in I'll find she's had a kidney removed."

"How long ago do you think it happened?"

"It seems more recent than the other girl's. Suturing is good, from what I can make out. Professional surgery."

"A doctor murdered her?"

"In my opinion a doctor, or someone medically trained, carried out the surgery. Doesn't mean that's who murdered her." Jane was scrutinizing the victim's legs. "She was a cutter."

"A cutter?"

"Self-harm," Jane explained. "Lacerations to her inner thighs. Despite the decomposition, I can just about make out old scars." An assistant took more photographs.

Lottie watched intently as Jane examined the entire body externally. As she lifted the victim's left breast, she hesitated and called her assistant.

"What is it?" Lottie asked, craning her neck to see.

"Looks like a deep scar on the outside of the breast. A knife wound maybe." Jane pointed to it, then checked the other breast. "Same here. Possibly self-inflicted."

"How could someone do this to themselves? God love her, she must have been going through such torment. Surely someone close to her would have known about this."

"It's easy to hide," Jane said.

"But wouldn't her family notice?"

"If she has any."

Lottie shook her head in dismay.

Jane said, "Sometimes the only way people can handle emotional pain is to cause themselves physical pain. In some cases, it can lead to suicide. But as we know, this girl was murdered."

Bile settled in Lottie's throat. She needed to escape.

"You okay?" Jane asked, raising her head, scalpel in her hand.

"Send me your report." Lottie pulled off her gown and gloves and stuffed them into the receptacle provided.

"Of course. Mind yourself," Jane said.

Lottie had to mentally slow down to prevent herself running out of the door. She wasn't afraid of visible scars; it was the invisible ones she couldn't handle.

* * *

She heard the commotion before she opened the door to the station.

"There you are!" Tracy Phillips propelled herself from the counter toward Lottie. "Where's my Maeve? Why haven't you found her? I'm worried sick. She should be back by now…"

"Mrs. Phillips. Tracy," Lottie said, clutching the woman's elbow and steering her to a bench. "Sit down for a minute."

Tracy wrenched her arm free. Hands on hips, she said, "I'm not sitting down. I want my daughter."

"We're doing all we can to find her." Lottie shook the rain from her hair, pulled her T-shirt free from her sopping jeans and wrung it out.

"Are you? Where is she, then? Have you questioned that good-for-nothing husband of mine? Out in the Costa del Sun, mixing with every class of criminal. He deserves to be locked up."

The smell of stale alcoholic breath threatened to overwhelm Lottie.

"Come with me," she said. She keyed in the code to the internal door and entered Interview Room 1. "Sit down, Tracy. Please."

"I just want you to find my Maeve." Tracy plopped her wet cloth handbag on the table and seated herself. Lottie pulled round a chair and angled it beside her.

"We've tried to make contact with your husband," she said,

"without success. However, I'm sure he has nothing to do with Maeve going missing." She would have said anything to placate the woman, but she wondered what had brought about the sudden change. Tracy Phillips was a mother, who for five days hadn't noticed her daughter was missing, and now here she was bordering on hysterical.

"I know different," Tracy said.

"What do you know?"

Tracy slumped back in the chair, hands shaking, lips trembling. "I had a visit last night."

"Your husband, Frank?" A whiff of unwashed flesh caused Lottie to shift away slightly.

"That bastard wouldn't leave his sunbed or his fancy women for anything. Not even for his daughter. No." She pulled at her loose hair. "You ever hear of Jamie McNally?"

Lottie tried to keep her face impassive while her heart skipped a beat.

"I've heard of him." She tried to be noncommittal. "Did he call to your house?"

"He did. There was I, ready for bed, and him outside banging on the window like a banshee."

"How do you know McNally?" Lottie asked. "What did he want?"

Tracy hesitated. "I...I don't know him, but that useless layabout in Spain does."

"Go on."

"I think he sent him over here asking about my Maeve."

"Frank sent Jamie McNally to talk to you about Maeve?"

"Are you listening to me at all?"

Lottie mulled over this information. They'd known McNally was around town, but so far they'd had no luck finding him. And now Tracy was giving her a specific link between Jamie McNally and Frank Phillips, and her missing daughter.

"Tracy, we know your husband is involved with criminal activity. And you know that too."

"Yes, I know he's a criminal and I hate every bone in his body. But I want my girl back. She should've been back by now if…"

"If what?"

"Nothing. I just want her home."

"Could Frank's activities be in any way connected to Maeve's disappearance?"

Tracy shook her head slowly. "I don't know, to tell you the truth."

"What did McNally say?" Lottie asked, now that Tracy had calmed down.

"That prick. All high and mighty and important in a black suit and tie. Looking like a proper businessman. Except his hair was slicked with a ton of gel, and he even had a ponytail yoke at the back of his head. The gobshite. He said…he said Frank asked him to check up on Maeve." She grasped Lottie's hand. "What's happened to my girl?"

"I guarantee you I intend to find out." Lottie pulled her hand away and debated taking a formal statement.

Tracy began fumbling around in her handbag. "I'm sorry, but I need a drink. I've tried to stay off it, but McNally scared me half to death. I thought Maeve had just run off. But now I'm not sure of anything."

I know the feeling, Lottie thought.

"Did McNally give you the impression he knew where Maeve might be, or if she had been abducted?"

"Abducted? No. He just wanted to know what you lot were doing, and if you'd taken anything from the house. I was afraid of him, so I let him have a look in Maeve's room when he asked."

"Did he say anything after that?"

"Just said, 'Maeve takes after her daddy.'"

"What did he mean by that?"

"Expensive tastes, that's what he said. Remember that blue dress you were interested in? He took it with him."

"Good God, whatever for?"

"I've no idea. I don't even know where Maeve got it from."

Shit, Lottie thought, they should have removed the dress from the house. Damn. Why was McNally interested in it?

Studying Tracy Phillips, trembling but dry-eyed, she said, "You know you can tell me anything. I promise no one will know but me, and my colleagues."

"What are you on about?"

"Is there anything at all that might point me in the right direction to find Maeve? Something you're not telling me?"

"Inspector, you have children, don't you?"

"Yes, I do."

"Can you honestly say you know everything about them?"

That got Lottie thinking for a moment.

Tracy said, "I drink a lot. I admit that. So there are things I don't know about my daughter and things I probably don't want to know, but I do know this. My Maeve wouldn't run away. If I were you, I'd try to find my bastard of a husband. If he doesn't know where she is, you can be sure he'll know someone who does."

* * *

After Tracy left, Lottie ran down to the basement and burst into the locker room. She had five minutes to get ready before the team meeting. Pulling off her damp T-shirt, she rummaged around for a clean one. When she was dressed, she walked toward the door.

Hearing someone on the other side of the room, she longed for the day when the building renovations were complete and she could have some privacy. Unisex lockers were not ideal. She looked over. Boyd was unbuttoning his shirt.

"What are you doing?" she asked, leaning against the door and folding her arms. She recalled Jackie at his apartment last night. Would he tell her what that had been about? Probably not. And she wasn't going to ask.

Boyd pulled on a clean shirt. "What does it look like? Got caught in the downpour."

"How's Jackie?" Why couldn't she keep her mouth shut?

"How would I know?"

"After all she put you through, Boyd, I thought you'd realize she's not your type."

"Are you my personal matchmaker now or what? She was my type when I married her. And how would you know what my type is anyway?"

He was right. What did she know? But she couldn't stop herself.

"I don't want you making a fool of yourself. Jackie arrives back in Ragmullin with her big baby eyes and you sleep with her." She unfolded her arms and shoved her hands into her jeans pockets.

Boyd banged the locker door and faced her. "Lottie, you're not my mother. Try being a mother to your own kids."

She stepped away from him, mouth open. "How...how can you say that?"

She saw his shoulders slump. He gripped her arm.

"I'm sorry. You know I didn't mean that. You just riled me—"

"Don't make excuses." She snapped her arm away.

"I'll make you a coffee." Boyd escaped up the stairs, heading for the makeshift kitchen.

"We have a team meeting," Lottie shouted after him, "and you better be there."

CHAPTER 45

Maeve's skin clung to her like a well-worn washcloth. She tried to turn over onto her side, but pain restricted her movements. Arms heavy, she traced her fingers beneath her body. She wasn't on the floor. Cold sheets beneath her. Damp. A bed. She lifted her hand. Blood. It smelled coppery, like corroded metal. Was it hers?

She turned her head. Solid walls. Bare concrete. No window that she could see. No furniture. A dusty fluorescent strip lined the center of the ceiling, casting a weak yellow streak downward, failing in its quest to brighten the room. Where was she?

Carefully she raised her head and glanced down her body. Naked, not even underwear. Instinctively she tried to cover herself, clasping her skin with weak fingers. An arrowhead of pain shot through her and she screamed, but only a strangled sob came from her throat.

Tentatively she caressed the spot where the stab of agony had erupted. A sticky wetness slid over her hand. She bit her lip to prevent another scream.

A wound across her abdomen, spread in an arc over her pelvis. Blood curled down her pubic bone and between her legs. The triangular illuminations from the stained-glass in a paneled door danced before her eyes, exploding in a thousand fireflies, fluttering in the dark.

She struggled to stay alert; to save herself from her unknown captor. What had he done to her?

I want to go home, she cried silently, before the light merged into one long line of blackness.

CHAPTER 46

The extended team members were gathered in the incident room. Lottie was glad when Superintendent Corrigan rang in to say he had to take a sick day. She hoped he wasn't too ill, but in all honesty he hadn't looked great all week. At least she wouldn't have to tell him about Milot.

Standing with the incident boards to her back, she looked at her team. Expectant faces stared back at her. She was about to give them a shit-load of information they already knew, and questions with no answers. She pointed to the photograph of the first murder victim and proceeded to outline the facts.

"Monday. First victim discovered at Bridge Street. Buried beneath the road. Found by water-main contract worker Andri Petrovci. From the postmortem results we know the victim had been undressed, shot, the wound washed, then she was re-dressed. Why would he do that?" She looked at the expectant faces. "Control? Power?"

"Because he could," Boyd said.

"To wash away evidence," Lynch suggested.

Lottie said, "The killer took a great risk burying her beneath the street where a few days earlier contractors had been digging. Did he know they would be back? If so, he wanted the body found. Why?

"The victim was about four months pregnant and aged between sixteen and twenty at best estimate. According to the pathologist, her bone structure suggests she is of Eastern European or Balkan origin. Moss was discovered under her nails but no DNA. She'd had a kidney surgically removed within the last twelve months. This detail must be kept from the media at all costs. Understood?"

A murmur of assent filtered throughout the room.

"A bullet was lodged in the victim's rib. No report from ballistics. Detective Lynch, you follow this up."

Lynch nodded as she scribbled notes. "Yes, boss."

"We've no idea who she is or where she lived, though we suspect she may have been a resident at the direct provision center run by an ex-army man, Dan Russell. We've got some information on him but I need you to dig deeper. Find anything you can on Russell and his venture."

Lynch said, "I'll work on that."

"Power and control," Boyd said. "Ex-army officer. Figures."

"We'll see." Lottie leaned against the board, considering where to go next with her spiel. She decided on Mimoza.

"Before the body was discovered on Monday morning, a young woman called Mimoza visited my home with her son before I left for work. She gave me a note. Roughly translated, it says that her friend Kaltrina is missing and this Mimoza is looking for help to escape. From what, I don't know. We still have no idea if Kaltrina is one of the murder victims. We've run the name, but no success. I have no idea where Mimoza is now." She decided against mentioning that Milot had mysteriously appeared at her door last night. "Just keep this in mind throughout your investigations. It may be linked."

Expectant faces stared up at her. Lottie took a sip of water and continued.

"On to Tuesday. At Bob Weir's car dismantler depot we found a bullet hole in a rear wall and blood was discovered on the ground nearby. To date, we've no report from ballistics, or analysis from the lab on whether the blood was animal or human. Kirby, can you hound them for results?"

"I'm doing it every day."

"Do it every five minutes."

"Yes, boss," Kirby groaned.

"Wednesday. We received a report that a seventeen-year-old girl, Maeve Phillips of Mellow Grove, was missing. Reported by her mother, Tracy Phillips. Maeve is the daughter of criminal-in-exile Frank Phillips, who we are currently trying to locate. As far as we can determine, the girl was last seen on Friday, a week ago today. We've interviewed her friends and appeals have been issued through social and national media. No sightings to date. It's possible she's been abducted. I must state also that Maeve's mother is an unreliable witness. Hard to believe anything she says.

"On Thursday, a second murder victim was discovered in Columb Street. Similar circumstances to our first victim. Buried beneath the road. Been dead at least four to five days. Unearthed by Andri Petrovci, who also found the first body."

"Number one suspect then?" Boyd asked.

"He's been questioned and a buccal swab taken for DNA, but to date we have nothing to hold him on."

"Jesus, he has to have some involvement. Bit odd finding not one but two bodies, isn't it?" Boyd stood and walked around. "Does his alibi hold up?"

Lottie clenched her fists to prevent herself from telling him to sit down. Best to let him wander.

"Petrovci lives alone and says he's at home every night. This morning I visited the pathologist, Jane Dore. She has yet to complete the postmortem but confirmed that the second victim has an abdominal scar, leading her to believe that she also had a kidney removed. This scar is newer than the other victim's, possibly six months. Again, I don't want to read about this on the web or anywhere in the media. Am I clear?"

"Crystal," Boyd said.

Lottie continued. "The sutures were professionally administered, which may indicate a qualified doctor—"

"Or a wannabe doctor," Boyd interrupted.

Digging her nails into the palms of her hands, Lottie said, "Keep it in mind as you compile a list of suspects."

"We don't even know who the victims are. How the hell can we get a suspect?" Boyd said.

Lottie shook her head. This wasn't going smoothly. Only good thing was that Corrigan wasn't around to witness it.

"Where was I? Bullet entered the second victim's back and exited just below the chest. Ballistics will confirm if it is the same weapon as used on victim number one. I'm sure it is. This girl is aged between eighteen and twenty-five. Undernourished also. But a difference to the first victim has been established."

A murmur of interest spread through the room.

"She has a lot of scars and cuts on her body. Self-inflicted? I'm waiting for Jane Dore to confirm all of the above, later today."

She sipped her water again before continuing.

"Recap time. Both bodies were found by Andri Petrovci. He works with the water-main contractors. He is a Kosovo national. Nothing to link him to the actual murders as yet. And I've confirmed he is not on the watch of any of our national crime teams. Columb Street is cordoned off and being searched, as is Weir's yard. A resident from that area, Willie Flynn, reported to Detective Kirby that the street was closed for a time on Monday night or Tuesday morning. He saw someone with a white van picking up road signs that had been used to shut it off."

Kirby piped up. "The security company employed by Bob Weir to patrol the area have no record of this being their van."

"Burial locations for both girls are under streets to the rear of the town, quiet areas, both easily blocked off in the dead of night. People are so used to disruptions occurring without advance warning that it wouldn't seem unusual. But we need to search through the CCTV from all the businesses that back onto these streets. Kirby, you again."

He nodded. "Nothing works, but I'll check again."

"As we have no reports on the missing persons database of anyone fitting the victims' descriptions, it's possible that both girls were residents at the DPC. We had a meeting with Dan Russell and he denied any knowledge of the first victim when shown her photograph. But when Detective Sergeant Boyd asked him about Mimoza, we think he lied in relation to not knowing her. So what is Russell up to? What's he hiding? Detective Lynch, please hurry up with your inquiries. I really need to know who I'm dealing with."

"Doing my best," Lynch replied.

"Have we enough for a search warrant for the DPC?" Kirby asked.

"Only suspicions," Lottie said. "Another thing to note is that Jamie McNally has returned to Ragmullin, as I'm sure you're all aware. Our best intel is that he entered the country last Wednesday week. Just before the bodies started turning up. Interesting, isn't it?" She pointed to McNally's photo pinned on the board and eyed Boyd.

"But if it is him, what's his motive?" Boyd asked.

"I don't know. The murders might have nothing to do with him, but last night McNally paid a visit to Maeve Phillips's mother. He took from the house an expensive dress that had been hanging in Maeve's wardrobe. We had already determined that it had been bought online and delivered on April fifth to Maeve's address. No idea as yet who purchased it. No idea why Jamie McNally would take it. But we now know from our intel that McNally works with Frank Phillips, Maeve's father. Is this criminal element related to the murders?" Lottie let that hang in the air for a moment.

"DS Boyd, see what you can find out. I believe you know someone who can help us."

Boyd unfolded his arms and squeezed his hands into fists. He didn't seem pleased with the task. Tough shit, Lottie thought. A muffled murmur rose among the assembled crew.

"Any questions?"

Detective Lynch stood up. "This Andri Petrovci seems like a prime suspect to me."

Lottie deliberated over this. "Besides McNally, and maybe Russell, he's the only suspect so far. But why would he unearth the bodies if he had buried them?"

"Looking for attention?" Lynch offered.

"Doesn't make sense. The whole way the murders and the bodies have been managed shrieks control freak to me. I'm not sure he fits the bill. But by finding the bodies he's already contaminated them. His DNA will probably prove worthless."

"He's getting off too lightly," Lynch protested. "I've spoken to him twice and he's definitely using the language barrier as a foil to keep us from digging too deep."

Lottie thought for a moment. She was usually a good reader of character but she wasn't at all sure about Andri Petrovci. Why had she asked him to translate the letter from Mimoza? A major mistake on her part? Jesus, she hoped not.

"Okay." She relented. "See what you can find out about him and we'll bring him in again. Anything else?"

"How does the killer pick his burial sites?" Boyd asked.

"He seems to know the contractor's routine," Lynch added.

"It's listed on the council website," Kirby said.

"What?" Lottie said.

"Traffic management section, online. Shows where they intend working a week in advance."

"It still points to Petrovci," Lynch said, sticking her pen into her ponytail.

"I've said we'll bring him in again." Lottie knew she was losing control of the meeting. "Has anyone got hold of a database from the Department of Justice listing the residents at the DPC?"

"I got a list emailed to me," Lynch said. "Took a lot of wheeling and dealing. Russell is running this as a private venture. But the Justice Department relented and sent it on."

"I suspect they believe he is compliant with their regulations, but I'm not so sure. We need to go through the names in detail."

"I did a quick scan. There's no one called Mimoza or Kaltrina on the list."

"Shit," Lottie said.

"Does that put Russell in the clear?" Boyd asked.

"Not in the least," Lottie said. "What's to stop him having his own unofficial list?"

"Why would he do that?" Kirby stood up, patting his shirt pocket for a cigar.

"Don't know yet, but it seems the obvious thing to do if you've something to hide."

Boyd said, "We don't know if he has anything to hide."

"If he has, I intend to find out."

Lottie spent some minutes going over all the details she had outlined and setting up a dedicated team to manage the Maeve Phillips disappearance. Then, with the chatter rising and the detectives shaking their heads, she sent everyone back to work.

A nagging doubt prickled beneath her skin. She hadn't told the team about Milot turning up at her house. She wouldn't like it if any of them withheld information, yet here she was doing it herself. Consoling herself that Boyd had said nothing about it, she knew she'd have to follow it up herself.

"Did you mention something about coffee?" she asked Boyd as she passed him.

CHAPTER 47

"I said I'm sorry." Boyd boiled the kettle. "About what I said earlier. But you insinuated I knew something about McNally—that was a bit low."

"I'm sorry too. We know McNally was at Maeve Phillips's house last night," she explained again. No point in fighting with the only person who listened to her grievances.

"Yes. Sent by the girl's father."

"When Jackie called to yours last night"—Lottie spooned hardened coffee from a jar into mugs—"did she mention anything about McNally?"

"No, she didn't." He poured the water. "I got rid of her immediately."

"So what are you going to do about McNally?"

"What are you going to do about the boy?"

"I wish you'd fuck off," Lottie said, with a grin.

"Be careful what you wish for," he said.

They carried their coffees back to the office. Boyd perched himself on the edge of Lottie's desk, mug of black coffee in hand, matching the dark rings beneath his eyes. She flicked through a file on her desk. He placed his hand on top of hers.

"Lottie?"

She looked up and caught the earnest look in his eyes.

"The Child and Family Agency? Did you contact them? You have the number."

She sighed. "Not yet."

"For God's sake—"

"Hear me out. The boy might know something, and once

he's in the system, he's lost to us. I'll have to buy time. Some-how. There's all the paperwork. In the meantime, we could question him."

"Question him? About what? A four-year-old kid without his mother? Get real."

Lottie stood up quickly, knocking the mug in Boyd's hand with her elbow. Coffee splashed over his white shirt. He leapt away from the desk. From the scalding liquid. From her?

"Sorry," she said.

"That's my last shirt."

"Look, Boyd." She placed her hand on his arm. He contin-ued wiping the stain without meeting her eye. She dropped her hand. "He's no more than four years old. He found my house having only been there once before. He must be living in town. Probably in the DPC. His mother came to me for help. I didn't give it enough attention at the time, but now I feel she really needs it."

"What're you going to do?" Boyd asked, giving up on sal-vaging his shirt. "Keep the boy? That's kidnapping."

"Know what you can do?" Lottie picked up her bag and brushed past him.

"Go fuck myself?"

She smiled back at him but still banged the door on her way out.

Even if Boyd didn't want to be part of it, she was going to find out why Milot had ended up at her house. Her gut was telling her Mimoza was in danger. And she knew her gut was always right. Well, almost always.

Standing in the corridor breathing deeply, she heard the office door open behind her and sensed Boyd approaching.

Without preamble he said, "Do you honestly think they were living in Russell's weird setup?"

"I don't know. But it makes sense. It's local. Mimoza was

walking and I saw her meeting up with a girl at the end of my road."

"What girl?"

"I've a vague recollection that she was small, black, but I'm not sure."

"Will I open a missing person file on Mimoza?"

"How? I know nothing about her. I need details, her photograph. I'm not even sure she's missing."

Pacing up and down the cluttered corridor, stepping around box files, she said, "We'll get an interpreter for the boy."

"You could ask the O'Hara fellow working at the DPC."

"Don't be daft. What if that's where they came from?" Lottie said. She added, "The DPC is within walking distance of my house. Not that far for a four-year-old, if he cut down by the canal or was brought that way. And the canal route is lined with cherry blossom trees." She took off down the corridor.

"There are petals everywhere after all that rain. Where the hell are you going now?"

Lottie kept walking. "To try and get past Dan Russell's stonewalling attitude."

"Lottie…"

"What?"

"Remember you told me what the superintendent said to you the other day, about standing on toes."

"Boyd, I think you have a hearing problem."

Running down the stairs before he could stop her again, she heard the sound of his fist banging against the wall.

CHAPTER 48

"Twenty Major," Boyd said. He needed a smoke. Badly. Lottie was getting on his nerves this morning. Opening his wallet, he handed over his bank card.

"Sorry," the shop assistant said. "We only take cash for cigarettes and Lotto."

"Really?"

"Yes. Bank charges, you know. Huge."

Sighing, Boyd flicked through his wallet looking for a tenner and counted out the odd change. He was sure he'd had a fifty. No sign of it.

He put the cigarettes into his pocket, and as he was closing his wallet he noticed a piece of white cloth sticking out from where he had pulled the notes.

The assistant handed him ten cents change. He waved it away and left the shop. As he walked toward the station, opening up the cigarette pack, he remembered the piece of cloth. He took out his wallet to have a look.

"Marcus! There you are."

Leaning against the barrier at the station steps, sun behind her head, Jackie appeared like a specter from the light.

"I need to talk to you," she said.

Boyd shoved the piece of material back into the wallet and tried to maneuver around her, but she grabbed his arm, pulling him back down the steps.

"What, Jackie?" he said.

"It wasn't very pleasant last night, you shoving me out and shutting the door in my face. Not nice at all, Marcus."

"Will you stop calling me that? What do you want?"

"A short chat."

Boyd took her by the elbow, wheeled her away from the station and walked in silence toward the canal bridge. He didn't want anyone overhearing what she might have to say.

"Glad I have my flat shoes on," Jackie said, when at last he stopped and leaned on the bridge.

Gazing into the murky green water reminded him of how he felt—murky and very green. He didn't like being wrong-footed, but Jackie had always been able to do it. He glanced at her, and despite everything she had done to him, a flicker of desire cut through him like a skewer. It's over, he reminded himself. Over.

"I haven't got all day, so come on, what is it you want to talk about?"

"I need to warn you…" she began.

"What?" He turned to her. As far as he could remember, Jackie only ever thought of herself.

"It's about Jamie."

"What about him?"

"He's very dangerous."

Boyd threw back his head and laughed. "Ah, go on, Jackie. Tell me something new."

"Don't you dare laugh at me, Marcus. I've noticed things recently. That's what I wanted to tell you last night. I called the night before also, but you were out. There are things you need to know about."

Her hand touched his arm. His skin tingled. Drawing away, he shoved his hands into his pockets. Safer there, he thought.

"I'm waiting," he said.

"Can we go somewhere else? Have a drink. Talk like adults," she said.

He stepped around her and backed away with his hands raised.

"You're playing games with me and I don't like it. I doubt you really have anything to tell me, so you know what, I'm going back to work." He started to walk.

"He's involved in smuggling."

"Jesus, sure I know that. McNally has had his hand in guns and drugs since he could walk," he said over his shoulder.

"But now it's women, girls."

Boyd stopped, turned around and stared at Jackie. He shrugged. He never could read his not-yet-ex-wife.

"Human trafficking? McNally? I'd have him down for a lot of things, but not that."

"I know. That's what scares me."

Boyd walked slowly back toward her. "Why are you telling me this?"

"I need to get away from him. You have to help me."

"Always a catch with you, isn't there?"

"Will you help me?" She fluttered her eyelashes like a little girl playing at being grown up.

Despite his best efforts to refuse, because Jackie was nothing but trouble, Boyd nodded.

"I'm busy now. I'll chat to you later. Give me your number. I'll text you."

Whatever he thought of her, he was compelled to listen to her. He needed to know what had brought Jamie McNally back to Ragmullin. His duty was to his job, no longer to Jackie. But if she genuinely was scared, he'd probably have to help her.

"Don't forget." She took his pen and wrote her number in his notebook before planting a kiss on his cheek and hurrying over the bridge.

He watched her go. What was he getting himself into? Taking after Lottie and jumping in with both feet. He knew he was going to get wet; he just hoped he didn't drown.

CHAPTER 49

The navy-blue sky was heavy with rain and inky clouds hung low as Lottie walked through the gates of the old army barracks.

Heading for Russell's office block, she couldn't help noticing how dilapidated the buildings had become since the army moved out. The damp gully along the footpath had vermin boxes nestling against the wall every couple of meters. Weeds and grass sprouted between the tarmac and the cobbled path.

A group of women clustered around the door to the cookhouse. Perfect, Lottie thought. Life at last. They might even speak a little English. She crossed over, heading toward them.

"Inspector, this way."

She swung around to see Dan Russell standing at the door to his office. His navy chinos, white shirt and dark blue tie made her feel shabby in her T-shirt and faded jeans. Damn.

She was debating whether to nab the women or obey his command when the small group hurried into the cookhouse, taking the decision away from her.

"Can I see what goes on here?" she asked.

Russell joined her. "Of course," he said. "Follow me. We're running a very interesting project at the moment."

She noticed his face visibly relaxing into a broad smile. Clearly he didn't want her talking to anyone without his say-so. They crossed the square toward a building she remembered from Adam's time as the NCOs' mess. Noticing even more vermin boxes along the outside walls, she asked, "Have you an infestation problem?"

"Yes, but it's not as bad as it was at the chicken farm."

"The chicken farm? I remember that from somewhere."

"It was our base camp in Kosovo. Awful place."

He pushed open the door to the mess and ushered her inside. Lottie looked around. The walls were covered with posters; paint was peeling from the ceiling. Very different from the evenings she and Adam had spent here. Back then there had been a fire blazing in the wide old hearth, groups of men playing pool and a handful of regulars hugging the bar, recounting sniper fire from some peacekeeping duty. She'd loved those evenings. Comradeship and friendship. Now it was gone, in every sense.

Russell led her through to the main function room. Rows of desks and chairs were lined up in perfect symmetry. Tables along one wall held four computers. She counted ten girls dressed in school uniform. What were schoolgirls doing in here? Tutoring the women? The girls sat at the desks, a woman beside each of them, poring over pages. The women wore cheap clothes similar to those Mimoza had worn. A young woman sat by the side wall, idly flipping through the pages of a magazine. Lottie thought she recognized her as a teacher from Chloe's school. As she went to speak with her, a man who had been showing one of the women something on a computer turned and stood up, blocking her view of the teacher.

"Hello," he said, approaching her and holding out his hand.

Lottie shook it, surprised at its coolness. "Detective Inspector Lottie Parker."

"I'm George O'Hara," he added.

"Pleased to meet you. Can you tell me what's going on here?"

"It's a language project."

"And you're the tutor?" Lottie asked. George O'Hara was older than she had anticipated, maybe early thirties. Head shaved closely, he wore clothing similar to Russell. Some sort of uniform? His feet were shod in brown leather shoes. No socks. Tanned ankles. She supposed it was better than Kirby's open-toed sandals.

O'Hara glanced at Russell. "Yes, I am. Part time at the moment."

A bustle of movement caught Lottie's eye at the back of the room. Emily Coyne, curls bobbing away, jumped out of her seat.

"Hiya, Mrs. Parker." Pushing her spectacles back up her nose, she said, "This is what Chloe will be doing next year."

"Is this the project you mentioned the other day?"

"Yes. It's great. We get to teach English."

"Seems a bit unusual, to say the least."

"It's all new. You can ask Miss Scully about it if you like." She pointed to the bored-looking teacher. "It's so exciting. All these women have such great stories. I think I'm going to write a book about their adventures."

Dan Russell moved between Emily and Lottie. "I don't think they would describe their experiences as adventures."

Was he dismissing the girl? Lottie wondered.

Emily was having none of it. "George is brilliant. I wish he could teach in our school."

"That's nice, Emily," George said. He stroked Emily's arm and Lottie gave a start. What type of class was this?

With a flick of her curls, Emily bopped back to her student.

Lottie concentrated on the tutor. "Can I talk to some of the women?"

"Their English is almost nonexistent," Russell interjected.

"I can interpret what they say for you," George said.

Their conversation was interrupted by a loud shriek from one of the schoolgirls. "I saw another one! I swear to God. He ran right over my foot."

"Calm down," Russell said. "It's only a mouse. Can't do you any harm. Sit down."

George O'Hara rushed to the girl, took her hand and helped her down off the chair. Once she was seated again, he stood beside her, kneading her shoulders, comforting her. Lottie felt queasy. She glanced at Miss Scully, who was still oblivious, engrossed in her magazine. Jesus, anything could be going on here.

"I need to talk to you," she said to Russell.

"Seen enough already?" he asked, moving round to stand by her side.

"More than enough."

"Come over to my office and we can have a chat."

* * *

When they were seated in his office, Lottie placed a photograph of the second dead girl on Russell's desk. She watched for his reaction. Frozen. That was how she would describe it. His hand stopped motionless in mid-air. A sheet of steel shifted over his eyes.

"What is this?" he asked.

"Another murder victim. Do you know her?"

"Know her? I can't even make out her features." He ran his fingers along his mustache, and beads of perspiration broke out on his forehead.

Lottie sat forward in the chair and folded her arms. The photograph lay on the desk between them like a weapon.

It only took him a few seconds to compose himself. "I don't know her. I'm sorry." He lowered his hand and pushed the photograph back at her. "You were asking me earlier in the week about a girl called Mimoza."

She held her breath and nodded.

"I did a little investigative work for you. I found out she was indeed a resident here."

Why was he suddenly deciding to be helpful? Lottie wondered. Now she could get that search warrant.

She kept her expression neutral and said, "I want to talk to her." But then a thought struck her. Maria Lynch had said Mimoza wasn't on the official database of residents. So was Russell lying?

"Impossible," he said.

"What? Why? I need to speak to her. Urgently."

"Mimoza Barbatovci *was* here, but unfortunately she appears to have run away."

"Mr. Russell—"

"Dan."

Lottie sighed, glad he'd interrupted her. If Mimoza was missing, it was clear Russell wanted her found. That was the only logical explanation for him revealing his knowledge of the girl's existence.

"When did she go missing?"

"I'm not sure. It was last night when we noticed that both she and the boy were gone."

"What boy?" Two could play his game.

"She has a son. He's gone also."

"You didn't report it at the time?"

"I'm telling you now." Russell smiled. It didn't reach his eyes.

"Do you have a photo of them? I need it to publicize their disappearance," she said.

"I thought you might do it without much publicity. I don't want my facility getting a bad name."

"A photo would be handy."

Russell flipped up his laptop, tapped the keys and a printer whirred out a page. He grabbed it and handed it over.

Lottie stared at the picture.

Mimoza with her son in her arms. The girl wore no hijab,

and her black hair flowed around her thin face. The boy had his thumb in his mouth; his other hand clutched the frayed toy rabbit. Folding the page, Lottie put it in her bag before Russell could change his mind.

"How do you have this?" she asked.

"It was taken when they arrived. Must have overlooked it when I checked before."

"I need to see her file," she said.

"That's confidential."

"I need to know everything about this girl if I'm to conduct a proper inquiry."

"There's no need for a major investigation. Just snoop around on your own. A woman of your ability should be well able to find them."

"Mr. Russell, I don't need you dictating how I do my business."

"I beg to differ, Detective Inspector Parker." He sat back in his chair, a certain smugness hardening his face. "You see, there are things I know about your husband. Things I think you would rather I kept quiet about. So it is in both our interests that you do what I say." He smiled that smile again.

Lottie jumped up, leaned across the desk. "Don't you dare threaten me. The absolute cheek of you to even—"

"I'm merely advising you that there are certain matters you most definitely do not want going public. Believe me, I know."

"What matters?" She remained standing. His calmness infuriated her. What was he insinuating? She had asked him about Adam before and he had been evasive. Now he was blatantly using her late husband as a threat. She opened her mouth to speak again. He raised a hand, silencing her.

"I don't want to go into details at the moment, as I'm very busy. Suffice to say, if you find this girl and her child, the information I have will never surface."

Lottie moved quickly to the door and looked back at him.

"I've no intention of surrendering to your vile intimidation. You'll be sorry you ever started this."

"I doubt that very much. If anyone is going to be sorry, it will be you. Now if that's all, close the door on your way out."

Unable to think of a suitable retort, Lottie walked out of the office, leaving the door wide open.

* * *

He watched the detective. Watched her run out of Block A as the clouds burst and the rain thundered down. She had a nice arse in her tight faded jeans. Did she think she was a teenager going around dressed like that? Who exactly did she think she was?

But he knew who she was, and all about her family.

He heard his dog behind him and turned.

"Did you get one, mutt?" he said. "Oh, it's a whopper this time."

The dog sat looking up at him with a dirty big rat in its mouth.

CHAPTER 50

The second victim's preliminary postmortem results were sitting in Lottie's email inbox when she returned to the office. As promised, Jane had dumbed down the language so Lottie could make sense of it immediately.

Cause of death: gunshot.

Entry through upper back.

Damage to lungs, heart and spleen.

Death instant.

Bullet exited below chest.

Bullet not recovered from body.

Left kidney removed surgically. Best estimate within the last three months.

Septicemia present.

Wound washed.

Traces of moss lodged in two toenails of right foot. Moss sent for analysis and soil analysis. Possibility that body was washed.

Old scars on body. Self-harm?

Imprint of letter K on right ankle. Maybe from a thin ankle bracelet on victim at time of death.

Interesting, Lottie thought, looking at the last point; the killer had missed that. Did it confirm that the second victim was Kaltrina? And what about the moss? What did that mean? Both girls had moss beneath their nails. She would have to follow up on the analysis.

She raised her head as Boyd entered the office.

He said, "You're soaking wet."

"I'm going home to get changed." She stood up. "Have a look at this. See what you make of it, in particular the bit about the moss."

"How did it go with Russell?"

She thought for a moment about Russell's threat. Should she say anything about Mimoza? But she decided she had nothing to fear from that pompous bastard. "He told me Mimoza was a resident and that she and her son seem to have disappeared."

"Did you tell him—"

"No, I didn't tell him about Milot. What do you take me for?"

"I don't know, but it would be interesting to hear what he had to say."

"I showed him the photo of the latest murder victim and—"

"I bet he knew her."

"Will you let me finish a sentence, Boyd?" When she was sure he would remain quiet, she said, "I think he knew her."

"Told you so."

"I'd better go and change. I'll see you in a bit and you can fill me in on your progress."

"What progress?"

"Exactly. Ring Jane. See how long the soil and moss analysis will take."

She left him shaking his head as he sat down at her desk to read the report.

* * *

Lottie rushed home and quickly changed into dry clothes. She checked in on Chloe but she was fast asleep.

Milot was sitting on Katie's knee in the kitchen, eating chicken nuggets. Lottie sat down and looked at her daughter.

She thought how it was only a few short years since Katie had been a child herself, and now she was just a shadow. Jason's death really had hit her hard.

"Granny went home," Katie told her. "I found these nuggets in the freezer and threw them in the oven. He seems to like them."

Milot smiled and a chunk of chicken fell out of his mouth.

"I've tissues somewhere." Lottie opened up her deep leather bag. She set aside the photo of Mimoza and Milot she'd got from Russell. It needed to go up on the incident board. Fishing around for the tissues, she pulled out receipts and chocolate bar wrappers.

"It doesn't matter, Mam." Katie found a kitchen roll. She tore off a piece and wiped Milot's mouth.

Lottie crumpled up the receipts. Her bag could do with a good clean-out. She glanced at the clock and scrabbled around in the mess. Pulling out a bundle of post, she scanned through it: mainly bills. She crumpled each one up, trying not to think of her depleted bank balance. Her hand stopped and she stared. The envelope that had held Mimoza's note. Suddenly she recalled that there had been something besides the letter in it. With everything that had happened, she'd totally forgotten about it.

"Mam, what are you at?" Katie tidied up the table and took Milot by the hand.

"It's such a mess," Lottie said. "Is Milot okay?"

"We're going to watch some television, aren't we, Milot?"

"Keep an eye on Chloe. I'm worried about her."

"Whatever."

Katie brought the child into the sitting room and Lottie heard the sounds of *The Lion King* blaring. I'm right to keep him here, she thought. Now I just need to find his mum.

Throwing everything else back into her bag, she opened

Mimoza's envelope and took out the material that was lying in the bottom fold. It was a narrow piece of green canvas about two and a half centimeters in depth and maybe fifteen centimeters in length. Velcro on one side. She turned it over. Deep green stitching embossed the edges. Her bag slid from her knee to the floor and she gasped as she realized what she was looking at. An army badge. Perfectly spaced capital letters, embroidered down the center, spelled out a name. PARKER.

"What's that?" Katie asked, coming back to the kitchen and opening the refrigerator.

Before her daughter could see it, Lottie picked up her bag and shoved the canvas badge inside.

"Nothing," she said. "Nothing at all."

Her hands shook fiercely and her legs twitched up and down. She took deep breaths, staring at the ceiling and trying to focus her thoughts. Why had Mimoza come to her house? What was her note all about? And how could she be in possession of Adam's army name badge? Was it really Adam's? Logic told her it had to be.

Her phone beeped a text from Boyd. *Meet at Weir's yard.*

Mimoza. She had to find Mimoza.

Only then could she find out the truth.

CHAPTER 51

Lottie rushed through the taped cordon at Weir's depot. The rain had ceased but its aftermath failed to lift the mugginess from the air.

Trying to keep her mind off the army badge burning a hole in the bottom of her bag, she looked at the white van with its door hanging off. It sat on top of two squashed cars and another appeared to totter precariously on top of it. Weir had assured them it was secure. She didn't know whether to believe him or not.

"What have we got here?" she asked.

"Small van. White. Ready for crushing," Boyd said.

"You know what I mean. What am I looking at?"

"Blood trace on the floor, near the rear door."

"Animal or human?"

"Samples have been taken by SOCOs. God knows when we'll get a result."

"I don't care about God. When will *I* know?" Lottie scanned the area. "Has everything been examined? Nothing else found? What have you been doing? Jesus." She paced around in small circles, then turned to face Boyd.

"What's wrong with you?" he said. "Calm down."

She shifted up close to him. "Do not tell me to calm down. Do you hear me?"

"Loud and clear."

Pacing again, she said, "Check Weir's records. Find out who owned the van, who brought it here and when."

The metal was giving off so much heat it was like electric charges, as if the sun was testing just how far it could go before melting everything.

Lottie sighed, rubbing her hand through her hair. "I'm having a bad day, Boyd."

"When do you ever have a good one? Rhetorical question."

"Anything else in the van?"

"SOCOs did a sweep. Clean. Too clean, really. Not a whisper of dirt. It's like it got a good valeting. Why do that if you're scrapping it? But whoever cleaned it missed the speck of blood."

"Maybe it was planted."

"What? Why would someone do that?"

"I've no idea, but the van needs further examination. Arrange it."

She took a few photos with her phone camera and noticed the time.

"Oh Jesus Christ."

"What now?" Boyd asked.

"Sean had a counseling session. I was to pick him up from school. It's too late now."

"You need to slow down, Lottie."

"You need to stay here and see if anything else turns up."

* * *

Back at the station, she scooted up the stairs to the incident room. Ignoring the phone conversations going on around her, she pinned up the photograph of Mimoza and Milot given to her by Dan Russell earlier.

Sitting on a wobbly-legged chair in front of the board, she thought about the army badge. Not now, she told herself. A torrent of tiredness washed up over her, and she felt she was about to fall.

"I'll have to go home," she said to Lynch, who waved a hand from behind a mound of paperwork. "See you for a few hours tomorrow. Is that okay?" she added.

"Really? Tomorrow's Saturday," Lynch said, looking up.

"I'm well aware of what day it is, but we're in the middle of two murder investigations and—"

"Okay, boss, no need for the lecture. I'll be here."

"I'm sorry. I didn't mean to snap."

"Go home. You're wrecked."

Picking up her bag, Lottie hoisted it over her shoulder. She had no idea how she could keep her work from impinging on her home life. Five days back, and already the hectic pace was catching up with her.

She was glad to be going home to her family. She wanted to hug her three children. Tightly.

With a sigh, she headed down the stairs, waved at the desk sergeant and went home.

* * *

Boyd stormed into the incident room. His mood didn't improve when he couldn't find Lottie.

Glancing at the board, he noticed a new photo pinned there. He moved closer to get a better look.

"Jesus Christ!" He stared and touched the photograph before pulling his hand away as if it was burned.

"What's up?" Kirby sauntered up behind him.

Sweat collected on the palms of Boyd's trembling hands. He stuffed them into his trouser pockets. Nodding at the photograph, he said, "Who are they?"

"Don't know. Only just got back."

"Boss put them up," Lynch said, raising her head, phone clutched between chin and shoulder.

"Where is she?" Boyd asked.

"Where I should be," Lynch said, gathering up an armload of files. "At home."

Boyd hurried back to their office, Kirby in tow.

"Spit it out," Kirby said.

"It's her."

"Who's her?"

"The photo."

"It's getting late and my brain is tired. What are you talking about?"

"The girl in the brothel," Boyd said.

"Shh. Will you be quiet? What girl in what brothel?" Kirby whispered.

"That den of iniquity you brought me to the other night. The girl in the photo is the one I saw there."

"That's shite!"

"It's not shite. I told you I wasn't with anyone. I remember waking up on the stairs. But I saw her before I left. I could never forget those eyes."

"You're serious. Why has the boss got her photo up on the noticeboard?"

Boyd thought for a moment. What was Lottie on to? Who was this girl?

Kirby was breathing down his neck. "At least you got your wallet back."

"What? Yes." Boyd shouldered Kirby away from him and sat at his desk. He got out the wallet, opened it and slid out the piece of material he'd seen when he paid for his cigarettes. He spread it on the desk. Smudged writing. From what he could make out, it wasn't in English.

"What's that?" Kirby asked.

"Don't even ask. Go away."

Kirby shrugged and strolled over to his own desk.

Boyd stared at the writing. Was the girl sending a message? How was he going to explain this to Lottie?

He placed the material into a small plastic evidence bag and slipped it inside his wallet. Leaning into his chair, hands interlocked behind his head, he closed his eyes. How was he going to talk his way out of this one?

CHAPTER 52

Katie had attempted to cook dinner. Eggs, sausages and oven chips. Milot liked it anyway. Sean took his plate to his room and Chloe hadn't appeared from her bedroom.

"Later," she shouted from upstairs.

"You'll eat down here, miss. Downstairs. Now!" Lottie shouted.

"Did you contact anyone about Milot?" Katie asked.

"I left a message," she lied. "They'll probably ring me tomorrow."

"Tomorrow is Saturday."

"I know. I'll try them again in the morning in any case."

"I hope you find his mum."

"Me too."

Chloe refused to come down for dinner. Lottie was too tired to push it. But soon she would have to lay down the law and regain control. Soon.

When she was alone in the kitchen, she took the badge out of her handbag, turned it round and round in her hand. PARKER. It had to have belonged to Adam. But how had Mimoza got it? And then there was Dan Russell with his insinuations and threats. So many intrusive thoughts throwing up disturbing questions with no answers. Wandering around her kitchen, closing windows that had been open all day, Lottie knew she had to do something.

Her mother had boxed up most of Adam's stuff after he had died. "You don't want to be looking at this in the state you're in," she had said. Lottie would have agreed to anything to get her mother off her radar so that she could drink away her pain. Those boxes were now in Rose's attic. Could they hold the answers? Without rationalizing her actions, she made her decision.

"I'm going to Granny's. Be back in a while," she called up the stairs and ran out to her car. She had to do this before she changed her mind.

* * *

The gate creaked as she pushed it inward. No sign of life. Windows closed. Curtains drawn.

She rang the doorbell. No response. Her mother was probably out on her do-good chores with the homeless.

Lottie had her own key. She unlocked the door and entered the dusky hallway. It was hollow with silence. The aroma of coffee drifted toward her. In the kitchen, she held her hand to the kettle. Warm. A mug with a crescent of coffee in the bottom sat in the sink along with a plate and knife. The hum of the refrigerator the only sound breaking the silence.

"Mother?" Lottie shouted, her voice reverberating around the bungalow.

No reply. Good, she thought and went back to the hall. The attic was fitted with a fold-down ladder. Taking the rod from the top of the living room door, she placed it in the brass hole and pulled. The steps hit the tiled floor with a thunk.

Standing on the top step, she felt around and found the light switch. A cool yellow beam cast eerie shadows as she hauled herself into the confined area. No dust or cobwebs. Just oppressive heat. Boxes were stacked on shelves, color-coded, and a clipboard lay on the floor in front of her.

The list was in alphabetical order, with a color linked to each name. There were four with "LOTTIE" in red. She noted one with "DAD" in black, and another with "EDWARD" in blue. Her heart flipped at the thought of her brother. She dearly wanted to root around in those, especially since her mother was not around. But she knew she would have to leave them for another day. Her immediate conundrum consumed her enough.

She drew her eyes back to the first entry on the list: "ADAM," the color green marked beside it. She only wanted to touch some of his things. To feel close to him again. To eradicate the misgivings Dan Russell's insinuations had planted in her brain.

Bracing herself, she put down the clipboard and crawled further into the claustrophobic attic.

* * *

"You took your time. Hope you weren't trying to avoid me."

Boyd locked his car and glanced over at Jackie, leaning against his apartment door, smoking a cigarette. She held a bottle of wine in her other hand and wore skin-tight jeans, with a black halter top accentuating her leathery tan. Boyd didn't need Jackie in his life right now, but Lottie had tasked him to find out about Jamie McNally.

"What do you want?" He went to put his key in the door, thought better of it. Didn't want her following him inside.

"You never rang me. You promised we could talk."

So he had.

"It's been a tough day, Jackie. Can we do this tomorrow?"

"Every day is a tough day with you, Marcus. Never a good time to put me first. Will you ever change?"

"Where you're concerned, the answer is no."

"Narky boots. Let me in. Even if you don't want to talk, I do." She stubbed out her cigarette.

Boyd turned the key and ushered her inside. For once, he hoped his phone would ring, summoning him back to work.

Knowing how his day had gone so far, he doubted his luck would turn.

With his back to Jackie, he phoned Lottie. Maybe she could rescue him. No answer. He'd try again in a few minutes.

He sighed and looked at his not-yet-ex-wife. "Want a drink?"

* * *

Searching through the attic, Lottie found two plastic boxes with a green mark. Two boxes for Adam's stuff. Not much to show for a lifetime, even one cut short. She double-checked. "ADAM" was written in black marker on the side.

They were midway up the rack. A see-through crate of ceramic ornaments sat on top of them. Hefting down the heavy box, she placed it behind her. She blew out a breath and removed the first box of Adam's things. Her phone vibrated in her jeans pocket; she ignored it.

Beneath the cracked lid she was faced with bundles of sympathy cards. Don't look at them, she told herself. She hadn't read them at the time; she wasn't going to do so now. Placing them behind her, she knelt down to search through the remaining items.

A sheaf of bills, invoices and checkbook stubs. Funeral expenses. A pile of Adam's ties and socks lined the bottom of the box. They'd been scattered through the house, she remembered, and after the funeral she'd gone around picking them up, determined to throw them in the bin. Her mother had stopped her. One day you'll thank me, she had said. Maybe today was that day.

Lottie held a tie in her hand, still knotted. She'd regularly tied the knot for him. Adam could never get it right, always with the inside bit longer than the outside bit. Smiling, she laid it to one side.

She found two of his work notebooks and remembered how he was forever writing things down. Flicking through one, she gulped back a sob. His handwriting seemed so familiar, yet she hadn't seen it in such a long time. Dates, events, names, vehicle registrations. Military work. Every page was full. Adam hadn't liked waste. Memories floated in front of her eyes. But no tears. They had already been shed, too many of them. She forced herself to focus. The dates were for the year before he died. Nothing any further back. No use to her now.

Pulling down the second carton, she noted it was lighter. Photograph albums. Old and well thumbed. Holidays. Sun and smiles. Years of family. Christmas, first day at school, hurling matches, fishing. A previous lifetime but all very familiar. She became so engrossed in the memories she didn't realize how long she'd been looking at them until she heard the front door open and bang shut. She jumped involuntarily, and the albums on top of the pile slid to the floor.

"Lottie Parker, what are you doing up there?"

"I'll be down in a minute."

Hurriedly Lottie returned the albums to the box and gathered up the ones she had dropped. Beside them, a faded photograph lay on the chipboard floor. She picked it up.

"Oh my God!" she cried, looking at it in shock.

"Lottie! What's wrong? Are you okay?" Rose shouted from the bottom rung of the ladder.

She had to get out of the attic. Without clearing up the mess she had made, she scuttled backward on hands and knees and made her way down the steps. Ignoring her mother, she rushed out of the house and into her car, where she rested her head on the steering wheel. What the hell had Adam done?

CHAPTER 53

Even though it was an hour to midnight, the sky still held a steely blue hue. The full moon cast an eerie glow, highlighting the leaves on trees at the bottom of the garden.

After she had fled her mother's house, Lottie had flung herself into her kitchen armchair and slipped into an uncomfortable sleep. She was awakened by her mother phoning to see if everything was all right.

"Yes, I'm fine. I was looking through Adam's stuff. Something Chloe wanted for a project."

"Why did you run out like that?"

"I saw a mouse. Sorry. It just frightened me."

"There's no mice in my house, Lottie. I've got those electronic sensors to keep them out. You sure you're okay?"

"Yes, Mother. I'll talk to you tomorrow," Lottie said and hung up.

And now she was wide awake and prowling her kitchen like a lioness. She took a once-white T-shirt from a bundle of folded clothes in the utility room and, dragging off her sweaty one, slipped on the clean cotton. It was like cardboard, having been first soaked in the deluge and then dried to a crisp in the sun. But at least it was clean and smelled fresh.

She felt a growing urge to drown herself in alcohol but knew she couldn't. Her children were in their bedrooms and she ran up the stairs to check on them. Milot was fast asleep in Katie's room. Tomorrow she would have to sort things out for him. She didn't even care what Superintendent Corrigan would say when he found out. Maybe she should ring him to see if he was feeling better. Not tonight. Too late. Tomorrow. Everything could wait until tomorrow. In her own bedroom she took her last half-Xanax from her nightstand drawer and swallowed it dry.

Back in the kitchen, her phone vibrated. She paid no heed to it. It stopped. Silence. She filled a glass of water from the tap and sat down in the armchair again, folding her legs beneath her. She placed the photograph face down on one knee and Mimoza's envelope on the other. Taking out the badge, she felt its rough edges between her fingers then laid it on the arm of the chair. Only then did she turn over the photograph.

Adam in a strange living room, dressed in his overseas uniform. A pregnant woman and a girl stood either side of him. His arms were draped lightly over both their shoulders. Two small boys at his feet. Another little girl, maybe aged two or three, sitting among them. Adam wore a smile broader than she ever remembered.

She studied the photo more closely.

Who were they?

Why was Adam with them?

Who had taken the photo and why hadn't she seen it before?

And the badge. How had Mimoza got it? Why had she brought it to Lottie?

Her mind thrummed with the mystery of it all. She noticed the faded orange numbers in the bottom right-hand corner of the photograph. A date.

Her phone buzzed again, and when she didn't pick up, it vibrated with a message.

She took no notice of it. It was as if she were in a different sphere. She sat there until the moon dipped low in the sky and the sun began its morning journey upward.

* * *

When her mother had peered around her door earlier, Chloe
had pretended to be asleep.

All day long she'd lain in bed and fretted about Maeve
and what might have happened to her. She knew the girl was
in danger, that was if she was still alive. But how could she
tell her mother? *What* could she tell her? Every scenario she
encountered meant revealing the pain she herself was endur-
ing, and she wasn't ready to tell anyone about that. Not yet.
She certainly couldn't burden her mother with it.

But how could she raise the alarm about Maeve? She had
no concrete evidence about what might have happened to
her. Did she? Of course there was *him*. Was he really dangerous? He had frightened the life out of Chloe all right, but she
couldn't make up her mind if that made him evil or not.

Tapping her phone, she brought up Twitter, put #cutfor
life into the search. No, she warned herself. Don't look at it.
Don't engage with him. She thrust the phone beneath her
pillow.

She turned over in bed and stared at the ceiling. She lay like
that with her eyes open until the light of dawn burst through
her window.

* * *

Boyd looked on as Jackie finished her bottle of wine and proceeded to raid his refrigerator of beer. He sipped a vodka and
tonic, hoping to be alert to her seduction.

"You're here an hour, Jackie, and all I've heard is how soft
the sand is, how hot the sun is and how fab the shops are in
Malaga. Talk to me about McNally and why he's come back
to Ragmullin."

She shooed him along the couch and sat down beside him.

She'd long since thrown off her shoes and changed out of her tight jeans and into one of his shirts. She stretched her tanned legs across his.

"Time enough for talk," she said, pouring beer into her wineglass.

"I think you've had enough to drink."

"You're still trying to be the boss of me," she sulked. "No change there."

Boyd yawned. "I'm tired. I've work in the morning."

"On Saturday?"

"It's all hands on deck twenty-four/seven until we get the murderer. If you're not going to talk, I'm going to bed."

"Great suggestion." She drained her glass and stuck her bare foot into his crotch.

Boyd jumped up. "I'll get a blanket. You can sleep in my bed."

"Even better."

"No, I mean I'll take the couch."

When he returned with a spare duvet, Jackie was biting her lip, tears flowing down her cheeks. Raising his eyes to the ceiling, Boyd silently cursed and sat down beside her.

"Why did you come back? Why do you need my help?"

She wiped her nose in the sleeve of his shirt and slurred, "It's Jamie. He's different. I'm scared."

Boyd scoffed. "You ran off with him. You knew he was a low-life criminal. What's changed?"

Sniffing, she said, "I'm not sure. He's involved in something gross. He's being a bastard."

"Jesus, Jackie, McNally always was a bastard and he was always into shady dealings. You said he was smuggling women. Can you tell me about it?"

"I don't know anything. He just said he was coming to Ragmullin to sort out something that had got out of hand.

He mentioned a brothel run by someone called Anya. That's all I know."

Shit, Boyd thought. How was he going to nail McNally for this without implicating himself?

"How do you want me to help you?" he asked at last.

"Can I stay here?"

"For tonight only. I'll see if I can find out anything concrete on McNally tomorrow. Where is he staying?"

"We've a room at the Parkview Hotel, but he's hardly been there since we arrived. I don't know what he's up to." Jackie threw her arms around Boyd's neck. "You can protect me."

Boyd recoiled from her drunken lunge. He took the glass from her hand, gently extricated himself and rested her down on the couch. By the time he pulled the duvet over her, she was asleep.

Grabbing the bottle of vodka from the counter, he went to his room, leaving the door open.

* * *

Maeve Phillips had thought she was dead. Opening her eyes to the dark, she whimpered. No, not dead. Not yet. Tensing her arm, she tried to move. She could feel the cool cotton of a sheet, damp from her perspiration. Silently she prayed for someone to take her away. She thought death would be a welcome release.

A soft scratching in the ceiling above her head kept her awake.

Gulping down tears of pain, Maeve remained powerless against the nighttime creatures that were invading her mind.

* * *

Kosovo 1999

The mice were everywhere. The boy was more afraid now. Not of the mice. Of the captain, and that creepy doctor. He was even afraid of the boy who had drawn a finger across his throat in a death threat.

Suddenly a mouse ran across his face. He shouted out. The soldiers in the room curled up laughing. He felt his face heat up.

His soldier friend came and sat on his bed.

"I'm going home soon, so you need to be a bit braver."

"I go with you?"

"No, son."

Son? The soldier had called him son again. The boy smiled. "Please. I go with you." He pursed his lips in a sulk.

"Not possible. You know what? You remind me of my baby daughter with that pout of yours. I've two little girls waiting for me at home."

The boy said nothing, but a feeling of intense jealousy flushed his cheeks.

"Look, you're a strong boy. You'll get plenty of work in Pristina. But I will miss you."

The soldier flicked his name badge from his shirt. The boy held his breath.

"Here, have this. Remember, I'm your friend. You can pretend to be a big strong warrior."

Smiling widely, the boy took the badge, pride pumping through his heart. Maybe his friend would change his mind. Take him home with him.

The smile died on his lips when the soldier stood up, saying, "I hope there's a good family somewhere who will take you in."

The boy's heart deflated. No one wanted him.

The soldier pulled his rifle to his shoulder and kicked out at the fleeing mice as he left the room.

Feeling the stiff green canvas in his hand, the boy traced his fingers over the thick stitches of the soldier's name. He wondered about the strange little family the soldier had brought him to visit last night. Would they take him in? Probably not. They looked too poor. But his soldier friend had given them money to buy food. He'd even got the boy to take a photograph of them all. Would he show it to his baby daughter when he got home?

Jumping out of the bunk, he stepped straight down on top of a mouse. He hated the chicken farm.

He had to get out of here.

Soon.

DAY SIX

Saturday, May 16, 2015

CHAPTER 54

"What's this?" Jackie asked.

Boyd raised himself on his elbow then flopped back down on the bed. His brain hopped around in his skull. Through the open door he saw Jackie in the living room, wearing one of his shirts open to the waist, naked underneath, with his wallet in her hand.

"What's what?" he asked.

"This?" She held up a plastic evidence bag.

Boyd jumped out of bed, the thud of his feet on the floor resonating in his head. He pulled his trousers on over his boxers and moved toward her.

"What gives you the right to go through my things?" He swiped the bag from her and then his wallet. Scrunching the plastic bag back into the leather, he said, "Get dressed."

She placed a hand on his shoulder, pulled him close and ran her bare leg up along his.

Pushing her away, Boyd turned and reached for the kettle. "I've to go to work."

He turned on the tap, the flow of water drowning out Jackie swearing and stamping through to the bedroom. He almost didn't hear the doorbell.

"Shit. Could that be McNally?" he said.

"If it is, he's a greater detective than you are."

Jackie was dragging on her skin-tight jeans. Boyd lunged into the bedroom and grabbed her by the elbow.

"It better not be. What are you playing at?"

"Pity you weren't this riled last night." She twisted away from his grip and pulled her top on over her head.

Hastily he zipped up his trousers and dragged on a shirt.

"Coward," she said, smoothing down her hair.

The bell shrieked out a persistent ring.

"Open the fucking door!" Jackie shouted as she searched for her bag.

Sighing loudly, Boyd did as he was told.

A man he'd only ever seen in a mug shot stood outside. Darkly tanned, hair slicked back and wearing a black three-piece suit despite the morning heat. Jamie McNally reached in and punched Boyd in the face. He was slammed back against the wall and watched through a swelling eye as McNally stormed into his home.

Gathering his wits quickly, Boyd followed. "I didn't invite scum into my house. Get out or I'll arrest you. Both of you."

Gripping Jackie by the wrist, McNally stuck his face into Boyd's, but Boyd grabbed his tie and pulled him closer.

"Get your hands off her and get the fuck out of Ragmullin. Otherwise, I promise I'll have you behind bars. Assault of a detective, breaking and—"

"You and whose fucking army?" McNally broke free of Boyd's grasp and pursed his lips into a snarl. "I'm back to help out a friend because you lot can't do your fucking job. Do ya fucking hear me?"

As spittle landed on his face, Boyd couldn't stop himself; he lashed out, catching McNally on the side of the head.

Before McNally could fall to the floor, Jackie clasped his arm and pushed him toward the door.

"I'll get you, you skinny fuck-face," McNally said over his shoulder.

"You need to listen, Marcus," Jackie said. "Listen to what's being said." And she followed McNally.

"Jackie! Wait! Where..."

But she was gone. With McNally. Had she a choice? Maybe he should have done more to protect her. Fuck.

After slamming the door, Boyd leaned against it. He didn't know what to make of the confrontation, and despite his confused feelings for Jackie, he feared for her. Why hadn't he arrested McNally? Shit.

Glancing at his reflection in the hall mirror, he knew he was going to have a serious black eye.

He headed to the shower.

CHAPTER 55

Lottie walked into the office.

"Boyd!" she yelled.

"Yes?" He entered, phone in hand.

"What happened to your face?"

"What're you on about?"

Grabbing him by his shirtsleeve, she careened him back out the door and down the stairs to the deserted locker room. Leaning against her battered locker, she folded her arms and glared.

"You've been drinking," she said with a sniff. "I can smell it. You've got the beginnings of a black eye and you're twisting your hands like it's going out of fashion."

It unsettled her that he wouldn't look at her. His lips remained sealed.

"Talk to me," she said.

"I've fucked up." Boyd took a step back and sat on the wooden bench in the center of the room.

Lottie unfolded her arms and sat beside him. "That's a new one."

"I'm serious. The photograph you pinned up in the incident room yesterday of the girl and the little boy..."

"What about it?" Lottie asked. This wasn't what she'd expected.

"It's that girl you were looking for, isn't it? The mother of Milot?"

"How do you know that?"

"Where did you get the photo?"

"Dan Russell. Remember I met with him yesterday; he eventually admitted that Mimoza was resident in the center but that she'd disappeared with her son. There's something not quite right…" She stopped, recalling how Boyd had started the conversation. She stood up. "Wait a minute. How did you know that photo was of Mimoza? You've never met her. Have you?"

Boyd ran trembling fingers through his hair. "I think…I think I might have met her. I'm not sure, but—"

"Jesus, Boyd. Where? Is she okay? When did you see her?"

Boyd's shoulders slumped and he took out his wallet. From it he extracted a small plastic bag and handed it to her. She sat back beside him and turned it over in her hands.

"What's this? Evidence?"

"It's a message of some sort. Written on a piece of cloth. I can't understand the language. You'll need to get it translated and forensically analyzed."

Lottie stared and waited for more.

He said, "The other night, Wednesday I think, I got drunk with Kirby. We ended up at this place over on Hill Point."

"What place?" She had a bad feeling about this.

"Some sort of…brothel."

"For fucks sake, Boyd. You didn't go in? Did you?"

He nodded.

"You did?" The reality hit her like a slap in the face. "And Mimoza…she was there?"

"I didn't know who she was at the time. Nothing happened…I think…I'm sure. I left."

"That's not the point."

Lottie struggled to sideline her feelings for Boyd and the fact that he'd visited a whorehouse. Jesus! Mimoza's well-being was the most important thing now. But Russell had said she was in the DPC, so how could she be in a brothel? Bracing herself to be shocked, she immediately switched into professional mode.

"Tell me about the girl and how you got this note."

And Boyd told her.

* * *

Boyd parked the car and led Lottie to the apartment where the brothel was located. Normal life was evident around her. Children on bicycles, squealing. Two women chatting across a yard through open windows. A man with his head under the raised bonnet of a car while a little boy handed him tools from a plastic container. Daily routines continued while evil lurked behind closed doors, she thought, as Boyd climbed the steps of a grimy-looking block of flats.

"You know I should have brought Lynch or someone else with me besides you. Both of us could end up in deep shit," she said as Boyd pressed his finger to the bell. They waited a while but there was no answer.

Lottie put her hand to the door. It creaked inward. Glancing back over her shoulder at Boyd, she stepped into the hallway.

"Hello? Anyone home?" she shouted. Her voice echoed back at her.

"Lottie..."

"Shh." Putting her finger to her lips, she stepped further into the gloom.

"There's no one here," Boyd said.

She went into the room at the end of the hall. Empty. Up the stairs, Boyd trailing. They tried each of the doors.

"No one home, so," he said.

Was he relieved? Scowling, she asked, "Which room was she in?"

He indicated the open door. "I was on the stairs. I didn't—"

She shook her head. "Don't even try to justify your actions."

"I wasn't going to."

"Jesus, how do men come into dingy places like this?"

She pulled on protective gloves. After giving the room a quick check, she lifted back the sheet, tugged it from the end of the mattress. As she shook it out, she noticed the ripped hem.

"She wrote on a piece of this." There was nothing under the bed or in the room to warrant further investigation. "I don't suppose it's worth getting forensics in here."

Boyd just shrugged, head drooping. "I doubt it. But what spooked them to leave?"

"You, Boyd. You did. You leaving your wallet behind. God damn it. How are we going to find her now?"

"I think I know someone who might be able to answer that."

Lottie somehow followed his train of thought. "McNally?"

"Yes."

"He has something to do with this?"

"I think so. Jackie mentioned he might be involved in human trafficking."

"Do you know where he is?" Lottie edged out past Boyd. The suffocating room was giving her a headache.

Boyd said, "I had a run-in with him this morning."

"Where? You know we've been trying to locate him for a week."

"He came to mine looking for Jackie."

"She stayed the night? Jesus, Boyd, will you never learn?"

"It wasn't like that. She's scared of him."

"A likely story. Where is he staying?"

"Parkview Hotel. Though Jackie says he hasn't really been there. He must have somewhere else to hide out."

"You had him, Boyd. Why didn't you arrest him?"

"For what? He has no outstanding warrants. Instructions were to watch him. Now we know where he's staying."

"He assaulted you, didn't he?"

"Yes, but..."

"Too late now." Lottie relented. "We'll check out the hotel. Send the note for analysis and get it translated immediately. We need to find Mimoza and I need to talk to Superintendent Corrigan about her son."

"Don't say anything about—"

"I'll say what the situation dictates I need to say." Lottie wiped the sweat from her nose and shook her head. "You're a grade-A eejit, Boyd." She held her hand palm upward and stepped away as he was about to speak. "And don't even try to blame Kirby."

CHAPTER 56

"You feckin' what?"

The tubed light fitting rattled with the force of Superintendent Corrigan's roar. He stood up, then crashed back down into his chair, a squeal of air escaping from the leather. He looked worse than he'd done all week, despite his day off work. A cotton swab was plastered crookedly across his sore eye behind his spectacles.

"Things just got ahead of me and I had no time to deal with him." Without an invitation to sit, Lottie remained standing, arms folded, trying to make herself look full of a confidence she didn't feel.

"You didn't even make a phone call, let alone fill out a form." Corrigan swept his hand over his forehead in despair. "You know the shite we had to deal with before with that shower."

"I know, sir. That's one of the reasons why I don't want Milot going into the system."

"You have to go by the book. You can't give them a reason to crucify us. I'm disappointed in you."

"If you'd let me explain—" she began.

He cut her off with a raised hand. "No, Inspector. You leave me no choice."

Lottie dropped her hands, leaned on his desk.

"Choice? What choice does that little boy have? What choice does his mother have, wherever she is? What choice do those unwanted souls in the DPC have? Don't talk to me about choice. Don't. Sir."

Stopping to catch her breath, it struck her with alarming clarity what she'd done. Bawled out her superior officer in his own office. He looked at her coldly, the silence seeming to last an eternity.

"Inspector," he said at last, his voice way too soft. She was in deep shit. "Inspector Parker," he repeated, "I don't take kindly to being spoken to like that. You have some nerve. I honestly don't know what to do with you. While I'm making up my mind, contact that feckin' agency and get a social worker to the child. Find his mother. And don't ever, ever speak to me like that again. Do you hear?"

"Yes, sir."

"And put a uniformed officer on every site those contractors are working on. I don't want to give this killer any opportunity to bury another body."

"Yes, sir."

"We need to find the bastard before he kills anyone else."

"Yes, sir. Thank you, sir." Lottie turned to leave.

"Don't thank me. This is your very last chance. Feck up again and don't even wait for me to suspend you. Take it as given."

"Yes, sir."

Reaching her office, Lottie spotted Maria Lynch hard at work.

"Lynch, can you get me the Child and Family Agency on the phone. I need to speak to a social worker."

* * *

The incident room was buzzing as Lottie entered. The agency had told her that a social worker, Eamon Carter, would call to her home. She had succeeded in putting him off until late afternoon.

"First things first," she said. "Superintendent Corrigan

wants uniforms active on every site the contractors are working on. I'm not sure we can spare the personnel, but he's not in
the mood to be disobeyed."

She pinned up a photocopy of Mimoza's note from Boyd's
wallet. It might only be a cry for help, but maybe it could tell
her something more. The cloth had been dispatched for forensic analysis. She looked up as Kirby sauntered in, swigging
from a bottle of Coca-Cola.

"The stud has at last decided to grace us with his presence,"
she mocked.

Kirby, with the bottle halfway between his lips and his
belly, stood with his mouth open.

She saw Boyd shake his head. Taking the hint, Kirby went
to answer the nearest ringing phone.

"When you finish that call, I want to see the two of you
in my office," Lottie said. "I mean our office. And the rest of
you better find something concrete before this day is out. I
want a warrant to search the DPC. And go back over all
the door-to-door reports; read interview transcripts; cross-
reference everything we have; check all the CCTV cameras
that work in this godforsaken town. Find out who owns that
van and how it came to be in Weir's yard. Someone is missing
those girls. Someone somewhere saw something, even if they
don't remember seeing it."

Pausing for no more than a single breath, she pointed to
Officer Gillian O'Donoghue. "You, talk to every retailer with
rear business entrances onto Columb Street again. That body
didn't get buried by itself. And you"—she singled out another
uniformed officer—"re-interview everyone who lives on Bridge
Street where the first victim was buried. Same thing applies.
Someone saw something. This is no invisible killer, though I
swear to God it feels like it."

A phone chirped away unanswered in the silence. "And

someone answer that phone. Am I working with a crowd of children? Am I?"

"No, Inspector," came the collective answer.

"Well you better prove it to me. If my arse is on the line, you can be damn sure all of yours are too."

Feeling her face burning and her heart thumping double beats, she slammed out of the room and marched down the corridor with Boyd and Kirby close behind.

* * *

"Detective Lynch, I need a moment alone with these two," Lottie said. "And I want that note translated."

"Who will I—"

"I don't care who you get, just get it done."

Lynch picked up a stack of files and left with a shake of her head.

Turning to face her other two detectives, Lottie paused, allowing them to sweat a little more. Condensation slid down the bottle in Kirby's hands. He placed it on the nearest desk. Boyd's. She heard Boyd sigh; watched him lift it up and wipe away the ring of damp with his fingers. He threw the bottle into the bin.

"Sit," Lottie said.

They did.

Walking around the cramped office, she said, "I'm disappointed in the two of you. Visiting a brothel is unacceptable behavior for men in your position. I'm sure you don't need me to remind you of ethics, codes of conduct, et cetera, et cetera." Jesus, she thought, I'm not a great one to be lecturing on conduct.

Kirby's eyes bulged toward Boyd. Of course Boyd hadn't had time to warn him. Lottie pounced.

"Brothel? Mean anything to you, Detective Kirby? Hill Point brothel in particular."

She had expected his rotund cheeks to flush with embarrassment, but they drained of all color.

"And don't even attempt to deny it."

Kirby slapped around his breast pocket, searching for a cigar.

"As you appear to have been well acquainted with this house of ill repute, tell me who ran it and where the fuck they are now."

"I...I...I've no idea," Kirby mumbled.

"Oh but you have. Anya. Isn't that the name of the lady of the house? Detective Sergeant Boyd filled me in on what he knows. I'm waiting to hear what *you* know."

Shaking his head of bushy hair, Kirby appeared to be arguing with himself, without looking in Boyd's direction. Eventually he spoke.

"I just knew her as Anya. I'd only been there once before... before the other night. She's Albanian, I think. Had four girls working for her. I got the same one the twice I visited. So there might not be a big turnover of... women."

With her stomach somersaulting, Lottie looked away from him. How could this grown man, a law-abiding citizen, an enforcer of the law, engage in such activity?

"You have a long way to climb to get back in my good books, Kirby. A long, long way. Do you know if Jamie McNally is involved?"

"McNally? No, never heard him mentioned in relation to it."

"Well, you can start by finding out everything about this Anya. Who she worked for. Who supplied her girls. Where she is now. And McNally's role. Got it?"

"But that's a job for either the anti-human trafficking team or the immigration bureau," Kirby spluttered.

"If I bring them in, I'll have to land you and Boyd right in the middle of it all. Do you want that?"

"No, Inspector, but—"

"No buts in my vocabulary. Get to it. Now!"

"With all due respect, boss, what has this got to do with the murders?"

Lottie breathed in deeply and exhaled long and loud. "For all we know, it could have everything to do with the murders. Boyd, you saw Mimoza in the brothel. Right?"

"I'm almost sure it was her," he said quietly.

"Mimoza communicated with me via a letter. She left you a note. She can't speak our language so it's her only way of communicating. I'm sure she's the key to the two murdered girls."

"It's the only lead we have," he agreed.

She left them to it, and went to find where Maria Lynch had buried herself.

* * *

"The lad who translated for me before isn't in today. Google Translate tells me this note is someone asking for help. It is Kosovar Albanian, though." Lynch handed over a printout.

Lottie read: *Help me. Find my son. Asylum center.*

"It has to have been written by Mimoza. She has a son," she said.

"Where did you get this note from?" Lynch eyed her with a furrowed brow.

Lottie debated bringing her in on Boyd's role in the whole debacle, but decided the fewer people who knew the better. For now.

"Doesn't matter, but it confirms what we already knew. Mimoza and her son were resident with the asylum seekers at the direct provision center. She came to me originally looking for a missing friend, Kaltrina. I now suspect this Kaltrina is our second unidentified victim though I've no idea who the first victim is. Somehow Mimoza ended up in a brothel after escaping from the DPC. Her son was left on my doorstep. Around the same time, the brothel residents shut up shop and disappeared, Mimoza along with them."

"People can't just disappear like that."

"But they do. All the time."

Lynch pored over the file in front of her. She looked utterly exhausted.

"I'm sorry," Lottie said, "for working you so hard."

"It's fine. We have to find this killer."

Checking the time on her phone, Lottie saw she still had a few hours before her meeting with the social worker about Milot.

"I'm going to see if Dan Russell is at work today. He definitely has some explaining to do."

"Want me to come with you?"

"No. This is something I'm going to handle my own way. There are a few things he needs to clarify for me."

"What things?"

"Things you don't need to concern yourself with." Lottie shoved her phone into her jeans pocket and moved to the door.

"Inspector?" Lynch said.

Lottie turned.

"Be careful."

CHAPTER 57

Chloe opened the refrigerator, glanced at the empty shelves and closed the door again. "We need groceries, Katie, and shut that whining child up." She filled a glass of water from the tap and stared out at the garden.

"You know it's about seventy-seven degrees out. Why're you going around wearing long sleeves?" Katie asked.

"Mind your own business." Chloe stomped barefoot out the back door.

"Whatever," Katie said, soothing Milot on her knee.

Sitting on a garden chair, Chloe sipped her water and chipped away at the varnish peeling from the table. The smell of barbecued food blew across the fence. Proper families having a proper Saturday, she thought. Her family was anything but proper. A tear escaped and fell unhindered down her face. Surrounded by so many, she had never felt so alone.

A train rumbled slowly along the tracks above as it made its way into the station. Maybe she should buy a one-way ticket out of Ragmullin. Could she leave her stress behind? Dodge her exams and escape her mother? With no more varnish to pick at, she felt her nail move toward the skin of her arm beneath her sleeve. There she found an old scab and worried away at it until dark red blood stained the white cotton. She felt no pain. Just unending numbness.

Looking up at the trees sheltering the garden, she thought she saw something glinting in the sunlight. As if the sun had caught a mirror and reflected a laser back at her. Squinting, her hand shielding her eyes, she spotted it again. Was someone up there among the trees? Watching her? Was it him? She gagged at the memory of when she'd last seen him. She could feel the heat of his tongue in her mouth. Retching, she stood up quickly, dropping the glass. It shattered on the patio, the fragments glittering like icicles in the sun. The tiny shards cut into her bare feet. She skidded across them and fell into the kitchen.

"Chloe! You're a fucking asshole. There's blood everywhere. Mam will have a fit."

"Clean it up then if you're so worried."

Chloe continued through to the hall and up the stairs, tears and blood flowing with her.

* * *

He shoved the binoculars back into their case, zipped it up and scanned his surroundings. She had seen him. Stared right up at him. No, she couldn't have seen him. But she had looked directly at his position. Then he knew. The sun. It must have reflected off the glass of the binoculars. He should have been more careful. Stupid mistake.

He comforted himself with the thought that she would only have noticed the reflection of light. There was no way she could have seen him. His camouflage clothes against the greenery had done their job. Of course they had.

Hoisting the black leather bag onto his shoulder, he moved back the way he had come that morning. He knew the train times. He remained hidden until the Dublin express exited the station and picked up speed as it headed on its journey. Crossing over the tracks, he walked down the well-worn slope into the rear garden of a deserted boarded-up house. Keeping close to the fence, he removed his hat and tugged off his jacket, and ran his fingers over his sweating head. After putting everything into his bag, he walked out the side gate and on to the footpath. Whistling as he went, he mingled with the Saturday shoppers and smiled as he made his way to the place he now called home.

Maybe he should go to work.

That sounded like a good idea.

CHAPTER 58

"Inspector Parker. What a pleasant surprise." Dan Russell was leaning against his car, parked outside Block A. "Why don't you come up to my office?" he continued, smirking.

"I'm fine here." Lottie was determined to keep control of the situation. "I need to confirm a couple of things with you."

Russell ceased his smirking. "Okay. What is it you want?" he asked shortly.

"Mimoza. What have you done with her?"

"Have you found her yet?"

"Answer the question."

"I told you she was resident here, along with her son. Now they're gone."

"What did you do with them?" Lottie repeated.

"Nothing. They were awaiting processing and they just disappeared."

"Well I'm processing a warrant to search this building, in particular your office files. I want to know everything there is to know about Mimoza, and believe me, I will find it out."

He took a step toward her. Lottie held up her hand to stop him. Her handbag slid down her other arm and fell to the ground, spilling its contents, including the photo of Adam she had found in her mother's attic.

"What's that?" He pointed to the photograph.

"Nothing." She picked it up, shoved it back into her bag along with the rest of her stuff. "I need all the information you have on Mimoza. We've got a new lead."

"What new lead?"

"I believe the girl is in danger. I want to know where she came from, how she ended up as an asylum seeker. Why her name isn't on the official database."

"She should be on it."

"Well, she isn't. I've checked it myself. Do you maintain a list of your own? A list of people here separate from the asylum seekers, for instance?"

"That's a preposterous accusation."

"You yourself informed me that Mimoza had been here, but her name doesn't appear on the Department of Justice database. Explain that."

"There must be some mistake."

"Yes. And you've made it, Mr. Russell. A big mistake."

For a moment she thought he looked worried before he recovered his composure.

"Come up to my office," he said, walking away from her.

Lottie debated turning on her heel and getting as far away as possible. Or at least calling for backup. Common sense disappeared.

At the door to Block A, Russell stopped and turned. Lottie could see him grinning when he noticed she was following him.

"Mimoza's in a brothel," she blurted, determined to wipe the smile off his face.

Bingo!

"What are you talking about?" His face blanched.

"Right here in Ragmullin," she said.

"I'd no idea. Is that where she is now? Oh, that poor boy. Surely she hasn't got him with her?"

Chewing on the inside of her lip, Lottie wondered if this was some grand act he was putting on for her benefit. She had a feeling he knew exactly what she was talking about.

"Are you providing girls to this brothel?"

He fiddled with his keys, unable to meet her gaze. "Inspector Parker, you do not want to go down that road."

"What road?" she asked crisply. She had no time for games now.

He stepped into her personal space. He was so close, she was sure she could smell what he'd had for breakfast.

"I'm calling for backup," she said, tapping her phone. "I don't like your threatening tone."

"No need. Come in and I'll see if I can find that file." He headed for the door.

Lottie sighed. At last she was getting somewhere. "Okay. You'd better be quick, though."

At the bottom of the stairs, he looked back over his shoulder. "And I need to discuss your husband's antics."

"What the—"

"There is a connection between him and that little whore Mimoza." He marched up the stairs.

Lottie stared up after him. What connection? She looked around her wildly. She should leave. Go back to the station. Get reinforcements, backup. Boyd.

Not yet.

She had to know what Russell was talking about.

CHAPTER 59

"Ah, Jaysus, not you again. Go away."

Boyd lit his cigarette and tried to sidestep Jackie. She followed him round the back of the station.

"You shouldn't be here," he said.

"Look, Marcus, I'm putting my life at risk talking to you."

He stopped walking. She held on to his arm, her fingers pressing into his skin. Glancing around, he expected to see Rat-Face McNally jumping out at him.

"I've already got one black eye. I don't need a match for it."

"It's about Maeve Phillips."

That stopped him. Throwing down his cigarette, he grabbed her by the shoulder. "What do you know about her?"

"Not much. I meant to say it last night, but... you know. I think I drank too much wine."

"Go on."

"Her father asked Jamie to look for her."

"We know that already."

"But you don't know why."

"Okay. I'm listening."

"Maeve has been kidnapped."

"Bollocks, Jackie. Why would I believe you?"

"I swear it's the truth. It has something to do with Jamie and Maeve's dad's... activities, call it what you like. I overheard him on the phone this morning."

Boyd thought for a moment.

"Human trafficking? For sex?"

"Yeah."

"You're telling me someone has taken Maeve to put her into sex work?"

"No, you dumb prick. That's what Frank Phillips and Jamie are up to. But something has gone wrong with their business recently. I don't know if it's money or drugs or women. But they have their knickers in a twist over something to do with all the refugees coming into Europe. And I do know that Frank Phillips is extremely worried about his daughter's whereabouts. He asked Jamie to try and find out where she is."

"Why won't Phillips come here himself?"

"He'd be arrested. Then he'd be no use to Maeve. He can operate better from Spain. Anyway, Jamie was already in the country. On other business."

"What other business?"

"I don't know."

Boyd walked around in circles digesting what Jackie had told him. He knew there was a warrant out on Phillips for a post-office robbery in Dublin about ten years ago. That was when he'd fled to Spain.

"So Rat-Face McNally is involved in looking for Maeve Phillips."

"Don't call him that." She pulled a pack of cigarettes from her bag, lit one for Boyd and one for herself. "But I think so. He's only doing what you're doing. Going round in circles. You need to speak to Frank."

"Chance would be a fine thing. He absconded years ago; I don't think he'd come back now."

Jackie said, "It's his daughter. Look Marcus, I accept that you and I are finished, but I can try to organize things for you to find the girl. And then maybe you can help me get away from Jamie."

Boyd looked at the woman who had once been the love of his life. He had to agree that they were finished for good. But he couldn't let her swim away with the sharks. Even though she was doing it for selfish reasons, something told him she could be jeopardizing her own life by helping him.

"Don't look at me like that," she said. "Let me help you."

"Thanks, Jackie." Boyd took a long, hard drag on his cigarette. "We have a team heading up Maeve's disappearance. It's at top priority. So if you can get Frank Phillips to talk to us, it would be a great help. And then you can give us whatever info you have on McNally to get him arrested."

"Okay," she said. "I'll let you know if I can get Frank to agree to speak with you. Then I'll see what I can rake up on Jamie." She reached up and kissed his cheek.

Boyd watched her walk away, then raced back inside. He had to tell Lottie about this. Hopefully it would take the scowl off her face. Then he remembered she wasn't there.

CHAPTER 60

The fan was whirring incessantly in Dan Russell's office.

"Tell me about Adam," Lottie said. She remained standing. "How did you come to the conclusion that Mimoza is linked to him?"

Russell eyed her speculatively from behind his desk. "Show me the photograph. I know you want me to tell you about it."

"I want you to tell me what the hell is going on in my town. Murdered girls, missing girls, stolen girls. You have something to do with it all and I want to know what."

"I have nothing to do with it."

She slammed the photograph on to his desk and sat down. "I've no time for games. That's Adam, as you well know. You served with him in Kosovo. It was taken there."

"How do you come to that conclusion?"

"The date in the corner. So don't lie to me. You were there then. Who are these other people with Adam?"

"I don't know."

She studied him closely. He was lying.

He pushed the photo back toward her. "Don't concern yourself with it."

"The woman is pregnant," she said. "That young girl looks pregnant too. And the toddlers seem terrified. I want to know more about them."

Russell pushed back his chair and stood with a sigh.

"Those were bad times in Kosovo. Despicable times. Atrocities were committed. Genocide...ethnic cleansing took many forms. Not just murder. Systematic rape. I don't know, but I'd guess that woman was a victim of rape and maybe Adam was helping the family, or..."

"Or what?"

"Or he might have been the perpetrator."

Lottie jumped up, knocking over her chair. She stared at him. Was this the lie he'd been threatening to expose? She snatched up the photograph. "How dare you!"

He moved around the desk and stood with his face inches from hers.

"You don't know what that country was like. I'm warning you, if you keep trying to drag me into your outrageous investigations, I will not hesitate to expose what your precious husband was up to."

"You're bluffing."

"Don't push me. A rumor can gather legs, you know. You find Mimoza and her son, and no one has to know about Adam Parker."

"You're a liar and a bastard, Russell. An out-and-out bastard."

"I've been called worse."

"And why do you want Mimoza found so badly? You wouldn't even acknowledge her existence a few days ago."

He hesitated. "My company runs this facility. I can't be seen to be negligent or I'll lose the contract."

"That's bullshit and you know it."

"I know my business."

"Really? You lost a girl and her son." Lottie wasn't buying his excuses. Her brain whirred, trying to find an airtight reason to arrest him. Shit, she should have brought Boyd with her. "She has a friend. A small, black girl. I want to speak with her. Now."

She watched as Russell's face paled before he quickly regained his deadpan look.

"I don't know anything about her," he said.

"Don't worry. I'll find her." Lottie thought for a moment. "What did Adam do that I'm supposed to be so afraid of?"

"If I tell you now, I think it will complicate matters."

Making her decision based on nothing other than rage, Lottie took the envelope out of her bag and waved the canvas badge.

"Mimoza brought me this. I believe it was Adam's name tag."

"How? Where? The little bitch."

Russell made to grab it, but Lottie stepped back, clutching the badge tightly.

"Little bitch? Come on!" she said. "I've two unidentified murder victims. Were they living here with Mimoza and Milot?"

"Of course not."

Thinking about the murdered girls, Lottie recalled the articles she'd read online. "Organ trafficking was rampant in Kosovo during and after the war. The two victims were missing kidneys. You were in Kosovo. Now you're here." She paused. Her thoughts were beginning to line up cohesively. At last. "Shit, Russell. Just what the hell are you mixed up in?"

"You need to find Mimoza's son. That photo you have of Adam—I think Mimoza is the girl in it."

Lottie shook her head in confusion. All reasonable thoughts splintered as Russell pointed to the photograph she held in her hand. She looked down at it. The girl who appeared pregnant had eyes similar to Mimoza; even the older woman had the same eyes.

She said, "But she is aged—"

"I'd say about nineteen now."

"She couldn't be this girl. The age is all wrong."

"Not her," Russell said.

He took the photograph from her. Laid it down on the desk. With his index finger he picked out the little girl sitting on the floor beside the two small boys.

"There. That's Mimoza. If you find her, I won't release the information I might have about your husband."

"I don't understand." Lottie frowned at the photograph. "So this older woman is Mimoza's mother? Why is my husband in this picture? What happened to this family? And why is Mimoza here in Ragmullin now?"

"What do you think your husband was up to in Kosovo? You need to think long and hard before you start hurling accusations at *me* about illegal organ harvesting and trafficking."

Lottie whipped up the photograph and ran to the door.

"You can threaten me all you like, Russell. I'll be back with that warrant."

CHAPTER 61

The sun, burning through what was left of the ozone layer, reddened Lottie's skin. Ignoring the heat, she strode quickly, phone clasped to her ear, trying to make sense of Boyd's rambling while internally churning up after her encounter with Russell.

"Slow down, Boyd. Where are you?"

"Waiting for you. Lynch and Kirby went on ahead. Uniforms have the scene cordoned off."

"What scene?"

"Have you been listening at all? There's another body."

"Fuck. Who discovered it this time?" Lottie ran across the canal footbridge and up over the railway bridge. She could see him up ahead, walking in circles outside the station. She kept running.

"I don't know yet. Call just came in."

Out of breath, she reached him. "It has to be Petrovci."

She was still talking into her phone. Boyd took it out of her hand, pressed the disconnect button and slid it into her shoulder bag.

"Calm down," he said.

"How many times have I been told that in the last few days? Each time it just makes me certifiably insane." She kept pace with him as they hurried past the cathedral and down the street. "Why are we walking?"

"Town is mental. Roadworks everywhere fucking with the traffic. We're quicker walking." He lit a cigarette.

"I'll have one," Lottie said.

He handed over his. "What had Russell to say for himself?" He lit another cigarette.

"I'll tell you later."

"Tell me now."

"Later, Boyd. Later." She could hardly get her own head around Russell's revelation, let alone try to explain it to someone else.

They reached the end of the street and took a left turn toward Chloe's school. Lottie hoped her daughter was studying hard for her exams. She understood the pressure the girl was under—at least she thought she did—so she didn't keep on about it. She trusted her. Maybe not as much as she had five months ago, though. Chloe had changed. Another thing to deal with. But first she had a body to see.

"Thank God there are no schoolchildren around. But why are the contractors working up here? Jesus, Boyd, they're all over the town. I thought we had eyes on all the work sites."

Traffic was clogged both ways. Horns blaring. Drivers shouting abuse, with no idea that another poor soul had been taken from their midst. They'd probably still shout even if they knew, she thought.

As they approached the bridge, uniforms were directing the traffic back down the road. White-and-blue crime-scene tape dangled without a flutter. The air hung in a stagnant state of humidity. She thought she smelled the pungent zing of a storm in the air. Hopefully SOCOs could get the scene examined before the deluge began.

They dipped their heads under the tape. At the top of the bridge Lottie surveyed the activity below. Beside the old lock gates, officers were erecting a tent against a building.

"Maybe it's a drowning. Or a suicide?" She couldn't see a body.

"I know as much as you do."

She reached Kirby first. "What's going on?"

"There's an old pump house over there. The contractors use it for storage. Two of the workers were fixing a lock and one of them noticed the body."

Behind Kirby, Lynch was taking notes from a tall man who had his back to Lottie. There was a familiarity about his stance, the way he held his head at an angle. Those broad, hardworking shoulders under his hi-vis vest.

She didn't need to see his face to know who had found their third body that week.

* * *

As if the gods, or indeed the devil himself, had ordained it, angry clouds blotted out the sun and sharp drops of rain spilled from the sky. No one had a jacket or an umbrella.

We're all going to get drenched, and worse still, evidence will be washed away, Lottie thought. She stood transfixed as Lynch grilled Andri Petrovci. This was no coincidence. He had been present at the discovery of their two previous murder victims. And here he was again at the scene of another suspicious death. His colleague had his head sunk into his chest, hands deep in his pockets.

Lottie needed time to gather her momentum to tackle Petrovci. Joining Boyd and Kirby at the entrance to the hastily erected tent, she asked, "What's the story?"

Kirby said, "Deceased female. Found inside the old pump house. From what we can gather from Jack Dermody, Petrovci's boss over there, she was lying behind an old excavator. They hauled her outside, thinking she could be revived. But one look at her in daylight, Dermody said, and he knew she was beyond CPR."

"Did Petrovci touch her?"

"The two of them carried her outside the door. Said the light wasn't working inside."

"Contaminating the body *again*." Lottie shook her head. She moved toward Petrovci but Boyd held her back by the arm, his fingers sliding down her wet skin.

"Let Lynch deal with the two of them for now," he said. "She's more than capable."

"And I'm not?" She swung around, rainwater flying from her hair.

"I'm not saying that and you know it." He lifted up the tent flap. "We need to see the body."

Lottie relented, and they pulled on gloves and overshoes. Before entering, she looked around the scene, spying Cathal Moroney remonstrating with uniformed officers guarding the site. "That's all I need," she muttered, making her way into the interior of the tent.

* * *

The body lay at an awkward angle, facing skyward, beside the red-brick wall of the old pump building.

"Recognize her?" Boyd asked.

Lottie stared. "It's not Maeve," she said.

"It's not Mimoza either."

She inched closer, careful not to disturb anything that might incur the wrath of Jim McGlynn and his crime-scene team, though she supposed it was too late now that Petrovci and company had had their hands all over the victim.

"Why wasn't she buried like the others?" she murmured.

The girl's eyes were closed and her body looked like a discarded rag doll. "Wish I could turn her over to see if she was shot in the back like the others. Look at those marks on her face and neck."

"Bite marks?"

"Looks like it. The first victim had similar marks, though

not as violent-looking. Jane got no DNA from the swabs." Lottie crouched down for a closer look. "Boyd, I think she could be the girl who was with Mimoza the morning she called to my house."

"Really? But you didn't get a close look at her, did you?"

"No, I didn't. I'm just saying she *could* be the same girl."

Boyd said, "We don't know the cause of death yet. Maybe she fell into the canal and then dragged herself into the pump house?"

"Such a beautiful girl. And if she's like the others, there'll be no one to claim her damaged body."

Boyd shook his head and ducked out of the tent. Lottie followed, and while Boyd waited for Jim McGlynn, she decided it was time to talk to Petrovci, the common denominator between all the victims.

As she reached him, he turned to face her. The scar on his face appeared more pronounced, deeper and darker in the rain. But his eyes were the same. Filled with pain and hurt.

"Mr. Petrovci. We meet again." She folded her arms.

"I tell detective." He pointed to Lynch, who was desperately trying to shield her notebook from disintegrating. Rain dripped from Petrovci's ears and nose. His T-shirt and singlet clung to his chest. Hands deep in sopping-wet jeans pockets. Black work boots covered in mud.

"Tell *me*," Lottie insisted.

He sighed but kept his lips tightly shut.

Lynch swung round to Lottie. "Mr. Dermody informed me they drove here to fix the lock and discovered the body. Together."

"When were you at this location before today?" Lottie directed her question to Dermody.

The man was a shivering wreck. "A few days ago. A week maybe. I'm not sure."

"Was it secured?"

"No. Lock was busted. We got a call to come and fix it this morning. Decided to pick up some tools at the same time. She's dead, isn't she? The girl."

Lottie nodded.

Lynch closed her sopping notebook. "That's the general gist of what he told me."

"This call you got. Who was it from?" Lottie asked Dermody.

"Some geezer from head office, I presume. I didn't know the number but he seemed to know what he was talking about." He stopped, his mouth hanging open. "You don't think..."

"At the moment, Mr. Dermody, I don't know what to think. And you?" Lottie inquired of Petrovci. "What have you to say?"

Andri Petrovci pulled his hands out of his pockets and raised them to the skies. "It evil," he cried. "So evil. Why I have to see all these bodies?"

"Do you know who this girl is?" Lottie asked him briskly.

Petrovci shook his head.

Lottie sniffed. "She was lying there waiting for you to come along and find her, was she?"

"I not know. She just there. Like she... asleep." His shoulders slumped. He looked small and beaten.

"I don't understand how you have found three bodies in the space of a week," Lottie said. "It makes no sense. Unless..."

"What?" he implored.

"Unless you killed them."

The wail from his lips took her by surprise and she stepped back as if his scream had physically propelled her. Words flowed from him. Unintelligible words. A language she had no knowledge of. Rain continued to fall in torrents. The ground at their feet swelled with turbid waters. The skies cracked with a flash of lightning and the air splintered with the explosion of thunder. It was not long past midday, but suddenly it was dark.

Petrovci screamed. "*Ju lutem!*"

Lottie said, "What is wrong with you? Take him to the station, Lynch."

The scene around her was like a negative. Everything inverted and obscure. With another streak of lightning cracking the black sky like shattered crockery, she wondered, had she been looking at this the wrong way round the whole time?

CHAPTER 62

In a blaze of blue flashing lights and screaming sirens, Detectives Lynch and Kirby took Andri Petrovci and Jack Dermody to the station to escape the rain and impatient reporters. Lottie ordered the two men's phones to be logged, then examined by the technical team. She wasn't sure what Petrovci had done, if anything, but having observed him becoming unhinged, she decided he needed to be in the safety of the station and checked over by a doctor before any further questioning.

She joined Jim McGlynn as he arrived on site. The rain had eased a little but the smell of thunder still lurked behind menacing clouds. Her clothes clung to her body, but she was oblivious to the dampness.

"Let's have a look at what you've cooked up for me today," McGlynn said.

Lottie followed him to the tent. He was suited up but she felt it was too little, too late. Everything had been contaminated, and anything that hadn't been was now washed away in the biblical deluge.

Boyd held the flap open and the two of them peered in as McGlynn began his work. His gloved hands measured and touched. He noted and muttered. Photographed. Eventually he flipped the dead girl gently onto her side.

Lottie stared at the girl's back. Beneath the thin cotton of her dress she could see the outline of a deep hole below her ribs.

McGlynn said, "You have another one. State pathologist will be here shortly."

"Shot and dressed," Boyd said.

"Shot and dressed," Lottie agreed, holding back her hand from smoothing down the crumpled dress.

* * *

Once the pump house had been searched, SOCOs began sweeping the old dirt floor for evidence. Lottie was convinced they wouldn't find a thing pointing them to the killer. Leaning against the outside wall, she thought of bumming a cigarette from Boyd. A shout from inside stopped her.

"Found something!"

She hurried back inside. A SOCO stood in front of a rusted piece of machinery. He looked like a ghost in his paper-thin white crime suit. In his gloved hand was something that Lottie instantly recognized.

Slowly she took a step toward him. He shook his head and opened an evidence bag, into which he dropped a soft, tatty toy rabbit. Just like the one Milot had. It was covered with blood.

* * *

Lottie rushed out of the pump house. She had to get back to the station.

"Inspector! Inspector, what's going on?" Cathal Moroney shouted from the outer cordon. He was standing in front of a scrum of journalists. Media vans, satellite dishes sticking up from their roofs, lined the road behind them.

She couldn't ignore him—she had to walk past him to get to the waiting patrol car.

"No comment." Keeping her head low, she continued up the canal bank toward the car. He clipped along at her heels, an eager posse of journalists behind him.

"Are the organs cut out of this victim also?" he shouted.

Where had he heard that from? He was persistent, she had to give him that. She kept on walking. He kept on talking.

"Is there a butcher stalking Ragmullin at the moment? Is it a serial killer?"

Lottie had had enough. She squared up to the journalist.

"The only one stalking anyone in Ragmullin at the moment is you, *Mister* Moroney. And if you continue shouting unsubstantiated statements like you've just done, I'll have you arrested for impeding my investigation. Got it?"

He stood with his mouth open, but quickly recovered. "So you're not denying there's a serial killer, then?"

"I'm not even going to dignify that with an answer. Now get out of my way."

She'd heard enough for one morning.

CHAPTER 63

Standing with Boyd in the station's makeshift kitchen, Lottie sipped a lukewarm coffee.

"Why did the killer put her in the pump house?" she said.

"He couldn't bury her in one of the existing excavation sites because we have them guarded," Boyd said.

"We only put uniforms on the sites today."

"I'd like to know how he picks where to dump the bodies."

"And are we ever going to find out who these victims are?" Lottie asked. "What about Milot's toy? What was it doing there?"

"You said you recognized today's dead girl from the morning Mimoza came to your house. Could she have delivered Milot to you?"

"I'm beginning to think so. She must have thought he was in danger. Maybe she forgot to bring his toy. But then why would the killer leave it with her?"

He shrugged.

"Boyd, I think the killer desperately wants to find Milot. I think it's Dan Russell. He seems very anxious about the boy. Perhaps he planted the toy with the body. Baiting us. He thinks we will lead him to the child."

"You really think it could be Russell?"

"Possibly. This victim was tortured." Lottie cradled her mug, grimacing. "You saw the bite marks . . . they were vicious. We need to go back over all the evidence. There's something there to lead us in the right direction."

"At this stage, I don't know what direction we are going in."

"Be positive," Lottie said. "We'll review everything." She put her mug into the basin.

Boyd picked it up and splashed in water from the kettle to rinse it out.

"Lottie, I saw Jackie earlier today..." he began.

"You don't have to explain anything to me."

She stared at him for a moment. With his saturated shirt clinging to his body, his short hair sleek from the rain and his black eye shining in the unnatural light, she thought he was the most handsome man she had met since Adam. Adam! Dear God, what had he been involved in? Had their life together been a complete lie? A gasp escaped her throat and she struggled to keep her tears in check before Boyd misread her.

"We need to talk," he said.

"Yes, we do. Change of clothes and incident room in five minutes. Team meeting."

She marched down the corridor without a backward glance. She knew he was watching her every step, waiting for her to come back to him.

Fuck you, Boyd. She kept on going.

* * *

Her team, all seated and eager, looked like Labradors ready to escape the leash. She would give them something to get their teeth into. The T-shirt she had changed into was the last one in her locker. Too tight and too short. Her jeans would have to do. She'd get another pair when or if she returned home. Her shoes were ruined, so she'd pulled on her boots.

Lynch reported first. "Duty doctor has given Mr. Petrovci a sedative. He's resting in a cell. I've put a guard outside. Just in case."

The holding cells were part of the new block and Lottie

knew there was nothing there that Petrovci could use to harm himself. Still, it was essential to have someone watch him.

Lynch continued. "Jack Dermody made a statement. He got a phone call at eleven thirty-five a.m. telling him to go to the pump house and fix the lock. His phone is being checked as we speak. He said Petrovci always works with him, so he was the obvious choice to bring along. Health and Safety procedures. When they got there, he went inside to check nothing was missing and to pick up some tools, and that's when he saw the body."

"Hold him for a while longer. See if he changes anything." Lottie glanced at the incident board. It now held a photograph of their most recent victim. "Let's recap on what we have and haven't got."

She marched along the floor, scanning the incident noticeboards.

"In addition to our two murder victims, the girl just found will be confirmed as murder later today. She has a gunshot wound to her back."

"Another one," Officer Gillian O'Donoghue said.

"Exactly. Three girls, none of whom has been reported missing. All shot in the back. The first two have had a kidney surgically removed, and victim number one was four months pregnant. The media circus, courtesy of that clown Moroney, now know about the organs being removed and are reporting it as a serial killer."

"Isn't that what we've got?" Boyd said.

"We didn't want the whole world knowing. Not until we had something substantial to bring to the public."

Lynch said, "We have a suspect currently sitting in the cells."

"I know. But I thought I asked for absolute secrecy on the organ removal issue." Lottie's eyes landed on Kirby. He'd been the source of information leaking to Moroney on her previous case, though he'd claimed it was accidental.

He shook his head, letting her know he wasn't the leak this time.

She sighed. "All I'm asking is that you do your jobs without causing panic on the streets. Okay?"

Murmurs rippled through the room.

"I'll get the press office to write up a piece. Try to keep the media chasing their own tail, not ours."

Kirby grunted but said nothing.

"These victims," Lottie said. "No one, not one single person, has reported them missing, so it is increasingly likely they were from the direct provision center."

Kirby said, "We've checked the official database and according to the Justice Department it's up to date. All accounted for."

"I believe there is an unofficial one. In the last few days I've become aware of a girl missing from the center." She pointed at Mimoza's picture, swallowing hard. She knew that once she went public with this, Russell could release the information he had on Adam. But the image of the soft toy rabbit and Milot with cherry blossoms stuck in his hair was more urgent. Whatever damage Russell intended, it affected the dead, not the living.

Coughing to clear her throat, she continued, "Mimoza hasn't been officially reported missing. However, Dan Russell has asked me to investigate. So we need to expedite that warrant to search the building, in particular the computers."

"It's down for the district court first thing Monday morning," Boyd said. "But I can't understand why Russell would want you to investigate Mimoza's disappearance if he's involved in these murders?"

"I don't know, but he also expressed concern for Mimoza's young son Milot."

"A missing child adds a new dimension," Lynch said.

"He's not missing," Lottie explained. "I know where he is." She remembered then that she had an appointment soon with the social worker.

"Phew," Lynch sighed. "Where is he?"

"You just need to know that he's safe. But SOCOs found a toy rabbit belonging to him at the site of the body discovered today."

"What?" A communal gasp.

"How can you be sure it belongs to the boy?" Kirby asked.

"Frayed label and ears. It's his." Lottie took a deep breath. "I don't know what it means yet. But bear it in mind when investigating the latest murder. I've also reason to believe Mimoza was kept for a time at a brothel. Detective Kirby, have you found out anything about this Anya who apparently ran the place?"

Kirby blushed bright red. "She's disappeared. We think she operated under a number of aliases. We've put the call out to ports and airports. But she's probably back in Albania by now. Neither sight nor sound of her or any of her girls. I ran it by anti-human trafficking and the other relevant bureaus. Nothing."

"Dead end." Lottie tapped another photo. "Maeve Phillips. Daughter of known criminal Frank Phillips. She was last seen over a week ago. No sighting of her anywhere despite widespread media alerts. We don't know yet if there is a connection to the murders or indeed to the recent disappearance of Mimoza."

"I think she is connected," Boyd said, shoving his hands in his trouser pockets.

"Explain," Lottie said, folding her arms.

"I tried to tell you earlier, but...Information has come my way that points to Jamie McNally's involvement with the brothel. Something was going wrong with the business; that's why he's in Ragmullin. It's hearsay, but I believe my source. We have an officer at the Parkview Hotel, where McNally's staying, but he hasn't been seen there all day."

Lottie held his gaze. "And Tracy Phillips told me McNally was at her house inquiring about Maeve's disappearance. Anything else to share?"

Boyd looked like he was about to speak, but shook his head.

"I tend to agree with DS Boyd regarding McNally's involvement with the brothel," Lottie said finally, clenching her fists under her arms to hide the fact that she was fuming at his reticence to share anything further. She'd get him on his own later. "Now, on to the blood and bullet hole in Weir's depot. Any updates?"

Kirby stood up, and as if the action made him feel awkward, promptly resumed his seat. "The blood isn't human. We think it's from an animal, maybe a fox. It's the same with the blood found in the white van. So that's a dead end."

"Interesting," Lottie mused. "Is the killer trying to distract us?"

"I took Buzz Flynn to see the van," Kirby said. "He lives down the road from the depot. Said it looks similar to the one he saw in the early hours of Tuesday morning when someone was picking up road signs. I double-checked with the security company. It's definitely not one of their fleet. But Buzz is elderly and he had been asleep, so I'm not sure about his accuracy."

"So who brought the van into Weir's yard?" Lottie scratched her chin and squinted down at Kirby.

"Weir says he paid some guy fifty euros for it. The bloke wanted it taken off his hands. No records. No recollection of who brought it in. Just remembers handing over a fifty. And I only got that info by threatening to arrest him for perverting the course of justice. Oh, and as you know, his CCTV is on the blink."

Lottie snorted her derision. "Why bury the body outside Weir's depot and then drop the van off there too? What type of lunatic are we dealing with?"

Boyd piped up. "We don't know for sure it was the killer's van."

"I think it was. He's playing mind games with us. Trying to show us he can do just about anything he wants. Like killing victim three and throwing her body into the old pump house as if she was a rotting fish." Lottie paced around the incident room. Everyone was silent. "Ignore the van. No point in wasting resources we don't have."

"But—" Kirby began.

"No buts. It's a diversion tactic. I'm sure of it. No more time wasted on the van for now."

"Right, boss." Kirby let out a grunt.

Lottie said, "Another thing I noticed. And this should be confirmed at the autopsy. I believe this latest victim was tortured. Her body has evidence of severe biting."

"But why?" Lynch asked.

"No idea. The first victim had one bite mark on her neck, but this latest victim has bites all over her face and neck. More frenzied. It adds a new dimension."

"We've enough fucking dimensions driving us all demented," Boyd exclaimed.

Letting her gaze land on Lynch, Lottie said, "We still haven't found the actual crime scenes where the girls were shot. Any information on that score?"

"No. Sorry." Lynch dipped her head.

Lottie said, "The moss under the murder victims' nails. Where did it come from?"

"It's the only clue left on the bodies," Boyd said.

"If the killer washed the wounds, he probably washed the bodies," Kirby said.

"He undressed them to shoot them, then washed and re-dressed them," Lottie said. "That's why Jane Dore couldn't get anything from the bite marks." She considered this. "He shot them somewhere no one would hear. A boggy field? A wood?"

"Has the moss been analyzed?" Boyd asked.

Lottie flicked through the forensic reports.

"Found it." It had been emailed that morning. She read through two pages. "Jesus, why didn't we get this earlier?"

"What?" asked Kirby.

"There are traces of crypto...I can't pronounce it." She spelled it out.

"Cryptosporidium," Lynch said. "Hold on, I'll google it."

"What did we do before Google?" Boyd said.

"A microscopic parasite that causes diarrhea." Lynch said. "Blah, blah, blah. Wait a minute. The parasite can be spread in several different ways—drinking water and recreational water. Swimming pools, lakes and rivers."

"That narrows it down," Boyd said sarcastically.

"It's unlikely these girls were taken to a swimming pool to be shot, so that leaves us with lakes and rivers." Lottie glared at him.

"Ragmullin is surrounded by lakes," he said.

She thought for a moment. "Lynch, go through every record we have of reports of unusual activities in or around all the lakes. Find out the dates of the shooting season and check with the county council to see if there's been any outbreak of crypto..."

"Cryptosporidium," Lynch prompted as she unfurled her ponytail. "What about all this?" She waved at the mound of interview transcripts on her desk.

"Leave it. This is urgent. Check back for about two weeks."
Lynch tied her hair back and grabbed the phone.

"It might be nothing," Boyd said.

"Don't go all pessimistic again," Lottie said.

"Well, just don't get your hopes up."

She studied the photographs. "Three girls are dead. Murdered. And we don't even know their names. Come on, lads. Cathal Moroney's telling his viewers there's a serial killer stalking Ragmullin. Butchering people for their organs."

"The internet is awash with new rumors," Kirby said, tapping his phone. "Twitter and—"

Lottie cut him off, "We need answers, not speculation. As soon as Jane Dore has the latest postmortem completed, we go public with what we have. And I want the victims' photographs everywhere. After Andri Petrovci, Dan Russell is our main suspect. We need something to bring him in. Get that warrant expedited, Boyd. Maybe the public will help—"

A ringtone cut through Lottie's words, causing her to lose her train of thought. She stared daggers at the assembled team. Boyd made for the door, phone to his ear.

"Detective Sergeant Boyd!" Lottie yelled.

But he was gone.

CHAPTER 64

She caught up with Boyd in their office as he finished his call.

"This'd better be good," Lottie began, standing with her hands resting on her desk.

"Jackie says Frank Phillips will talk to us. In person. Tomorrow."

Lottie expelled pent-up anger with a burst of air through her nose. A few deep breaths before she could talk.

"I'm not sure Phillips has anything to do with three murders in Ragmullin seeing as he is currently sunning his arse in Spain," she said.

"His daughter is missing. He's sent his head honcho McNally to look for her. He wouldn't do that lightly." Boyd sat at his desk and pulled on a tie he found in his desk drawer.

"Boyd, Frank Phillips's head honcho, as you call him, has been in Ragmullin since last Wednesday week. Before Maeve went missing."

Boyd paused with his hand mid-air before bringing it down to his chin. "I know that, but he was here to look into Frank's business affairs."

"That's what Jackie told you. Can you honestly believe her, Boyd?"

He didn't answer.

She said, "We need to know his real reason for being in Ragmullin."

"So we should meet Frank Phillips anyway?"

"Yes, I think so. It can't do any harm. What flight is he

getting? We'll meet him at the airport." Lottie sat at her desk, pulled out a bottom drawer and rested her feet on it.

"He's not coming to Ireland because then we'd have to arrest him. We've to go see him." Boyd sat down on the corner of Lottie's desk. "In Malaga."

"You're joking."

"He might be able to throw some light on these murders. Why else would he talk to us? It can't do any harm. Can it? Would you at least ask Corrigan?"

Ignoring the pleading in his voice, Lottie grabbed her bag. "I've a social worker to meet about Milot."

Boyd followed her to the door and blocked her way. "Jackie is scared. There's something big going on here, but she doesn't know what it is. I think we have to go talk to Frank Phillips."

"Why can't his wife talk to him? It's their daughter."

"This has to do with more than Maeve."

"*You* ask Corrigan, then. If he approves it, we'll go, otherwise it's a no. For now, see if Petrovci's medically fit and get Lynch or someone to interview him with you. And go back over everything. We've missed something important, Boyd. Find it. That will serve us better than flying to Malaga."

Superintendent Corrigan appeared outside the open door.

"No one's flying to feckin' Malaga. No one!"

* * *

When Lottie got home, Milot was sitting on the couch beside Katie watching Cartoon Network. He was dressed in a new T-shirt and trousers. Lottie questioned her daughter with a raised eyebrow.

"I asked Chloe to go into town and get him something to wear," Katie said. "She wouldn't budge. Sean went and got him these. Only eight euros."

"Sean? That's great. Though I wish I knew what's bugging Chloe."

"Have you time to cook something for dinner? Granny hasn't appeared today and he won't let me out of his sight." Katie hugged the boy.

"Maybe chips?" Lottie said. "You like chips, Milot?"

The little boy stared up at her, his wide eyes soft with unshed tears. Missing his mummy. God, she thought, where would he end up once he was taken into care? She hoped he'd at least be safe from the likes of Dan Russell.

"Where are Sean and Chloe now?" she asked.

Katie glanced toward the ceiling.

"Be back in a min." Lottie flew upstairs to check on them.

Sean's headphones blotted out her query about what he wanted for dinner, so she made for Chloe's room. The door was locked.

"Chloe, let me in."

"Go away."

Leaning against the wood, Lottie tried again. "Please, Chloe. Open the door."

"I'm studying. Talk to you later."

With a heavy sigh, Lottie gave up and headed for the shower. Even though it was warm out, she was shivering since the soaking she'd got at the pump house. Tiredness chewed through her bones. Eventually the water eased her flesh. She pulled on clean clothes and felt ready for the social worker.

Entering the kitchen, she noticed a trail of dried blood leading to the back door. It appeared streaked, as if someone had unsuccessfully tried to clean it up.

"Chloe! Katie! What happened in here?" she yelled.

A door opened upstairs and Chloe ran down to the kitchen. "I let a glass fall and stepped into it."

"Are you okay? Let me have a look."

"No! Go away." Chloe held out a hand, backing away.

"What's going on with you? Is it the exams?" Lottie asked.

"What exams?"

"Don't be smart with me, missy."

"I'm trying to study, and the minute you come home it's a row," Chloe snapped. "Always the same." She glanced into the refrigerator, but finding nothing she liked, slammed it shut and turned toward the hall.

Lottie caught her by the arm. "Don't talk to me like that."

"Whatever." Chloe wriggled out of her grasp and fled up the stairs.

Standing with her mouth open, Lottie caught sight of Milot at the sitting room door, choking away sobs, tears flowing down his cheeks.

Before she could comfort him, the doorbell rang.

* * *

The man on the doorstep looked too young to be a social worker. That was Lottie's first impression. Too young to be dealing with all this shit.

He showed his ID and she welcomed him in, apologizing for the mess. Katie had picked up Milot before Lottie opened the door, and was comforting him in the sitting room.

He introduced himself as Eamon Carter and sat at the kitchen table. His blonde hair was neatly trimmed around small ears. Lottie thought the stubble on his chin was by design, like the skinny black trousers he wore.

"Tea?"

"A glass of water would be good," he said in a sharp Dublin accent. "It's sweltering out there again."

She let the tap run until the water was cold.

"In the job long?" she asked.

"A couple of months," he replied.

Not long enough to have got used to the harshness of the work he was embarking on. Such an inexperienced young man to be tasked with the difficult case of Milot. She silently wished him luck.

"Now, about Milot," he began and opened a file with a solitary page. "He turned up on your doorstep and you have no idea where his family might be. Do you know them?"

"His mother initially called with him last Monday morning. She had a query for me to sort. I had never met her before and I haven't seen her since. Her name is Mimoza Barbatovci, and I believe she's resident in the direct provision center in town."

"And you've tried—"

"Yes, I've made inquiries. She seems to have disappeared." Suddenly Lottie thought of the toy rabbit found beside their third victim. Once she handed Milot over, the killer could easily find out his whereabouts. She couldn't risk his life. "Eamon, it's Saturday and it must be hard to find places for very young children at the best of times. Why don't you leave the boy here, for the weekend at least? Give yourself time to find him a proper placement and me time to locate his mother."

He rubbed a hand over his mouth and down his chin. Thinking.

"Can I see the child?"

"Sure."

Lottie went to get Milot. When she returned, Eamon was scribbling notes in the file.

He looked up. "Hello, little man." The boy snuggled his head into Lottie's shoulder. Carter continued, "He seems comfortable here. Where would you get the time to look after him?"

Katie walked into the kitchen. "I'll help out." She flashed a wide grin. Carter blushed.

Lottie mouthed a thank-you to her daughter.

Carter fiddled with his phone and dialed a number. He waited impatiently, tapping his pen on the table. "No one answering."

"What are you going to do? Milot is perfectly safe here." I hope, Lottie thought.

"This is against all my training but I think I'll make an...an executive decision." He drank the remainder of his water. Lottie held her breath. "You can keep him here until Monday. If his mother hasn't turned up by then, I'll have to place him with a registered carer or in a foster home. I'll work on it over the weekend."

Katie ran forward and whipped Milot from Lottie's arms. "Did you hear that, Milot? You can stay a little bit longer." The little boy smiled, as if he understood.

Eamon stood and Lottie shook his hand.

"Thank you. I honestly don't want that little boy transferring from one system into another. I'll do my best to find his mother."

"Please do. It'll make my job a whole lot easier." At the front door he added, "What's with the blood on the floor in there?"

"Just cut my hand on a glass," Lottie said, crossing her fingers behind her back for the lie.

He frowned, nodded and left.

"Thank God," Lottie said. But she wondered if he had scribbled it in his notes.

CHAPTER 65

"So Mr. Petrovci. Our good doctor says you're okay to speak with us. Do you want a solicitor?" Boyd sat down beside Lynch in front of Andri Petrovci in the interview room.

"No, sir," Petrovci said, twisting his hands together.

"You have now been present at three sites where the bodies of young women have been discovered. What do you say to that?"

"I not kill them."

"What was that phrase you shouted out earlier? *Ju lutem?*" Boyd asked.

Petrovci hung his head.

"Speak up for the tape," Lynch ordered.

"Please, it mean please."

Boyd glanced a warning at Lynch. "Are you going to tell me about this latest girl you found? Do you know her?"

Petrovci shook his head.

"I not know her. I go now?"

Lynch said, "Do you have an alibi for every night last week?"

"At my home. Most nights."

"Can anyone verify that?" Boyd asked, then, noting the confusion on Petrovci's face, added, "Do you live with anyone who can say that's where you were every night?"

"I live alone."

Boyd rubbed his hand across his nose and mouth. He actually wanted to shake the answers out of the man.

"Do you like to shoot?"

"What?"

"You know. With a gun. Shoot rabbits in the fields. Or ducks out on a lake. Anything like that."

"I not shoot. I not go on lake. What you mean?"

Boyd slapped the table. "Come on, prick. Tell me. Where did you kill those girls?"

"I kill no one."

"Is there anything you can tell us that would help clear you of involvement in these girls' deaths?" Lynch asked.

"I not kill them. You have nothing. You let me go." Petrovci leaned back in his chair, folded his arms and closed his eyes.

He stayed silent for four minutes.

Kicking back his own chair, Boyd jumped up. Lynch cautioned him with a look.

"I'm going to have a word with Superintendent Corrigan and we'll see what he wants to do with you. Interview terminated."

Without waiting for Lynch, Boyd stormed out of the room.

* * *

The man packed up his new van. The traffic was beginning to ease. People were getting wise and avoiding the town center, he thought as he spied the workers making safe a section of road until they returned on Monday. And he would give them something to find.

Driving by the railway station, he glanced over at the car dismantler's yard. He knew the guards wouldn't find anything there. The old van was bleached clean except for what he'd left in it, and he congratulated himself on his stroke of genius. Planting the blood and shooting at the wall. He'd fired the gun with a silencer as the night train was exiting the station. The sound had been well muffled. Took them long enough to find the body, though!

He drove within the speed limit. No point in attracting attention. Skirting the town through the industrial estate, he took a left by the greyhound stadium, allowing himself a glance up Windmill Road where DI Parker lived. Interesting woman, with her long legs in tight jeans, and her crazy daughter.

He thrust a hand between his legs to quell the pulsating hardness. Not long now. Though he knew he would have to wait until darkness descended.

He could wait. He was used to waiting.

The prize at the end was worth it.

CHAPTER 66

It was eight thirty before Lottie got her house in order and Milot tucked up in bed. Katie cajoled Sean downstairs to watch a particularly gory episode of *CSI*. When she looked in on them, both were slumped in armchairs. Just as she was about to go upstairs to talk to Chloe, her phone beeped. Boyd.

"It better be good news," she warned.

"Not a bit. We released Andri Petrovci. Doc said he was fit and I attempted an interview with him."

"What'd he say?"

"Said *ju lutem* means 'please.' No alibi and he refused to say anything further."

"Shit."

"Corrigan said we had nothing to hold him on, once he gave his statement."

"I wonder if we can link him to the DPC in some way. He knows something."

"*I* know something. He's a fucking killer."

"Moving on from Petrovci, did you go over all the evidence again?"

"With a fine toothpick."

"Tooth comb."

"Whatever."

"You sound like my Chloe." Lottie felt a stab to her heart. She needed to get to the bottom of Chloe's anger and distance. And she needed to comprehend Russell's insinuations about Adam too.

"Any sightings of Maeve Phillips or Mimoza?"

"Not a thing. How did it go with the social worker?" Boyd asked.

"I can keep Milot until Monday. Did you talk to Corrigan about Malaga?"

"Yup."

"And?" If the superintendent had okayed it, could she really go? She had to keep a close eye on Milot. And Chloe, for that matter.

"I had to use my magnificent charm and flattering vocabulary," Boyd said.

"So he said yes."

"Flight's at six fifteen in the morning. I'll pick you up at four. And we fly back tomorrow evening."

Lottie asked, "What about Europol?"

"We're not interviewing Frank Phillips in an official capacity. The superintendent spoke to someone he knows who knows someone who's in the know, so we're good to go."

Despite everything, Lottie couldn't help but laugh.

"Go on, say it," Boyd urged.

"You're a tonic, do you know that?"

"So you keep telling me."

"See you in the morning. And bring the Petrovci interview transcript. It'll give me something to read on the plane."

"And here was I thinking you'd be snuggling up on my shoulder."

"Goodnight, Boyd."

She ended the call and paced the kitchen. A glass of wine would be good. A vodka maybe? No way. A pill? She rooted around in her bag. Tried the zip pocket. Found half a pill crumbling in the bottom. Rescuing what was left of it, she poured a glass of water from the tap and swallowed.

Sitting in her armchair, she hoped the pill would help ease the memory of Russell making his threats about Adam. His words were ingrained on her consciousness. She knew Russell had been implying her husband had been complicit in human organ harvesting. No way. Adam would never have been involved in something like that. Russell was a liar.

Closing her eyes, she listened for the wind. Nothing. Rain? Birds in the trees? Nothing.

The night was silent.

She fell into an uneasy sleep, disturbed by noisy dreams.

* * *

Mimoza had been tied up and a black bin bag drawn over her head. The plastic stuck to the blood oozing from her wounds, but there was a tear in it allowing her to breathe.

Bundled into the boot of a car, she hadn't the energy or the will to fight back or to try and figure out where she was being taken. She was beyond caring about herself. And such was her physical pain and emotional desolation, she momentarily thought that she didn't even care about Milot. But that wasn't true. No matter what they did to her body, she vowed they would not break her spirit. All she could do was hope. If she could survive, she might have a chance of finding Milot. If she was dead, all bets were off.

When the car stopped, she was hauled out of the boot and hoisted over a man's shoulder. Through her pain she felt herself being carried before being flung down. She hit a wooden structure and it rocked. She heard water splashing and further rocking as he nudged her out of the way and joined her.

She was in a boat.

* * *

When she awoke, Maeve knew instantly that she was in a different place. The air was fresh and she could see the dark sky. Dozens of stars twinkling. She was outside, lying on damp grass.

The pain in her side was intense. Her fingers lingered in the feathery softness of the earth and she felt cold. Naked. She tried to raise herself onto her elbows, but she didn't have the physical energy to move. Pain seared through her body. Her head nestled into a bed of heather. She could smell it. Earthy. She desperately wanted to go home.

Turning her head slightly, she heard water rippling and tiny waves splashing. Through the shadows of the trees she noticed a shape, hunched over, walking beneath the branches toward her. It looked like a caricature of the hunchback of Notre-Dame. It was a man, carrying something on his shoulder.

She lay deathly still as he dumped the bundle on the ground beside her. The plastic split.

And then she screamed.

* * *

Kosovo 1999

The captain was driving too fast while talking frantically into a bulky mobile phone.

Deep in his broken heart the boy knew he was being brought back to the clinic. The road led to Pristina and he wasn't stupid. Sinking into the hot upholstery of the seat, he watched the countryside disappearing in a blur until they entered the battered city. The captain parked the jeep at the clinic door.

"Out."

He was shoved down the corridor and through the door at the end. The doctor stood there holding a file with a sheaf of papers sticking out.

"Good work. This candidate is ideal."

The captain said, "I want more for this one."

"No way."

The boy shuffled from one foot to the other, the leather of his sandals causing a blister to pop up on his heel. He wetted his fin-ger and, bending down, rubbed it like his mama had shown him.

"Stop that," the doctor said, pointing with a bony finger.

Skulking into the corner, the boy buried his hands into his jeans pocket, and there, he felt the canvas badge. Rubbing the stitched name, he didn't feel so alone. He had a friend.

The captain said, "You told me his blood is a perfect match. No impurities. Not like some of the others. So it's double for this one or I'll drop him at a whorehouse."

The boy watched as the doctor opened a drawer. Taking out a wallet, he counted the money as a fly buzzed, trapped in the plas-tic covering of the fluorescent light.

"Take it and go," the doctor said.

Folding the notes, the captain pushed them into the top pocket of his camouflage shirt without counting.

The boy felt a shove on his shoulder as he was prodded toward the doctor. He smelled the man's clammy body but he felt no fear. He had already endured the torture of watching his family mas-sacred. What could be worse?

The door banged shut as the captain exited.

He was alone with the white-coated man.

His chin was tipped upward.

He gagged from the odor of dry fish coming from the doctor's mouth.

"Time to get you ready. Come, boy."

Shoulders drooping, the boy followed him to another room.

The sign on the door said: TEATRI.

DAY SEVEN

Sunday, May 17, 2015

CHAPTER 67

Lottie listened at the bottom of the stairs. Silence. All asleep. She pulled the door closed quietly behind her.

She'd warned Katie not to let Milot out of her sight, to stay with him at all times, even inside the house. The back garden was a no-go area for today. She had been thinking of calling her mother to come over for the day, but decided they would be all right.

Boyd looked fresher than she'd seen him in days.

Throwing her bag at her feet in his freshly hoovered car, she sat in and said, "You're looking sprightly."

"And how are you, beautiful lady, on this fine dark morning?"

"It's three fifty-five and I've hardly slept a wink, so can you quell the sunshine for an hour? I'm so tired I feel my bones are about to concertina into each other and I'll collapse like a puppet. Drive the car, and shut up."

"Your wish is my—"

"Boyd!"

"Okay, okay."

Resting her head into the upholstery, she stared straight ahead as the yellow hue of the street lamps gave way to the white glare from the motorway lights. For some reason she wanted to shout at Boyd, to bang her fists against his chest and tell him... tell him what? That she really did like him? That he was making a big mistake rekindling his relationship with Jackie? Bottom line, she didn't want to see him get hurt.

She chanced a glance. He was concentrating on driving. She bit her lip to keep herself from saying something stupid.

"What's the matter?" Boyd turned to her.

"Watch the road."

He hunched his shoulders and, setting his mouth in a serious line, increased his speed to slightly above the legal limit.

Turning her head to the window, she closed her eyes.

"Wake me when we get to the airport," she mumbled.

"I'll wake you when we get to Malaga."

* * *

Frank Phillips owned many properties in the Costa del Sol, but had opted to live in a brand-new complex on Malaga's beachfront.

With Boyd by her side, Lottie entered the gray-stone building, smelling the newness, drinking in the view, appreciating the cool after the pulsating early-morning sun. They took the lift up to the sixth floor and stepped out to a massive hallway, the wall mirroring their reflections. She turned away from the offending glass only to find she was looking at herself again. One wall slipped away silently to the right and a man came out to usher them inside. He looked to be around seven foot tall, but she estimated he was probably about six ten.

"Mr. Phillips will see you shortly." As quickly as he had appeared, the giant vanished.

"It's like the bloody *Wizard of Oz*," Boyd muttered.

"Shh," Lottie whispered. But she had to agree with him as she surveyed the room. Everything was emerald green. The sparkling marble tiles, the columns supporting the ceiling, the couch with its three-foot cushions. The paintings, all by renowned Irish artist Paul Henry.

"They look like originals." Millions of euros' worth of artwork. Sweet Jesus!

"Yes, they are originals."

Wheeling around, Lottie recognized Frank Phillips immediately. The long black hair, the nose, even the eyes. Maeve was the image of her father. But Frank was all of five foot, with skin so tanned he looked like a wooden whiskey keg.

He ambled toward them, tightening the belt of his trousers.

"Sit down," he said expansively. His starched white shirt crinkled over a protruding belly. He directed them to three chairs strategically placed in front of floor-to-ceiling windows, the Mediterranean providing the backdrop. "Tea, anyone?"

He didn't wait for a response. The tall man appeared at his side. Little and large.

"Manuel, tea for three. Now, Detective Inspector—or should I call you Mrs. Parker?—you're here in an unofficial capacity, I believe."

"Inspector will be just fine." She noticed that Phillips was ignoring Boyd and focusing his attention on her.

"My wife, Tracy, chose the life of an alcoholic. If you can even call it a life. My daughter feels some sort of duty to her. When she's eighteen, I intend to bring her over here. Show her all she'll inherit and maybe then she might leave her good-for-nothing mother in the gutter where she belongs and come live with me. What teenager wouldn't?"

"One with decent morals?" Boyd piped up. Lottie tried to nudge him with her elbow but his chair was strategically placed too far away.

"Morals fly out the window in the face of wealth," Phillips said. "My Maeve can have everything she ever dreamed of here. And more."

"Except maybe freedom?" Boyd again.

"Money sets you free." Phillips motioned for Manuel to set the white china cups on the wooden table painted in the tricolor. Carved Celtic crosses for legs.

"Surely you're a prisoner in your own castle?" Lottie said.

"I have all I want." His tone rose an octave. "Right here."

He's angry now, she thought. "Except you don't have your daughter." How far could she push him?

"It's your job to find her. Which you haven't been too successful at so far."

"Maybe that's because you sent your minion McNally to interfere in our work."

"How can you interfere in something that's not being done? Unless you've come to tell me you've found Maeve. Have you?"

Lottie shook her head. "We think your business ventures are linked to Maeve's disappearance."

"So she hasn't run away with her invisible boyfriend, like you had us believe?"

"We haven't found any boyfriend. Yet." With the sea outside and the green inside playing games on the walls, Lottie felt almost seasick. "May I use your bathroom?"

"If that's a ploy to snoop around my home, you're out of luck. There's nothing to find here. I'm—"

"No, it's not that. I suddenly feel a little queasy."

Phillips clicked his fingers and Manuel materialized.

"Show her to the guest bathroom."

Standing up, Lottie grabbed Boyd's shoulder for support.

"You okay?" he asked.

"I'll be fine in a minute."

Phillips had been right. She did want to snoop. Following Manuel around a pillar and down a wide corridor, greener than the room she'd just left, she hoped the bathroom was painted white or pink. Otherwise she would definitely spill her guts.

It was canary yellow.

* * *

After a quick scout around, without going into any of the rooms, Lottie returned to the living area. Tea had been poured but lay untouched.

"I was just saying to Sergeant Boyd here, you have to put things in perspective." Frank Phillips was standing at the window, his arm resting on what looked like a gold-plated telescope. He trailed his short fingers through his long hair, now tied back in a ponytail. Shades of gray pricked above pointed ears and at his temple. Otherwise it was a shimmering black. And she was sure he'd had a face lift or possibly Botox. Not a crease or a line anywhere on his leathery face.

"See that gull there," he said, pointing to a fat bird on the sill, plucking at the scales of a fish. "Now look up into the sky at the planes taking off from the airport."

Lottie squinted into the sunlight. Boyd leaned forward in his chair.

"That tiny dot of white snaking across the blue. See it?"

She nodded. What type of game was he playing?

Phillips put his eye to the telescope. "That is a 737 Boeing. Ryanair. A dozen or more flights from all over Europe daily in and out of Malaga. Full of people. And yet the plane looks smaller than that seagull there."

"What's your point?" Boyd voiced Lottie's thoughts.

Drawing away from the telescope, Phillips said, "Sometimes what's in front of our eyes is so close, we can't see the full picture."

"I've lost you there," Lottie said.

"The seagull looks huge standing close. Just like a plane with a load of people waiting on the tarmac. But when it flies way up in the sky it's just a dot. One of many way up there." Phillips tapped the window. The bird dropped the fish and flew away with loud squawks. Phillips laughed.

"I suspect you're dealing with something big in Ragmullin.

But believe me when I say you have no idea how massive it really is."

"Has this got something to do with the murders?" Lottie asked, glancing at Boyd to see if he was following Phillips. "We've found three murder victims in the last week. Do you know anything about them?" She was bored with his talk of seagulls and planes.

"I heard about them and I think you don't know what's really going on."

"Explain," Boyd said, blowing out his cheeks in exasperation.

"Can you confirm I'd be free from prosecution and get witness protection? That I could go home and look for my daughter?"

Lottie exchanged another glance with Boyd. She said, "It might take a while. Tell us what you know and I'll see what I can do."

"Not good enough."

"We've come all this way for information that might help us save Maeve. I'm disappointed in you."

"Save her from what? Inspector, if I told you all I suspect, I would be dead in a matter of days, then I'd be no use to Maeve at all. I need to get home and look for her myself. You don't understand the complexities."

"Enlighten us," Lottie said.

"I can only point you in a certain direction."

"Point away." Lottie tried to hide her exasperation.

"Walk along the docks." He swept his short arm toward the port. "It's in front of your eyes. That's all I can say. I've decided I'm getting out of my current business, and believe me it won't be in a coffin. Construction. That's how I'm going to make my money from now on."

Lottie looked at him directly. "I need more."

"I have people scouring every rat-hole looking for Maeve.

He's taken her. He's going to come for me too. I can't leave my home without a bodyguard."

"He? Who are you talking about?"

Phillips snorted. "A man called Fatjon. He's been involved in human trafficking for the sex trade for years. I believe he could be involved in the murders."

"Does he work for you?"

"Not anymore."

"Why do you think he's involved?"

"I only suspect it, Inspector. I need to be careful what I say unless you can guarantee me immunity."

"You know that takes time and paperwork. Tell me what you can." There was no way he was going anywhere without a set of handcuffs, Lottie silently vowed.

Phillips looked out of the window at the great expanse of sea. His voice was low and gravelly as he spoke.

"A couple of my…the girls brought into Ireland, earmarked for the sex trade, have disappeared. Without a trace. I'm losing money. Fatjon was the middleman."

Lottie let out a sigh of frustration. Phillips was leaving out more than he was telling her. She decided to plow ahead.

"Two of the bodies we found had organs removed. Is this Fatjon involved in that?"

Phillips opened his mouth to speak, but paused. Taking a deep breath, he said, "I don't know. Organ removal? Really? Perhaps it's a doctor, or a wannabe doctor."

"And this Fatjon, he's not a doctor, is he?"

Phillips laughed wryly. "I doubt it."

"What does he look like? Where does he live?"

"I don't know where he lives. He is a very tall man; muscular, a brute. And he has extremely crooked teeth."

Lottie looked at Boyd. He shook his head. They hadn't come across anyone like that so far in their investigations.

She tried again. "What about Dan Russell? He used to be a commandant in the army. Do you know him?"

"Scum of the earth."

"I thought he was doing well with his company managing the direct provision center."

Phillips snorted. "He's paying for his sins. Look beneath the surface of the man. Have you investigated him?"

"We have. Nothing major. He retired from the army and set up his company."

"Sloppy work, Inspector." Phillips tut-tutted. "He was kicked out for bringing the good name of the Irish army into disrepute. Do your job properly and you might find my daughter. Before it's too late."

Lottie glanced around the room. Where to go from here? She didn't want this to be a wasted journey, or Corrigan would be at the arrivals gate of Dublin airport with her termination papers.

She said, "Maeve had a new, expensive dress in her wardrobe. Do you know anything about that?"

"A dress?"

"Yes. McNally took it."

Phillips seemed to deliberate over this, his eyes glaring. At last he said, "I've no idea why he would do that."

"I think you do." Lottie walked around in a circle and came to a stop, towering over the criminal. "Why was McNally in Ragmullin two days before Maeve went missing?"

"Interesting you should ask that." He moved away from her. "Maybe you're not so stupid after all."

"Let me spell it out for you," Lottie said. "McNally arrives in Ragmullin. Your daughter goes missing and three girls end up being murdered. I'd say that is very interesting, wouldn't you?"

"As I told you already, there's someone much bigger than me involved here. McNally traveled over to sort out a job."

He stood in front of one of his Paul Henry paintings, put out a hand and straightened the frame. "I needed to get out of a particular line of business. I was threatened. My family threatened. Shit, I don't give a fuck about my alcoholic wife. But my daughter—she's everything to me. I sent my man to sort it out."

"But McNally fucked it up."

"Maybe he did. Maybe he jolted someone into action earlier than might have been intended."

"Who is this mysterious someone?"

"Your killer?"

Lottie began joining the dots in her head. "You provide girls for the sex trade. You traffic them. But some of them are used by this . . . doctor to harvest organs for sale on the black market."

"Now you're getting somewhere."

"Who is he, this doctor?"

"I don't know. I only deal with the man with the crooked teeth, Fatjon."

"Where is Fatjon from?"

"Kosovo, originally. There was illegal trade in human organs during and after the Balkans war. Look it up. I'm sure even you can find out about it. Try Wikipedia."

Another Kosovo link.

"Did you ever hear of Andri Petrovci?"

"No."

Lottie thought over everything Phillips had told them. Could this Fatjon be in league with Petrovci? It looked likely. "You said your family was threatened. How and when?"

Sighing loudly, Phillips said, "Suffice to say, I didn't take it seriously enough. Otherwise Maeve would be safe. You'd better find her, Inspector."

"Tell me about this threat."

"I'm dealing with it. Enough said."

"Mr. Phillips, I'm not here to make trouble for you. You agreed to speak with us. Can't you be candid?"

"Mrs. Parker, I've told you more than I intended. You need to find my daughter. And quickly. If you don't, you will be responsible for the war I will wage on your town."

"I'll take that as a threat so."

"Take it any way you like, but I think it's time the pair of you left. Manuel will show you out." Phillips turned to look out of the window. "And don't forget to visit the docks. Interesting place."

* * *

Stepping out on to the burning pavement, Boyd asked, "Did you discover anything interesting in Chez Phillips with your snooping?"

"Manuel wasn't too far away so I didn't get a chance to look."

"I don't believe that for a minute."

"Oh shit," Lottie said.

"What now?"

"Wait here. I left my phone in the bathroom."

"What? Lottie! Come back."

She disappeared inside the glass doors, leaving Boyd behind.

The door to the apartment opened immediately. Manuel directed her inside when she asked. Frank Phillips was still standing, staring out at the sea.

"My phone, I think I left it in the bathroom," she said, breathlessly. "I'll only be a minute."

With a wave of his hand, he acknowledged her without turning. "You know the way."

There was no sign of Manuel as she hurried down the corridor, patting her bag where her phone was safely stashed. Five doors plus the bathroom. She quickly checked them out.

The first one was a kitchen with dining area. Manuel sat at a marble-topped table reading a newspaper.

"Oh, sorry. Bathroom?"

"You passed it. First on the left."

"Thanks." Lottie pulled the door shut.

She opened another three doors. A bedroom, probably Manuel's; two guest rooms. She surmised that the last door was the master bedroom.

With a glance around, she stepped inside. The contrast with the green reception room was startling. A long space spread out before her, decorated in baby-blue. Ignoring the corner housing a desk overflowing with books and files, her eyes were drawn to the super-king-sized bed on the furthest wall. On one side the pale linen was rumpled and tossed; on the other a small, dark figure lay curled like a baby in the womb.

Lottie crept toward the bed. A child, a girl of maybe ten or eleven, snored with soft, even breaths, skin like chocolate fondant shimmering through the sheer baby-doll negligee. Her hair was tightly woven to her scalp, and short lashes fluttered as her chest rose and fell. A film of perspiration glinted on her upper lip despite the coolness of the room.

Dear God, Lottie thought. A dank smell hung in the air. The smell Phillips had tried to mask with his cologne.

The girl turned in her sleep, but her breathing remained regular as the snores subsided.

What could she do? With no jurisdiction, she was powerless. She would have to wait until she got home and tell Superintendent Corrigan, who could inform his Spanish colleagues. Monsters, she thought, I'm dealing with monsters.

She eased back out of the room; tried to keep her footsteps normal as she made her way through to the living room.

"I hope you found it." Frank Phillips turned, his eyes dark green balls of glass.

The air con muttered a constant tune in the silence. Lottie nodded, unable to trust her voice. The crispness of the air suddenly turned into a raw chill and her skin prickled.

He knows, she thought. He knows that I know and I can't do a damn thing about it. We'll see about that.

She reached the front door. Manuel appeared by her side. Keyed in a code. The door glided back soundlessly.

She put one foot out into the hallway.

"No matter what you think of me, Inspector, I'm still a father with a daughter who has disappeared. Find her."

She took a deep breath. Moved like a sleepwalker toward the elevator to the sound of the door closing on Frank Phillips's warped world. And she knew exactly who the child in the bed reminded her of—the girl they'd found yesterday at the pump house.

CHAPTER 68

They turned left into the shade of a side street, walking hurriedly away from the beach and back toward the city.

When she could trust her voice, Lottie said, "Okay so. There are five rooms and all appear normal except for one that I presume is his. A bed, probably the size of my bedroom at home. Beside it, a small marble table lined up with heroin paraphernalia." She knew she was avoiding the other horror in the room.

"So he dips into his own product?"

"Phillips doesn't deal only in drugs anymore. You know he deals in people. Girls…children. Oh Boyd, it was awful."

"What did you see?"

"This wee girl on that monster's bed…she looked no more than eleven."

Boyd stopped, grabbed her arm and pulled her to face him. Lottie saw the rage in his eyes.

"We're going back. I don't care about this being unofficial; we need to take that girl out of there."

"Stop, Boyd. We'd mess it up. I'll tell Corrigan the minute we get back. Let him do it through the correct channels. It's the best way to get Phillips once and for all."

"She'll be long gone by then."

"No. I think he's brazen enough to think we can do nothing."

"If you say so."

She started walking again.

Boyd said, "So this analogy he used, about the birds and planes…was he trying to tell us to back off?"

"I think he was trying to say that what's going on in Ragmullin is only the tip of the proverbial. His main concern is finding his daughter."

"So he definitely didn't have her abducted?"

"No. He wouldn't have agreed to meet us otherwise. I think he genuinely loves Maeve and wants her with him, but he hasn't taken her."

"So what's the story then?"

"His sex trade business. He's upset players bigger than him by wanting to change direction. To stop supplying them with girls for sex or organs or whatever they want to do with them. I think that taking Maeve is their way of getting him to play ball."

"Damn expensive ball."

They walked over the dry riverbed toward the train station. "Let's go to the port," Lottie said, changing direction.

"Why there?"

"Because he told us to. And it's one of the key areas for smuggling people into Europe."

As they walked, Lottie thought about the little girl on Frank Phillips's bed. How pathetic she had looked, dressed up in a baby-blue negligee. And the stench of sex in the air. She felt her heart breaking for the frightfulness of the world and feared for the very soul of the human race. And she felt powerless to do anything about it.

* * *

A ruffling breeze cooled her burning skin as they walked along the paved promenade.

"The architecture is beautiful," Lottie said, glancing up at the wavy concrete canopy above their heads.

A cruise ship blared a foghorn, slipping away from the dock. A flotilla of tug boats heralded the route. Lottie stood beside the glass panel skirting the harbor. She saw a cargo ship. Containers stacked high. Gigantic cranes, maneuvering, lowering, lifting. The skyline appeared like a contemporary piece of art. Lines and arcs. Mesmerizing.

"So what was Phillips trying to tell us?" Boyd asked.

"Look over there." Lottie pointed. "The ferry. Can you see the name on the side?"

Boyd squinted beneath the shade of his hand. "Melilla. Never heard of it. Is it the name of the ship or her home port?"

"Wait a minute." Taking out her phone, Lottie switched on her mobile data and googled the name. "It's a port in Africa. Bordered by the sea and Morocco. Owned by Spain." She tapped off her data.

Boyd held up his hands. "We're not going to Africa. No matter how important you think it is. We'd have to get malaria shots. And I've read about what that stuff does to your sex drive."

Lottie said, "I've worked out how Phillips operated the human trafficking. And it's way too big for him alone."

"So who's the boss? Our doctor killer?"

"I don't know."

"Neither do I." Boyd scratched at his jaw.

"I'm starving." She grabbed Boyd's arm. "Let's find somewhere to eat."

"Best suggestion you've made all day."

"There." She pointed to tables outside an eatery facing the port. "That will do. It has free Wi-Fi."

They ordered two omelets and got the Wi-Fi code from the waiter. Lottie's phone pinged with three emails.

"Who's writing to you?" Boyd asked.

"Jane Dore." She opened the first email, the latest one to arrive.

"Read."

"It's a bit convoluted." Lottie scrolled to the end, where Jane had summarized her findings. "The last victim we found. She's different to the others."

"Different?" Boyd took his plate from the waiter and ordered a glass of red wine. Lottie declined with a shake of her head without looking up.

"She was shot and the wound washed. The bullet was lodged in her heart. But no organs missing."

"Plus she wasn't buried underground." Boyd munched.

Lottie ignored her food. "A rush job? Why?"

"Was the same weapon used?"

"Yet to be determined." She tapped open the next email. "This one is just Jane's preliminary autopsy." Glancing at the last message, she raised an eyebrow. "Dan Russell?" She read the missive before hurriedly closing her email and slapping the phone into her bag.

"Must be personal," Boyd said.

"It's not personal. Not really." Lottie picked up her fork and dug it into the hard omelet. Suddenly she had no appetite.

"What's up?" Boyd asked.

"Forget it."

"Lottie Parker, I know when something is upsetting you. What had Russell to say for himself?"

"Nothing to do with you."

"Nothing to do with me? Come on."

"It's to do with his time in Kosovo." And Adam, she thought. Was Russell really telling bare-faced lies? She'd have to find out.

"Kosovo? Is it to do with Petrovci?"

"It might have to do with Adam."

"Your Adam? You'd better explain."

"Not now, okay? And I honestly don't think it is connected to our investigations."

"You're such a crap liar. You already said this Melilla place links back to Kosovo."

"That's not what I said. I think they bring some of the girls through Melilla into Spain and from there to wherever they need them to operate. It's the murders that have something to do with Kosovo."

"And Andri Petrovci is from Kosovo."

"And so are Mimoza and Milot. And this mysterious man with crooked teeth. It's like something out of an Agatha Christie novel." She set her lips in a thin line, threw down her napkin and picked up her bag. "Are you finished eating?"

"I am now." He laid down his cutlery and gulped the remainder of his wine.

Lottie paid with her card. Boyd asked for the receipt.

Without speaking to each other, they walked the short distance to the main road, jumped into a taxi and headed to the airport.

* * *

On the plane, Boyd twisted sideways to look directly at her.

"So how does Adam fit into all this?" he asked.

Buckling her seat belt, Lottie said, "I knew the silence was too good to last. I could ask you how does Jackie's boyfriend McNally fit into all this too."

"He's just trying to find the boss's daughter."

"Maybe he killed three girls, having first extracted the kidneys from two of them."

Lottie sighed. It didn't make sense. Closing her eyes, she hoped Boyd would take the hint: conversation over.

"How long are you going to be allowed to keep Milot?"

She opened her eyes. "Monday. Shit, that's tomorrow. I wish I knew where Mimoza is."

"I think she's been murdered," he said.

"If she's dead, where's her body?"

"We just haven't found it yet."

"Well if she's not dead, she's in terrible danger. First thing tomorrow, I'm bringing in Russell and then I'm hauling in Andri Petrovci. This time he's going to talk."

"Maybe we should follow up with his boss, too. This Jack Dermody."

"You do that, and check out all his friends and acquaintances. Someone got his phone number in order to send him to the pump house. He doesn't strike me as a killer, though."

"And pray tell, who does?"

"Boyd, close your eyes and go to sleep."

The seat belt sign remained on for the full flight. Turbulence bucketed the plane through the sky and it was half an hour late landing at Dublin airport.

It was 7:30 p.m.

Lottie felt like she'd been up for a week.

CHAPTER 69

Chloe didn't want to go out; Emily Coyne was begging her. On a Sunday night? With school tomorrow? Madness. But her mother was away in Spain or somewhere, so it might be okay.

After pulling tops, skirts and jeans from her wardrobe she looked at the heap of clothes on the floor. Too warm for long sleeves, she thought, but she had to cover the scars. Frustration welled up like a balloon in her chest. She sank to her knees and flung the clothes to the four corners of her room. On the bed, her phone vibrated with an insistent chirp.

"Go away, Emily," Chloe shouted at it.

She stumbled to her feet. Maybe it was Maeve. She checked. It wasn't Maeve.

Twitter alert: #cutforlife.

Her bottom lip trembled. She had wanted to delete the app. But she couldn't do it.

Now she tapped it and read the tweet.

"No," she cried. "No! Leave me alone."

She threw herself onto the bed and howled.

* * *

Boyd dropped Lottie off at her house at 9 p.m. Sean opened the door.

"Missed you," he said, hugging her tightly.

"I was only away for the day." She hugged him back. "It's nice to be missed, though. Everything all right?"

"Yup."

"Hi, Mam," Katie shouted from the sitting room. The remnants of a pizza takeaway littered the floor. Milot smiled, a rim of ketchup on his lips.

"Hello, little man." Lottie threw her bag on an armchair and ruffled his hair. She needed a shower but didn't think she could move her legs up the stairs yet.

"Where's Chloe?"

That was when she heard a scream from above.

Crashing into Chloe's room, she shouted, "What's wrong? What happened?"

"Go away," Chloe sobbed into her pillow.

"I'm going nowhere until you tell me why you're screaming at the top of your voice." Lottie stood inside the door and surveyed the mounds of clothing scattered everywhere. "What's happened here?" She began picking up T-shirts, folding them over her arm. Initially she thought they were dirty, but they smelled fresh, unlike another underlying scent that she couldn't place. Dirt? Dust? Blood? "I leave for one day and the roof caves in."

Chloe cried, "For God's sake, leave me alone. I thought you were away."

"You'd better tell me what's going on, missy. Are you ill?"

Chloe thrust her head under her pillows. Placing the folded clothes on the bed, Lottie noticed the phone and fought an urge to pick it up and have a look.

"If it's your period, I can get you Tylenol. Is your head hurting?" She sat on the bed, placing a hand on Chloe's shoulder, but was shrugged off. A muffled sound came from beneath the pillows. Pulling them away, Lottie patted the girl's damp hair. "Talk to me. Please."

Chloe turned round and hauled herself into a sitting position, dragging the long sleeves of her jumper down over her fingers.

"You're sweating," Lottie said. "Take that off and put on something lighter."

"I can't find anything to wear." Chloe kicked out, knocking the newly folded bundle to the floor.

Lottie ignored the childish act, conscious that there was something serious at play.

"I love you so much and I'll do anything to help you. But you have to talk to me," she pleaded.

Scrunching her eyes shut as if considering the consequences of her actions, Chloe picked up her phone, tapped the screen and handed it over.

"What am I supposed to be looking at?" Lottie furrowed her brow.

"Twitter."

"I know that, but what do you want me to see?"

"That hashtag? Cutforlife. Jesus."

Lottie looked down at the phone, and then back up at her daughter. "Oh my God, Chloe. You're not cutting yourself, are you? Self-harming? What's going on?"

"It's k-kind of like a f-forum," the girl said, choking down tears. "F-for people with d-difficulties in their life. I can have a rant on it or whatever."

"*You're* on it?" Lottie asked, horrified. She could think of a hundred and one different places to get help besides Twitter. She stared helplessly at the girl. At the smooth, youthful face, the big blue eyes, the image of her dad. She couldn't bear to think that her daughter was going through serious mental trauma. "Chloe, what's the matter?"

"It's Maeve. She regularly posted stuff on it. There's been nothing from her since she d-disappeared. But two minutes ago, this p-popped up."

Lottie looked at the last post under the hashtag: *U r next Chloe @ADAM99.* "Who is @ADAM99?" she asked.

"Me. I set it up in Dad's name. Just to be anonymous, like. But someone seems to have sussed who I am. As far as I'm aware, only two people know about the @ADAM99 tag."

"Who knows?"

"Maeve and this guy. I think he set up the hashtag."

"What guy?" Lottie grabbed Chloe by the shoulders and stared into her eyes. "Who is he?"

"Don't go all detective on me."

"This is serious." What had her daughter got herself into? Chloe hesitated. "I...I don't think I can tell you."

"This is a blatant threat against you," Lottie said. "A threat to your safety, especially as we don't know where Maeve is. Tell me who this guy is."

"He calls himself Lipjan on Twitter. I don't know his real name..."

"Go on," Lottie coaxed.

"I thought he might know where Maeve was. I thought he might have been her boyfriend. I sent him a message and he told me to meet him."

"You didn't..."

"I'm so sorry."

"Oh Chloe. Who is he? Where does he live?" Lottie fumbled for her own phone, ready to call in her team.

"Will you listen?"

She put the phone down and grasped Chloe's hand. "I'm listening."

"I don't know his real name. He was nice online. But he was horrible in real life." Chloe scrunched her face in disgust.

"Did he touch you? So help me God, I'll kill him if he did."

"He tried to kiss me. I got away. No harm done." Chloe rubbed a hand along her arm.

"When was this? Did he know where Maeve was? Are you sure you're okay?"

"Mam! Stop it!" Chloe cried. "It was a few days ago. It was awful but I'll be okay."

"Where did you meet him?"

"In the town park. Mam, what if he took Maeve?"

Chloe broke down in sobs. Lottie held her to her chest and soothed her, running her fingers through her long hair. She wanted to hear more, but she knew her daughter had had enough trauma for one night.

CHAPTER 70

Lottie sat on the side of the bed and watched until Chloe eventually fell asleep. She recalled how only two days ago she had looked at the body of the second murder victim, with its evidence of self-inflicted wounds. What had she said then? "Surely someone close to her would have known." Right.

Her daughter needed help. The child was suffering. Chloe had been too strong over the last few years. Ironic, then, how it had been Sean's ordeal that had broken her.

With a weary sigh, she kissed the girl's forehead and went to her own room. She stripped off and had a quick shower but was unable to wash away the mental strain of the last hour, the day, the last week. She pulled on an old T-shirt of Adam's and a pair of leggings. In her bare feet she padded down to the kitchen, found her iPad and switched it on. Sitting at the table, she entered the word "Lipjan" into Google. Tapping open the first line of articles, she began to read.

Lipjan—a town in Kosovo. She sat up straight, hand trembling on the iPad. After a few minutes, she jumped up.

The chicken farm? Something Dan Russell had mentioned when she'd been to see him at the barracks. He had said the mice reminded him of the chicken farm. Now here she was, reading about it on an online article. The chicken farm was based outside the town called Lipjan.

"Got you, Russell," she cried, clapping her hands together.

* * *

"Come again," Boyd said. "What hashtag are you on about?"

Lottie poured two cups of tea. Boyd had arrived ten minutes after she rang him. Patiently she explained what Chloe had told her.

"And Maeve was using it too?" he asked.

"According to Chloe, yes. We need to trace everyone who uses it. Warn them."

"That's a big job."

"It might save a life."

"This Lipjan, who do you think he is?"

"Because it is in Kosovo, I think it has to be either Russell, who worked there, or Petrovci who is from there."

"What reason would either of them have?"

"A means of luring in vulnerable girls."

"I hope your Chloe isn't one of them."

Lottie could feel tears searching for release. Her shoulders sagged with exhaustion but her brain was wide awake.

"I'm sorry. I wasn't thinking. Chloe will be fine." Boyd reached out to touch her hand. She pulled it back and gripped her mug.

"She better be, Boyd. I'm not letting her out of this house until we solve this."

"That's wise. So what do we do now?"

"We have to figure out Dan Russell's role."

"That email he sent you? What was it about?"

Toying with the handle of her mug, Lottie considered how much she could tell him. Silence lingered in the air. She lifted her head and found him staring at her.

She picked her bag up from the floor and took out the photograph she'd found in her mother's attic and the badge she'd got from Mimoza.

"According to Russell, that girl there, the little one, is

Mimoza. And that is Adam's army name badge. Russell insinuated that Adam had something to do with illegal organ harvesting in Kosovo."

Boyd's eyes looked like they were about to pop out of his head. "Back up there a minute. Surely you don't believe that?"

"I don't know what to believe anymore."

"Lottie, you knew Adam better than anyone. This isn't true."

"If it's not true, why is Russell threatening to expose it?"

"He's fucking with you. Twisting the truth."

Lottie stood up and walked around. She looked at her wedding photo gathering dust on the wall.

"You're right. I'm stupid. Russell is trying to compromise me with lies. He's diverting me from the truth."

"And Petrovci is slap-bang in the middle of it all."

"I can't figure it out. That's the awful thing."

"You know what you need?"

"A good night's sleep?"

"Exactly."

"I'm not so sure I'll manage to sleep, Boyd, but I'll try. Thank you." She gave him a tight hug.

After he had left, Lottie knew there was no way she could sleep and opened up her laptop. Following hours of research into the night, she discovered something that caused her jaw to drop. Hurriedly, she sent off an email, hoping the reply wouldn't take long. It might just help solve her case.

* * *

Mimoza stared up at the sky and shivered. The stars blended into each other. One big blinding light. She wanted to shield her eyes but her arms were tethered to her sides with thick rope. Then she realized the light wasn't the stars at all but a flashlight. Beaming straight down into her eyes through the darkness.

She tried to speak but her mouth was bound with a rough

cloth. The light turned away from her and she tried to follow its glow. He was shining it onto the other silent bundle.

She wondered where Milot might be. She hoped he was being treated better than she was.

Against the sound of shallow waves lapping against a distant shoreline, she cried silent tears under the starlit sky.

And she wished she had never left her homeland.

* * *

Kosovo 1999

Images flitted behind his closed eyes. Lights, colors, shapes. Then voices.

He screamed. "Mama!"

No one answered him. Slowly he opened his eyes. Mama was dead. Papa and Rhea too. He wished he was dead. Pain. Searing red-hot pain shot through his belly, around his back and down his legs. He tentatively moved his fingers along his skin. A clear plastic tube protruded from the back of his hand. He found the source of the pain. Low on his side, a series of bandages curving around his hip. What had the doctor done to him?

He tried to remember.

A room with bright lights. A trolley. He'd been made to lie down on it. The doctor had put a needle in his hand and the last thing he recalled was the boy he'd seen in the corridor approaching him with a scalpel.

That was it. Now he was here. Where? He turned his head. A small room with paint curling in the corner of the ceiling. A memory fought to gain control of his brain. Scratching away like the mice in the chicken farm. Mama and Rhea, screaming in pain as their bodies were sliced and their life organs torn so easily from them. With quivering fingers he eased back the bandage and felt beneath it. He touched the rises and bumps. Stitches. Pulling his fingers away, he held his hand up in the air and saw a smear of blood.

The door opened. He squeezed his eyes shut.

"Wake up." The voice was that of the doctor.

The boy obeyed and looked up into the eyes of the gray-faced man. Gobbling up spit from deep in his throat, he let it fly.

The doctor wiped it away with his coat sleeve. "You shouldn't have done that. Believe me."

"What did you take from me?"

"A kidney. And seeing how you are reacting, I'm sorry I didn't take both."

The boy laughed. It was easier than crying. "You will pay for this."

"Where you are going, boy, you will soon forget me. You are nothing. You hear me? Like all the others who come through my doors. I use them to save those worthy of saving. And you are worthless."

Hearing movement at the door, the boy twisted round. The young lad stood there, holding a steel case similar to those he'd seen at his home the day his family had been murdered.

"Father," the lad said, "are you ready? We need to hurry or the ice will melt."

The doctor slid a long bony finger along the boy's face.

"I will be back for you."

"Let me go!"

"Only when I am ready."

The boy felt the skin on the back of his hand tingle as the doctor inserted a syringe into the cannula and the liquid trickled into his body. He had no control. Before a dead weight caused his eyelids to close, he saw the emotionless black eyes of the boy at the door, his face sporting a smirk of pure evil.

Eventually he slipped into darkness.

DAY EIGHT

Monday, May 18, 2015

CHAPTER 71

"Chloe, I think it's safer if you stay home from school today, and I'm going to arrange a squad car to patrol the area."

Placing a mug of coffee on the nightstand, Lottie sat down on the edge of the bed. Chloe's eyes were swollen from crying.

"Did you sleep much?"

"Not a lot. Thanks for understanding, Mam."

"Darling, I'll help you any way I can. I have to go to work now, but ring me if you need anything."

Chloe smiled and Lottie felt her heart constrict. She squeezed the girl's hand and feathered her cheek with a kiss. "I love you."

"Love you too."

"How come she gets to stay home and I've to go to school. It's not fair." Sean stood on the landing, rucksack flung at his feet, hands stuffed into his pockets. "I'm sick too."

Lottie mussed his hair and appraised her tall son. "Image of your dad."

"Do I still have to go?"

"I'm afraid so. Come on. I'm late and I don't want you late too."

"Fuck."

"Sean! Language," Lottie said.

Katie was at the bottom of the stairs, holding Milot on her hip.

"Fuck," the little boy said.

"Dear God," Lottie sighed. "What will that social worker think of this family?"

"His name is Eamon," Katie said.

"Is it now?" Lottie folded her arms.

Her daughter blushed.

"Fuck," Milot said again.

And Lottie had to agree with him.

CHAPTER 72

Lottie informed Superintendent Corrigan about the girl she'd seen in Frank Phillips's bedroom. He lifted the phone immediately to contact his Spanish colleagues. Relief soared through her as she entered the office.

"Right. We've got three murder victims and two girls missing, Maeve Phillips and Mimoza Barbatovci. The only things that seem to link them are the DPC, Dan Russell and Andri Petrovci. We're going through everything from day one right up to date."

Kirby and Lynch flustered around. Boyd sauntered in with two Styrofoam cups of coffee and handed one to Lottie. She placed it on top of a stack of files.

"We're solving this mess today. Today!" she said. Taking a sheet of paper from her bag, she laid it out in front of her. She'd worked for hours last night, listing things they had to do, reading up on Kosovo, sending off emails.

"Where's that warrant for the DPC?" she asked.

"It's before the judge this morning," Boyd said.

Lottie told the team about Chloe's revelations regarding the man calling himself Lipjan.

"I did some research on Kosovo last night. During the war back in the nineties, illegal harvesting of human organs was endemic. Organs were torn from the living bodies of captive soldiers and ordinary civilians. People were brought to a doctor in Pristina by the KLA and others. Big-money business. This disgraced doctor, Gjon Jashari, was brought to trial a few years ago for crimes against humanity, but he suffered a heart attack and died before anyone could give evidence."

"Rough justice," Boyd said.

"I've emailed the prosecutor for details of those involved. It's a long shot, but seeing as we have two dead girls with organs removed, and links to Kosovo in town, it's worth a try."

"Real long shot," Kirby said.

"Get everything we have so far, and a fine-tooth comb. Come on, lads. Today!"

After an hour trawling through reports, transcripts and evidence, Lottie sat back.

"Anything on the crypto and reports of illegal shootings on lakes?" she asked Lynch.

"I'm working my way through the reports. I'll have a list ready for you later."

"Be as quick as you can. The shore of a lake could be our primary crime scene. Kirby, if you haven't already done it, look up Jack Dermody's phone contacts." Lottie marked off a list she'd made last night. "See if anyone crops up who could be involved in all this."

"Yes, boss. Will I do the same for Petrovci?"

"We ran his phone on day one, so now I want you to cross-reference his contacts against Dermody's. Calls and texts also."

"Yes, boss."

"And check if any unit dealing with organized crime or human trafficking know of this Fatjon whom Frank Phillips mentioned."

"Jaysus, boss, I've all this stuff to do and—"

"I don't want to hear it." Lottie caught the roll of Kirby's eyes as he made his way out of the office. "I'm heading off to see Dan Russell." She ticked another item on her list.

"I'll go with you." Boyd stood up.

"Of course."

"Good cop, bad cop?"

"I'm the bad one this time." Lottie picked up her bag and headed for the door.

"You're the bad cop all the time."

"Who's a bad cop?" Superintendent Corrigan filled the doorway with his oversized bulk. Beneath his spectacles, one eye sported a black patch.

Lottie escaped out under his arm before she said anything about pirates.

CHAPTER 73

"So you haven't found Mimoza yet?" Dan Russell said.

They'd refused his invitation to sit. Boyd leaned against the wall to the left of the ex-army man. Lottie stood to the right, her back to him, and perused the line of hanging photos. She spun round. "I want to know the truth."

"Don't know what you're talking about." Russell ran a finger round the inside of his collar.

She felt a shiver scurry along her bones. "Do you traffic girls illegally for the sex trade?"

"I'll report you for slander," he retorted.

"Report away. It was just a question." Lottie paused, arranging her thoughts. "I've been speaking to Frank Phillips. You know him?"

"I've heard of him. Nothing to do with me."

"Know anyone by the name of Fatjon?" She watched him intently. His eyes flickered, nothing more.

"Can't say that I do. Why?"

"He's involved in trafficking girls and women for sex. I suspect your management company facilitates it. Be easy for you to hide them among genuine asylum seekers so that they remain undocumented. Never appearing on any official register. What I don't understand is why. Why would you do it? It's such a high-risk operation. Money? How much do you make? Is it per girl or per the hour?"

Russell lifted the phone on his desk.

"Don't bother ringing my boss. He knows I'm here," Lottie said.

Russell's finger hovered over the keypad.

"Lipjan." Lottie pounced. "What does it mean to you?"

Tilting his chair back, Russell rested his hands behind his head. She could see gray hair poking out where his shirt stretched across his abdomen. His thin mustache wobbled on his upper lip as he laughed.

"What's so funny, Mr. Russell?"

"You are. You've researched it, so you know Lipjan is a town in Kosovo where peacekeeping troops were based under the NATO flag. The camp was built beside an old chicken farm. Your husband was based there. Not far from Pristina."

"You're right. I have researched it. Wasn't it in Pristina where a doctor illegally harvested human organs?" She thought of her late night on the computer. "More like barbaric butchery. And let me tell you, Mr. Russell, it had nothing to do with Adam Parker." She threw him a meaningful look. "But the fact that you insinuated he was involved leads me to believe *you* had something to do with it." She had no evidence if he had or not, but she needed to see his reaction.

"How do you reach that conclusion? Your detective skills? Don't make me laugh again." His face remained neutral.

Lottie paced for a moment before stopping behind him. She fought an urge to upend his chair. Leaning so close to his ear she could see hair sprouting inside, she whispered, "Gjon Jashari."

The effect of her words was instant. Russell pulled his hands out from behind his head, almost hitting her, and leapt up. She jumped back against the wall.

He turned and pressed his face close to hers. "You have no idea what you're talking about."

Spittle landed on her face. Lottie edged sideways, threw a glance to Boyd telling him to stay where he was and faced Russell.

"Gjon Jashari," she repeated. "He lived and worked in Pristina during and after the war, at the time of your tour duties. Interesting, don't you think?"

Russell opened and shut his mouth. Boyd did likewise. Lottie forced a weak smile. Hopefully she'd soon have a reply to the email she'd dispatched in the early hours. Until then, everything was speculation.

"Get out! Get out of my office," Russell commanded, pointing to the door. His mustache now drooped with sweat and spit. His sleek hair fell across his forehead. He looked demented.

"Frank Phillips told me he knows you." Keep going while you're ahead, Lottie thought.

"That bastard."

"So you do know him?"

"Know *of* him." Russell backed down. "Before you accuse me, I read about his missing daughter and it has nothing to do with me."

"Interesting." Lottie moved away, ignoring Boyd's questioning eyes. She gazed along the line of photographs for the second time since she'd arrived. "Is he in any of these?"

"Phillips was never in the army." Russell folded his arms.

"Not Phillips. Your friend. The one with the crooked teeth."

"You're insane. Fishing expedition, that's what you're on."

Nail on the head, but she wasn't about to admit it. Continue catching him off balance, hoping he slipped up. "I have murder victims with severe bite marks. This Fatjon has crooked teeth. We can match up the bites with forensics. Tell me about him."

"I'm telling you to get out. Now." This time, when he lifted the phone, he punched in a number.

"Let's go, DS Boyd. I've got what I need for now."

"You got nothing from me," Russell sneered.

Lottie hoisted her bag up her shoulder and walked to the door. "That's what you think. Don't leave town. I'll be back for you."

* * *

Keeping his hand around the dog's mouth to stop him from yelping, the man melted into the shadows at the side of the cookhouse. He watched the two detectives walk quickly out of Block A, down the path and out the gate.

He looked up at the window on the first floor. Dan Russell stood there, staring out, holding a phone in his hand. What had he told the detectives? Time to find out.

He bent over the dog.

"Sorry about this, mutt," he said. With a jerk of his hand, he broke the dog's neck. He laughed. The dog had been a prop, helping him blend into normality. The time for blending in was now past.

Releasing the small furry body, he unfastened the lead and wrapped it around his hand. He kicked the dog into the gully beside a vermin trap and headed across the square to Block A.

* * *

"I could do with a cigarette," Lottie said, pausing on the footbridge. The sun blazed down from the morning sky. The cherry blossom trees were all but bare, their petals drowning in the turbid waters of the canal. Unlike her mind, which at last was beginning to clear.

Boyd lit two cigarettes and handed her one in silence.

She dragged hard on it and puffed out a curl of smoke. "I need to speak with Andri Petrovci."

Boyd said nothing.

"I have to find out how he fits into all this. And we need to find Maeve Phillips."

"Being practical, I'd say she's dead."

"Never give up. Never lose hope, Boyd. Otherwise you may as well hand in your badge."

"I was only saying."

"Well, don't. I'm going to speak with Petrovci. After that debacle with Russell I now suspect Petrovci's the Lipjan character on Twitter, so he must know something about Maeve."

"Corrigan will have a field day if he finds out about all this. I suppose you think Petrovci is involved in smuggling human organs too."

"He was only a boy when the war was raging in Kosovo. He couldn't have been involved then, could he? I don't know about now." She flipped her cigarette into the water below. "Are you coming?"

"I suppose I am." He sighed.

"Knew I could count on you."

* * *

They cut down by the canal towpath and on to Main Street, where the warm air was clogged with dust and the noise of diggers. Traffic shuffled along like a little old lady.

"After we released him on Saturday night, we put a tail on Petrovci," Boyd said.

"I know. Find out if he's at work now."

Skirting round the corner of the Malloca Café, Lottie marched down Columb Street. The remnants of crime-scene tape trailed from lampposts, but SOCOs had moved on to the old pump house. Bob Weir's gates were open and it seemed business was returning to normal. A sheet of metal covered the crater in the ground where the second body had been found. Cars avoiding the congestion on Main Street passed over it, oblivious.

Boyd talked animatedly into his phone as he walked. He

ended the call and Lottie looked over at him without breaking stride.

"They lost him?" she said.

"How did you..." he began.

Lottie shook her head. "*How* could they lose him? He's one man, not an army. Now Corrigan will have that field day you were going on about."

"Shit, I don't know. The squad car stayed outside his apartment Saturday night, and all day and night Sunday. Said he never left, not even for work this morning. They've just knocked on his door. No answer." He paused for breath.

"We'd better go up there." Turning round, she began striding back the way they'd come. "He could be dead inside." She broke into a run.

"Slow down. If he's dead, he's not going anywhere," Boyd panted.

She kept running.

CHAPTER 74

Dan Russell heard the door open and turned away from the window. The phone slid from his fingers when he saw the man entering his office twisting a leather dog lead round and round his hand.

Rooted to the spot, Russell said, "How are..."

The words died on his lips when Fatjon stepped into the office behind the first man.

"Wh-what's going on?" Russell asked, backing up against the wall, knocking down two of his prized photographs.

The man with the dog lead spoke. "I was hoping you could tell me that, Dan." He moved further into the office until he stood beneath the motionless ceiling fan. "Why don't you sit and make yourself comfortable." He unfurled the lead and slapped it against his thigh. "This won't take long. Will it?"

"I told the police nothing. Do you hear? *Nothing*. There's no need to be threatening me."

"I thought I could trust you," the man said. "Instead you bring the pigs sniffing and grunting into our business. And you know I don't like pigs."

"I swear to God, I didn't say a thing. That girl, Mimoza, *she* involved them. It's all her fault."

"Come on. You promised me you would do what you were told. The one thing—" the man slapped the leather against the palm of his hand—"the only thing you had to do was keep that girl and boy safe for me. Did you do that?" He turned to Fatjon. "Did he?"

Russell didn't like the sneering tone. He gulped spit down his throat, tried to speak, but the words wouldn't form.

"It's his fault." He pointed at Fatjon.

"Fatjon here is a sex-mad lunatic. He couldn't organize a... What do you Irish call it? A piss-up in a brewery."

Russell prided himself on never begging for anything, but this was a time to plead.

"I'll find the boy. I promise. Just give me today and I'll bring him back to you."   .

"Too late, my friend. I already know where he is and will deal with him myself. And as you've reneged on our agreement, I will have to deal with you like I dealt with the other troublemakers."

"You can't do that. We agreed—"

"Deal's off. You lost the boy."

"I got his mother for you, and that other bitch. I only involved the detective to try to find the boy for you. She doesn't know you have his mother."

"Too little, too late, my friend."

"But you promised that if I let you take who you wanted, you would never tell anyone what I was involved in, in Pristina. Please. The only thing I have left is my reputation."

"Reputation? You didn't care back then that you could drag the name of peacekeepers through the mud. You only saw the color of the dollar flashing before your eyes. I don't care about your reputation, *Captain*, it's your life I want." The man laughed loudly, the sinister sound cutting through the air.

Russell heard the crack of the lead before he felt it lash his face, the prong from the brass catch hooking into his eye. He sensed the second strike without hearing it. Sinking to the floor, his legs like jellied eels, he raised a hand to shield his face. As he touched his eye, he felt it hanging from its socket like a smashed ping-pong ball.

CHAPTER 75

"Open up! Come on, Petrovci. I know you're in there."

Lottie banged hard on the door. Neighbors stared. Boyd rocked from foot to foot beside her. Two uniformed police officers stood in the hall shooing onlookers away.

"This is your last chance. I'm counting to three, then I'm breaking down the door."

"You're not breaking down anything," Boyd said.

"No, but you are, smart-arse. Get the enforcer from the trunk of the patrol car. Hurry up." Lottie continued banging on the door. It remained firmly shut. Shit, hopefully he wasn't dead. Not because she felt anything for the foreigner with the pained eyes. No. She needed him alive to get information. And possibly charge him with three murders, two abductions and attacking her daughter. Bastard.

Boyd returned hauling a battering ram.

Lottie shouted at the door, "Andri Petrovci, this is your final warning. We're coming in on the count of three." She counted loudly, then stepped out of the way and gestured for Boyd to proceed.

The door splintered with the force of his strike. Lottie pulled on gloves, put her hand through the fragmented wood and unlocked the latch. Boyd dropped the enforcer, gloved up and followed her into the silence of the one-bedroom flat.

* * *

Katie opened the front door.

"Hi, Eamon," she said. "Are you here for Milot?"

"I'm afraid I am."

"Mum isn't here. I can't let you in until she gets home from work. Sorry."

He glanced around nervously. "I have documents which allow me to take the boy. We've found a good home for him. He can live there until his mother is located."

Katie smiled her sweetest smile. "All the same, I can't let you in. Come back later when Mum is home. There's a squad car patrolling the area, so I think you should go."

The social worker looked over his shoulder. Katie followed his gaze, but saw no police car. Nor was there a car parked outside the house.

"Did you walk over here?" she asked in surprise.

"Er, no. Yes."

"Which? You can't take Milot with you. He's only a child. He can't walk far. It's too warm. He'll get heat stroke." She pushed the door, but his foot stopped it closing fully.

"What are you doing?" Katie asked, her skin prickling.

"I have to take him with me. Now."

"I'm sorry, but—"

She was hurled back into the hall as Eamon Carter pushed the door inward. Landing on her side, she squealed loudly. "What the—"

His hand clamped over her mouth. "Shh. I don't want to hurt you."

Her eyes bulged.

He said, "I'm going to take my hand away and close the door. Do not scream. Understand?"

She tried to nod.

"Good girl."

When he removed his hand, Katie gasped for air and screamed as loudly as her lungs would allow. His fist crashed into the side of her head and stars floated in front of her eyes.

He slammed the door and drew the safety chain across.

"I asked you to be quiet." He knelt down beside her. "I shouldn't have hit you. But it's not my fault. I have to get the boy. Let me help you up and I'll explain."

"Who the fuck are you?" Chloe shouted from the top of the stairs, brandishing Sean's hurley stick like it was a sword. "Don't you dare touch my sister or I'll fucking kill you."

She leaped down, three steps at a time, and cracked the hurley across his knees as he raised his hands to his face to protect himself.

"Chloe! Stop, you'll kill him," Katie shouted.

Eamon Carter staggered against the wall. "Fucking mad bitches."

"You haven't seen the half of it," Chloe said. "Now what the hell are you doing here? Tell me before I hit you again."

* * *

The room was neat and tidy. Two wooden chairs pushed in against the table. Floor swept. One mug, a bowl and spoon drying on the draining board. Couch with throws neatly folded. A coffee table free from clutter.

No one home. No sign of a struggle. Nothing out of place.

Lottie looked in the bin. A few empty Coke cans, a sliced-bread wrapper and a chunk of hard cheese in cling film. She opened the refrigerator. Milk in date, tomatoes, ham and butter. Slamming it shut, she went to the bedroom.

Single bed. Not a wrinkle on the sheets. Military-style. Wardrobe open. Empty. Dresser drawers hanging out. All empty.

"Not even a mothball," she said.

Boyd stuck his head into a small bathroom. "Likewise in here."

"Where did he go?"

"Well, he wasn't dragged out against his will," Boyd said.

"Not through the front door anyway, unless those two feckers were asleep on the job."

Lottie pulled Boyd out of her way and entered the small bathroom.

"Here," she said, pointing up to the window hanging open on its hinges. "It's about two feet by three. Plenty of room to squeeze out."

"This is the fourth floor. What did he do? Sprout wings?" Boyd ran one hand through his hair and the other along his chin.

Lottie flipped down the toilet seat, stood on it and looked out. "He wouldn't have to be Superman. There are fire-escape steps right outside."

"Shit." Boyd jumped up beside her. "You're right. Fuck."

"Did they not think to watch the back of the building?" Lottie shook her head and inadvertently knocked Boyd off the seat.

He banged his elbow off the wall. "They probably thought there was no exit."

"Thought? They should have checked." She stepped down beside Boyd in the confined space. "What a cock-up!"

Boyd said, "He could be in Timbuktu by now."

Lottie brushed past him and re-entered the living-room-cum-kitchen. "He's not gone far. He has to finish what he came here for." She picked a book from the shelves, flicked through the pages.

"And what might that be?"

"If I knew that, I'd be God. Get SOCOs to give the place a going-over. He might have held the girls here." She shoved the book back in place. "Let's see if Kirby found out anything from the phone records and if Lynch has got us a crime scene."

* * *

Katie ran upstairs to check on Milot, leaving Chloe watching Eamon Carter. When she'd gone to answer the door, she'd left the boy in Sean's room playing a game on the computer. Sean would have a canary when he got home from school, but it kept the youngster occupied. Looking in now, she saw that Milot had mastered the keyboard and was engrossed in Minecraft.

Easing the door shut, she ran back to the kitchen. Eamon was sitting at the table. Chloe had placed a glass of water in front of him and stood with the hurley across her chest like a soldier on guard duty.

"I'm telling you the truth," he said. "I think you broke my kneecap."

"Did you ring Mam?" Katie asked Chloe.

"She's not answering."

"Probably busy with work. What's he saying?"

"I'm right here," Eamon Carter said, rubbing his knee furiously.

"So you are. Why did you hit me?"

"I said I'm sorry. I didn't mean to do that. I was told to pick up the boy."

"What are you talking about?" Chloe slammed the hurley against the side of the table.

Carter jumped, banging his other knee on the underside of the table. "Ouch. Will you stop?"

Katie said, "Chloe, take it easy."

"He's telling lies. I don't know what he's up to. Probably going to take Milot and sell him to a gang of pedophiles."

"What pedophiles?" Katie and Carter said together.

"Just saying," Chloe said.

Eamon Carter made to stand up. Katie put her hand on his shoulder. He sat back down.

"I'm sorry. Honestly. I'm not long in this job. I didn't ask for all this."

"Tell us what you didn't ask for." Katie pulled out a chair and sat opposite him.

He looked around.

"There's only the three of us. Go ahead," Chloe encouraged.

He didn't look at all sure but he said, "Okay so. I think there must've been someone either watching your house or following me, because in the middle of Saturday night I got a phone call from someone. Threatening me and my mum."

"What?" Chloe said. "Who?"

"I don't know." He wrung his hands into each other. "My mum lives with me since my dad died. Up in Rathfarnham. I commute to Ragmullin for work. I don't know how they got my phone number let alone my address."

"What did this mysterious caller say to you?" Chloe remained standing, hurley clasped in both hands.

"He told me to come here today, when your mum's at work, and take Milot."

"If I believed that, I'd believe in Santa Claus," Chloe said.

"Shut up and listen." Katie scowled at her sister.

"I told him to get lost. He was very angry. Started swearing and shouting at me. I couldn't understand him. But then he said . . . he said he'd hurt my mum to show me just how serious he was. I was so terrified, I actually hung up on him."

"Did you ring the police?" Katie asked.

He shook his head. "Sure, what was I going to tell them?"

"There have been three murders in Ragmullin and two girls missing, including Milot's mother. Why wouldn't you ring the police? You shit-head." Chloe slammed the hurley against the table again.

"I have to take the boy with me. I've no choice. Please listen to me."

"I'm all ears," Chloe said.

"Yesterday afternoon I was sitting down with my mum

to watch a football game on the telly and these two guys march in."

"What two guys?"

"I don't know who they were. Dressed in black jeans and T-shirts. They came in the back door, walked through the kitchen and into the sitting room. My poor mum nearly had a heart attack. They dragged me out of the room, told me I was to get the boy. They said I wouldn't raise any suspicions because it was my job, and I was to tell no one. Or else..."

"Or else what?"

"They'd come back and kill my mum."

"Jesus." Katie felt the blood draining out of her face. "And you still haven't contacted the police?"

"No. I can't, that's what they said. No police or Mum gets it."

Chloe asked, "What happened after that?"

"That's it. They went out the back door and over the wall."

"What were you supposed to do when you had Milot?"

"They gave me a number. I've to text it when I have him and then I'll get further instructions."

"Do they think you're Superman or what?" Chloe was met with a steely stare. "I can't believe you'd do this to an innocent child, and you a social worker and all."

"What choice do I have?"

Katie went to the door. Listened. She could hear Milot shouting at his game. Just like Sean.

Carter pleaded, "You have to let me take him."

Chloe walked around the table, hurley under her arm. She tried ringing her mother again. Engaged. So much for contacting her any time she needed to.

"I don't get how they knew who you were. They even followed you to Dublin? It sounds made-up to me."

"You have to believe me. This man, when he rang me, he

sounded like a guy who knows everything and everyone. He must have pull somewhere."

"Even so, you're not getting Milot. Pretend you have him. Text and see what instructions you get."

"Are you mad? I don't want my mum to die." He ran his hands through his hair, pulling at the roots.

"We don't want Milot to die either. I'm scared, but we have to think of something," Chloe said, thinking there had to be a way she could fix this.

"Ring Boyd," Katie said.

Chloe tapped her contacts with a tremor in her fingers, found Boyd's number and rang. This time the phone was answered.

"Boyd, thank God. It's Chloe here. I can't reach Mam. Tell her to come home quickly. It's urgent. Carter's here. I'm scared." She could hear Boyd arguing with her mother. "Fuck this," she said, and hung up. Her phone pinged.

"What's that?" Katie asked.

Chloe checked. "Shit, I thought I deleted this app. It's just a Twitter notification." She handed the hurley to Katie. "Here, you hold this and don't let him out of your sight. I'm going to check on Milot." She rushed up the stairs, stuffing the phone into her jeans pocket.

CHAPTER 76

Waiting on the steps outside Andri Petrovci's home for the SOCOs to arrive, Lottie took her phone out of her bag to ring Kirby. The display showed that she had two missed calls from Chloe. Before she could ring her daughter back, her phone chirped. Kirby.

"What's up?" Lottie shielded her face from the sun with one hand. Boyd ran down the steps to give the two uniforms a talking-to.

"The call to Petrovci's boss Dermody telling him to go to the pump house was made via a pay-as-you-go," Kirby said.

"Impossible to trace. What's the good news?"

"I cross-checked Petrovci's contacts with Dermody's. No matches."

"That's the good news?"

"No, but then I cross-referenced their calls. Incoming and outgoing."

"Lottie," Boyd shouted up the steps, holding his phone out to her.

"Not now, Boyd." She turned back into the doorway. "Sorry, go ahead, Kirby."

"So what do you want me to do about it?" Kirby asked.

"You'll have to repeat that. Someone with no manners was shouting at me."

Boyd reached the top step, shoved his phone into her hand. "It's Chloe. It's urgent."

Lottie took his phone. Had something happened? Her children had Boyd's number for emergencies only. Oh my God, she thought. She'd never organized a watch on her house.

"Chloe, hun, what's the matter?" Looking at Boyd, she said, "She's gone. The line's dead."

Boyd said, "She sounded frantic. Do you know someone called Carter?"

"That's the social worker. I hope he hasn't come for Milot already. I warned Katie not to let the boy go."

"She said she was scared. I'll call round to your house now."

"No, I'll go. You see what Kirby was on about. Then get your car and follow me."

"You've no car either."

"I'll get Mutt or Jeff here to drive me. I'm sure the other one can watch a broken front door until SOCOs arrive. Oh, and when you speak to Kirby, get him to check Petrovci's online history. There's no laptop in there." She pointed back to the apartment. "He may have taken it with him or he might've used his phone."

"What for? Twitter?"

"That and flights abroad. We need to work out where the hell he is."

Lottie sat into the squad car, yelling instructions at the uniformed police.

Boyd shouted, "And show Chloe a photo of Petrovci, if you have one."

She pulled the door shut. Why hadn't she thought of that before now?

* * *

Jumping out of the car, Lottie ran up the front path and was struggling to get her key in the door just as Katie opened it.

"What's wrong, Katie? Is Milot here? Where's Chloe? Jesus, what are you doing with Sean's hurley?"

"Mam, slow down. Come inside."

"And what happened to your face?" Lottie followed her into the kitchen and saw Carter. "What are you doing here?"

Eamon Carter stood up, put out his hand, then seemed to think better of it. He thrust it into his jeans pocket.

"I'm sorry, Mrs. Parker. Detective Inspector."

"Sit down and tell me what's going on. And I'm very busy at the moment, so you'd better make it quick."

* * *

After speaking on the phone with Kirby, Boyd ran back to the station car park. As he sat into his car, he saw Lynch running round the side of the building.

"It's impossible to get either you or the boss," she panted, bending down to the open window.

"You have me now," Boyd said.

"About those reports concerning unusual activity around the lakes." She shoved a page of print at him. "See there. Lough Cullion." She pointed.

"I can read, Lynch. What do you want me to look at?"

"Firstly, the lake supplies the town's water. The council confirmed that recent samples have traces of cryptosporidium and if it gets any worse they'll be issuing boil water notices."

"Okay. And?"

"It's not shooting season yet and there've been three reports of gunshots at night. Two reports of lights. Out on Monk Island."

"Never heard of it."

"Not many people have. It's one of two islands on the lake. Church Island is more frequented as it has a little harbor area for fishing boats. But Monk Island is further out, a lot less accessible. In the Middle Ages it was used to incarcerate people—"

"Okay, okay, Lynch. Anything else I need to know?"

"Kirby wants to talk to the boss about phone records. Oh, and your ex-wife was here earlier, asking for you."

"She's not my ex yet. What'd she want?"

"Something about Jamie McNally. She couldn't get through to you on your phone. You've to give her a call. Sounded urgent."

"Okay. I'll be back shortly. Tell Kirby to keep digging."

"What will I do?"

"Find out everything you can about Monk Island."

* * *

Lottie ended her call with Rathfarnham Police and faced the social worker.

"Now, Eamon, your mother is safe. My colleagues in Rathfarnham have dispatched an officer to stay with her."

"But if they see a squad car, they'll know I've told you," he cried.

"Give us some credit. It'll be an unmarked car. Anyway, your mother is safe. Milot is safe. And I'm going to arrest you for attempted kidnap and assaulting my daughter."

Katie said, "It's okay, Mam, it was just a misunderstanding. I don't want to press charges."

"You're going over to Granny's house, and this time I'll make sure there's an officer with you. I don't like the idea of someone watching for this eejit here to leave with Milot."

"What about Sean?" Katie asked.

"Boyd can pick him up from school."

Boyd walked into the house. "Will I go for him now?"

"Just a minute," Lottie said. "Katie, run up and get Chloe and Milot."

"What about me?" Eamon Carter leaned against the back door. Looking for a quick exit?

"You're coming to the station. We need to trace the number of whoever contacted you." She shoved him toward the door. "You have to give a statement. And a description of the two men. Then we'll see about letting you go home to your mum."

Katie rushed into the kitchen. "I can't find them!"

"What?"

"They're gone. I can't find them anywhere."

Lottie rushed past her daughter into the hallway. "It's not a feckin' mansion. Chloe! Come down here this instant."

"Mam," Katie said, rubbing her hands up and down her arms. "I think Chloe's a bit unhinged. She was like a lunatic with that hurley. I thought she was going to kill Eamon."

"She thought he was going to kill you." Lottie took the stairs two at a time. "Chloe?"

Minecraft flickered on Sean's computer. No Milot. She glanced into Chloe's room. Empty. Katie's room too, as was her own. Running back into Chloe's, she noticed the bed pushed up to the open window. The curtain hung limply, no breeze to blow it around.

She leaned out, shouting hysterically, "Chloe? Chloe, where are you?"

* * *

"Shh, Milot. I won't let the bad man take you."

Chloe didn't trust Eamon Carter. She hadn't believed one word out of his mouth. She'd seen what had almost happened to Sean in January at the hands of a madman. Knew what had happened to Jason, Katie's boyfriend. She wasn't taking any chances with little Milot. She had been so caught up in her own misery, cutting herself, causing herself pain, that she'd ignored the little boy since he'd come into her home. Now was her chance to be brave and get him to safety. Her mother was too busy; she had to do this herself.

Her biggest fear was the man who called himself Lipjan. She'd felt an awful helplessness when he'd pinned her to the tree, and she believed he knew where Maeve was. He possibly had her captive and maybe he'd already killed her. She gulped down a cry. No, she couldn't take any chances with Milot. The message she'd received on her phone moments earlier confirmed it.

A surge of fear fueled by adrenaline had intensified her need to get out of her room, and not via the front door. Grabbing Milot from Sean's room, she'd brought him into hers and dragged the bed over to the window. Wrapping the boy's arms round her neck and his legs around her waist, she'd stood on the bed, eased out of the window and dropped onto the garden shed roof. Her ankles had jarred with the thud. At least she hadn't fallen through. Disregarding the mild pain, she'd edged to the eaves, hauled herself over and slipped to the ground. She'd shrunk into a narrow space behind the oil tank and hunkered down with Milot snug to her body. Above her head she heard the rumble of the railway and knew a train was slowing down to enter the station.

Milot whimpered. Chloe held him closer. The poor child. What must he have gone through in his short life? Too much, she thought. While all she had done was indulge in self-pity. She physically shook herself and the boy let out a small cry.

"It's okay, little man. I won't let anyone take you."

A voice rang into the evening air. "Chloe? Chloe, where are you?"

She looked up to see her mother hanging halfway out of her bedroom window. Should she go back? Should she stay hidden? What was best for Milot?

No sound of sirens. No guards rushing around her house to protect them. What could her mother do? She began to cry, and Milot looked at her, his dark brown eyes filling up.

"It's all right, petal. I'll mind you. No one will hurt you ever again."

Sniffing away her tears, she momentarily wished she had her little blade. Just one cut. To feel the blood oozing slowly from her flesh. Giving her relief from her mental anguish. But the little boy needed her more than she needed her blade.

Chloe took her phone from her jeans pocket. Checked the text once more and made her decision.

"We're going somewhere safe and I need you to do what I tell you."

She put the boy on her back. Winding his arms and legs tightly around her body, she scrambled up the bank at the rear of the house and through the bramble hedge. Once she was on the railway tracks, she began to run.

CHAPTER 77

"Boyd! Boyd!" Lottie ran down the stairs. "They're gone. Where could they go? Oh God. Chloe. What will I do?"

Boyd gripped her by the upper arms and shook her. "Breathe, Lottie. Look into my eyes. Now, slow breaths."

Lottie stared into the brown depths with their hazel flecks. She took her breaths and counted every one. Feeling slightly calmer, she said, "We have to find them. Quick. Look out the back. She must have jumped onto the shed from her bedroom window. It's not that far, is it? I hope she's not lying hurt somewhere. Oh God."

"Wait here." Boyd ran out the door. He returned in a few minutes.

"No sign. She could've run round the side of the house or through the neighbor's garden. I've contacted the station. The whole force will be searching. We'll find them."

"But why would she do something like that?"

"Maybe she feared for Milot's safety. She didn't stop to think."

"It's more than that. All that stuff I went through over my brother, everything that happened with Sean, even Maeve…I think it's seriously impacted on Chloe."

"Don't go there, Lottie. Now's not the time for analysis. First we have to find them. Are you all right?"

She scrunched up her shoulders and blew out a long, loud breath. "I'm okay. Honestly." She thought for a moment. "I need Sean picked up from school. He's to be brought to my mother's house along with Katie. Get someone to guard her house and at least I'll know they're safe there."

Boyd made another call. When he hung up he said, "Lynch is on her way to the school. Lottie, I think you need a cup of tea."

"For fuck's sake, Boyd. I don't want tea. Are you mad?"

She turned to see Officer Gillian O'Donoghue standing at the table with Carter. "How did you get here so fast?"

"You phoned me on your way over," the officer said. "To come and watch Milot while you sorted out whatever Chloe was ringing you about."

"So I did." She didn't know what she was doing anymore. She needed to get out and look for her daughter. "Boyd, you drive. My car's at the station. I have to think where Chloe would go."

"Maybe Katie knows," Boyd said.

Katie was at the table, slumped over with her head resting on her arms.

"Katie, are you all right?" Lottie rushed to her daughter.

"I'm fine." She raised her head. "Go find Milot and Chloe."

"Have you any idea where she might be?" Lottie pulled out a chair and sat beside Katie, taking the girl's hand in her own. It was clammy with sweat.

"You know Chloe doesn't talk to me, Mam. She just yells most of the time."

Lottie noticed the exhaustion in her daughter's eyes. "Katie, I'm sorry, for landing Milot on you and—"

"Don't be sorry for me," Katie interrupted. "I loved looking after the little fellow. Sean's even taken to him. He's been good therapy for us. Helped us to forget about ourselves for a while. Oh Mam, where is he? Surely Chloe wouldn't harm him?"

"Chloe's a good girl. She thinks she's protecting him. I need to figure out where she's gone."

"Mrs. Parker." Carter spoke. "Before she went upstairs, Chloe said something about Twitter."

Katie stood up and grabbed Lottie's arm. "I forgot about that. Her phone pinged and I asked her what it was and she said it was some Twitter notification."

"Do you have Twitter?" Lottie asked.

Katie opened the app. "What am I looking for?"

"See if there's anything from @Lipjan or @ADAM99. Check under #cutforlife."

Katie tapped a few times. "Nothing today. What's this about?"

"I don't know. Can you see Chloe's account?"

"She hasn't posted anything."

Lottie paced, twisting her hands through her hair. She couldn't think straight. She stopped in front of Officer O'Donoghue.

"Head back to the station with Carter and trace the number of whoever was contacting him." She hurriedly scribbled on a page of O'Donoghue's notebook. "This is Chloe's phone number. I want a transcript of all activity on it, and on Twitter, Facebook and whatever else she might have been on."

She rushed O'Donoghue and Carter out the door.

"Cup of tea," Boyd said, placing two steaming cups on the table.

"I don't want fucking tea," Lottie said. She heard O'Donoghue talking in the hall before Superintendent Corrigan marched in through the open door.

"What's this I hear about a boy who shouldn't have been in your house disappearing from it? For feck's sake."

"Oh, shit," Lottie said.

"Would you like a cup of tea, sir?" Boyd asked.

* * *

The man left Fatjon to clean up the mess.

In the downstairs bathroom, he took off his shirt and

turned on the hot tap. There was no soap. He took a complimentary hotel bar from his pocket, unwrapped it and lathered up under the flowing water. He scrubbed his hands up to his elbows for two minutes before drying them with paper from a roll sitting on top of the toilet. Checking his shirt for blood, he noticed a couple of splashes. He turned it inside out and left it flapping open over his white vest, then strode out without turning off the tap. Glancing at his phone, he noted there was still no message from the social worker, Carter. Just as well he had taken extra precautions in case the young shit balked at the task he'd been set.

Moving out through the main gate, he smiled to himself. The sun was beginning to dip. An impressionistic sky of purple and orange tinged the horizon, but the heat of the day still hung in the air. At the canal he noticed an evening fog misting over the green water.

He'd have to hurry and get his van. Night would fall in a few hours and then he could start on the beginning of the end.

CHAPTER 78

When Boyd had left to take Katie to her granny's house, Lottie went to the cupboard and counted the mugs while Corrigan proceeded to give her an earful.

"I told you. Didn't I tell you to put that boy in care? And what do you do? Whatever you feckin' want as usual. A loose cannon. That's what you are. I despair over you." He paused for breath. "Any word on your daughter?"

She felt his hand on her arm as he led her to a chair.

"Why did you come here?" Lottie sat down and gazed up at her superior officer.

"I might only have the use of one eye at the moment, but I'm not blind. Nor deaf either. All hell was raging at the station and I wanted to talk to you about it." He wiped his eye and winced. "So your daughter and the boy. Tell me."

Lottie explained what had happened.

"This Eamon Carter, is he our killer?"

"No, sir. I think my house was being watched. They knew the boy, Milot, was here. I'd say Mimoza's friend brought him here and they tortured her to find out."

"The girl found dead at the pump house?"

"Yes, sir. I believe they then targeted Carter so they could take Milot without raising suspicion."

"So who are 'they'?"

"I don't know for sure." She stood up. How could she be sitting here talking so calmly when she should be searching for her daughter? She had to get out.

"Sit down, Lottie."

"Look, sir, with all due respect, my daughter is out there somewhere with the little boy these men are after. Someone is stalking her on Twitter. I think it's linked to the missing girls. She's traumatized and terrified. Can I please go and do my job?"

Corrigan said, "I've mobilized every officer in the district. They're turning this town upside down looking for your daughter and the little boy. You're coming to the station with me. When we find them, I'll decide what to do with you."

"Sir—"

"Don't feckin' 'sir' me. No argument. I'm not letting you out of my sight again. Leave the investigating to the others. You're in no state to be doing anything other than sitting under my watchful eye."

She didn't have much choice. Lottie sighed, grabbed her bag and followed him out, pulling the door closed behind her.

* * *

The station was buzzing. Superintendent Corrigan bustled through, giving everyone orders and snapping his fingers. Lottie escaped to her own office.

Boyd was pulling files from a cabinet. He slammed the drawer shut and leaned on top of it, staring at her.

Lottie returned his stare. "What?"

"I've been given the shitty job of babysitting you while everyone else is out there hunting for Chloe and Milot. So you can either sit down and we try to solve this together, or you can stand there moaning."

"If I wanted a lecture—"

"You'd get one from your mother. Yeah, I know. I had to listen to her when I dropped off Katie."

"Sean was there too, wasn't he?"

"Yes, they're both safe with two detectives watching over them."

"Good. Thank you."

"Sit."

"I can't, Boyd. I need to find—"

"You need to do what you're told."

Lottie sighed and sat at her desk. Of course he was right. But how could she concentrate when she didn't know where Chloe had gone?

Boyd said, "Chloe is a wise girl. She's doing what she thinks is best for Milot. She's—"

"Scared. She's terrified. Where is she, Boyd?" Lottie gulped down a sob.

"We've checked with her friend Emily Coyne and she hasn't seen her."

"What about Maeve's mother? Tracy Phillips. Chloe might have gone to her."

"Checked also. Not there. That woman's a mess. Why would Chloe go to her anyway?" Boyd sighed. "She'll be fine. You have to keep telling yourself that. Okay?" He clasped her fingers.

Lottie nodded and extracted her hand. She didn't trust herself to speak.

"Listen. Have you ever heard of Monk Island?" Boyd asked.

"Is Chloe there?" She jumped up. He gently pushed her down again.

Perched on the edge of her desk, he said, "Not unless she's an Olympic swimmer or can manage a boat. Lynch was looking at the reports of unusual activity around the lakes. There were a few about Monk Island."

"Which lake?"

"Lough Cullion. Anyway, there were complaints about shots being fired outside the shooting season."

"Has anyone followed up on this yet?"

"We were stretched to the limit and it seemed a low priority at the time, so no."

"Is someone out there now?"

"All manpower is assigned to tracing your daughter."

She thought for a moment. "Chloe's phone! Has her GPS been tracked yet?" Pulling her desk phone to her, she lifted the receiver.

Boyd stopped her. "It's being done. And we'll check Monk Island as soon as resources are freed up."

"But it needs to be checked now!"

"We'll try and find Chloe and Milot first."

"Why haven't I got a transcript from Chloe's phone? What are they at upstairs?"

"It takes time."

"What about the social worker's phone? Any trace on the number he was supposed to text when he had Milot?"

"Tech guys are working on that too."

"I need to get out of here. I can't just sit around."

She blinked as an email pinged. Glanced at her inbox. "I don't need this now."

"What is it?"

"It's just a reply to the email I sent last night to Besim Mehmedi."

"Who?"

"The prosecutor of the illegal human organ harvesting case in Pristina about five years ago. I told you about it."

"Relevant to our cases?"

"Could be."

"Open it."

As she clicked the email open, Officer Gillian O'Donoghue put her head around the door.

"Detective Inspector? Eamon Carter is throwing a tantrum down in the interview room. He's insisting he needs to send a text message to the guy who forced him to abduct the young boy. He doesn't believe his mother will be safe unless he does it."

Lottie looked up at Boyd. "What do you think? Draw the bastard out?"

Boyd stood up. "Exactly."

Ignoring the email from the prosecutor in Pristina, she hit the screen-save button.

"Later," she said to the computer.

* * *

The heat in Interview Room One was usually oppressive. This evening it was overwhelming. Perspiration stained Carter's shirt dark gray between his shoulder blades and under his armpits. Boyd appeared to be cool, but Lottie knew he was as anxious as she was. She had to find Chloe and the boy. And the only way to do this might be by snaring the man in contact with Carter.

She had ripped the phone out of the plastic evidence bag and dictated the message for Carter to put in his own words. No point in spooking the recipient. Now she felt the phone slip around in her hand as she waited for a reply.

A text came in: *St. Declan's. Ten minutes. Wait behind gatehouse.*

"Let's go." Lottie ran to the door.

"Doesn't give us time to get a team together," Boyd said.

"You and me. That's team enough."

"What about me?" Carter said.

For a moment, Lottie thought about bringing him with them to draw out the kidnappers, but she couldn't risk his life.

"Stay here where you can't get into any more trouble," she said over her shoulder.

"Watch him," Boyd told O'Donoghue.

Lottie ran through reception and out the station door. "Where's your car?"

"Round the back."

"Hurry up." She streaked around the side of the building.

"Ten minutes in this traffic. It's madness." Boyd clicked the car unlocked and they jumped in. "Blue light and siren?"

"Yes. No." Lottie clasped the dashboard as he swung the car out of the yard at an acute angle. "We don't know where he is. He could be watching us for all we know. Better not to warn him."

* * *

He'd parked his van in the cathedral car park. Right under the noses of the Keystone Cops across the road. He'd lived dangerously all his life. No need to change now.

He pulled off his soft leather shoes and shoved his feet into steel-toe-capped boots. As he was turning the key to start the van, he heard the message vibrating in his phone.

Glancing at the screen, he banged the steering wheel. "Yes!"

He read through the text again: *Got the kid. What will I do now? Don't hurt my mum.* He thought for a moment before keying in his reply.

As he drove out through the cathedral gates, he glanced over at the police station. Why were Lottie Parker and her sidekick running so fast?

He wondered about it as he traveled down the street. It gnawed at the back of his brain. Did they know something? Surely not.

His mind ticked over as he thought of ways to manage the situation if they were on to him. He'd been careful, but was there something he'd overlooked? Had Russell blabbed to the cops? He'd said he hadn't and now he was in no state to answer any questions. Too bad.

He would just have to think on his feet. Like any good surgeon would do.

* * *

The traffic wasn't the problem. It was the fog. Out of nowhere it seemed to drop like a heavy veil over the town. Ensnaring everything in its web. The sun was shrouded out and darkness descended.

"It's like the end of the fucking world," Boyd said, turning up by the Dublin bridge.

"Where the hell are Kirby and Lynch?" Lottie said tensely.

"Nothing from either."

Lottie tapped Kirby's name on her speed dial. "Come on, big man, answer."

"Boss?"

"Thank God. Where are you? Any sign of Chloe?"

"We've completed a search of the railway line from the back of your house. Think she climbed up there and walked along the tracks. Haven't found her yet. Or the little boy."

"Why would she go up there?" Lottie widened her eyes. "Why were *you* up there, for that matter?"

"Tracked her phone. She'd dropped it just outside the train station."

"Whereabouts?"

"The little footbridge. The one that goes over the canal to Hill Point. We're searching the area now."

"That's where Petrovci lives." Lottie shook her head, trying to insert some logic into the equation. "Why was her phone there?"

"Don't know. Maybe she was running and it fell out of her pocket. I'll let you know as soon as. This fog is slowing us down, though."

"Lynch with you?"

"Yes, boss."

Lottie sighed a long breath. "Keep at it." She hung up. "Keep driving," she told Boyd.

"I can't see a thing."

"Just follow the tail lights of that van in front."

"That's what I'm doing."

"Faster, Boyd. Can't you go faster?"

"Not unless I grow wings."

* * *

He could see the police behind him. Pulling in at a corner shop, half a mile from St. Declan's, he let them pass.

Where were they off to? Surely not St. Declan's Hospital, once an asylum for the mentally insane. They had no reason to go there, had they? Closed down for ten years, as far as he knew. Crumbling in on itself until he had stumbled upon it a year ago and brought its operating room back to life. He couldn't let them find it. Not yet. Not until he had finished. He had a job to complete.

Maneuvering the van back into the line of traffic, he continued his short journey. He had to concentrate on the job in hand. He needed to take delivery of the boy. And deal with Eamon Carter. No loose ends.

Driving through the rusted gates of St. Declan's, he saw no sign of the unmarked police car. He parked behind the gatehouse, switched off the engine and sat waiting for the biggest prize of all. Mimoza's boy. Milot.

CHAPTER 79

Boyd drove around the roundabout that led to the motorway and came back down on the opposite side of the road.

"Stop!" Lottie cried. "In there."

"Someone will crash into the back of me in this fog," he protested.

"Park the fucking car, Boyd!"

With a swerve of the steering wheel he banked the car up on the grass verge.

"And switch off the lights. Have you a jacket I can wear?"

Boyd leaned into the back seat and found a black fleece. "This any good?"

"It'll do." Lottie unbuckled her seat belt and zipped up the fleece.

"You're not going out there alone."

"Stay here. You need to keep in touch with Kirby," she said, ignoring his concern.

"I'm going with you." He opened his door.

Grasping his arm, Lottie pulled him close. "Listen, Boyd. I need you to monitor the phone and the radio. I have my gun."

"That's what I'm afraid of. I don't want it to end up like the O. K. Corral."

"I'm not that stupid."

He groaned. "You're the boss."

"This guy might have Chloe or know where she is."

"He might also be the same guy who has killed three girls and abducted two more."

"You think I don't know that?"

Boyd held her hand. "Be careful."

Lottie opened the door and stood out into the damp fog.

"I'm coming for you, you bastard," she whispered into the mist.

* * *

Smothered, that was what it felt like. Lottie couldn't breathe with the fog and couldn't see through the darkness. She panned her arms around her like a madwoman in a padded cell. Right place for that, she thought. Her hands touched air. No walls. The only thing she felt was the ground beneath her feet.

Baby steps, heel to toe, she moved forward. Four steps. Nothing. Why was it so dark? A blackout? There was no hint of the yellow shadow from the street lights in the distance. She knew you could normally see it from almost five kilometers away. But now it was as if the town had been plucked from its foundations and spirited away in an ethereal haze. Her hands swiped down a spiderweb, its gossamer trail hanging from the trash can to her right. She counted three industrial-sized bins with her fingertips.

Feeling a presence behind her, she paused. Held her breath. Listened. The slow hum of traffic on the N4. No other sound. I'm definitely raving mad, she told herself.

Easing her way forward, she couldn't shake off the feeling that someone was right behind her.

Where was he?

* * *

He saw the detective through the fog. She was close. What to do? He couldn't let her find anything. It would be endgame for sure. He eased around the side of the building after her. She couldn't prevent him from finishing his quest. A promise was a promise. It didn't matter that he'd made it to himself. He had started this and he was going to finish it.

He was now so close he could smell her scent. He crept nearer. Heard her breathing, low and fast. Was she afraid? He didn't believe that for one moment. She was a fine adversary. But now wasn't the time to test her fortitude. He had to act.

Stealthily he edged closer, holding his breath so she wouldn't sense him. With precision and accuracy he slid his arm around her throat, pulled her into his chest and squeezed.

Her arms flailed about, trying to dislodge his, before they fell slowly to her sides without finding a target. Feeling her head slump against his shoulder, he released her and she fell at his feet. Moving quickly, he hurried away from the bins and back to his van.

The bastard Carter had squealed after all.

* * *

Lottie didn't know how long she had been unconscious. She opened her eyes and rubbed her throat, trying to breathe through the tightness and pain. Clutching her under-arm holster, she felt her gun. At least that was something. He hadn't got away with her weapon. He had stolen her pride but replaced it with a dogged resolution to catch him.

Sliding her phone from the back pocket of her jeans, she saw the screen was cracked, but she could still make the call.

CHAPTER 80

"Jesus, Boyd, faster." Lottie stamped her foot to the floor as if the accelerator was on her side.

"Shut up. I'm concentrating on the road. I can't see a thing." He switched the wipers on to clear the mist from the windscreen.

She swallowed hard. Her throat felt like someone had thrust broken glass down it. Boyd had seen the van screech out of the hospital grounds and down on to the dual carriageway. He'd put the car in gear and rushed over to find her fumbling with her phone among the trash cans. She'd insisted they follow the van.

"I don't know where I'm going," he said. "I've lost him."

The fog was dense, the road twisty; she could hardly blame him.

"If he turned left onto the N4, he could be heading for Lough Cullion and Monk Island. Maybe that's where he brought Chloe."

"You have no idea if Monk Island has anything to do with anything."

"Where else could he be heading?" Lottie said. "It has to be Petrovci."

"It could be anyone."

She thought for a moment. She remembered the strength of the arm that had choked the breath from her.

"I don't know who it was," she admitted. But she knew she couldn't let him get away.

The car skidded up from the main road on to the slip road.

"It's the wrong turn, Boyd," Lottie screeched. "Ouch." Her throat blazed in pain.

"Shit!" He kept driving. "I can't go back down. I'll cut across the link road."

With blue light flashing and siren blaring, Boyd sped across the ring road. Lottie planted her feet firmly in the footwell and held on to the dashboard. Around a corner, past the cemetery and along a narrow road. He righted the vehicle and its lights bounced off the fog, blinding them. Red tail lights up ahead.

"There he is," Lottie said.

The lights disappeared.

"That could be anyone," Boyd said, and the car swerved into the center of the road. "Sorry."

"Follow the verge," Lottie shouted.

He said nothing, his hands white as they clutched the steering wheel.

"Hail Mary, full of grace," Lottie whispered.

She caught his glance and screamed as the car mounted the grass before sliding back on to the road.

"Jesus Christ, Boyd. Watch where you're going."

"He's getting away."

Rounding the next corner, Lottie knew the railway crossing was ahead. "Dear God in heaven, whom I don't always believe in, don't let there be a train. Please."

Flashing lights through the fog. Amber, amber, red.

Boyd slammed the brakes to the floor. The seat belt cut into Lottie's shoulder and chest with the impact. The barriers slid down with a clunk in the night air.

She leapt out of the car to see the tail lights of the van crest the hill and disappear.

"Fuck. What do we do now?"

"Radio for backup and wait for the train to pass."

"Five minutes. That's how long it takes." She was helpless to stop the tears. "Five fucking minutes until the train passes."

She felt Boyd put his arm around her shoulders. He led her back to the car.

"I hope he doesn't do anything while we're stuck here," he said, resting his head on the steering wheel.

"Hope is a fine thing," Lottie said. "He could have Milot or Chloe. Couldn't he?"

"He hasn't got them, Lottie. He was meeting Carter to get the boy," Boyd said with a level-headedness she couldn't manage at the moment.

She turned to look at him. "Then where are they?"

* * *

He shifted his hands along the oars, tightening his grip as he rowed. He never risked using an engine, but this was a time he knew he could do with one. Soft ripples swam away from the boat, a watery swish trailing in their wake. Arm muscles trembled with each heave as his journey inched along. The fog began to lift and he could see the orange shimmer of the setting sun reflecting on the small waves. He was aware of the trees surrounding the shoreline, which appeared black in the shadows, and the dock hidden through a river of reeds. He aimed straight ahead.

It had been a close-run thing with the police. The train had saved him. He'd been lucky. This time. But now he was sure they knew about his killing ground. A little water swirled beneath his booted feet, splashed in from the lake, as he squinted through the disappearing fog. Monk Island. He shivered with anticipation. Maybe this time he would succeed in a fulfilling his destiny. But without the boy. Pity.

As he docked the boat a few minutes later, he thought about the clear water. Water he'd used to wash away the impurities from the bodies. He had two more to cleanse. He hoped they hadn't succumbed to starvation. It was a few days since he'd been here. It would be a pity if they died before he could send them on their way to redemption. He laughed out loud. Redemption? Only he could achieve it.

He jumped up onto the short wooden jetty shielded by wild shrubbery and hauled the boat astern with a thick rope. He wrapped it carefully around a stick jutting from the edge of the worn slats and tightened it in a double knot. He filled his lungs with fresh air, exhaled; repeated the exercise three times.

Ducking under the leafy trees, he followed a pathway of trodden grass. He had made this journey on numerous occasions and knew the grass suffered only the trampling of his own feet. No one else ventured to this island. He had reconnoitered it well. Church Island, two kilometers to his right, was where the indecent escapades occurred, leaving his island to birds and badgers. An unofficial sanctuary for wildlife, he was the only interloper, with, of course, his own prey.

Almost there, and he couldn't dampen the excitement throbbing through his veins, from the follicles of the hair on his head to the tips of his toes. And for once the swelling inside his trousers comforted him.

At last the clearing opened up before him, illuminated by the rising moon, a blue haze around its rim. A bird skittered from a tree with a loud flapping of wings. He slumped to his knees. The two bundles were where he'd left them. Unmoving. No, he was wrong. He checked one, then the other. Soft, labored breaths. They were still alive. He looked skyward and gave thanks. Slowly he unwound the tape from the first bundle, peeled back the fringed folds of woven wool. At last she lay before him.

A bruise had risen on her forehead where he had kicked her.

He traced his finger over her face, pausing as he felt the indentations of the wounds on her cheek.

"Damaged bird, your wings are broken but I can set you free and let you fly again," he whispered.

He unwrapped the covering from her body and marveled at her nakedness. Allowing his finger to linger on her deepest scar, his salty tears dropped silently on to the wound. His actions had caused this and now he would heal her. Forever. He would release her from her pain and bring her peace and eternal salvation. Pity she wouldn't be able to thank him. He sacrificed them in order to save others who paid him well for it. But that wasn't why he did what he did. Was it? He was following in footsteps. It was ordained. And with her death, she would make the evil one pay for causing his father's death.

Rising to his feet, he moved through the undergrowth and hauled out his steel toolbox. He took a key from his inside jacket pocket, unlocked the lid and opened it. From under a soft cloth he extracted the gun wrapped in leather. Checking the magazine was empty, he counted the bullets from a cardboard box, loading each one carefully. Then he clicked the magazine back into the semi-automatic and chambered the first bullet. One was all he required, but he liked the feel of a fully loaded weapon. Power and control.

Clouds moved swiftly across the sky and a warm mist caressed his skin.

With his gun in one hand and the silencer in the other, he turned around.

CHAPTER 81

When the train eventually passed and the barrier lifted, Boyd put the car in gear and set off again.

"Where did he go?" Lottie asked. "Did he keep on driving? Or did he turn off for Monk Island?"

"Wish I knew." Boyd exhaled in exasperation.

"Stop!" Lottie shouted.

The car screeched and Boyd skewed it up on the verge. "What now?"

"There." She pointed to the narrow slip road at the side of the rail track. With the fog lifting, the lake sparkled like molten glass beyond it. Jumping out of the car, she disappeared into the vegetation.

"Wait," Boyd shouted, slamming the car door.

"His van." Lottie stood beside a small white vehicle. She tried the door. "Locked."

Boyd reached her side and stood with his hands on his hips, looking out over the lake.

"There's Monk Island," he said.

"How are we going to get over there?" she asked. The bleat of her phone broke though the air. "Kirby. Have you found her?"

"Not yet, boss. But you need to get back to the station."

"I'm in pursuit of a suspect. I think it's Andri Petrovci."

"That's not possible."

"Why not?"

"We've just found Petrovci attempting to get into his apartment."

Lottie turned to look at Boyd, then let her gaze span the lake.

"So who the hell is over there?"

* * *

Mimoza heard the click of the magazine going into the gun. She knew what it meant. She sensed him moving, aware of him leaning over her, touching her.

"Ah, little Mimoza. I've waited for this moment to set you free."

"Milot?" she whispered, her voice a thin wheeze.

"I wanted to bring him to join you, but fate intervened. Or should I say a cop called Lottie Parker. She is on my list once I finish here."

The lady detective had not forgotten about her after all. Mimoza tried to smile. Her lips cracked and her throat seized up. Don't let me die yet, she thought. Just let me see my little boy one last time. Was that his apple shampoo she could smell? The man was lying. He was certainly cruel enough. Milot was here.

"Milot? Please," she begged.

"Shut up. I've told you I haven't got him."

She had to do something. Milot needed her. She needed him. She willed strength into her body. The act of opening her eyes was torture. She had to, though. Had to force herself to act. Otherwise she was going to die.

Shifting her elbows underneath herself, she tried to sit up. "Please..."

"Oh, will you shut up?"

She squinted through half-open eyes. He was right there. On one knee. Looking down at her. Gun in his hand. She'd seen plenty of guns in her short life. It didn't frighten her. What did frighten her was the thought of never seeing her son again.

That thought infused a superhuman energy into her body. At last she was half sitting up, leaning on her elbows. He seemed to find it amusing and laughed. Why would he think that was funny? Because he's mad, a voice in her head told her. Mad. And how do you fight madness? With madness, she thought.

"I ... I know you ..." she began.

"Of course you do." He laughed again. A manic sound.

Good, she thought. Now I can act. For Milot. She took one last look at the stars in the sky. She saw only the smile on her son's face and the light in his eyes as she brought her leg up and kicked out as hard as she could with the little energy she had left. And an image of her son smiling and giggling lit up in front of her like a miraculous icon.

"Mama loves you, Milot."

* * *

The sound of a gunshot split the silence of the night.

"What the..." Lottie ducked, automatically reaching for her gun.

The trees above her head shook with the flutter of birds taking flight. Boyd dragged her up.

"Over there," he said. "On the island."

She threw her arms up helplessly. "He's there and we're here. Blare the siren. Quickly. Up as loud as it can go. And where is our backup?"

She stared across the water as Boyd ran to the car and switched on the siren.

The fog returned as quickly as it had vanished, falling in a soft sheen around them. Only the light flashing on the car told her where it was. She strained her ears above the screeching noise. No further shots. Had they scared him off?

"We need a boat," she shouted above the din.

"What?"

"A boat. Where can we get one? The shore. I'll try along the shore."

Without waiting for Boyd, she climbed over the rail tracks and down the other side. Slipping and sliding, she ended up on the rocky shore. In the dense fog, she couldn't see further than her hand. She took out her phone to switch on its flashlight and realized Kirby was still on the line.

"Kirby. We need a boat. Quick."

* * *

They killed the motor and the boat glided to the island shore. It was half an hour since they'd heard the shot. A man living nearby had run out of his house to investigate the siren just as two squad cars pulled up. Lottie had told him what they needed and he'd returned immediately with an engine and quickly rigged it to one of the boats pulled up on the shore.

Now he jumped out and secured the boat. "It's a hidden dock," he said. "Not many know about it. Best that way. Enough interfering bastards—"

"Thanks," Lottie interrupted. "Wait here."

Taking Boyd's hand, she stepped on to dry land. With their weapons at the ready, they crouched under low-hanging branches and made their way along a grassy path.

"This vest is fucking heavy." Lottie hated wearing the ballistic vest Boyd had taken from the trunk of the car, but she knew she was no use to anyone dead.

"How did he find this place?" Boyd said.

"Shh. I've no idea."

"Why was there only one shot?"

"Will you shush? Listen." She put out her hand and pulled him back toward her by the belt of his trousers. "Did you hear that?"

"It's only damn birds."

"No. Stop. It's like someone crying. Dear God. Chloe?"

"Wait," Boyd said.

But Lottie ran past him, falling through the undergrowth. "Chloe!" she shouted, all her training vanishing with the night. "Chloe?"

Charging into a clearing, she stopped suddenly, sending Boyd crashing into her.

"Jesus Christ," he said.

He switched on his flashlight, scanning it over the scene. The light bounced off the fog, but Lottie could see three prone bodies in front of her. Her hands and legs trembled uncontrollably. "Please God, no. No!"

She turned away. Couldn't look.

"Tell me, Boyd. Is it Chloe?" She thought his pause went on forever.

Eventually he said, "It's not Chloe. None of them are Chloe. But I know who they are."

Blowing air through her nose, she tried to regain control. She moved toward him on her hands and knees.

"Who are they? Are they alive? I heard someone crying." Pulling aside a ragged blanket, she stared into a young face. "Maeve Phillips. She's alive, Boyd, but unconscious. We need help. He could be here."

"He is." Boyd pointed. "Bullet through the belly."

Lottie cradled Maeve to her chest. "He's dead? What about the other one?"

Boyd moved away from the man and edged to the other person. "Can't see a bullet wound."

Lottie laid Maeve down gently and looked at the naked body of the girl at Boyd's feet. Clutched in her lifeless hand was a semi-automatic pistol.

"It's Mimoza," she whispered. She felt for a pulse. "Oh my God, Boyd, she's dead. The brave girl killed him."

A groan rose from the man lying on the ground. Boyd swung back toward him.

"He's still alive." He checked him again, then snapped on handcuffs. "You're going nowhere, you bastard, except jail for the rest of your life."

"I recognize him," Lottie said.

"You do? Who the fuck is he?"

"George O'Hara, the tutor at the DPC."

She turned her head away. Hauling off her heavy vest and Boyd's fleece, she wrapped the warm clothing around Maeve and held her close.

"You're safe now," she soothed through her tears. "But where is my Chloe?"

CHAPTER 82

"It's going to take some time before McGlynn and his SOCOs get working on Monk Island," Lottie said.

She watched the blue lights of the ambulance swirl through the mist. Maeve Phillips was on her way to hospital. Lottie knew the girl would survive her physical injuries but wasn't sure if her mental scars would ever heal. A second ambulance carried George O'Hara, with two armed detectives for company. Mimoza's body remained on the island. Alone.

Boyd lit two cigarettes. He handed one to Lottie and leaned against the bonnet of the car.

Inhaling deeply, she said, "We need to get back to base and see what this is about Petrovci. And I need to know if there's any sign of Chloe and Milot."

"Smoke your cigarette first."

"But—"

"No buts." He pulled her close. "Thirty seconds' rest. My orders."

Leaning her head on his chest, Lottie fought the intense fatigue rushing through her.

Boyd's phone buzzed.

"It's Jackie. I forgot she'd been trying to contact me."

"Better answer her." Throwing down her cigarette, Lottie ground it with the heel of her boot.

Boyd turned away. "Jackie, you were looking for me. What's up?"

Sitting into the car, Lottie started up the engine. She didn't want to hear whatever Boyd was saying. She had to find her daughter.

* * *

Back at the station, she flew up the stairs. It was almost midnight. She felt like she'd throw up if there wasn't word of Chloe soon. Boyd was parking the car. Silence had ensued during the drive back to town. Jackie had been cut off and he had no idea what she wanted.

"Where the feck did you go?" Corrigan stormed down the corridor. "Didn't I give you a direct order to stay here?"

She didn't have time for this. She rushed past him into the incident room without saying anything. It was as quiet as the Dead House. Corrigan followed her.

"Oh God," Lottie said. Looking up at the incident board, her eyes had landed on the photograph of Mimoza holding Milot in her arms. A little boy without a mother. What would happen to him now?

"What are you looking at, Parker?"

Lottie indicated the board. "Sir, we have everyone pinned up here except George O'Hara, our killer. He never even crossed our radar."

"Clever fox, then."

She phoned Kirby. "Carry out a thorough background check on George O'Hara. I want to know everything about him. Like five minutes ago."

Feeling a surge of adrenaline, she turned back to Corrigan. "I think he had others working with him. He needed someone to get the girls for him." Pointing first to Dan Russell's photograph, then Petrovci's. "These two. One or both of them has Chloe and Milot."

"Petrovci is in a cell," Corrigan said.

"I need to see him, sir. Right away. He might know where Chloe is."

She waited, counting in her head. She got to five before he moved to one side. She was out the door before he could change his mind.

"Detective Inspector Parker! By the book. You hear me. By the book."

"Yes, sir," Lottie shouted back with her fingers crossed.

* * *

The three-inch-thick steel door clanged shut behind Lottie.

Petrovci made to get up from his stone bed.

"Stay where you are." She propped herself against the wall, crossed her feet. No chairs.

"I sorry. I do nothing." He swung his legs to the side and sat up straight.

Flipping through the pages that Kirby had given her on her way to the cells, Lottie said, without looking up, "The guy who rang your boss Jack Dermody telling him to go to the pump house where you found the third body, his number came up on your call list. Explain."

"I not know what you mean."

"We believe his name is George O'Hara. Familiar?"

Petrovci shook his head. "I not know him."

She folded the pages and stuffed them into the back pocket of her jeans. "You expect me to believe that?"

"I not know."

"Your friend George O'Hara is in hospital. Shot."

He raised an eyebrow and rubbed a hand over his shaved head. "I not know anyone by that name."

"Oh come on. We found two phones on him. There was a call to you on Saturday night from one of them. Why did he contact you?"

Petrovci looked puzzled, remained mute.

Lottie said, "I'll explain it for you. You're working with this man, George O Hara. Reeling in girls from Kosovo, Africa and God knows where, for him to operate on and dump in the sex trade. Were you grooming them?"

"I not know...grooming."

With two steps Lottie was on him, dragging him upright by the elbow. He jerked his hand free easily and moved to the wall.

"You angry. Why?" he asked.

"I haven't time for this. My daughter is missing. I believe you know where she is. So out with it." She slapped her hand against the wall beside his head.

He didn't flinch. "Daughter?" He turned to her.

"For fuck's sake. This is impossible." Lottie sat on the bed. "Please. You have nothing to lose now. You're going to prison for helping this murderer. However the two of you did it, I'll find out. But you can help yourself. A shorter sentence. I'll see what I can do. Please, tell me where she is."

"I kill no one. I not take your daughter."

With an exasperated sigh, Lottie knew she was getting nothing out of him. She stood up and gave the signal for the door to be opened.

"Such a waste of life. But at least Maeve survived. She will tell me everything."

"Maeve? I confused."

"You recognized her photograph."

He shook his head. "I not know name."

"You don't know much of anything."

"Who...Maeve?"

She knew she shouldn't play along, but she took out her phone and scrolled. Turning the photo toward him, she said, "This is Maeve."

He stared at it for a moment then raised his eyes to meet hers.

"I remember you show me. She look like a girl I know once. It scare me. I fear for her. I think she one of them. In ground."

"I haven't time for your lies." Lottie snapped away the phone.

He put out a hand and held on to her arm. Thick fingers, ingrained with dirt from his work, pressed into her skin. "I no lie. I never lie. I not kill girls. I come to Ragmullin. I work and I look for my girl. Every day. But I not find her."

Shrugging off his grip, Lottie said, "What girl? Why did you leave your apartment? You took your stuff." She needed to get away from him. To get out and search for Chloe and Milot.

"I a boy in war." He pulled up his T-shirt. "War do this to me."

Lottie gasped. A neat scar stretched from his abdomen up over his hip and round his back. Similar to the scars borne by the first two victims. "Who? Who did that to you?"

"Many years ago. In the war. It not matter now. Hurt my brain. My head." He knocked at his skull with his fist. Three times. Hard. "So many things happen. I not remember. You understand. What you call… blackout. I not remember."

She ran her hands through her hair. "It still doesn't explain why you left your apartment and came back again."

He shuffled around the small cell, constantly tapping and rubbing his head, leaving dark streaks of dirt and sweat. In the confined space he appeared like a lonely, sad giant. Lottie shook herself. She shouldn't be feeling sorry for him. God knows what he'd done.

Facing the wall, he said, "I find that little girl dead by the water and you lock me up. Your detective, he ask me lot of questions. He let me go. I afraid. I not want to be locked up again. I get phone call. This man, he say my girl in town. He say he kill her and me. That all he say. I pack and I go. I have to look for her."

"Where did you go?"

Petrovci shrugged his shoulders. "I walk around. I sleep by the rail tracks. But I got nowhere to go. I come back to my apartment. Only place I know. I got nowhere." He banged the wall with his knuckles. "I come back. That is all I know." He started to sob. "She is near."

"Who is near? What are you talking about?"

"He tell me she is near. That is why I look for her. The man on the phone. But he not tell me where she is."

Give me strength, Lottie thought. "When you're ready to speak without the riddles, I'll be back." She opened the door.

As she stepped out into the brightly lit hallway, she heard Andri Petrovci cry out.

"One day. One day I see my Mimoza again."

* * *

Boyd clasped the phone to his ear and walked up and down the station yard.

"Start from the beginning, Jackie, you're making no sense."

"I haven't seen Jamie for hours. He rushed off after getting a phone call. When he'd left, I found this phone on the couch. Not his usual iPhone. A bulky Nokia. It was unlocked. I thought maybe he used it for another woman, you know…"

"So you checked it. Right?"

"Right. The only text sent said: 'Boy not safe at yours. Leave. Meet at canal footbridge.' That's all."

"You sure. No name? Anything?"

"Just the number." She read it out to him.

Boyd recognized it. "I'm sending someone to yours for the phone. Don't leave."

"Okay. And one other thing…"

"What?"

"There are only two names in the contact list. One is Tracy Phillips and the other is George O'H. Mean anything to you?"

"I need that phone," Boyd said.

CHAPTER 83

"Boyd. Boyd!" Lottie ran up the stairs and into the incident room. "Have you seen Boyd?"

Lynch and Kirby were there, rings as black as nuggets of coal circling their eyes.

"Chloe?" Lottie gasped.

"No, boss," said Kirby. "We've searched high up and low down."

"Her phone. Anything on it?"

"We got a number, but it's another one of those throwaway yokes."

"Pre-pay," Lynch said.

"Yes. And it's not the same number that contacted Dermody or Carter," Kirby said with a yawn.

"Guys, I'm so sorry," Lottie said. "You've been working day and night. I need Boyd."

"I'm here." He walked in.

If anything, Lottie thought he looked worse than her other two detectives. She said, "It's Petrovci. You won't believe what he's just told me."

"Can it wait? I've something important to tell you all."

"You're looking too serious. It's Chloe. Tell me!" Gulping air so as not to get hysterical, Lottie pleaded with her eyes. "I can handle it."

Boyd slumped into the nearest chair, plucked at the growing stubble on his chin. "It's Jackie—" he began.

"Boyd! My daughter and a child are missing and you're on about Jackie. Give me a break."

"Will you calm—"

"Don't tell me to calm down." Lottie kicked over the nearest chair. "This is shit. All shit." Near to tears, she picked up the chair and sat down. "Sorry. Go on."

"Turns out Jamie McNally is in this up to his greasy little ponytail."

"What?" Lottie jumped up again.

"The slimy little fucker," Kirby said, sticking an unlit cigar into his mouth.

Boyd told them about the phone Jackie had found.

Lottie counted silently, trying to ease the tension building in her chest. She said, "McNally has Chloe and Milot."

"How did he get Chloe's number?" Kirby asked.

"Kids have their numbers on Facebook and Twitter and stuff," Lynch said. "Never aware of how vulnerable it leaves them." At the incident board she pushed a pin slap-bang in the middle of McNally's face.

"I should have been more careful. I suspected someone was watching me, watching my house," Lottie said. "Why would Chloe respond to that message if she didn't know who it was from?"

"Unless he is Lipjan," Boyd said.

"Where is McNally now?" Lynch said.

"Is Jackie with him?" Lottie said. "Why are we still here? Come on. Let's go."

Boyd stopped her at the door. "I don't know where McNally is. Jackie's alone. I've sent officers over to get the phone and sit with her."

"Could McNally be with Russell? Up at the DPC?" Lynch asked.

"I thought I told someone to pick up Russell," Lottie said.

"We went in with the warrant," Kirby said. "I left a crew of detectives searching. Ongoing as we speak. But Russell wasn't there. Last seen early afternoon."

"Check his home."

"Done. Not there either. His car is still at the DPC."

Lottie paused, banging her forehead with her knuckles.

"Could he be at St. Declan's? That's where O'Hara wanted to pick the boy up from Carter. And Jackie said that O'Hara's name is in McNally's phone."

"You're right." Boyd passed her at the door. "Two cars. No sirens. Come on."

"Right." Lottie wondered where she was getting her energy from. She hadn't eaten all day and she was still going.

Fear, she thought.

Fear for her daughter and that little boy.

* * *

The three-story Victorian asylum for the mentally insane rose in front of them like a monster in the fog as they parked the cars outside the front door. They couldn't see lights anywhere in the building.

Huddling in a group, Lottie quelled a rush of anxiety taking a tight hold of her heart.

"It's a horrible-looking place," she said.

"There's an annex-type building to the back. It was built in the early 1900s," Lynch said.

Lottie, Boyd and Kirby stared at her.

"I studied for a diploma in local history a few years ago," she explained. "Far as I can remember, the annex housed an operating theater."

They set off round the side of the building, staying close to the wall.

"You all right?" Boyd asked Lottie.

"No."

She stopped abruptly as they turned the corner. A long single-story building jutted out from the main hospital. A light glared from a window at the very end.

"Looks like it's shining through plastic or something," Kirby said.

"It's the fog," Lynch said.

"No, I think Kirby's right," Boyd said.

"Quiet," Lottie warned. "Be ready with your weapons." She eased her gun into her hand.

The door opened silently. No creak.

"Not a sound," Lottie whispered. "No flashlights. Follow me."

"Shouldn't we get the ballistic vests?" Kirby asked.

"I said, not a sound." She entered a narrow hallway.

High ceilings. Thick pipes snaking along the walls by her feet. Concrete floor. Stopping at a tall door, which seemed to cut the hall in half, she looked up at the strip of stained glass at the top. To her left, the floor sloped away into a dark, cavernous hole. She ignored it and put her hand to the hard wood of the door. It opened inward without resistance.

Stepping inside, she found the wall to guide her, sensing the three detectives behind. Trailing her hand as she walked, she felt an indent. A door. Kept on walking. Twenty-seven steps. Another high door with glass on top. The light they'd seen outside was coming from here. Would this door be locked? She hoped not.

"On the count of three," she whispered.

"Fuck that," Boyd said, and kicked in the door. "Armed police!" he shouted and entered running. He halted immediately. They all did.

"Jesus Christ," Kirby said.

"What the—" Lynch dropped her arm, letting the gun fall to her side.

Lottie stared, her mouth opening and shutting, no words coming out. Whirling toward Boyd, she tried to comprehend what she was witnessing.

Windows sheathed with plexiglass, solidified blood like a Jackson Pollock reject. White ceramic tiles grouted in blood. Ceiling pebble-dashed red. She lifted her foot from the plastic-covered floor, dark remnants stuck to her boots. Blood and more blood.

At the end of the L-shaped room were two iron-framed hospital beds. One was empty. Not even a mattress. Base springs rusted green under the fluorescent light. From the other bed saturated sheets dripped blood to the floor. Pools of it.

Picking her way slowly, so as not to slip, she inched forward. Slow. Slow. Slower. She reached the bed. Gasped. Swallowed bile back down to the pit of her stomach.

Dan Russell.

Naked, except for navy socks with gold logos. Prostrate on the bed, a wide canvas strap across his chest. He didn't need restraining. Not anymore. The socket of one eye was sunk flaccid in his head. She dragged her eyes to the source of the blood. Stomach sliced open, entrails and intestines hanging out across fatty flesh.

She heard Lynch retching behind her.

"Don't contaminate the evidence," she said, her voice sounding like someone else's entirely.

"It's like a…like a…" Kirby stammered.

"An abattoir," Boyd said.

Breathe, Lottie, breathe, she commanded herself. The fetid stench in the room clogged her throat and she thought for a moment she'd be joining Lynch. But she had nothing in her stomach to bring up.

Edging by the beds, gun in hand, carefully avoiding the viscera, she rounded the corner at the end of the room.

"Boyd!" she yelled. "Quick. Here."

He joined her. Lottie put out an arm to hold him back. They stared.

She said, "McNally?"

Slumped on the floor, knees to his chest, sat Jamie McNally. Black hair streamed greasily around his neck. Face covered in blood spatter, he waved a scalpel through the air.

"Get the fuck away from me, bitch," he snarled.

Lottie leaned in as far as she deemed safe. "Where is my daughter? What did you do with her, you piece of shit? Tell me. Now!"

"Who?"

"Chloe."

"Her? I didn't touch that little bitch."

"I know you texted her. You asked her to bring Milot to you."

"Is that the little shit's name?" He laughed. "I'd a cat once called that. Gutted the little fucker, I did."

"Like you did to Russell?"

"I didn't do that," he snickered. "For a detective, you're mighty stupid, woman."

With one hand holding her gun, Lottie dug her nails into the palm of the other. She wanted to lash out and shove the weapon down McNally's throat and pull the trigger. But she remained outwardly calm. Professional.

"Where are they? Are they safe? That's all I want to know. That my daughter is safe."

"I don't know where she went. Freaked the hell out when I brought her in here. Fatjon freaked her a bit too."

"Fatjon?" Lottie looked round at Boyd.

"Russell and O'Hara's right-hand man. Big dude with a mouth full of crooked teeth. Bastard attacked me after he'd gutted Russell."

Nice and slow. Unemotional. "Where is Fatjon now?" Dear God, she prayed, don't let him have Chloe.

"You don't give up, do you?" McNally pulled at his chin with the hand holding the scalpel. Nicked himself. Smiled crookedly. "I'd been watching your house, and when there was no sign of Carter coming out with the boy, I knew your kids had probably called the police. I couldn't tell O'Hara I'd fucked up, and my last chance to get the boy for him was through your daughter."

"I still don't understand why O'Hara wanted Milot," Lottie muttered.

McNally was still talking. "When O'Hara didn't show up, Fatjon started on Dan the Man. Time is of the essence, O'Hara always said when he was slicing and dicing, according to Fatjon." McNally whimpered. "He handed me a scalpel. I couldn't do it. He said he couldn't waste a good set of kidneys."

"So this Fatjon killed Russell," Lottie said. Keep cool. I want to rip his heart out.

"He got the kidneys out and put them in one of those icebox things. Locked it up to wait for the good doctor, but when he didn't turn up, Fatjon got other ideas."

"Like what?"

"Beat me up, took the product and left."

"Where did he go with the...product?"

"Dublin. Flies them out on a private jet to Greece or Italy. Wherever the highest bidder is."

"I think you should come with us now," Boyd said, his voice even and calmer than Lottie's. "You don't need that scalpel anymore." He reached over and swiped the knife from McNally. Twisting the criminal's arm behind him, he hauled him to his feet and slammed him up against the wall. "You're the scum of the earth. You know that?"

"Your wife's a good ride. Do *you* know *that*?" McNally laughed.

"Shut your filthy mouth." Boyd cracked McNally's face into the wall.

"Stop, Boyd. Stop." Lottie dragged him off.

McNally fell to the floor, blood spurting from his broken nose. He curled up like a baby, hands clasping his head, shielding himself.

"Coward." Boyd kicked him.

"Wait, Boyd. Look." Lottie bent down and picked up a piece of material that McNally had been sitting on.

"Maeve Phillips's blue dress. What are you doing with it?"

"An incentive. To butter her up."

"But you took it from her house. Why?"

"Thought you lot might track it back to me."

"Why did Tracy even let you into her house?"

"You'd better talk to Tracy, hadn't you?"

Lottie looked at him quizzically. "What do you mean?"

McNally shook his head. "You didn't figure that out, smart-arse detective."

She noticed his arms then. Long, thin cuts. Knife cuts.

"I figured out that you're Lipjan," she said, flatly.

"O'Hara's idea. He gave me the name. I had to show solidarity with the little wimps. That's what Tracy said. She wanted to fuck over her husband for money. She'd sell her soul to the devil, that one, never mind her own daughter."

Lottie and Boyd exchanged glances.

McNally laughed. "Ah, you had no idea, did you? Maeve was telling her drunk mother all about her cutting. Looking for attention. Told her all about your precious daughter too. And—"

"Boss, come quickly. I've found them. Chloe and Milot." Lynch's voice cut through the room.

Lottie froze. Blue silk shivering in her hand.

"Alive?" she whispered.

"Yes," shouted Lynch. "Both of them."

Lottie felt her knees give way, and as she sank with relief, Boyd caught her before she fell.

CHAPTER 84

"I'm okay. Let me go." Lottie twisted away from Boyd and ran. Slipping and sliding on the wet floor. "Arrest that McNally bastard. Cuff him."

She followed Lynch back up the corridor, now lit with the fluorescent tubes hanging on chains from the high ceiling. Down the sloped floor she'd noticed earlier. Through a low, narrow passageway and into a room.

Chairs upside down on tables. Beds piled high on top of each other along the walls. Boxes and crates. A line of cupboards along the furthest wall. And sitting on the floor, Chloe with Milot asleep on her chest.

Blue eyes. Adam's eyes. She smiled sadly. "Hi, Mam. Sorry about the fuss."

"I'm going to kill you," Lottie cried as she flung herself to the floor and folded her daughter into her arms. "Are you hurt? Did he do anything to you? Are you okay?"

"I'm fine and so is Milot. We got a bit scared."

"Don't you ever do anything like this again. You hear?"

"I hear."

Lynch hovered over them. "I've called an ambulance. Be here in a few minutes."

"I don't need to go to hospital." Chloe looked up into Lottie's eyes. "I want to go home."

"You'll have to be checked over by a doctor. Milot too."

"I saved him, Mam, I saved Milot. I tried to fix it. I like to fix things, but I'm sorry if I messed up. I'm—"

"It's okay, darling. You did what you thought was right."

But Lottie knew Chloe had run head-first into the arms of death rather than away from it. What mattered now was that both of them were alive and physically unharmed. She didn't want to think of the hard journey ahead for Chloe. Not now. Not yet. And what would happen to Milot? Too many questions for the middle of the night.

"Time to go," Kirby said. "Ambulance is here." He whispered in Lottie's ear. "And so is the Super."

"For feck's sake," Lottie said.

* * *

Kosovo 2010

He lived with the image of his mother and sister. With the image of the bloody scene of their murder. But he had never tried to avenge their deaths.

He remembered the day he woke from whatever the mad doctor, Gjon Jashari, and his son, Gjergi, had done to him. He wrecked everything in the clinic. Movable and immovable objects. With his bare hands he tore it down. He found his clothes, dressed himself and walked out the door. Alone.

In his pocket he had his soldier friend's badge. He didn't know how long had passed, but he supposed the soldier had gone home to his family.

Over the years, he worked hard. Rebuilding his beautiful country. And then, one summer's day, he saw her standing outside a brothel in Pristina. Long black hair, glistening in the sunlight. Big brown eyes. And he remembered her. He'd seen her before. That evening when the soldier had asked him to take the photo of the family. The little girl sitting on the floor.

He spoke to her, and they became friends and eventually lovers.

He loved her more than anything he could imagine loving. She was his world. He worked even harder after he rescued her from the brothel. She was the light at the end of every tough day.

Then one day: "I'm home," he said, walking into their apartment.

It was empty. He checked everywhere.

He ran to the stairs. Taking three steps at a time, he ran down the four flights and out the front door.

"Have you seen her?" he shouted at the girls on the outside step.

"Your little concubine?"

"Run away, has she?"

Ignoring an invective of abuse, he ran to the street. Cars honked and swerved. Frantically, he looked all around. Where could she have gone?

Rounding the corner, he ran into a darkened alley. Shadows emerged at the end and he sped toward them. So intent on finding her, he forgot his street-wariness.

The first blow knocked him straight to the ground. The next caught him on the side of the head. A heavy boot into his face followed. He saw the sheen of a slim blade slashing toward him.

Before he blacked out, he heard them say, "She is gone. Shipped away to make big money. Don't give evidence at the trial."

He didn't know how long he lay there. Groaning, he pulled himself upright and leaned against the wall. The stillness of the night clawed at his heart; even the traffic seemed to have evaporated. He tracked back along the way he had run.

He dragged himself up the four flights of stairs. His door was swinging open.

The emptiness crawled from the corners of the room and settled into the chambers of his heart.

He would not be used again.

He would give evidence.

And then he would find her.

DAY NINE

Tuesday, May 19, 2015

CHAPTER 85

After briefing Superintendent Corrigan, and once Chloe and Milot had been checked over at the hospital, Lottie drove to her mother's house. She laid Milot beside a sleeping Katie in her own old bed. Sean was asleep on the floor wrapped in a duvet. Chloe had gone straight to the spare room and was asleep in seconds.

"I'll be back later, Mam," Lottie said. "I'm leaving the detectives on guard for the night until everything is resolved."

"Lottie, I need to talk to you." Her mother stood in the hall, blocking her exit.

"Can't it wait?"

"It's about Katie. She had a chat with me tonight. Told me she hasn't been well these last few months."

"I noticed," Lottie said. "She's grieving for Jason."

"It's more than that." Rose pulled her dressing gown across her chest.

"I'll bring her to the doctor. Get her checked over." Lottie fiddled anxiously with her keys.

"She's already been to the doctor."

"What?" Lottie stared at her mother.

"Katie is pregnant. It's Jason's. She's over four months gone and was afraid to tell you. She—"

"Oh God. No," Lottie cried, dropping her keys. She bent to pick them up and her mother took her elbow and pulled her close.

"She asked me to tell you. You go and do your job now. I'll watch over your children and you and Katie can have a long chat tomorrow. Okay?"

"I…I…Okay. I'm going. I can't deal with this right now."

"And you need to sleep," Rose said.

"I will, when all this is over. Thanks for looking after my children and Milot. I don't know what I would do without you." Lottie leaned over and kissed Rose's forehead. Rose reached out to hug her daughter, but Lottie was already out the door.

* * *

They banged on the door of 251 Mellow Grove. And banged again. A light shone out from the hallway but the rest of the place was shrouded in darkness.

"Try again," Lottie said, and walked back to the car, where two uniforms and Kirby stood sentry. "The enforcer, please," she said.

Boyd lugged the battering ram to the door.

"Mrs. Phillips? Tracy? If you don't answer, we will have to break the door down."

"I'm coming. For fuck's sake, what's all the racket about?"

"Ah, at last," Lottie said. "Can we come in? Why aren't you at the hospital watching over your daughter?"

"I rang to check on her. She's unconscious. Not much use to her there, so I stayed home."

"Couldn't leave your drink?" Lottie leaned against the door frame as Kirby took the battering ram back to the car. Boyd looked like he was going to fall over where he stood. But Lottie was suddenly filled with adrenaline and wanted to smash her fist into Tracy Phillips's drunken face.

"No need to be like that now. Thanks for finding her. Can I go back to bed now?"

"Get your coat. I'd like to ask you a few questions. Down at the station."

"Fuck off, you long lank of misery," Tracy spat.

Catching her by the shoulder, Lottie wrenched Tracy's arm up her back.

"Tracy Phillips, I'm arresting you on suspicion of kidnapping. You don't have to say anything—"

"Fuck off, bitch," Tracy yelled. "What are you talking about? Let me go."

Lottie finished her spiel and Boyd handcuffed the woman. As he led her to the car, Lottie looked on and shook her head. Kirby opened the door and they pushed Tracy into the back seat.

The car sped off and Boyd joined Lottie as she closed the front door of the house.

"How did she come up with that scheme?" he asked.

"Saw an opportunity to make her husband pay up for the years of 'hardship' she'd suffered."

"I still don't get how she did it."

"We'll ask her in the morning." Lottie walked down the path, a cone of yellow from the street light leading the way.

"It is the morning," Boyd said.

"In the real morning, after we get a few hours' sleep. Got a cigarette?"

* * *

Refusing Rose's offer of her bed, Lottie lay down on the couch and fell into a fitful sleep of nightmares until she was awoken with a bowl of porridge and a mug of coffee, and her mother's sad face. Neither said anything about Katie's pregnancy.

Refreshed but exhausted after only three hours' rest, Lottie escaped to work. Reaching her desk, she roused the computer from sleep mode. The email from the Kosovo prosecutor, Besim Mehmedi, was open, waiting. She read it.

"You look like death warmed up this morning," Boyd said, placing a Diet Coke on her desk.

"No coffee?"

"You're lucky to get that. Lucky I'm here at all."

"Why's that?" Lottie stretched into the back of her chair, only half listening to Boyd. Her mind was in overload, having read the contents of the email. She was desperately trying to keep busy, to concentrate on work. Then she wouldn't have to think of her pregnant daughter.

Boyd said, "I've just brought McNally back. The doctors released him to my care an hour ago. My care? I wanted to smash the bastard's face under my shoe. And jump up and down on it until—"

"Enough. I get the picture. Where is he now?"

"Cell Two. Beside your friend."

"Petrovci? Shit, Boyd, he needs to be released."

"And you reached that conclusion how?"

Lottie stood up and beckoned for him to sit. "Read that."

Boyd sat down and looked at the screen. "Who is Gjergi Jashari?"

"The son of a doctor called Gjon Jashari. Infamous illegal organ harvester and trafficker in Kosovo. Ran a clinic in Pristina. A front for his butchery. During and after the war. Look at the attached photograph."

She tapped the mouse and waited for the penny to drop. When it did, Boyd shot up out of the chair.

"George O'Hara? He's this Gjergi character. I don't get it."

"Use your brain." Lottie opened the can and drank.

"Tell me. My head is too tired to think," Boyd said, rolling up his shirtsleeves to his elbows.

Lottie sat on the edge of the desk and crossed her legs at the ankle. "Gjergi Jashari was a qualified surgeon, like his father. From that email it is clear that Andri Petrovci was one of those who, as a child, had a kidney taken from him. What happened in the years up to the trial I don't know. But Petrovci was the state's key witness against Jashari senior—probably the only living witness—and then the old man keeled over and died the day the trial was due to begin."

Boyd said, "But what brought the doctor's son to Ragmullin?"

"I believe Dan Russell was in cahoots with old man Jashari in the years after the war in Kosovo. Bastard tried to blacken Adam's name with his own dastardly deeds." She cringed at the thought of what Russell had been implying. "When Russell took over the direct provision center, Gjergi, who was probably in contact with Russell down through the years, saw an opportunity to continue his father's work. I'm sure he will confirm all this when he recovers from Mimoza's bullet."

"I can't see a man like Russell agreeing to be involved in that carry-on again."

"There's millions of dollars available on the black market for anything you can sell. So it was either money or fear. Maybe Gjergi threatened him with exposure for what he'd previously done in Kosovo. Or he was just a greedy bastard. Got his comeuppance either way. Can George O'Hara talk yet?"

"He's in intensive care, last I heard. But explain to me again how Frank Phillips is linked to all this?"

"Superintendent Corrigan tells me the Spanish police have Phillips cooperating with them. Phillips supplied girls, initially for the sex trade, and then for organ harvesting. Trafficked some of them via Melilla through Malaga. Others he moved overland from the Balkans and Eastern Europe. When the girls arrived, Russell mingled them in with genuine asylum seekers. A great cover."

"But what brought Gjergi O'Hara to—"

"Gjergi Jashari," Lottie corrected.

"What brought the butchering bastard to Ragmullin in the first place?"

"Revenge."

"On Russell?"

"No. I believe Gjergi was involved in trafficking Mimoza and her son to Ragmullin. She was Andri Petrovci's girl-friend. Petrovci discovered she was in Ireland and followed but couldn't find her. Petrovci suffers blackouts from the trauma of having his kidney removed and I don't think he knows what's real and what's not half the time. I think Gjergi wanted to fuck with his mind because he'd been about to give evidence against his father at his trial. He was going to torture and kill Mimoza and set Andri up to take the blame. He'd already set him up for the other girls' murders."

"But McNally wanted a piece of the action," Boyd said. "He knew Frank Phillips was pulling out of the deal so he muscled into the gap due to become vacant. Makes sense."

"Aided by Tracy Phillips. She planned for McNally to kid-nap Maeve and demand money from Frank in return for his daughter. When we were in Malaga, Frank told us his fam-ily had been threatened. We should have pushed him then for more information."

"If Maeve was in danger he wasn't going to tell us any-thing," Boyd said. "But I wonder what went wrong."

"Tracy had it all nicely set up, but McNally got greedy. Sold Maeve off to the doctor to get back at Frank Phillips and get into Gjergi's good books."

"That's why she came to the station urging you to find her."

"She knew McNally had double-crossed her, but she couldn't say anything without implicating herself."

"And McNally became the Lipjan Twitter guy," Boyd said. "to ensnare Maeve."

"Yes. I think McNally's actions motivated Gjergi to start killing the girls he stole organs from. It was an ideal way of framing Andri Petrovci for murder. His *coup de grâce* was to be Petrovci finding Mimoza and Milot dead in a trench under a street."

"Mad bastard in his own insane world."

"And Chloe walked straight into it. She confided in Maeve about her self-harm and was targeted after Maeve's abduction. I think in Gjergi's warped mind he believed he was saving the girls he killed. But it was all motivated by revenge."

"Against Petrovci."

"Yes. Is he still here?"

"With everything going on we never got to release him."

"We need to speak with him again," she said.

"I think we do," Boyd agreed.

CHAPTER 86

"I remember now. Sometimes it like that. The blackouts first, then memory come back."

"What do you remember, Andri?"

Lottie sipped a mug of coffee brought in by Boyd. Andri Petrovci had declined the offer of a drink. The three of them sat at the steel table in the suffocating heat of the interview room.

Andri said, "I get headache. I leave apartment because man ring me. You ask what he say."

"Yes. We've checked all the phone records and you were called by the same number that contacted Jack Dermody and Eamon Carter."

"He say I never see my Mimoza again."

"Andri. I'm sorry to tell you but Mimoza is dead. She died fighting off a very evil man."

He began to shiver. His hands quivered and he shook his head. "No! It not true."

"I'm afraid it is true."

"Why? Why this happen?" After a moment he said, "This man, he say...I never see son again." Tears gathered at the corners of his pained eyes. Hastily he wiped them away and sniffed. "I not have son." Lifting his hands, pleading, he said, "Why he lie? Why?"

Lottie looked at Boyd.

"But Andri—" she began.

Boyd shook his head and mouthed, "Outside."

They stood in the corridor.

"I have to tell him about Milot." Lottie folded her arms and leaned against the wall.

"At least wait until DNA confirms it or otherwise." Boyd paced in front of her.

"But he's the boy's father. He needs to know."

"He's a mental wreck, Lottie. How is he going to care for a little boy? Be realistic."

"We can't not tell him."

Back in the interview room, Lottie picked up her bag. She took out the photograph she'd found in Adam's belongings and placed it on the table.

Andri took it. "Where you get this? I take this photo. When I a boy. I remember. Why I never see it before?"

"I'm not sure, Andri," Lottie said softly. She handed him the name badge Mimoza had brought her over a week ago.

Andri turned it over and over in his hand, tracing the tight green stitches marking out the name on the canvas. He looked up at Lottie and smiled through his pain.

"Friend. Soldier friend. He good man."

Tears spilled from Lottie's eyes. "You knew Adam?"

"Soldier friend, he give me this. He tell me, ever in trouble, come look for him. I give it to my Mimoza. I tell her look for him if anything happen to me. One day I come from work, she gone. Now she truly gone." He smiled sadly. "Soldier friend, I not forget him."

"Adam died nearly four years ago," Lottie whispered. "But he would have helped you."

"You help me. You believe me when I say I not kill girls. You help my Mimoza?"

Lottie shook her head. Tears dripped from the end of her nose to her chin and down on to her chest.

"I tried, Andri, but not hard enough. I couldn't save her." She glanced over at Boyd, and he nodded.

"Andri, I've something to tell you. Something that will make you very happy."

"Nothing make me happy. My Mimoza gone."

She choked back a sob. "Listen to me, Andri. You do have a son. He is a beautiful little boy. His name is Milot."

Andri reached out and wiped the tears from her cheek. "You tell truth? I have a son?"

"Yes, Andri, you have a son."

And when Lottie looked at him, all the black pain had left his eyes, and he smiled.

"I have a son."

* * *

Kosovo, May 2011

Andri's plain black suit had been hired. The collar of his shirt cut into his neck. Though his head was newly shaved and gleamed bright under the artificial lights, his eyes were dark with pain. He shifted on the chair and rubbed his hands together. He could feel someone watching him. Without turning round, he knew Gjergi Jashari was staring at him from the back of the packed courtroom. Seeking out his soul.

A hush descended as the defendant was led into court, followed by the judges taking their seats. Everyone rose and sat as directed.

Bracing himself for the trauma he would have to relive, Andri closed his eyes and remembered her eyes. The girl he'd met and loved. The girl someone had taken away from him. He would search the world for her. Once the trial was over.

But before proceedings could commence, a commotion from the dock caused a flurry of activity. Andri looked over. Old Gjon Jashari had crumpled over on himself, his head smashing against the floor. Both hands clutched his chest as the life shot out of him in a long, hoarse groan. The man who had taken life from others for tainted dollars left the world without paying for his actions.

As people ran and fetched and carried and shouted, Andri sat motionless and emotionless. He wouldn't have to give his testimony. Maybe now he could begin his search for his beloved Mimoza.

As he sat there, above the commotion he heard a door bang shut. He turned around.

Gjergi was gone. He hadn't waited to see if his father lived or died.

And Andri realized that Gjergi had only two goals in life. One was to follow in his father's footsteps making money from illegal human organ harvesting; the other to make Andri Petrovci suffer.

EPILOGUE

May 31, 2015

Four white coffins stood behind the brass altar gates of Ragmullin Cathedral for the prayer service.

Three of them bore names on copper plates. *Kaltrina. Sara. Mimoza.*

The fourth held the unidentified female with her unborn child. A silver angel holding a white dove sat on top of the wood where their names should have been.

In the front pew, Andri Petrovci had Milot on his knee. The little boy held a new white rabbit with floppy ears. With one hand he fingered the toy's label, over and back, over and back. His dark eyes searched for his mother in the crowd behind him.

Lottie and her children were in the next row. Katie held out her hand to Milot and he smiled at her. Lottie's heart was breaking for her daughter, but Katie was happy now her pregnancy was out in the open. Chloe kept her head down. Milot reached out and rubbed her hair until she looked up at him. He said something to his father, and Andri turned round and acknowledged Chloe with a nod.

At least Milot is with his dad now, thought Lottie. Katie's baby wouldn't have a dad. Her own children no longer had their father, but her heart soared with pride at the stories Andri had related to her of his time with Adam at the chicken farm.

The sound of murmuring rippled through the congregation as the tap-tap of crutches approached on the marble floor.

Maeve Phillips stood beside Lottie's pew.

"Thank you, Inspector," she said. "For saving my life."

Lottie stood and touched the girl's elbow as she edged into the seat. "I don't know what you're going to do, Maeve," she whispered, "but when your dad gets out of prison, don't go to live with him. Believe me, he is not a good man, no matter how much money he has."

Maeve said, "I thought he sent me that expensive dress. Just look how wrong I was." She moved weakly along the row.

Lottie felt Boyd slip his hand into hers.

Glancing across the aisle, she saw Jackie staring at them.

She squeezed Boyd's hand.

For now, it was comfort enough.

Tomorrow it might be different.

A LETTER FROM PATRICIA

Hello dear reader,

I wish to sincerely thank you for reading my second novel, *The Stolen Girls*.

I'm so grateful to you for sharing your precious time with Lottie Parker and company. I do hope you enjoyed it and that you will follow Lottie throughout the series. To those of you who have already read the first Lottie Parker book, *The Missing Ones*, I thank you for your support and reviews.

All characters in this story are fictional, as is the town of Ragmullin, though life events have deeply influenced my writing.

I'm a little embarrassed to ask, but if you liked *The Stolen Girls*, I would love it if you could post a review online. It would mean so much to me.

Your amazing reviews for *The Missing Ones* really inspired me to do the best that I could in writing *The Stolen Girls*.

You can connect with me via my blog, which I endeavor to keep up to date, or on Facebook or Twitter.

Thanks again, and I hope you will join me for book three in the series.

Love
Patricia

www.patriciagibney.com

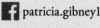 patricia.gibney1

 @trisha460

ACKNOWLEDGMENTS

Writing *The Stolen Girls* was a completely different experience for me than writing my debut novel, *The Missing Ones*. I could not have accomplished it without the support and encouragement of many people along the way.

Firstly, I want to thank you, my readers, for taking the time to read *The Stolen Girls*. Without you, my writing would be in vain. To everyone who posted reviews for *The Missing Ones*, your words bestowed on me the confidence to believe in my writing ability.

The Bookouture team, in particular my editors Lydia, Jenny and Helen, for your tremendous work in helping me whip *The Stolen Girls* into shape. To everyone else from Bookouture who worked with me along the way, thank you, including Hachette and Grand Central Publishing staff.

A special thank you to Kim Nash of Bookouture for her amazing ability to market and publicize my books, and for answering my most asinine emails. Your infectious good humor makes even the dullest day shine bright. One awesome lady.

My fellow Bookouture authors, you are an incredible bunch of people, supporting each other. I am honored to be among you.

Thank you to each and every blogger and reviewer who read and reviewed *The Missing Ones*.

My agent, Ger Nichol of The Book Bureau, for signing me up and then giving me so much encouragement.

My writer friends, Jackie Walsh, Niamh Brennan and my

sister Marie, for reading early copies of *The Stolen Girls* and offering worthwhile comment and advice.

Grainne Daly, Tara Sparling, Louise Phillips, Jax Miller and Carolann Copeland for always encouraging and supporting me.

Sean Lynch and the staff of Mullingar Arts Centre.

Paula and the staff of Westmeath County Libraries.

All my friends in Westmeath County Council.

Westmeath Topic and *Westmeath Examiner*, for interviews and articles.

Claire O'Brien of Midlands 103, for the interviews and broadcasts.

Martin McCabe, John Quinn and Alan Murray, for advice on policing matters; any mistakes are entirely my own. In order to help the story flow, I took many liberties with police procedures.

David O'Malley for bringing me out on a shooting range and letting me fire real live guns! Must do it again soon. All for research purposes!

Antoinette and Jo, for being my best friends forever.

My mother and father, Kathleen and William Ward, my brother and sisters for unwavering support and belief in me.

My mother-in-law Lily Gibney and family, always behind me.

My children, Aisling, Orla and Cathal. You make me so proud, and now I have my four adorable grandchildren, Daisy, Shay, Caitlyn and Lola, who bring me down to earth whenever I see their gorgeous smiles.

Aidan, my dear husband, who never doubted I would be a published author. I miss your wisdom and advice. But every so often, I get a sign that you are by my side, guiding me and protecting me. I just know you are bursting with pride. Thank you for being part of my life. I miss you, but you are always in my heart.

ABOUT THE AUTHOR

Patricia yearned to be a writer after reading Enid Blyton and Carolyn Keene and even wanted to be Nancy Drew when she grew up. She has now grown up (she thinks) but the closest she's come to Nancy Drew is writing crime!

In 2009, after her husband died, she retired from her job and started writing seriously. Fascinated by people and their quirky characteristics, she always carries a notebook to scribble down observations.

Patricia also loves to paint in watercolor and lives in the Irish midlands with her children.